Fanny Blake was a publisher for many years, editing both fiction and non-fiction before becoming a freelance journalist and writer. She has written various non-fiction titles, as well as acting as ghost writer for a number of celebrities. She was Books Editor of *Woman & Home* magazine until recently, regularly reviews fiction in the *Daily Mail* and has been a judge for the Costa Novel Award, the British Book Awards and the Comedy Women in Print Award, among others. She is the commissioning editor for Quick Reads, a series of short books by well-known authors. She has written eight novels, including *An Italian Summer* and *A Summer Reunion*.

To find out more visit www.fannyblake.co.uk or follow her on Twitter @FannyBlake1

Also by Fanny Blake

What Women Want
Women of a Dangerous Age
The Secrets Women Keep
With a Friend Like You
House of Dreams
Our Summer Together
An Italian Summer

Praise for *Fanny Blake*

'I adored *An Itali*... ...t only writes beautifully about relationships, but the descriptions of Rome and Naples are so ravishing that you not only marvel at the scenery, but also taste the delectable food and feel the hot sun on your back. A most beguiling read'
Jilly Cooper

'Intelligent, grown-up and cheering, Fanny has cornered the market in "real" stories told well'   Fern Britton

'A glorious jaunt around Italy with characters I didn't want to leave'   Clare Mackintosh

'Fanny Blake's writing is absorbing, intelligent and an absolute joy to read... Building to an unexpected and clever twist, this heart-warming and compelling novel is the perfect summer read'   *Daily Express*

'The clever plot, set in gorgeous Rome and Naples and full of glorious food and wine, has the group dynamics continually shifting... A perfect summer read, full of heart and sunshine'   *Bella*

'As themes of friendship and love intertwine with mystery, the plot reels you in until you have no choice but to devour every word'   *Heat*

'You'll be enveloped in Italian sunshine with this great read full of warmth and insight'   *Fabulous*

A Summer Reunion

Fanny Blake

ORION

First published in Great Britain in 2019 by Orion Fiction,
an imprint of The Orion Publishing Group Ltd
Carmelite House, 50 Victoria Embankment
London EC4Y 0DZ

An Hachette UK Company

1 3 5 7 9 10 8 6 4 2

A CIP catalogue record for this book is
available from the British Library.

ISBN 978 1 4091 7714 2

Typeset at The Spartan Press Ltd,
Lymington, Hants

Printed and bound in Great Britain by Clays Ltd, Elcograf S.p.A.

MIX
Paper from
responsible sources
FSC® C104740
www.fsc.org

www.orionbooks.co.uk

For Lisa, Samantha and Fran
with much love

I

I still remember that morning, the morning my life changed irrevocably and not for the first time. I had driven to Monkton Combe where I went for a long walk, one of my 'inspiration hunts' as my husband Rob calls them. Sometimes, removing myself from the demands of my interior design business and the internet gives me the distance I need to find inspiration for a new collection or solve any work problems. The business can be stressful, and I feel the pressure to keep the designs fresh, the turnover up and the staff happy. I set up Amy Green, my first interiors shop, about thirty years ago and since then we've gone from strength to strength, opening shops in three other cities and selling my fabrics through department stores throughout the country. Of course, the biggest change has come through the internet, so our thriving online shop sells fabric and our products throughout the world.

When I got back to the house, I made some coffee and settled with my laptop in the sitting room, trying not to let my usual guilt from having been away from the business for a few hours take hold. Silly, really. As silly as biting down on an aching tooth.

As soon as I logged into my inbox, I could see that Kerry, our marketing director, had emailed me repeatedly, her messages all flagged as high priority. I was immediately on alert. Since she enjoyed being in control, she usually kept communication to the bare minimum while I was out of the office. She liked proving she could cope without me.

I opened the most recent one.

> Amy! Where are you? For God's sake get in touch when you get this.

I quickly checked back to her first email and started from the beginning of the thread. She must have sent it the previous evening.

> The accountants have found a discrepancy of almost £200,000.

I had to pause and read the sentence again. That was impossible. Rob looked after the financial side of things for me and would never let a figure like that go unnoticed. All the same, I felt a nasty shiver of unease.

> They're investigating several accounts that we've paid money into that I don't recognise. Need your help urgently!'

I trusted everyone who worked for me implicitly so I was sure it was some kind of error. However, I knew Kerry well enough to know that she wouldn't go anywhere until this was straightened out. She would blame herself if anything went wrong on her watch.

I skyped her and she picked up immediately. Seeing her tidy office was oddly reassuring. She was a woman who believed in delegation and a clear desk if a business was to be run efficiently. I did my best to set the same example, but had never succeeded in quite the same way. She looked more harassed than I'd ever seen her; her hair, usually neatly pinned up, hung messily around her face. She looked exhausted, though relieved to see me.

'Amy! Thank God! I've been trying to get hold of you all day. I know you switch off when you're working from home but I've been going out of my mind.'

'Tell me what's happened.'

She pushed her hair back off her face. 'I got a call from the accountants. I explained you and Rob were away, so they told me we're missing around two hundred thousand pounds and asked if I could explain it. Someone's been transferring money to themselves but recording it as payments to suppliers.'

'Who would do that?' No one I employed would. 'Who *could* do that?' I stopped. Only three of us were signatories to the company accounts. If neither Kerry nor I had requested those transfers, that left one person. Rob.

I was only too aware that business had being going through a bit of a dip. I'd been meaning to sit down with Rob to discuss new strategies but he'd been away a lot recently and we'd delayed the discussion. At that moment he was in France, at one of those trade fairs that I hated so much.

'There's no point hating them,' he'd say. 'It's new business. Don't you want new business?' Sometimes he frowned, sometimes he kissed me. 'Even if you don't, I do. For us both.'

'There must be an explanation.' I tried to hide my concern from Kerry, because revealing any kind of discord between Rob and me would affect staff morale. We had to show a solid front at all times.

Her raised eyebrows were sufficient comment. 'Do you check the accounts yourself?'

'Not recently. I've left that all to him.' How stupid I sounded. Amy Green was *my* business, for God's sake. How could I not have involved myself in every aspect? Because I believed in giving people responsibilities and letting them have their heads, and because I trusted Rob. 'If Rob's done this, he must have had a reason.'

'I hope so. Have you spoken to him? He's not been answering either.'

'I'll call him now. Leave it with me. There's nothing more you can do.' I hung up and called Rob.

He picked up immediately. 'Darling. What's up?' Those languid public school tones always made my stomach turn over. They belonged to a world very different from the one I knew when I was growing up.

'Kerry's been trying to get hold of us all morning. The accountants are saying our figures are out of synch.' I didn't imagine his sharp intake of breath. 'Any idea what's going on?'

His silence told me he did have, and that I wasn't going to like it.

'Ah . . . yes.' He paused. 'Perhaps we shouldn't do this over the phone.' His voice didn't sound quite right.

'Do what over the phone?'

'I'll be a back in a couple of days.'

'But this is urgent. We need to sort this out now.' I was alarmed. 'The fair finished today.'

He lowered his voice so I could barely hear him. 'There are one or two things that I need to finish off here first. I'll be home as soon as I can.'

'What's going on, Rob?' Panic washed through me. A distance had been growing between us over the last I-don't-know-how-long but I'd put that down to the pressures of work.

In the background, I heard a door slam and a woman's voice that was disconcertingly familiar, although I didn't immediately put two and two together. 'Coffee, Rob? We haven't got long.'

'Who's that?' I asked. 'Where are you?' He'd told me he was staying in a hotel that was so cheap and cheerful it wouldn't impinge on the company's balance sheet.

'A friend.'

I knew my husband well enough to know that there was something he wasn't telling me. 'Who? What's going on?'

'I can't explain now.'

'Where are you?' I insisted.

'Look, Amy. This isn't a conversation that I want to have over the phone. I'll be back for a few days.'

'*For* a few days?' I repeated, helpless. 'Where are you going after that?'

'I'll explain then.'

When he ended the call, I realised I should have pushed him harder for an explanation.

Of course I should have done but the truth was, I didn't want to hear.

That voice had driven everything else out of my head. Just hearing her was enough to make me doubt him. I'm not a jealous person. Really, I'm not. But Rob hadn't always been the most faithful of husbands. We'd got over his last affair (a hotel receipt in a jacket pocket was the only clichéd clue required) with apologies, counselling and determination on both sides.

I had convinced myself we had been devoted to each other since then. Though for both of us, Amy Green came a close second, because the business gave us the life we both wanted. But there was something else niggling at me that I couldn't quite get a hold of. I ran through our conversation again, trying to read between the lines. If he had been defrauding the company – and I couldn't accept that – what did he need the money for? He had everything he needed. When I had set up the company with his help thirty-odd years ago, we'd agreed that I'd stick to the creative side of things and remove myself from the financial. It wasn't that I was unable, but he knew what he was doing, and it was a fair division of labour that suited us and let us play to our strengths.

I typed Kerry a quick email.

> He's not picking up for me either. I'll be in touch as soon as I've heard from him. Try not to worry. I'm sure he'll have a good reason. Ax

I hesitated before pressing send. This would be the first time I had lied to her. The business had always benefited from our honesty with one another, although I was plagued by sudden doubt. In any event, I thought it was better not to worry her further by reporting an inconclusive conversation. I knew Rob better than he imagined. Something wasn't right.

I opened a new email and began to type.

> Rob, you didn't answer my question about the accounts. Why so evasive? Kerry and I are worried about this money. I'm sure there must be an explanation but we need you to share it with us.

Was that too passive aggressive? I was never sure.

> Who was that with you? Did I recognise her voice?

I hoped I hadn't but that might nudge him into telling me.

> I know you're busy and it's not a good idea to catch you on the hop, but if you could email ASAP and explain all before you're back, it would go down well at this end! Looking forward to having you back.

I wasn't. Not really.

It took him two days to come home. Two days during which he never got in touch and I reassured myself frantically that he wasn't guilty of . . . what? Fraud? Stealing? Having an affair?

Which was the worst? I wasn't sure. All of the possibilities hurt.

I heard the front door closing and the sound of him dumping his bag in the hall.

'I'm in the kitchen,' I called. I was ready. If he had been stealing from the company, no excuse would do. At the same time, I couldn't believe he was guilty, and I wanted him to say so. But if not him, who else could it be?

He stood in the open doorway looking hesitant but also unexpectedly determined. His dark hair was showing signs of silver around his temples and his face was unusually pale. His hand moved to the back of his neck. That's when I knew something was definitely wrong. I had seen him make that gesture numerous times over the years, always prefacing a difficult conversation.

'This is so hard.' His hand didn't move. 'I don't know how to say it . . .'

I suspected that was an understatement. 'Then you'd better come and sit down.' My heart was racing.

We pulled out a bar stool each and sat facing each other round a corner of the kitchen island. Behind his head, the large hand of the skeleton station clock tick-tocked the minutes as they passed. Between us, a bunch of bright red, orange and yellow ranunculi flowered in an earthenware vase.

'I'm not going to make excuses, I'm just going to come clean.'

Nothing coming after that sentence was going to be good.

'What's going on? I thought everything was OK between us.' I don't know why I said that. Because I wanted it to be true, I suppose.

'Come on, Amy. You know as well as I do that things haven't been right for ages. When did we last have sex?' He paused. 'Think about it.'

He waited for me to deflect that arrow. But I couldn't.

7

Rushing. Snatched meals. Late nights. When had we last spoken to each other properly? Made love?

'Exactly. So this shouldn't come as too much of a shock to you.'

'You're having an affair.' A pat on the back for perception, though I was feeling sick with apprehension. I studied the veins in the quartz worktop, my finger tracing one of them.

'Yes. I'm sorry, but Morag and I want to move to Edinburgh with the kids and start a business together.'

'Morag!' I twisted in my seat. 'You can't mean it?'

He had the grace to look away. 'I do.'

'Morag who I hired to do our publicity?' He nodded as if I was an imbecile – which at this moment I felt I was. I had so much wanted that voice not to have been hers. 'The Morag who has a vile ex-husband, three children and is my friend?'

We'd invited them to spend that first Christmas with us when she had nowhere else to celebrate. She was often in our house for supper or weekend brunch while her kids went to her ex. We had gone on mad shopping trips together, spent hours dissecting the business, the new ranges and the staff we did and didn't need. And all that time, I had never once suspected that she and Rob . . .

'For how long?'

'Nearly two years now.'

Two years! What a blinkered, trusting idiot I'd been.

'And the money? Tell me you haven't been stealing from the business, too.' I was reeling, unable to get a purchase, but I had to sort this out for everyone else's sake, too.

That got to him and something like shame crossed his features. 'I thought I'd be able to pay it back before anything was noticed.'

'But why? What do you need it for?' Perhaps he would tell me this was all a terrible joke.

8

He took a deep breath. 'We're setting up our own interiors business and needed it for the start-up costs.'

I was so shocked, I could barely take in what he was saying. 'But why you didn't get a loan or go to an investment company?'

'I was going to, but the ideal premises came up and we had to move fast. I thought I'd have time to pay the money back before anything was noticed.' He shrugged. 'But either way, let's face it, it's the least you owe me.'

'What does that mean?' I was punch drunk from one shock after another. They were setting up in competition!

'I've worked for you for years and you've never given me so much as a share in the company.'

'You've never asked.'

'More fool me.'

'I didn't know that was what you wanted. We agreed that it was my company and I should retain ownership of it. I thought you were happy with that.'

'We're soulmates,' Rob had once said to me. 'We'll beat the world together, whatever it throws at us.'

I had been crazy in love then. 'Promise me we'll never not talk. Never hide anything. Never be dishonest with one another.'

He promised.

But now, apart from wrecking our marriage, he was torpedoing our business, too.

'What are you going to do?' He swept his hand through his hair.

I looked into those eyes that I thought I knew so well but there was no reaction. However, I had him in the palm of my hand.

'Am I going to report you to the police? Is that what you mean?'

He nodded. 'But you don't have to.' Desperation had crept

into his voice. 'I'll pay you back. I can't do it all at once but I can do it.'

My anger and hurt were indescribable but, despite everything, I didn't want to be responsible for him going to prison. 'Then do that.' I hesitated. 'If you haven't repaid it in full within one month, I'm going to the police.'

'You wouldn't.'

'Don't push me too far.' However devastated I might feel, I hadn't lost my reason. 'I'll do whatever's necessary. I won't let you ruin my business.'

'That's impossible. We've spent some and some of it's already committed. I don't know how we'll be able to. I was going to suggest—'

'No!'

He flinched: a man used to getting his way in negotiations. 'No?' As if he couldn't believe I was contradicting him.

'You'd better go home and discuss it with Morag.' I had to get him out of there before I broke down. I didn't want him to see the tears that were stinging my eyes. 'That's my only offer.'

He thought for a moment. Then: 'Very well.' He reached out across the table. 'Perhaps we can be friends again when this blows over.'

I ignored his hand and got to my feet. 'Can you hear yourself, Rob?' I didn't want his apologies and self-justification and meaningless hopes for the future. 'I think you should get out now. Take what you need and we'll sort out the rest later.' I didn't want him in the house any longer than necessary.

'I'm sorry.' He hovered, as if he wasn't quite sure, despite what he'd said.

'Out. Now.'

I watched his retreating figure. 'I'll get that money back,' I called after him. 'I'm not letting Amy Green go. Not after all those years.'

After he left, the tears started. And they didn't stop for days.

Now, I could not stop Rob and the business parading through my head as I veered between disbelief, hurt and fury. The pain was all-consuming. I thought about taking myself to our house in Mallorca, although the idea of being on my own there was unbearable.

Once, when I was much younger, I survived what seemed a life-changing turn of events. Although it was over forty years ago, I still remember what led to my expulsion from St Catherine's School for Girls quite clearly. The art teacher's word against mine. His missing watch found in my desk. I hadn't a hope.

At the time, I thought my life was over; the ambitions I had to be a doctor scattered, my parents' faith in me shaken. But I was wrong. My life hadn't been over at all, though I ended up having a different career to the one I'd imagined for myself. I survived. But now I found my life was falling apart again, I looked back once more, and I found myself wondering if there was anything I could learn from what happened then that might help me now?

Of our gang of four – Linda, Kate, and Jane and me – I was pretty sure one of them had set me up by planting that watch, and I had a fair idea of who it might have been. But I could never prove it. Despite that, prompted by Kate, three of us had started to keep in touch sporadically, Christmas cards, round robins and the odd phone call, so I knew the barest bones of their lives and Kate relayed snippets of Jane's. Recently she had suggested we all meet up but none of us had done anything about it.

Through my distress, an idea stuck in my mind. While Kerry and I were in limbo as we waited for Rob to pay back what he owed, I could take my mind off the present by sorting out what had really happened in my past. I appreciated the symmetry of that. That's when I decided to take the initiative and act on Kate's suggestion. I would suggest a small reunion. None of them knew Rob, so my personal life could be as off-limits as I made it, and their company would distract me.

This year the four of us were all going to have a milestone birthday – that merited something special, didn't it? A long weekend away, for example. So why didn't I take them to Mallorca with me? The house was standing empty, just a budget airline flight away with all expenses paid (by me, quite happily) when we got there.

This was utter madness. Why on earth should the four of us want to spend a weekend in each other's company after so many years of managing quite happily without? On the other hand, I'd be offering a cheap weekend in a beautiful spot with sunshine, an infinity pool, to-die-for scenery and great food (even the King of Spain was said to frequent one of the excellent nearby restaurants) all laid on. Besides, what was four or five days in the great scheme of things? How terrible could they be?

2

Coming in from work, Linda went straight to the fridge, stepping over the post that lay on the mat as she went. There wouldn't be anything interesting. Never was. Later, wine in hand, she went back to pick up the envelopes, only because it seemed wickedly lazy to leave them lying in situ. Among the mail-order catalogues, a bill and her monthly copy of *Which?* was a thick white envelope addressed in handwriting she couldn't place. She took it to the sitting-room table and slit it open with a paperknife once given to her by someone. She unfolded the sheet of paper inside and stared at the blur of words. Unable to decipher it, she reached for the reading glasses she pretended not to need.

> Come to Mallorca for a long weekend!
> We can stay in our house and could catch up at last with no interruptions. What do you think? If you like the idea, I'd suggest we go next month when the weather's lovely and the island is less crowded. I'm asking Kate and Jane too.
> I hope you'll all be able to come
> Love
> Amy x

Linda frowned, piecing together some memories. Jane once had a habit of snapping her fingers behind people's backs, if

13

she remembered rightly. *And* she had pinched a mascara of hers when she thought Linda wasn't looking. At least she had given it back with an apology.

It was always the small details which stuck in Linda's mind.

She read Amy's invitation again, noting the expensive notepaper. What an extraordinary suggestion. The last thing she wanted to do was remember that time in her life any more than a Christmas card or round robin might prompt. But she couldn't resist pulling her atlas from the shelf and opening it at a map of Spain. Sasha, fat and tortoiseshell, immediately jumped up and stretched herself out right across the Balearics so the sun fell directly on her. She extended a front leg and began cleaning herself, her purr a familiar engine.

'Get off. I'm looking at that.' Linda lifted her up and put her gently on the floor. 'Go and do something useful.'

Sasha considered her for a moment before jumping straight back up onto the table and settling herself on the atlas again.

This time Linda removed her to her lap where she stroked her until Sasha's purr was at full throttle. 'Mallorca. What do you think, Sasha? You'd have to go into a cattery, and I don't know if you'd like that.'

She took a sip of her wine. 'Mike and I once talked about going to Mallorca for a long weekend when his wife was visiting her parents.' She made a point of not using her name. 'Remember? But then her plans fell through, so we never did. He should have been braver.' She thought for a moment. 'But how could he have been? And anyway, it was all talk, I see that now.'

Sasha stared at her.

'But if he had been, my life might be so different.'

She put her elbows on the table and her head in her hands.

Was she turning into a mad old cat lady?

The thought was enough to make her want to phone Mike. She scanned the contacts on her mobile.

Stop. No. The last time she'd called him, he'd suggested in that kind voice he put on when he was dismissing an argument from a colleague that it wasn't a good idea to phone him at home. Now he'd retired, his wife wouldn't understand why Linda would be calling him. She had never suspected a thing over the ten or so years of their affair, but they had always had the pretext of work as an excuse. With the funding for his project withdrawn, Linda had eventually been relocated to the enquiries desk, which was a very different and much less enjoyable role, and he had taken early retirement.

She loved him. Still, after everything. And hated him too.

But mostly she missed him. She also missed their work together on the Tom Florence Collection – a unique compilation of local recipes and culinary records. If only the sponsoring restaurant hadn't gone belly up. The Robin Hood Library was an emptier place without him. Her life was emptier. She felt disoriented without his reassuring presence there. He had always been the one she had been able to rely on for support and advice when she was floundering. Without him she had no one at her back.

Her colleagues wanted change. They had kowtowed to Mike while he worked there as Head of Collections, but now he had left, his replacement, Simon, was bent on modernising the systems and making cuts. There was a rumour going round that the University HR department was going to be looking for candidates for voluntary redundancy. What would she say if asked? That she would prefer a cataloguing role to answering endless queries on the desk? That was what Mike had originally hired her to do, after all, and it was where her skills lay. But if she ever quoted Mike, there was a certain amount of eye-rolling, as if he was old wood that should have been cut out long ago. She too.

She was aware that the others whispered behind her back, speculating about their relationship, questioning whether she was pulling her weight. That last was outrageous, when she looked back and thought about everything she had brought to the job. The Tom Florence collection was respected nationwide. Michelin-starred chef Florence had funded the project to collect recipes from all the local communities with 1 per cent of his restaurant's profits, and she had been brought in just as it started. She stood up, tipping Sasha to the floor, and went through to the kitchen to refill her glass.

Mike.

She'd met him when he'd been a rare books librarian and had taken her under his wing. He'd introduced her to cataloguing before she went off to Aberystwyth where she'd got her MA in Librarianship, specialising in special collections. After several blissful years working in the London Library, he had written to her.

> I've secured funding for a new project and we're looking for a cataloguer. You'd be perfect. We're advertising very soon, but I hope you'll apply.

That letter had changed her life. She had got the job and they'd worked together ever since. Over time, as they collaborated on the Florence collection, their relationship changed. She had only experienced that kind of electrical charge once before. Long ago. Mike was married with children and the shine on his marriage was wearing thin, or so he led her to believe. All such a cliché – but she hadn't seen that then.

At first she had tried to avoid him but he'd seek her out, ask her about her work, but also about the other librarians. Gradually she became his unofficial spy without even realising. When something needed to be discussed with no danger of being overheard, they started going out for lunch or having a quick drink after work. She remembered Veneziano, the little Italian restaurant that had become their favourite, with a pang. Now deemed hopelessly out of fashion with its checked tablecloths and candles in bottles, it had been their private place.

'They'll never find us here,' he'd joked on their first visit.

At the time, she had revelled in the secrecy that added a definite frisson to their meeting. She hadn't thought he meant anything else until a long time later when his hand brushed her knee under the table. She jumped as if she had been electrocuted.

'So you feel it too?' He leaned forward, his smile broad.

She'd nodded, not sure what to say. He was married, after all. She knew what people said: *never shit on your own doorstep.* And experience had taught her something. But they didn't act on the feeling for years.

Living out of town had meant that occasionally, after a work do, he missed the last train and had to check into a hotel. The Premier Inn wasn't the most salubrious of starts but back then, that was all his expenses ran to. That first evening held a special place in her memory.

'Another?' He had leaned towards her, to scoop up her empty glass. He smelled of woodsmoke and something citrusy. She still missed the scent of his aftershave.

'I ought to go home,' she said, not moving.

'Just one more.'

She watched as he ordered their drinks. Most of the team had drifted off home a little earlier but she had barely noticed, so engrossed she had been in their conversation. He'd been telling her about being in the 1989 train crash at Purley that had injured many and killed five. His face had changed as he told her about the casualties he'd seen. 'I'll never forget the sound of one woman screaming.' His eyes glazed with tears. 'Never.'

She wanted to reach out to him, to hug him close. But that would have been highly inappropriate, especially with the last of their colleagues still propping up the bar, so she held back.

But he had looked at her with such sadness, her heart carried on melting.

'You understand?' he said.

She nodded, appalled by what he had seen and the effect on him.

'Gemma, my wife, thinks I should be able to forget what happened. Maybe she's right. But . . .' He looked down at the table, tracing his finger round the marks left by the glasses.

Still she resisted reaching out to touch him.

'It isn't something that's easy to forget.' He shook his head.

'Have you talked to anyone, I mean professionally?' How buttoned-up and formal she sounded.

'No. But talking to you is a help.' He took her hand in both of his.

Startled, she pulled back but then as he looked up at her, his eyes intent, she relaxed.

She could still remember how she'd felt as she'd given herself up to him, not something that she had done lightly. Married men were off her agenda. Her fingers had been burned before. But look at her now. She had nothing. They would never be a couple and soon she would be out of the job that had kept her going for so long. If she didn't have him, at least she had work. But not for much longer. If she didn't offer herself up on the altar of voluntary redundancy, they'd find another less pleasant way of making her go, and that would be without a financial cushion. She hadn't even reached retirement age.

She returned to her tiny sitting room, where Sasha had reclaimed her position on the atlas. She straightened one of the pictures on the wall before sitting down again.

'You know what?' she said to the cat. 'Maybe a few days away would do me good.' She opened her laptop and googled Amy Green. 'Let's see.'

Her search took her straight to the Amy Green website, but she found nothing about the villa there. She flicked through the pages to check. She had read Amy's biog so many times she almost knew it off by heart but looked at it again. Their lives had taken completely opposite and unexpected paths. When they were at school, Linda was the one who carried everyone's high hopes whereas Amy was ambitious but blew it. Stealing from a teacher was a stupid thing to have done. She typed in 'Mallorca Amy Green' and clicked on Images. And there it was.

She had imagined the place as a modernist white box, minimally but expensively furnished, accessorised by pieces from the Amy Green range but this was something much more comfortable looking. A sandy-coloured stone building stood against a backdrop of wooded mountains, a glittering blue pool in front of it with views stretching across a deep valley and, as far she could make out, a large terrace for dining outside. Plants grew in pots around the place, everything from brightly coloured flowers to exotic-looking palms. Below the house, she could make out the terracotta rooftops of a small village trapped in the folds of the hillside. She caught her breath.

This was a house that was asking to be visited. Linda longed to be able to step inside, to find out more about Amy's life and how she'd got here from such an unpromising start.

More than anything, she wanted to escape her own and have a taste of it.

'You should have seen where she grew up,' she said to Sasha, under her breath. Then she raised her voice. 'Nothing like this. I used to go round there and we'd spend hours listening to records, dancing in front of the mirror, trying out make-up and talking about the boys we fancied.' What a world away that was. Amy's mother would be downstairs in the front room measuring up clients or sewing furiously. Everything was accompanied by the whirr of her sewing machine as she ran up wedding dresses, evening dresses, suits and day dresses, costumes for school plays or dance school performances.

She made almost all of Amy's clothes too until Amy begged

her to stop. After that, Amy had taken a weekend job at the local pub so she could save up to buy clothes mail order from Biba. When the catalogue arrived, they would spend hours browsing through it, picking one thing each that they couldn't live without. She still remembered her knee-high kingfisher-blue suede boots. Those were the days: the days when she had loved colour and fashion and excitement.

She sipped her wine. 'I'm going to accept. Sorry, Sacha, but I'll soon be back. I deserve this.' Opening her email, she typed one quickly to the care agency who came to her aunt every morning, asking if they would step up the visits for the five days she'd be away.

3

The post was late that day. Kate had been clearing away break-fast when she heard the snap of the letterbox and the post falling on to the mat. She loved receiving birthday cards, all the more from people she hadn't seen for ages, so she rushed into the hall. Five, including one from Amy. She recognised the writing and saved it till last. No card, but what she read surprised her.

> Come to Mallorca for a long weekend!
> We can stay in our house and could catch up at last with no interruptions. What do you think? If you like the idea, I'd suggest we go next month when the weather's lovely and it's less crowded.
> I hope you'll all be able to come. I'm asking Linda and Jane too.
> Love
> Amy x
> PS Kate: I don't have Jane's address but I think you do. Would you mind sending the enclosed invitation on to her?

Nice idea.

She closed her eyes and thought about it.

The farm was busy in the late summer, bringing in the hay, doing the repair jobs in time for the winter, preparing the sheep for sale or show. She was expected to be there, doing her bit in the office, answering the phone, making sure the accounts were up to date, helping outside if need be, putting hearty meals on the table for her husband and children.

The answer would have to be 'no'. Instead of throwing the invitation away, she put it behind the mantle clock so she would remember to reply, then got on with her birthday preparations.

But as she moved through the day, one question kept resurrecting itself. Was she the only one who remembered what had happened that last spring term of school?

Much later she had changed out of her farm clothes, three of her children were home and Alan her husband came through the back door into the kitchen as she took the chicken chasseur out of the oven.

'Looks good.' This was his habitual refrain when she put supper on the table, as if today was the same as any other. She remembered the restaurant he had taken her to when they had visited London the year before. She'd have liked to celebrate her special birthday by going somewhere like that again, in York perhaps, or that fancy pub in Oulsted, but he wasn't one for going out if he didn't have to.

'Special occasion or something?'

She flapped her new oven gloves at him. He knew perfectly well.

'Have you put out the glasses, Kit?' she called to the twin she could see through the hatch in the dining room.

'Just about.' A flurry of movement and the clink of glass suggested that he was just starting.

'Not stew again?' Noah, the older of the twins by twenty minutes, came into the kitchen, and draped his arm round Kate's shoulders, planting a kiss on her cheek. 'Happy birthday.'

'This is no stew, you philistine! This is chicken chasseur – your father's favourite,' she protested. She had been looking forward to this evening for ages. Having the whole family home together didn't happen often any more but this was her birthday so they were making the effort. 'Is Lara here yet?'

Noah raised his eyebrows and shook his head. 'What do you think?' The day his eldest sister was on time for something would be another cause for celebration. 'She's probably forgotten.'

'Don't worry, Mum. She'll be here.' That meant Kit must have had a quiet word with her.

'Can I do anything?' Noah tried to make amends for his tactlessness.

'Get everyone a drink,' said Alan as he left the room. 'I'll be back in a minute.'

'Why can't he . . . ?' Noah turned angrily.

'Don't,' warned Kate. 'Your father's had a long day working outside . . . let him have his shower in peace.' She didn't add, *and he's used to me doing everything for him when he gets in, so that's what he's come to expect. My fault.*

'So have I.' Noah had gone straight into the family business after completing his agriculture and animal science degree. She would have preferred him to widen his experience by working somewhere else first but Alan was keen to get him learning on home turf. 'Might as well get him used to the business. No point him working anywhere else. Won't be long till I retire.' This seemed so short-sighted to Kate. Wouldn't learning different methods and ideas bring new life to the farm? But there was little point in arguing over what was not her domain. Those boundaries had been set years ago.

'And it's my birthday, so no arguments,' she added. She loved every member of her family in different ways but each of them had moments when they could be more demanding than the others. She watched Noah get out seven champagne glasses and dust them off. 'Champagne? What a treat.' Her heart lifted.

'Nothing but the best, Ma.' He gave her one of those long, lazy smiles that had made her heart melt since he was a baby.

'Kit and I brought a couple of bottles. I smuggled them into the freezer.' He went down the steps to the larder and returned with one of them.

'Yes, please.' Molly, their youngest, came in and sat at the kitchen table, pulling a glass towards her. 'Ma, I asked Donal if he wanted to come. That's cool isn't it? The others thought it was.'

Kate didn't miss Noah's imperceptible shake of the head. 'Of course.' Although, much as she loved Molly's boyfriend, she felt a flicker of disappointment. She had been looking forward to one evening of being surrounded by family only. But, she reasoned, Donal was as good as. So what did it matter? He'd been going out with Molly for four years, since they got together at their school dance just after Molly had completed her A levels. They had weathered going to different universities and their relationship seemed as solid as it could be, given Molly was back living at home while she worked out what she wanted to do with her life. Presumably she wouldn't be working as a waitress in Bumbles café forever. Kate hoped she wasn't simply waiting for Donal to propose. She wanted more for her daughter than marriage and children.

'Nice hair.' Her daughter was the only one to have noticed the change.

'Thanks. You don't think it's too short?' She had nervously watched her hairdresser snip away until he was satisfied. Yes, she could have stopped him but she had said she wanted a change . . .

'Not at all. It's quite funky.'

'Really?!' Funky wasn't a word Kate would normally associate with her middle-aged, somewhat overweight self. She wasn't sure anyone else apart from Molly would either. She touched the unfamiliarly naked nape of her neck.

'Champagne?' As Noah filled the last glass, Kit came into the room. She should be used to how different the two boys were from one another even for non-identical twins, not just because Noah was dark and built like a prop forward and Kit was fair, finer boned and sharp-featured. Where Noah was chilled, Kit was wound up like a coiled spring. As far as Noah was concerned, anything went, but Kit was a perfectionist who liked everything just so – right down to the last detail of his appearance. Tonight Noah was in his usual work clothes of T-shirt and jeans – what was the point of changing? – whereas Kit was wearing a shirt and trousers. Instead of following his brother into the family business, he had struck out on his own, much to his father's incredulity and relief. He read economics at university to become a civil servant. He studied hard, took his ambition seriously – very different from her other children – so that she knew he would make it, despite his only having achieved a lowly job in local government so far.

He crossed the room and draped his arm round her shoulder. 'All done.'

She felt herself relax. 'Thanks, darling.'

At that moment, Alan reappeared and put a huge parcel with pieces of mismatched wrapping paper stuck over it on the kitchen table. 'Happy birthday to my one and only!'

'You old smoothy,' said Noah, passing him a glass of champagne.

Alan grinned, smug that he'd remembered.

'Shouldn't we wait for Lara?' asked Kate, touched by her husband's gesture. So often he had forgotten, or given her presents weeks late.

'We could be waiting all night,' said Kit, tapping his fingers on the table. 'You know what she's like. *Time has no meaning for me any more.*' He pressed the back of his hand to his forehead as if he was about to faint away.

They all laughed.

'What about Donal? We'd better lay another place.'

'He's got football tonight so he won't be here till much later. I said we'd keep something for him.'

'That's fine', said Kate. 'We'll keep something warm in the oven.' She was pleased to have her immediate family on their own for a while.

'Happy birthday, Mum!' Molly raised her glass and the others followed suit.

'Aren't you going to open it?' said Alan, shunting his present across the table towards her.

She felt herself blushing. Being the centre of attention did not come easily. She was happier in the background.

'Not jewellery, then?' She joked, but how she would love a new pair of earrings or a necklace. Alan would never take that risk, not even if guided by the girls. As the paper tore off and she realised what the box held, she composed her face into a beam of pleasure and tried to sound surprised rather than disappointed.

'A duvet! How...' Words failed her.

'Yes,' he said, clearly pleased with himself. 'You said we needed a new one.'

'We do.' But not as my birthday present. The words remained unspoken. She forced a smile and kissed him. 'Thank you. That's lovely.'

The front door slammed and Lara blew in, slim, pretty in a floaty floral dress. 'Hey.' She smiled at the room then looked at Alan's present. 'You haven't given Mum a duvet for her birthday? Dad, honestly!' She picked up a glass of champagne. 'Cheers, everyone. Happy birthday!'

Alan looked indignant. 'It's what she wanted.'

'Even so. You could have been a bit more imaginative. I would have helped you.'

'You can't just walk in here and start criticising.' Molly leaped to her father's defence.

'I can do whatever I like.' Lara tossed her blonde hair back over her shoulder. 'Anyway I'm sure it'll be very cosy. I got you something, too.' She reached into her bag to produce a small box. So not another set of oven gloves (Noah) or apron (Kit) or kitchen knife (Molly). Kate was touched they'd all remembered but the message involving domestic drudgery was coming over loud and clear. How had she let herself be so stereotyped?

'Thanks, darling.' Inside the box were a pair of gorgeous beaded and tasselled gold earrings. She held them up. 'They're beautiful.' Although she couldn't imagine when she would ever wear them.

'Nipple covers. I can't imagine you taking up stripping for a living, Mum!' said Noah, laughing.

'Noah!' Molly punched his arm.

'Earrings, you dummy.' Lara gave him that withering look that needed no words. 'They'll look great on you. Come and see.'

Lara went out with Kate to the cloakroom. 'Go on, put them on.' Lara stood at the door, watching as Kate struggled to get the pins through her rarely used pierced ears. She never had much reason to dress up.

Lara clapped. 'They look brilliant! I knew they would.'

Kate swung round and hugged her daughter. 'I love them. They make me feel quite different and they're not at all heavy.' When she moved her head, the gold threads glinted in the light.

'Good. I thought you deserved something a bit glamorous. Let's show the others.'

In the kitchen, the men were laughing.

'Perhaps they don't look their best with this old shirt.' Kate hesitated, running her hands over the faded blue cotton.

'Then treat yourself to something new. You deserve it, Mum. All you do is wait on this lot. It's time you did something for yourself.'

'That's not quite true.' Kate laughed, but Lara's words hit home. She loved looking after her family, had never had much ambition to do anything else after Lara was born. Just occasionally she did dream of striking out, doing something for herself but the opportunity never arose. Or was it rather that she had never grasped it? That's why she worried about Molly still being at home. Lara meanwhile was working in hospitality at York racecourse and sharing a flat in the city. When they went back in the kitchen, the men were bent over the table, studying something in the paper.

Alan looked up. 'Whoa!' He gave a stagey blink or two. 'Look who's just walked in! You look...' He paused.

'Amazing,' said Kit. 'They suit you.'

'Aren't they a bit young for you?' Noah often spoke his mind without thinking of the person on the receiving end.

Kate took a step back but felt Lara's hand pushing her forward and remembered what she had said. Yes, she did deserve a bit of glamour in her mundane life. Why not?

'I don't care,' said Kate, suddenly emboldened. 'I like them and I'm going to wear them.' She shook her head from side to side so the tassels caught the light again.

'Go, Mum,' said Kit. 'Mata Hari in the kitchen.'

'Mata who?' said Noah.

Kit put him down with a glance.

'Oh, piss off.' Noah drained his glass.

'Boys! Please. Not tonight.' Kate nodded towards the casserole. 'Can you take this through to the dining room?' Lara was right. It wasn't the most special of menus but, if it was a family favourite, what did it matter?

Alan picked up the dish. 'Chicken.' Matter of fact.

'I thought chicken chasseur was your favourite.' Kate was indignant. He knew perfectly well what it was. Although the meal was for her birthday, she had cooked for the family.

'Ooh, lah-di-dah! Just thinking you might ring the changes once in a while.'

'Perhaps you should cook once in a while, Dad.' Lara's voice

28

was steely. It occurred to Kate that her daughter's job had given her new strength of character.

'Get you and your feminist ways,' said Noah as they all went through to the dining room and took their places at the table.

'Don't be silly. It's a simple question of equality. Why should Mum always be the one in the kitchen?'

'We're out all day, working. That's her side of the bargain,' said Alan, making Kate feel as if their marriage had been reduced to a business arrangement – although she knew he didn't mean it.

'I didn't notice you arriving early so you could help.' Molly started pouring out the water.

'I don't live here any more, in case you hadn't noticed.'

'Thank God.' Noah's voice was low but loud enough for them to hear. He took a bottle of wine, going round from glass to glass.

'Children!' Kate's voice was sharp with anger. 'How old are you?' And why was it always her who stepped in rather than Alan who was sitting at his end of the table, checking football results on his phone under the table. She could tell by the way he was totally focused on his lap.

'Sorry, Mum.' Both Lara and Noah looked sheepish, although Kate didn't miss the flicker of anger in Lara's eyes.

'Give your mother a rest.' Alan looked up and entered the fray too late to be of any real use. He got up and went to stand behind Kate with his hands on her shoulders. 'It's her birthday.'

Kate lifted her glass of wine. She had a vision of sitting at the table on her own in a fancy restaurant with asparagus, a half lobster and salad, raspberries. She would eat every mouthful in silence, savouring each one. The wine would be exquisite, white, crisp and delicate on the palate. Not the rich red that Alan favoured that they were drinking tonight.

'You know what? I'd rather have white,' she heard herself say, turning her head up to face him and pushing her glass away.

He looked surprised. 'But I thought . . . of course. What-ever you want.' He left the room to return with a bottle of Sauvignon.

She hadn't the heart to say anything. But how, after more than thirty years of marriage, had he not registered that was the one white wine she didn't particularly like. It was the same with carnations and chrysanthemums. Her non-appreciation of them hadn't sunk in either, judging by the garage flowers he returned home with from time to time. But of course, it was her fault. She had never made her objections clear enough. 'Is that all there is?'

He looked puzzled and held the corkscrew away from the neck of the bottle.

'I don't really like Sauvignon.' There. And she felt better for saying it.

'You've never said.' He sounded hurt.

'I'm sure I have. You just never listened.' She reached up to squeeze his hand to reassure him she was joking. Except she wasn't. And, judging by the look on his face that disappeared almost as soon as it arrived, he knew it. At least he was trying.

While he went to get the one and only bottle of Chardonnay, the conversation began to dart round the table, stopping at one member of the family, then another – never for long enough for any disagreement to flare up. Kate began to relax. Alan unscrewed the top from the bottle of white wine and poured it for her before taking his place back at the head of the table. This was where she was most comfortable, in the heart of her family. She raised her hand to feel her new earrings and caught Lara smiling at her.

'Not on my watch, you won't.' Alan's voice rose above the rest. 'The old tractor's got a few years left in her yet.'

'Investing in the future makes perfect business sense,' Noah said.

'When you've been farming as long as I have, you'll find

experience is better than theory.' Alan's fist banged down on the table.

'In Germany...' Noah was not going to give up.

'Boys, please.' Kate had had enough.

'No work at the table,' said Molly, quoting her mother's oft-used phrase. 'It's your birthday, Mum. What would you like to talk about?'

'Actually I've got a surprise for you.' Conscious of everyone's eyes on her, she was almost as surprised by the decision she had just taken as they would be. But this evening had made up her mind. Instead of being taken for granted and turning into a drudge, she would do something for herself. Strike out. They were waiting...

'I'm going to Spain.' The words fell from her mouth before she had time to deliberate any further. 'That's going to be my birthday treat to me.'

Alan stared at her. 'When? We can't go now. The farm needs me.'

She smiled down the table at him. 'Actually I've been invited away for a long weekend. Just me and my three best friends from school.'

They had never gone away, one without the other. She had booked holidays, found lost passports, washed and ironed and packed for two. Not this time.

'In Spain?' His disbelief was almost comical.

'Mallorca, to be exact. I'm going to Amy Green's place. Just for four days so I won't be gone for long.'

'Amy Green of *Amy Green*?!' Molly sounded astonished. 'I read a piece about her online somewhere.'

Kate nodded as a smile spread across her face. She really was going to go.

'How do you know *her*?' Lara's estimation of her had obviously risen a notch. 'You've never said.'

'Old school friends. I haven't seen her for over forty years but we've kept in touch. I sometimes see what she's up to on Twitter.'

'Twitter?' Alan's astonishment had reduced him to bluster. 'Since when?'

'Since Molly showed me. I don't tweet though.' She glanced round the table. 'What's so funny?'

She had to wait till her family stopped laughing before she could go on. 'Amy's asked three of us out to her villa for a long weekend.' When she had first read Amy's letter, Kate had been far from convinced by the idea. Not that she would ever bring up what happened, of course. But what did it matter? That was years ago. This was Amy holding out a hand to show there were no hard feelings, presenting her with an opportunity on a plate.

The time had come to stretch her wings: to do something unexpected of her. To live a little.

There was a moment of silence as the others took it in. Then: 'Good for you.' Kit raised his glass in her direction. 'It's time you did something for yourself. Here's to Mum's reunion.'

Kate could have hugged him as the others raised their glasses in support. Only Alan looked uncomfortable. She shouldn't have sprung it on them like that but she would rationalise the speed of her decision to him later, and get him to understand. After all, it wasn't as if she was going to be away for weeks. She'd soon be back to enjoy the new duvet and 'ring the changes' with the cooking. She gritted her teeth. This was something she wanted to do. For herself. She shook her head again, so her earrings jiggled.

'And these bad boys are coming with me!'

4

Jane's office was a soulless box of a room, with grubby windows that were jammed shut, yet it was the one place where she could get a moment's respite from her hospital duties. She had brightened it as best she could with a couple of photos of David and Paul, their son, and one or two of the ornaments given to her by grateful patients. That was enough. On the shelves behind her desk were a number of hefty medical textbooks and piles of back numbers of the *BMJ* and the *Lancet*. She pulled a letter out of her handbag. Why on earth was Kate writing to her? She had brought the letter into work with her, uncomfortably aware that she hadn't phoned back after the voicemail Kate had left months earlier. Work and life – those two most demanding of creatures – had got in the way. Now she had a moment to herself, she tore off the Sellotape that stuck down the back of the reused envelope, and pulled out a note and another envelope.

Amy sent me this for you. Let's go. Yes? It should be fun.
Love, Kate x

Puzzled, Jane opened the second.

Come to Mallorca for a long weekend!
We can stay in our house and could catch up at last with

no interruptions. What do you think? If you like the idea, I'd suggest we go in September when the weather's lovely and it's less crowded. I'm asking Linda and Kate too.

I hope you'll all be able to come.

Love

Amy x

Jane groaned. Kate always got so overenthusiastic when there was something she wanted to do. The last thing like this she'd tried to persuade her to go to was when she got excited about returning to school for an old girls' reunion that had then been cancelled a fortnight before due to lack of interest. Admittedly that was twenty years ago.

She put the letters into her bag. She would think it over when she got home although she already knew her conclusion: *No thanks.* She needed to finish up before she went home. She never tired of her job as a medical oncologist that remained as fascinating, stimulating and humbling as she had found it when she first started out. She logged into her personal inbox to find a stream of messages.

Among them was one from Kate, asking her to call her when she had a moment. She understood how demanding Jane's job was. As her personal life was becoming too. She checked the list again. Yes, Rick had called to confirm he was in town that evening. They didn't need to speak, just the fact that he'd made the call was enough. They'd been snatching these rare times together long enough for her to know that. She also knew she should call time on their relationship and yet she couldn't bring herself to, despite her fear that David must be close to realising what had been going on under his nose for years.

How had she got herself into this position of being torn between two men, neither of whom she could live without? David was the husband she had wanted Rick to be: thoughtful, kind, loving. He would do anything for her and she could rely on him one hundred per cent. And she loved him back with almost all her heart. But the little bit left over went to Rick, the ex-husband David would never be: unpredictable, charismatic and irresistible. They had made a hopeless partnership in every way except one. She couldn't help smiling as she remembered the time they had punted their boat into an overhanging willow tree to make out under its branches. And that time years later in St Helen's Passage after a late one in Oxford's Turf Tavern – urgent, fast, thrilling. Then she remembered the hurt on David's face when she turned up half an hour late for dinner with his friends who were over from New York. She felt ashamed and yet addicted. But to keep David, she knew it couldn't go on.

She looked at her watch. Six-thirty. She only had a few minutes before she had to leave so there was little point in attacking the mound of admin that was waiting for her – that would wait till the morning – so she just had time to return Kate's call.

Kate picked up immediately. 'I shouldn't call you at work but I wanted to check you got Amy's invitation to Mallorca?'

'I did just now.' She straightened the ornaments on her desk into a neat line, turned the photo of Paul, her son, to face her. 'I've decided to go. I've told the family.'

'You have?' It was unlike Kate to take the initiative. 'I haven't given it much thought yet. If it was just an evening somewhere, then maybe. But I don't have time for a whole weekend.'

'The thing is, I've been thinking about it, and I don't much want to go on my own so I was thinking if you . . .'

'No. Really, no.' She may not have given Amy a thought for years but the unexpected reminder of her existence had forced what had happened between them back through the haze of memory. A whole lot of growing up had happened since then.

'Aren't you curious?'

'A bit. But not so much that I'd want to risk spending all

that time together.' She scrolled through her emails to see if there was anything that couldn't wait till tomorrow.

'But I'd be there and it might be fun.'

Kate had always been there. Since they were children, they had been best friends but they couldn't be more different. Kate's life was so unlike hers. She had been married to the same man for years, stuck out in the Yorkshire Dales, popping out children until she had the family she so longed for. When she and Alan had asked Jane to be godmother to Lara, their first, she had been delighted and touched. That had come at a time when she had been convinced she wouldn't ever have children herself. Before David. Before Paul, their son. But it was always Jane who took the important decisions in their friendship and Kate went along with that. This was a first. They might live hundreds of miles apart but they talked occasionally, saw each other when they could and told each other about everything in their lives. Or almost everything.

How disbelieving and disapproving Kate would be if she ever got wind of Jane's continuing on-off relationship with Rick. Marriage and family meant everything to her.

'I don't think so.'

'At least think about it. I think we'd enjoy it.'

She couldn't remember when Kate had last sounded so determined. Every now and then she stood her ground, but usually ended up caving in for a quiet life. She had always shied away from confrontation.

'I've checked the flights and they're not too expensive. What's the worst that can happen?'

'None of us get on and we have a terrible time?' She folded up the letter again as if she hadn't opened it.

'That won't happen. We're not kids any more. You can always get a flight home or check into a hotel if things go that badly. But why should they? I'll be there.'

But Jane's attention had wandered back to one particular

email from one of the surgeons, asking her opinion on an aspect of the treatment plan discussed at that morning's multi-disciplinary meeting for a woman recently admitted to the hospital with metastatic cancer. She should read it and reply before she left. 'Look, can I call you back? Something's come up.'

'Of course. But we'll need to book soon before the prices go up.'

'I'll call you back in the morning.'

'Truly?' She heard the note of hope in Kate's voice. 'You'll think about it then?'

'Yes, I'll think about it but no promises.' She would have to be content with that.

Twenty minutes later she was at Rick's flat, a neat pied-a-terre for the man whose real life took place in the enormous country pile that she'd seen in a photograph on a shelf once. The next time she came it had been removed so there was no longer any sign of his other life. She hesitated for a second before ringing the bell. She shouldn't be doing this. But, as always, when he opened the door, those thoughts flew out of her head, leaving the residual question: occasionally sleeping with the man you'd been married to for seven years didn't really count. Did it? Their relationship could hardly be termed an affair – after all they only met very occasionally, when he happened to be in town and their schedules coincided. Sometimes they caught up on the phone.

The door opened and he stood there, smiling. His face was lined, his hair grey but his eyes had never lost that twinkle that made him so attractive.

She kissed him, felt that familiar flip of her stomach and walked into the flat. This was the best stress buster there was and just what she needed. Any day now she'd receive a letter from the General Medical Council summoning her to a tribunal that had the power to kibosh her career. Although, if she were honest with herself, she had to acknowledge if anyone was responsible for that, she was. If she wasn't at work, that was all she could think about so coming here would take her mind off what was to come.

He followed her into the living room where a chilled bottle of her favourite Sauvignon stood beside two empty glasses. He quickly did the honours and passed her one.

'Shall we?'

She nodded and went into the bedroom where she put her glass on the bedside table. Sometimes it was like this. Almost wordless. Adrenaline-fuelled and satisfying. Tonight she might talk to him about what she'd done that day, ask his advice, but she could tell by the way he was looking at her that he wouldn't be in the mood. And, in fact, she didn't want anyone, least of all him, knowing about what she'd done. His day in meetings would have been as testing as hers. She didn't ask him. Instead she removed her clothes, those belonging to a well-respected member of the medical fraternity. No one would have any idea that underneath them, she was someone else altogether. Her body was well-toned, thanks to the rigorous demands of her personal trainer, whom she saw in the gym at least twice a week before work, and a regimented personal regime. Her underwear was brief but expensive and (she hoped) seductive. Judging by the look on Rick's face, her hopes were satisfied.

They fell on the bed as if for the first time and she forgot everything else. They knew each other's bodies intimately, knew the shortcuts to each other's pleasure. Afterwards, they lay back, exhausted and fulfilled, the stresses of the day disappeared.

Rick propped himself up on one elbow. 'You look amazing and that was . . .'

'Amazing too?' she offered.

He grinned. 'As always.'

'We should stop doing this.' She rolled onto her side to look at him.

'You always say that.' He ran his hand over her breast, stopping at her nipple, teasing it, watching her respond. 'But no one's going to find out. If they haven't before, why would they now?'

'Oh, I don't know.' She spoke lazily, losing herself in his kiss before she tore herself away. Every time she was surprised that he still found her attractive. Her body had changed so much since they first met but then, so had his. They had both done their best to keep ageing at bay. HRT and exercise seemed to do the trick for her, but she had no idea what his secret was. Nor had she any idea who else he might be having an affair with. She never asked him because it didn't matter. What they had together was unique and what he did with the rest of his life was his business, not hers.

She had never regretted the break-up of their marriage, recognising that they could not live together. He had been an infuriating mix of possessive, quick-tempered and unfaithful, determined to get to the top of his career as an orthopaedic surgeon. She had been equally career-focused and refused to let his demands get in her way. Her friends might accuse her of being selfish but that was the person she had been and it had got her to where she wanted to be. Her parents had been proud and supportive – she had been an only child in a medical family and given every encouragement. They had been delighted when she had married Rick, another member of the profession, although they would be spinning in their graves if they knew she was still involved with him. Not that they had carried any particular brief for David. As far as her father had been concerned, her second husband – an advertising man through and through – stood for everything he didn't approve of: crass commercialism. For as long as she had been married to him, they had said nothing but had made their feelings quite plain.

They lay facing each other, almost touching. She could smell the wine on his breath.

'How's David?'

'He's well.' She disliked talking about her husband with him. Any such conversation brought her guilt racing to the surface. 'And Paul got that job at Masters and McAusland.' She named the marketing company that her only son had worked so hard to get in to. Somehow she felt easier talking about him. 'Remember I told you about that away day he had to go to – team-building stuff.'

His hand ran down the curve of her side, halting on her hip bone. 'Good for him.' But she could tell he wasn't really interested. His hand was back on the move.

'I should go.'

'So soon?' He turned down the corners of his mouth like a spoiled child. 'I may not be back for a while.'

'You will.' She smiled at him, moving her head so their noses touched. Her tongue touched his lips, until he responded.

Sex for sixty-year-olds was severely underrated, she thought fleetingly as they kissed, long and hard. Perhaps she didn't have to be back precisely on time after all. What were a few minutes either way? And anyway David had said he was going to be late tonight...

By the time Jane got home, David was in the kitchen cracking eggs into a bowl, James Taylor on the sound system. He turned as she came in, looking at her over the thick dark frames of his specs. In her hand was the letter she'd picked up off the table in the hall. It had arrived at last. Sometimes apologies and lies weren't enough. The word 'tribunal' had jumped out at her immediately. If only she hadn't transgressed all hospital protocol and succumbed to temptation. If only... But she had been thinking not about herself but about Paul, her son. And her grandchild.

She read through the letter carefully. It confirmed the date of the tribunal in four weeks' time. Type of case – Misconduct. Thank God her father was no longer around. He would have been aghast however she tried to justify her actions.

As she changed into her fleecy slippers, she reflected on what she'd done. It had only taken a moment. A moment that broke all the codes of her profession. And when Paul had found out what she'd done – for him – he had been appalled. However she would defend herself to the end so her reputation would remain intact. That was everything to her. She was so close to retirement that she couldn't go out with a cloud hanging over her.

'Good day? Scrambled eggs, okay?' We don't seem to have anything else.' That wasn't a reproach, just a statement of fact. They worked on the premise that they had equal responsibility when it came to running the house and their lives together. Both of them held down demanding jobs so everything they had together should be shared.

She went over to him, and put her arms around him, feeling the sort of warm affection that she had never felt for Rick. 'Perfect.'

'Have you heard from Paul?' He turned down the volume on the speaker dock. 'Is he getting on okay?'

'He hasn't rung, but that's a good sign, I'm sure. I'll try him in a minute.' She got out the bread, cut a couple of slices and stuck them in the toaster.

'Is something wrong?'

'Just they've sent me notice of the hearing at last.' She pulled out a chair at the kitchen table and sat down, suddenly feeling exhausted.

He swung round, stopping his stirring. 'You don't think they'll take it seriously? Extenuating circumstances and all that.'

'They have to. There's no getting away from the fact that I

accessed patient records without consent and that's enough for them to find my fitness to practice impaired.'

He returned his attention to the pan. 'But, all the same, they might be sympathetic. You've been in the game for so long.'

But she was realistic. 'Long enough to know way better. They may well judge that breaching confidentiality of medical records is a threat to public confidence in our profession, and whatever they decide will be on my records for ever.' The thought almost paralysed her with dread. She ran her finger round the top of her glass. 'Please let's talk about something else. How was your day?'

He patted the top of her hand, comforting her, knowing nothing he could say would make things better. 'Same as. Martin was being a complete prat about a new account one of the young directors has brought to the agency. Thinks it'll tarnish our brand if we take it on. But he's operating in the dark ages. Even I can see that. If anything we need to be seen to be taking on new products.' He brought their supper to the table. 'Bring on retirement is all I can say.'

'You don't mean that.' How often she had heard him say this over the last few years. 'You founded the company with him, you can't hand over the reins to someone else. You'd hate that.'

'Oh, I don't know.' He rubbed a hand over his head as if expecting to find the hair he'd lost years earlier. 'Sometimes you have to move on or call a halt. And I'm beginning to think that it would be nice for us to spend more time together.'

She looked at him in astonishment. 'What's brought this on?' The idea of retirement had crossed her own mind but she always dismissed it immediately. What would she *do*? Of course she didn't want to go on practising if she had become a liability but even then she felt sure she'd find other work. She wasn't one to sit at home twiddling her thumbs when she wasn't gardening, reading or travelling the world with all the other pensioners with nothing else to do.

'Think about it. We see so little of each other really. We're both always working, and look how late you come home from the hospital.' He nodded towards the kitchen clock.

She studied him closely, feeling her guilt come knocking. But he didn't look as if there was any underlying meaning to what he was saying. Besides, she was extremely careful – something that had always marked her life. He couldn't possibly know about Rick.

'I phoned, by the way. You must have been busy.'

'When?'

'About seven-thirty.'

She thought fast, her heart beating quicker. 'I had to go and see a patient's husband on the ward.' She quickly used something she'd done earlier in the day to cover herself. That wasn't exactly lying, was it? And better that than have David suspect.

'Will she be OK?' He was concerned, as he always was when hearing her talk about her patients.

'She should be.' She thought of the woman she'd looked in on at four-thirty, lying so peacefully while her anxious family gathered round her bed. She had done everything she could for the moment. Now the night staff would take over. She would check in on her as soon as she got in the following morning.

'Even after all this time, I still don't know how you do it.' His pride in what she did always embarrassed her.

'It's what I trained for,' she said simply. 'I had Kate on the phone today. She wants me to go to Mallorca for a long weekend – school reunion. Can you imagine?'

'What did you say?'

'No, of course. Not my thing at all, although I do feel I should support her.'

He looked thoughtful as he forked up the last of his eggs. 'Why don't you go? You need a break. You could go and then I could fly out and join you for a few days. Why not?'

'I can't take time off just like that.'

43

He tipped his head to one side, questioning, expectant. He knew that wasn't strictly true. 'You've done it before and Terry and Raina covered brilliantly. They don't need that much notice.'

'It's not fair.' She stopped herself. 'And anyway, I don't want to go. Imagine being cooped up with women I don't even know for four days. Being at school together shouldn't bind you for life.' Besides there were aspects of her schooldays that she would rather forget.

'But Kate does.' He got up, took the plates and put them in the dishwasher. 'Bed?'

Her mind flicked back to Rick. Only a couple of hours earlier they were... *Stop it!* 'In a minute. I want to call the ward to check everything's OK and then take a look at Tim's article. I promised I would. My registrar,' she reminded him.

'Don't you ever stop?' For the first time, she heard the disappointment in David's voice.

'Not unless I have to. You know me, busy saving lives.' She made the joke that had accompanied them throughout their marriage.

But this time he didn't laugh. His face was sad or resigned (she wasn't sure which) as he went out. 'I'll leave you to it then.'

She was ashamed of the way she treated him. He didn't deserve her apparent indifference, yet she couldn't help it. He knew what a workaholic she was when they married, but now she was even refusing him a few days away as he reached a turning point in his own life and would probably value the time they could spend discussing their future. Still, they could always do that without her having to join a school reunion. She would say so in the morning.

5

Rob had swiftly and effectively removed himself from my life. Over one weekend, he packed up his belongings and gave me his key. I still felt numb. When I looked back, without my rose-tinted glasses, I could see our relationship for what it was. I had managed to ignore the fact that our lives were lived in parallel. We got on well enough, but love had become a habit, not a raison d'être. The business was what had brought us together in the beginning but was also what had split us up in the end. Once we agreed we didn't want children and threw all our energies into making Amy Green work, we didn't consider the consequences. I saw that now. If I ever had doubts and suggested we changed our minds, he reminded me of all the reasons why we shouldn't. Just as I did when he wavered. Apart from making the initial decision, we were never in synch. What hurt was that, despite having persuaded ourselves that we were enough for each other, he was moving on to a ready-made family, leaving me alone.

As for the money, he promised he'd pay me back, every last penny. Despite everything, I wanted to believe him. Involving the police and charging my own husband with fraud was the last thing on earth I wanted to do. Kerry was quietly furious but she went along with the plan for my sake. Our staff's livelihoods were of paramount importance so I had to keep the business running for them, apart from my own interest in it. Whatever

I felt about Rob, and there was little positive left there, I didn't want him going to prison. I couldn't do that.

I was finding it impossible to concentrate at work and Kerry had been encouraging me to take some time off. I was still waiting to hear back from the others about Mallorca. To be honest, I was getting cold feet about the whole thing by this stage. I only knew them as teenagers. What would they be like now? And what if they didn't love the villa and the village as much as I did?

Linda was the first to email me.

What a great idea. I'd love to come. I can take time off work, I've got extra care for my aunt and my neighbour's going to look after Sacha, my cat...

I've never understood the attraction of pets myself – just another domestic responsibility and tie. I know that makes me sound like an uncaring person, but I'm really not. I would never have once nursed that childhood ambition of becoming a doctor if that were true. I don't mind other people's pets but I can't stand it when they're sentimentalised and treated like little people. They're animals, for God's sake. However, Linda wasn't bringing her cat with her.

In answer to her question: So what do I need to bring? I emailed back

Just yourself. Everything else is there. We're in the mountains just above a village called Fornalutx. You'll love it. At least I hope you will.

I'm sure I will. Can't wait, came the reply.

Suddenly I was praying the other two would accept. A long weekend alone with Linda was not what I'd had in mind at all. I had a feeling that what we once had in common might

46

have evaporated. I couldn't imagine the two of us pubbing and clubbing together in the way we used to when Jane had turned her fleeting attention to others of her acolytes. We never minded because we knew we'd come back into favour in the end. And we always did. Almost always.

You can imagine my relief when Kate emailed to say she would love to come too. Then, slightly to my surprise, Jane wrote saying she was on board as well. So I would have my chance to straighten out the record. Last time all four of us were together, I had been accused of being a liar and a thief. And last time we four were together, the others had watched as I was punished.

This long weekend was happening! I checked the flights, confirmed dates with them all and called Carmen, our housekeeper who lived in the nearby town of Sóller, and warned her we would be arriving in just under four weeks.

'The pool and garden will be OK?'

'Yes, of course. I make sure Fernando goes up there as he should. You want me cook for you?' I could tell she didn't want to.

'Thank you, Carmen. But I don't think we'll need that. Perhaps something for the night we arrive, but that's all.' That would give me an excuse to withdraw from the others if it was all getting a bit much. Or, if it was going well, there were several restaurants in the village. 'Just something simple.'

I ended the call, reassured that the place would be ready for us in a month's time. When I thought of Ca'n Amy – 'Amy's home' – Rob's and my *folie de grandeur*, I couldn't help feeling more relaxed about what I was arranging. We bought it on a whim, twenty years earlier, after we'd been on holiday in Sóller, one of the prettiest towns in Mallorca. We'd seen the house in the window of an estate agent and spent the remainder of that day going up to see it and debating the madness of owning a property abroad. But its position and character completely did for us. When I say 'character' I mean that it was almost a ruin – an old farmhouse that had been waiting for a long time until the members of the family who owned it had all agreed on the sale. While they fought, it fell down. Well, not down exactly, but let's just say it was badly in need of the TLC which we wanted to give it.

The weeks passed in a flash. Everyone booked their own flights, and Jane and Kate hired a car. The rest was up to me. I flew out a few days early, partly so I could make sure the house was at its best and ready, but I also wanted to see how I would cope on my own. I was pleasantly surprised. The house soon worked its magic and I found myself falling into my usual routines. Of course I missed Rob, but I made myself think about other things. My studio here was where I had done some of my best, or at least my favourite work. I was often most inspired on the island. The light, the colours, the natural world – they all combined to give me the basis of some of my best fabric designs. Once I'd done the basic sketches then I'd sometimes get the team out to work on their development with me. I wanted them to see where they came from so the finished fabric and colourways ended up exactly as I imagined. Then they went out into the world as soft furnishings, fabric and cushions to provide various different and now sought-after looks.

So finally the day dawned. I had offered to meet Linda off the early flight. First thing in the morning is the most beautiful time of the day here for me. I left Fernando cleaning the pool when I set off for the airport.

Would they all be as nervous as I was? I'd thought a lot about the idea of revisiting one's past. Why do it? Those days were over; but the more I reflected on them, the more they mattered. Although I hadn't seen these three women for years, we had once been virtually inseparable. In some ways, they knew more about me than any of the friends I'd made since then.

They knew my parents – my postman father and dressmaker mother. They knew the home I'd come from with its small front room taken over by my mother's business, the kitchen where my dad sat smoking, listening to the radio; the small bedroom I had which was the result of dividing a large room into two so Dan, my brother, and I had one each. My parents shared a tiny bedroom at the back of the house. They knew my brother – in fact I think Kate might have had a thing for him once but he'd never tell me – and all the things that shaped me. And I knew the same things about them.

I knew Kate would do anything for an easy life, even taking the blame and the detentions for Jane when, for example, a tennis ball flew through the window of the Head's office or confessing to cheating when Jane had copied her work, not the other way round.

I knew Linda was the smartest of us all and something had gone very wrong in her life. She had been the brightest and liveliest too. Despite remaining single, she seemed to have found a career that fulfilled her, although messing about with books all day wouldn't float my boat.

I knew Jane lied to get her way out of trouble as if it was the truth. I think she often believed it was. Isn't that what compulsive liars do? With her, it was all about image, about being the best.

Why did they want to come? I thought a lot about that too. Perhaps because they had the same sorts of feelings as me. Unfinished business. Curiosity. A need to tie up loose ends. We all like to know how a story finishes, and this was our chance to find that out. Never mind a few days of escape from the humdrum routine of our daily lives.

I always liked the drive down to the airport. I took the main road down from the mountains, through the tunnel and along the wide main road flanked with almond, olive and citrus groves until they met the outskirts of Palma, skirting the city and ending up at the airport. I left the car in the multi-storey car park and crossed into the airport building to wait at the arrivals gate. How many times had I done this? Countless. I loved taking visitors and friends, some dazed from the early flight, up to the house. Back along the main road with the mountains looming ahead, then through the tunnel, and it all changed. I loved the pleasure on their faces when they saw where they'd be staying.

Linda came uncertainly through the arrivals doors, looking round as if worried there would be no one to meet her. I needn't have worried I wouldn't recognise her. Her hair was different, cut short and tucked behind her ears, but her face hadn't changed. Still the same oval shape though her features were older. Unlike the other people pouring through, she was dressed for an English summer in a black linen dress and jacket, with a scarf wrapped round and round her neck. I felt almost naked in my summer dress by comparison. I waved and the frown left her face.

We sized each other up. We knew each other so well once but who were we now? She was slightly stooped, as if she'd hunched over a desk for years. Her expression was serious, anxious as she came towards me.

'Amy!' She pulled her case behind her. 'Thanks for meeting me. I thought you might have forgotten. You must be so busy.'

We exchanged polite kisses. I caught the faint scent of sweat and something reminiscent of my mother's 4711 cologne.

'It's no distance. Well, you'll see.' I led her out of the airport to the car.

She squinted against the sun, as if shocked at its brightness. 'Like an idiot, I've packed my sunglasses.'

I passed her the spare pair I kept in the car door. 'Try these.'

'Thanks,' she said, putting them on. 'Have you had the house here long?'

'About twenty years. It's changed a lot since we bought it

though. When Amy Green started to make money we were able to transform our romantic hideaway into something else: somewhere we could be ourselves and recharge our batteries. We've had it extended and redesigned, keeping as many of the original features as we could. You know . . . fireplaces, shutters, ceiling beams – that sort of thing. You'll see when we get there.'

'Your husband doesn't mind us being here?'

What a funny question. 'Not at all. He's delighted.'

I don't think I'd bothered to tell him.

She glanced at me as my voice rose a notch. 'Is he at home. In the UK I mean?'

'Yes. He's got work to do.' I should have thought about what my reply would be when they asked me about Rob. I didn't want them to know what was happening between us. I didn't want them to know that my life wasn't as perfect as it had been a few weeks ago. If I'm honest, I wanted them to see where I'd got to in life after such an unpromising start. 'It was always intended to be a girls only weekend.'

'Of course.' She went back to staring out of the window.

'You never married?' I said, in an attempt to steer the conversation in another direction.

'No,' she said, not offering anything more. This wasn't the most promising of starts. I hoped that once she relaxed, things would get easier. It was just a question of time. There was something magical about Ca'n Amy and I didn't know anyone who hadn't been able to relax and forget about whatever shit they'd left behind them. As the countryside streamed past, Linda occasionally commented on what she saw, asking me what the orchards were, were we near the sea, that sort of thing and nothing more about me or Rob. When we reached our destination, her eyes widened as we crawled down the stony drive and the house was revealed. 'Amy! This is amazing.'

When someone reacted like that, I always saw the house as if for the first time. The first time since the builders finally moved out, that is. And it was beautiful. Under that brilliant blue sky, the honey-coloured Mallorquin stone building blended with the landscape. The shutters at each window were the traditional shiny forest green and the hard edges of the house were softened by the surrounding palms and large pots filled with plants and trailing with flowers, the walls partially hidden by the profusion of bougainvillea. The shadows cut sharply across the stone paving outside the front door. I noticed a bead of sweat making its way down the side of her face

'Come in. I'll show you your room. You can change and I'll have a cold drink ready for you. We can have a swim or just lie by the pool.'

She followed me through the house, up the stairs, down the cool pale corridor, past the paintings of Mallorquin landscapes that I had collected over the years, as many by local artists as I could find. I opened the door to her room, dark and cool inside.

'This is yours. I hope you'll be comfortable.' I threw open the shutters and light flooded in. I'd decorated it using fabrics from my Seascape range; the blues and greens sang against the brilliant white walls. In her funereal black, Linda resembled a moth that had fluttered into the wrong habitat. 'I usually keep the shutters closed until the sun moves round in the afternoon. But it's up to you of course. This switches on the fan.' I flicked the switch so the ceiling fan began to turn, cutting through the air with a loud creak. 'But there's aircon too. I prefer the old-fashioned way, but that's just me. There.' I pointed to the control panel.

Linda gasped. 'This is all so beautiful. It's perfect.'

'I'm glad you like it. I'll leave you to it. Come and find me when you're ready.' I left her yanking her case onto the wooden luggage rack.

In the kitchen, I exchanged my driving pumps for my flip-flops with stones that glittered in the sunshine. I took the lemonade (home-made by Carmen) from the fridge and put it on the tray with the glasses, added a few oaty biscuits on a plate, and took the lot outside. I hoped it wouldn't be long before the place started working its magic and she began to relax. Otherwise it was going to be a very awkward few days.

I was reading the paper at the table on the main terrace when I heard footsteps. With a slight sinking feeling, I half-turned my head and said, 'Come and sit down.'

'Thanks.' A man's voice answered.

I spun round. 'William! I didn't know you were going to be out here this week.' Our neighbour, a renowned pianist, led a peripatetic life that took him all over the world on tour. When one ended, he and his wife, Fleur, came to hide away from the glare of publicity that had accompanied them for the previous weeks.

'Yes. We came here after Paris for a month.'

He sat beside me. Even in his seventies, he looked great in shorts and T-shirt with his messy grey hair and face as fascinating and lined as Samuel Beckett's. His broad hands rested on his thighs – insured for over a million at the last count. I couldn't help staring at them. I always wondered how he dared go anywhere without wrapping them in bubble wrap to protect them from injury.

'Lemonade?'

'No, thanks. I've got to get back, but Fleur asked me to see if you were here and if you and Rob would like to come over on Saturday night. We're having a drinks party. Johnny's got one of his artists over for an exhibition in the Valldemossa gallery and asked us to introduce him to some likely patrons.' He winked at me, knowing my interest. 'Do come.'

'You know I would—' I would never be going to a party with Rob ever again and I wasn't sure how I felt about that. Odd? Bereft?

'But...' he interrupted me, lifting his hands into the air, palms towards me.

I smiled. 'But Rob's not here and I've got three girlfriends staying for a long weekend.'

'Bring them.' He stood up. 'Any friend of yours...'

'Well, if you're sure...' I couldn't imagine how the three of them would greet the news that they were being swept off to a party where they would know no one.

'Of course I am. We'd love to see you. It'll be the usual crowd plus a few.' The usual crowd would be a mix of wealthy expats, many of them temporary residents with fancy houses like mine, plus the more bohemian arty community who lived on the island permanently. William's parties were never dull.

I hesitated for a moment too long.

'That's settled then.' He grinned. 'About seven-thirty?'

I watched him disappear round the corner of the house. As for Linda, Kate and Jane – I hoped they might be intrigued to see a little of that side of island life. They might even enjoy it.

And so it began.

6

In her room, Linda picked up the soap and sniffed it. She
shut her eyes as the scent of a thousand tea roses lifted her
spirits. A fat bumblebee buzzed in and out of the window,
leading her gaze to the view that stretched down the hillside to
the mountains across the valley. In the foreground, olive trees
moved in the breeze, their leaves silvery green in the sunlight.
Beyond them the dark shiny leaves of a citrus orchard. Directly
beneath sprawled the sandy-coloured buildings of what must
be Fornalutx.

The last time she was anywhere as beautiful as this was when
she had gone on a walking holiday in Sicily. But since she began
her affair with Mike her life had been spent waiting, full of
hope and disappointment. Exotic holidays were talked about
then not taken because something always came up. Perhaps she
should have taken the reins of her life and gone away on her
own or with friends, but it was doubly hard to escape when
her elderly aunt had demanded so much of her. How could she
turn her back on her Aunt Pat after she had been a mother to
her for most of her life?

She remembered once cornering her. 'I'm thinking of going
away. A couple of weeks, that's all.'

Aunt Pat's colour rose and her lips tightened. 'Oh, Lin, I was
about to tell you I'm not feeling too good.'

Her heart had sunk. Somehow, always somehow, she rarely got away.

Now she was actually here, she wasn't sure how to be or what was expected of her. She was aware that Amy must be wondering how one of the most popular girls in the school – hard though that was to imagine now – had ended up as she had. There was a time when the four of them – Amy, Jane, Kate and her – had the world in the palm of their hands. Everyone believed they could have anything that they asked for. Until that last year of the sixth form. That's when it all went wrong. And yet they had stayed in touch, as if nothing had happened. But of course, the others didn't know half of what really went on.

She picked her navy swimsuit, newly bought for the weekend, off the bed. She had better change so she could join Amy in the pool. Swimming had been off Linda's radar for years. Her swimming captain days were well behind her now. Public swimming pools were out of the question ever since she'd read an article about the skin particles and other unthinkable bits of human residue that floated around in them. And lying sunning herself was not something she'd ever done much of. The few holidays she had taken were occupied with her aunt and trips to English towns where there was a cathedral and a decent tea shop. She hung up her dress – perhaps black was rather sombre now she was here. She'd felt like one of those heavy black beetles beside Amy's butterfly while they made polite small talk, both impatient for the other two to arrive. One thing she had registered was Amy's reluctance to talk about her husband. In the old days they had confided everything to one another. But that was a long time ago, and they were different now.

Her swimsuit seemed to be made of yards of material ruched over the front to disguise the less than perfect bits of any woman's anatomy. She stepped into it, wiggling it up her legs then ... Jesus! ... it was like pulling on an iron corset. Bit by discouraging fat-fighting bit, she yanked it up her body, twisting herself, jumping up and down (twice) to persuade it over the more stubborn bits. Finally, it was on. She caught sight of herself in the mirror. She might be in danger of asphyxiating but her stomach looked almost flat. Almost.

But her eyes were tired, her body heavy with exhaustion. Her nights were spent lying awake worrying about the decision ahead of her. Her future hung in the balance. What to do? Her constant deliberations and the early start had caught up with her at last. She sat on the bed, just for a second, then let herself fall sideways so her head was on the pillow – as soft as a cloud. Bliss. She shut her eyes, lifting her legs on to the bed so she was lying on her back. Immediately her stomach flattened and she relaxed. Just for a minute. No more.

The rhythmic whirr of the fan above her head was soothing. This room was the haven she'd never had and was all she'd imagined a room in Amy Green's house would be. Everything was perfect, colour co-ordinated, with light-green towels that hadn't been hardened by being hung out to dry, soap that hadn't dried or cracked from not enough use, a chair covered in a pale fabric in a shell design that matched the flimsy curtains fluttering in the breeze. On her bedside table were a couple of recently published novels. On the distressed chest of drawers, a vase of fresh flowers. She had touched them earlier and, yes, they were real. Every detail had been thought of, right down to the hairdryer in the top drawer, the hot water bottle – did it ever get cold here? – the soaps, shampoo and conditioner. On the white walls hung framed photographs of seascapes. Her eyes closed.

She was startled awake by her phone. Aunt Pat's number, though her aunt rarely used her mobile.

'It's Judy. I've come in to look after your aunt. Everything's fine but your aunt would like to speak to you.' Her voice was calm, patient: qualities Linda tried to harness but that soon turned to impatience when dealing with her elderly relative.

'Linda! Where are you? Will you be here soon?' Aunt Pat's voice was sharp with anxiety.

Linda braced herself. 'I'm in Spain, Aunt Pat. Remember? I'll be back in five days.'

'There's a strange woman in the house. I don't know what she's doing here. She's eating my biscuits.'

Deep breath. Keep calm. She can't help it. 'That's Judy. She's looking after you. She does the shopping, just like I do, and she can eat the biscuits too.'

'But I don't want her here.'

Her aunt's protest was like a drill boring through her brain. Exerting as much patience as she could muster, she said, 'I can't visit you this week. I'm on holiday now. Judy's there to help you.'

'I'm all right on my own.' Defiant but despairing.

'No, you're not. We've talked about this before.' So many times, Linda had lost count. 'If I hadn't come and switched the gas off last week, you might have blown the place up and your wrist's only just properly better from your fall in the living room. It's much better if there's someone there, making sure you're safe and you've got everything you need.'

They went round and round in circles until Aunt Pat finally caved in and Linda hung up, exhausted and as upset as her aunt. She should never have come here. Her responsibilities at home were too great.

A brisk knock at the door brought her back to where she was. Startled, she looked at her watch. She had been asleep for two hours! What would Amy think of her? The door handle turned.

'Are you awake? Can I come in?' Amy entered carrying a glass of water that rattled with ice and a slice of cucumber. She was wearing a bikini with a brightly coloured sarong tied at her waist. Linda envied her poise, her chin-length blond bob that said fashionable and attractive, against her own less studied appearance.

She sat up. Despite the fan, her whole body was covered in a thin film of sweat and . . . she was wearing her swimsuit. 'I was about to come for a swim but . . . I'm so sorry.'

'I know. That early flight's a killer.' Amy put the water down beside her. Her nails were painted the palest of pinks. 'I thought I'd leave you to recover. But the others have arrived, so we wondered if you were ready to join us. We're going to have lunch quite soon. But today's all about lounging around, getting the hang of the place so, if you need to sleep for longer . . .'

'No, no. I'd woken up just before you knocked.' She didn't want to burden anyone else with her concerns over Aunt Pat. 'Perhaps I'll have that swim first though.' The idea of wiggling herself out of her costume for a shower was too much. A swim was the answer. 'Give me a minute.'

'Of course. You can find your way?'

'I think so.' Linda nodded as Amy left the room, straightening the vase of flowers on her way past.

As she walked down the corridor, after several minutes wrestling with her swimsuit in the loo, Linda could hear unfamiliar voices and laughter. She froze. Of course, none of them were who they once were either. Time would have changed everyone. What was she doing here? She wouldn't fit in any more. The others were more successful, far more at home in this sort of environment than she was. Four days of being the odd one out lay ahead of her. She turned into the living room, another room straight out of a magazine. It was as if the stylists had just walked off set. White sofas, plumped cushions with an angular terracotta-coloured pattern, terracotta tiles, Moroccan mosaic tiles framing the windows, judiciously placed ornaments, vases and a couple of photo frames. She approached one of them. He must be Mr Amy Green, squinting into the sunlight, tousled grey hair, raised glass in hand, laughing. Nice.

She took a deep breath, slipped on her sunglasses and walked through the open glass doors into the brightness of outside.

There was an excited gasp. 'Linda!'

At the table with Amy were two women, one of whom Linda recognised immediately. 'Hello, Kate.'

'You recognise me?' Kate sounded surprised and a little disappointed.

'You haven't changed *that* much,' said the other woman, who must be Jane. Her once long dark brown hair was streaked blonde like Amy's but in a shorter layered cut. Her face was lean, her lips thinner than Linda remembered. It was as if she'd been through a stretcher. She extended a long lean leg so her varnished toenails gleamed blood red in the sun. Like Amy, she was wearing a bikini. Linda folded her arms so her towel covered her stomach.

'It's your smile,' she said to Kate. It was true. Linda had immediately recognised the infectious grin that lit up Kate's face. However much weight she might have put on, however different her hair (a pepper-and-salt crop), however lined her face, that smile had remained unchanged.

'I'm Jane,' Jane said unnecessarily.

'I had a funny feeling you might be.' That hadn't come out quite as wittily as she'd intended. But the others laughed all the same. Linda joined in, relieved. Looking at Jane she suddenly saw the teenage girl beneath the adult's face: indulged, confident, middle-class, secure in the knowledge that she was still the leader of this particular pack.

'You swimming?' said Kate. 'I've been dying to get in since we arrived. Shall we?' She stood up. Linda could feel the wiring in her swimsuit pinching the skin underneath her breasts.

'You should have said.' Amy got up too. 'I'll just put some

lunch together. Nothing much. No, no.' This to Jane who had swung her legs off the lounger. 'You stay there.'

'But I thought I might walk around the garden.'

'Oh, sorry. I thought you were offering... never mind.' Amy smiled before turning on her heel and leaving them to it.

Linda wondered whether she should follow her inside but Kate was egging her on down the paved path to the pool.

She laid her glasses and towel on the edge and got in as quickly as she could, trying not to fuss as she inched her way down the steps and the cold water rose up her legs. At the deep end, Kate plunged in with a giant splash while Linda dithered then slid under. Eventually submerged, the world seemed a better place altogether. She watched as a pair of yellow butterflies danced up into the clear sky over her head.

'Isn't this place something else?' said Kate swimming up beside her. They swam a stately breaststroke back down the pool together.

'I've never been anywhere like it.'

'To think I almost didn't come.' Kate rolled over and floated on her back like a contented seal.

'Why not?' Linda remembered her own hesitation.

'Oh, they need me at home.' Her eyes were shut. After a second she turned her head to look at Linda. 'Four children and a husband who all take me for granted. So I decided this was the perfect excuse and they can discover for themselves exactly how much I do for them.' She paused. 'You never married, of course.'

Linda shook her head. 'No. I never did.'

'Lucky escape.'

In that second, Linda loathed her. That was the kind of remark thrown out by smug marrieds as a joke but that could cut the recipient to shreds. At least Amy had not done that. Linda's own situation felt far from any kind of escape. If Mike had announced he was leaving his wife to marry her, she would

61

have agreed like a shot. But he never did. And she had never pushed him, just waited. And now it was too late for anyone else. 'Not really,' she said, and swam to the steps.

Kate came after her, wading out of the pool with her. 'Listen. I'm sorry. I didn't think. It's the excitement of being here. Almost five whole days on my own, with no one to think about but myself. I feel quite giddy.' Her smile was enough to make Linda forgive her.

'That's okay. I'm used to it. It's just not a great time for me at the moment.'

Kate looked understanding. 'Man trouble?'

'Partly. But that trouble's over.' Mike was the last thing she wanted to talk about. To her horror, she felt tears stinging her eyes so picked up her dark glasses and slid them on. 'I've got trouble at work.'

'Then we must make the most of your time away from it.' Kate wrapped a sarong around herself. 'Look. They've laid the table.'

Linda was grateful she didn't quiz her for more information, but then most people did dismiss librarianship as boring when in fact it was anything but.

'Do you want to change first? It's all cold so it can wait.' There was something in Amy's voice that said she would rather they didn't. Her finger tapped a beat on the table.

'No, no.' Kate took the hint. 'We're fine.'

Linda's costume clung like an immoveable damp second skin. Despite her self-consciousness, she removed her towel in the hope she would dry faster. Nobody turned a hair.

'This looks amazing.' Kate eyed the two salads, the cheeses and bread. 'Shall I?' She picked up the bottle of water.

'Anyone for wine?' Amy nodded towards a bottle of rosé in an ice bucket.

'Yes, please.' Immediately Linda realised she'd replied too fast. 'If anyone else is,' she added.

Jane put her hand over her glass and Linda's heart sank. A glass of wine would make getting to know each other again so much easier.

'That would be great.' To Linda's relief Kate spoke up, ignoring Jane's raised eyebrow. 'I know it's lunchtime but we're on holiday and we haven't seen each other for years.'

'Not since I . . .' Amy began to pour.

'I've never forgotten your Mum's front room.' Kate spoke over Amy, whether deliberately or not, Linda couldn't tell. 'All that fabric piled up all over the place, dresses hanging everywhere and her at her sewing machine in the middle of it all. There was hardly room to sit down.'

'That's where you must have got it from.' Jane extended a lazy hand towards their surroundings. 'All this.'

'Maybe, and she'll never know. That's my one sadness. That she died before Amy Green really took off.' Amy laughed. 'Well, OK, four-town-wide and online. But that's enough for me. You know, if someone had predicted what would happen, I'd never have believed it. I was so embarrassed by that front room.'

'You shouldn't have been. She made Mum an amazing suit once. Pink with pockets. And all those costumes for Mrs Jay's dance shows.'

'Mrs Jay . . .'

And they were off, reminiscing about one teacher then another. 'Remember how we put deodorant in Miss Wesley's locker?' Linda remembered how Amy had tried to persuade them not to and Jane had sworn blind she had nothing to do with it when questions were asked.

'Yes. And I took the flak for it,' said Kate, laughing.

'We were doing her a favour. How bad was her BO?'

'She probably couldn't help it. Some people do have a real problem.' Jane spoke in all seriousness.

The three of them turned on her in astonishment.

63

'That wasn't what you said at the time. You were the one who put us up to it. Remember?' Kate dared contradict her.

Jane looked puzzled. 'Me? I don't think so.'

'Yes! You got us into so much trouble. But somehow you were always the one who came out smelling of roses.'

'That's not true.' Jane took off her sunglasses, anchoring them by sticking one of the arms in the centre of her cleavage. 'Guys?' she appealed to the other two. 'Support me.'

'What about the time you and Amy were caught shoplifting?' Linda saw the twist in Amy's mouth as she looked down and realised she'd said the wrong thing.

'I had to do that.' Jane looked away.

'What? Put the blusher and lipstick into my bag so I'd take the rap?' Amy's voice was controlled as she passed round the salad.

Jane grimaced as if she didn't like what she was hearing. 'But my dad would have gone mental if I'd been caught.'

'And it didn't matter if mine did?' The salad bowl was banged onto the table.

'Of course it did.' Jane picked up her knife and sliced through the melting butter. 'I was selfish, I suppose. I do see that now.'

'And we were in school uniform.' Amy ran a finger along the chain round her neck. 'So it didn't do me any favours with Minters. "You've brought the school into disrepute",' She mocked the Scottish accent of their draconian headmistress, Miss Minton. 'She had it in for me after that.'

'And when she caught you smoking behind the gym.' Kate put two fingers to her mouth and puffed.

'God! She was *so* unforgiving.'

'Can you imagine what it must be like faced with all those rebellious sixth-formers though? I suppose you have to set an example if you want to maintain any semblance of order.' Kate took the middle path as usual.

Amy looked as if she was going to say something else but changed her mind. 'Ghastly,' she said before lifting her glass. 'Cheers.'

'Here's to a wonderful weekend.' Linda followed suit, appreciating the chilled wine as it ran down her throat. Just the ticket. Like the others she was avoiding the subject of Amy's expulsion. She had her own reasons for not wanting to revisit it but, nonetheless, there it sat like the elephant in the room.

'And thanks for having us here. It's just...' Kate looked around her. 'Well, just thank you.'

Amy smiled, smug like the Cheshire Cat in Linda's well-thumbed childhood copy of *Alice's Adventures in Wonderland*. 'My pleasure. I hope you'll all have an unforgettable time.'

Linda tried to ignore a flicker of unwelcome unease. If nothing else, she was sure they would do that.

7

After lunch Kate excused herself to make a call home. If she didn't, Alan would panic and do something daft like call in Interpol to mount a search for her. She walked up to the top of the garden where she found a rustic wooden table and a low-slung chair. Sitting there looking down the slope to the house and to the valley beyond, she was the queen of all she surveyed. Four more days weren't going to be enough. And then again . . . But things were bound to get easier as they got to know each other once more.

She called up Alan's number, taking pleasure in the sight of the photo she kept as his caller ID. Not a conventionally handsome man perhaps but his steadfastness and kindness shone from his face. Those were two of the reasons she married him, or at least had stayed married to him once the first flush had dimmed a little and the demands of a working sheep farm and young family took over.

'Kate!' His voice immediately took her home.

'Of course it's me. I promised I'd call when I got here so here I am.'

'I thought something might have happened.'

'You needn't have worried. The plane didn't crash and Jane drove like an angel. I didn't know you cared so much.' That was a little harsh, and she was pleased he did, even though it could be suffocating at times.

'Of course I do.' He sounded hurt, but recovered himself. 'So how are the harpies?'

'Don't call them that.' But he did have a point. Despite their friendship, Jane had been very chilly towards everyone. Linda wasn't at ease and Amy was nervous. 'It's all a bit odd. We're in the most stunning villa on the side of a valley though. And it's all so green.'

'But . . . ?' He knew her too well.

'But it's not as easy as I'd hoped. Jane's being too aloof. And that's making all of us uncomfortable.' With her foot, she nudged an overturned black beetle back on to its legs and watched as it lumbered off. 'She could be like that when we were kids. Weirdly, it's probably what made us all want to be her friend. Such a thrill when she thawed and you were in her warmth again. But right now, it's just unpleasant.'

'But she's Lara's godmother. You've known her for years.'

'Yes, but you know we don't see each other as much as we used to and, honestly, we don't really have that much in common now.' She wondered why she hadn't registered it before.

'What about the other two?' Alan rarely went anywhere apart from the farm and the pub in the village, so when Kate brought back news from the outside world, he lapped it up, although his interest never lasted long.

'Linda's a funny one. The future looked so bright for her and yet she's never married, and now she's facing redundancy. But she won't talk about it.' Perhaps she hadn't tried hard enough to draw her out. 'She used to be so confident. We all wanted to be like her. As for Amy, having got us all here, she's so desperately anxious for us to have such a good time that she's like a cat on hot bricks. I can't help feeling that she's waiting for something to happen. I'm making it sound awful but I'm sure it'll all be much better when everyone relaxes.'

'A few drinks should do it.' He laughed, gruff and hearty.

'Maybe tonight.' But she could tell he'd finished with that subject.

'I'm glad you called, because there's something I want to ask you.'

She hadn't been away for a day but already she was missed. She stared up at the sky as two birds flew high above her towards the mountains on the other side of the valley. 'What's that?'

'Molly and Donal want to have a party, putting up tents in the lower field. I said I'd ask you.'

Kate shut her eyes, despairing. They had discussed what they were and weren't prepared to let their children get up to while living under their roof countless times. Did he never listen? Or was it that he did, knowing he could forget and rely on her. 'You're in charge, Alan. What do *you* think?'

'Well, I . . .' Katie knew exactly what was going through his mind. The disruption, the noise, the people, the mess. He wanted her to say no.

'They're twenty-two, darling.' Just a brief reminder. 'They ought to be able to clear up afterwards. What were you doing at that age?'

'So you think it's OK?'

'I think it's fine. Just lay down some ground rules.' Surely he could do that on his own, or at least wait till she got back.

'You're so sensible. As always.' He had no idea how dull and how irritated that made her feel. 'And Tom and Sarah have taken pity on us and asked me and Noah over for supper.'

Katie gritted her teeth at the word 'pity'. She had made and frozen five dinners for them both before she left. She had left a pan of soup in the fridge and a newly baked loaf of bread in the bin and two in the freezer. Their neighbours wouldn't think Alan was so helpless if he didn't play the part. If he was ever away for a rare night or two, they didn't invite her unless they were having a dinner party for friends. They assumed she could cope on her own. 'That's nice.' She listened to her own voice with some scorn. If anyone had encouraged Alan in this role of helpless husband it was her. By looking after her family all their lives, attending to all their needs and most of his, she had taught them to rely on her. Kit had barely been able to boil an egg when he moved away from home. Whose fault was that?

'You did do the wages before you left?'

She sighed. 'Yes, I did. They're in the desk as usual. Don't worry, everything's done and, anyway, I'll be back soon. There's nothing that can't wait.'

'Oh, I know. I'm fussing. Sorry.' He sounded as if he meant it. 'Have a good time and forget about us.'

'As if.'

When she'd ended the call, she sat for a while enjoying the solitude. She was often on her own nowadays, but this was quite different. Having absolutely nothing to do and no one waiting on her was a novelty. There were children playing in a neighbouring garden, their shouts interrupting the quiet, but no one was expecting her to wade in and separate them, find them something else to do. How could she possibly forget about her family? They might treat her like an old tea towel but they were all she had.

She had always been a family woman, unlike the other three. She had grown up in the middle of a large and messy family of five and loved her childhood enough to want to carry it on. On leaving school, she had imagined she would have a career first but she and Alan had met at university and the die was cast. He was studying agriculture and once they'd decided to get married, there was no alternative to going with him to his family farm where he worked until his father retired and passed the business to him. She had learned to help with lambing, weaning the motherless lambs, shearing, everything else that went towards maintaining the farm, from venturing out in the harshest weather to feed or even rescue animals struggling to survive to tweezering the stray white hairs from the sheep's faces for showing. She had thrown herself into it all, imagining that the farm would then be taken over by one of their children – Noah, as it had turned out. The girls and Kit were going to make their own way. And her? Kate? What was there for her now?

She was the only one of the three women who much of the time worked outdoors. Every day she got to walk outside, come rain and shine, dogs at her heels, children once tumbling around her, appreciating the astonishing beauty of her surroundings. Her life was such a lucky contrast to the cool deskbound nature of theirs. She considered them.

Neither Amy nor Linda, for all their job satisfaction, had children. And there was something funny going on in Amy's personal life because Kate had noticed the photo of Rob had been removed when she last went through the living room. And, for all she had gathered so far, Linda's was currently empty. And Jane? As difficult and unpredictable as ever. Her friendliness on the flight had turned almost to indifference when they arrived at the house, as if, at the sight of Amy and then Linda, a tap had been turned off. But then, why had she come?

Unable to sit still a moment longer, Kate walked back through the garden, stopping to pick up a windfallen lemon on the way. She held it to her nose, inhaling the fresh, biting sweet smell before spotting Amy by the pool, waving at her. 'Come and join me.'

With the delightful realisation that she had absolutely nothing else calling on her time, she went over and took another lounger. Although they were lying in the shade of parasols, the air was warm. Kate gave a deep sigh.

'She hasn't changed, has she?' Amy fiddled with the controls of a small radio until a song Kate didn't recognise, sung by a woman in a smoky contralto, played in the background.

'Who?'

'Jane.'

'I don't think any of us have really. Not underneath.'

'Not even Linda? She was such a star at school. It's as if the life's been washed out of her. I wonder what happened.'

'You'll never get it out of her.'

'She's here though. Which is brilliant. I'm glad you all came.'

'What made you ask us? After what happened, I'd have expected you never to want to see us again. But you even kept in touch with me and Linda.'

'I didn't steal that watch.'

'That's what you always said, and I believe you. But does it really matter any more? You've had a great life whatever happened then.'

Amy propped herself up on an elbow and stared at her. 'I'd almost forgotten about it but I've had a bit of a crisis at home.' She raised a hand to stop Kate from asking anything. 'I don't want to talk about that, but I was reminded and I've realised that having the slur on my character does still matter. My parents died without seeing my name cleared. I can at least try to straighten it out for me, if not for them.'

'I guess.' The quiet fury in Amy's voice unsettled Kate. 'But we didn't have to come all this way for that.' She was beginning to wish she had stayed at home. But then, as she looked around her, no she didn't. 'Isn't this meant to be a relaxing weekend?'

Amy grinned. 'It will be. Don't worry, I won't do anything to spoil it.'

'That's a relief.' Kate returned the smile while trying to imagine what could have happened in Amy's perfect life to make her want to dig up the past. She was dying to know more but she would ferret about a little later. Of course she remembered when Amy was expelled. She had claimed Mr Wilson, the art teacher, had offered her high marks for sex and then his expensive watch had been found in her desk. All her claims of innocence had been dismissed, and with one term left before the A levels, she had gone to the comp and screwed them up.

Let's move off the subject.

'How did you start Amy Green?'

Amy shifted so that she was more comfortable and began to talk as they both gazed towards the other side of the valley. 'I was so angry about the injustice of everything when I was expelled and reckoned that if everyone believed I was a liar and a thief, I might as well live up to their expectations. My poor old Mum and Dad. I got in with Mick Kirby's lot . . .'

Kate remembered the band of punks who hung out in the Museum Gardens in York, smoking weed and taking God knows what else. They dyed their spiky mohicans the colours of the rainbow, shredded their clothes and hung around looking threatening. She and her siblings had always been told to stay well clear of them, and had. But Amy had dyed her hair yellow and pink and run with the gang for some time. Kate had once bumped into her in Browns and barely recognised her in her torn tights and short tartan skirt.

'I hung out with them until Billy May died from that overdose. Remember him? That shocked me into seeing some sort of sense, thank God. Some of the others were getting into heroin then but I got out before it was too late. Unlike Billy.'

'God, I'd no idea.'

'Mmm, not the part of my life I'm proudest of. But my parents were amazing. I needed a job and no one wanted to give me one, not surprisingly. I'd given up all interest in academic success – didn't think I was capable. So being a doctor was out of the question then. But, despite everything, Mum threw me a lifeline and I started working with her.'

'So you got over your embarrassment?'

Amy laughed. 'No choice! I hated it to start with but I had to do something and gradually I got more and more involved. I loved the fabrics: all those textures and patterns and colours. I used to dream of being able to design my own and spent hours in my room, painting my ideas, never thinking I'd actually get there in the end. After Dad died, Mum and I carried on working together until she couldn't cope any more and went to live with her sister. I moved down to Bath to be near her. I lived in a bedsit, kept my head above water with every job you can think of: waitressing, chambermaiding, barwork, shop work – anything that would pay. No one knew me there so it was like starting again. I used to spend ages trawling car boot sales, charity shops and jumble sales for bits and pieces I could furnish my room with for next to nothing. It turned out I had something of an eye and my new friends began to ask me to help them. Eventually I enrolled in evening textile design classes. It was like coming home. A door was opened and I knew what it was that I wanted to do.'

'I wish I'd had a calling like that.'

'But you've got a family. I forfeited that.'

'Deliberately?' Kate couldn't believe that anyone would forgo the all-consuming pleasure of children.

'Yes. Rob and I decided that we would throw all our energies into making the business work. And it did.'

'Did?' Kate hadn't missed the catch in her voice.

'Yes, did. We're not going to be working together any longer.' She was not inviting questions. 'We disagree about the direction we should take so I'll be looking after the business on my own from now on.'

Kate looked at her, but Amy's eyes were hidden by her sunglasses, and the rest of her face gave nothing away.

'That's brave.'

'Not really. I've got a great team.' She sat up quickly. 'In fact, talking of them, I ought to just catch up with emails before everyone surfaces again. Do you mind?'

'Not at all. You go ahead. I'm very happy here.' Kate shut her eyes again as Amy went inside. Left alone to her thoughts,

Kate had to try to shake off the apprehension she was feeling. The next few days didn't look as if they were going to be quite the restful time promised. If Amy planned to confront Jane or Linda over what happened, things could get pretty uncomfortable. Jane was not someone who backed away from confrontation. Kate, on the other hand preferred an easy life. And she'd put money on Linda doing the same. What was more, there was definitely something that Amy was not saying. If it emerged over the next days, however much she might prefer it not to, Kate would support her if she could.

8

Jane shut her bedroom door, thankful to be on her own at last. She pulled off the short kaftan that she'd brought back with her from Pondicherry when she and David had spent a couple of weeks in Tamil Nadu. That was the last big holiday they'd taken together. A couple of years ago now. She lay flat on the rug near the end of her bed. A few stretches would help get rid of the residual stiffness from the flight. She pulled her knees up to her chest and rocked gently from side to side, feeling the pull on her spine.

Very soon, she'd be meeting Rick in Barcelona. That had been the final deciding factor in making this trip. That and the fact that she wanted to get away before the tribunal. She would have to face up to what she'd done just a few days after she got back. What better reason to escape and recharge her batteries?

When he called her, she had mentioned that she ought to come to Mallorca for Kate's sake even though she didn't want to. Quick as a flash, he'd said: 'Why don't we meet up while you're out there? Perfect excuse . . . Just a suggestion,' he added when she didn't immediately reply.

'We couldn't.' But the temptation was almost irresistible.

'Not in Mallorca. But you could fly to Barcelona.'

'What about David?' A flicker of guilt troubled the edge of

her conscience. After all, he had suggested they take a break together, too.

'What about him?' Rick's voice was like warm chocolate. 'Tell him you're at a conference for a couple of days. He'll never know.'

Caught by the spirit of his idea, she had caved in. David hadn't questioned her. Quite the opposite.

'This gives me just the excuse I need for a couple of bridge evenings and that concert I said I wanted to go to,' he'd said a couple of days later.

'But you don't play bridge.'

'I'm going to learn. Might be a good thing to do of an evening when there aren't any emails to answer.' She said nothing. Though she shouldn't, she wanted both men in her life – they complemented one another and between them gave her everything she couldn't find in just one of them. Selfish? Perhaps. But practical too.

He had driven her to the airport, kissed her cheek as she got out of the car. 'See you next week, love. Enjoy your reunion and I hope you get something out of the conference.' He didn't ask any more about the subject of the conference or who would be there. He'd long ago given up trying to involve himself in the gritty detail of her job, easily satisfied with the basic generalities. He didn't have the stomach for half the cases she dealt with. Of course, with his medical background, Rick did.

She stretched out her legs, then twisted her torso from one side to the other and back, feeling the stress ease from her body. Rather than think about the impending tribunal, she turned her mind to David and what he would be doing now. She bet he'd be in the garden with the newspapers, a cup of coffee, music drifting outside from the speakers in the living room. Content.

After a few more stretches, she got up and lay on the bed, able to relax at last. She looked down at herself, pleased with what she saw. She worked hard to keep her body in this good shape. David had taken it for granted for years. Rick was the one who still appreciated it. The thought made her breath catch. How ridiculous to feel like this about the man she had married and then let go. But this way was better for both of them. She picked up her phone and started to text him then deleted it. Instead she sat up, arranged her body so she looked her most seductive and took a selfie. When she'd finished editing it and changing the filters, she texted it to Rick.

Thinking of you. Only four days to go and she pressed send.

She lay back, eyes closed, remembering the last time they were together. Drifting, her hand slipped into her bikini bottom, touching, imagining. She was brought back to the present when her phone pinged with Rick's response. She picked it up.

Are you feeling all right?

Not the response she'd been expecting. She was working on a pithy rejoinder when her eye caught the name of the sender. *Shit!* She checked again. *No!* Not possible. But it was.

David.

She had sent the photo to David by mistake.

Suddenly she was wide awake. How could she have done that? She checked the thread, disbelieving, only to confirm that was exactly what she had done. Her photo sat right underneath the last text she'd sent to him, asking if he'd bring back some onions for supper three nights earlier. How could she have been so careless? After so many years of extreme caution, of warning Rick to be nothing but discreet when communicating with her, in one unguarded moment, she had been the exact opposite. She would have to reply. Say something. She thought quickly and typed...

Fabulous. Just thought you should see what you're missing

She sent it. Would that wash?

Another ping alerted her to a photo of a cup of coffee and a newspaper.

I wasn't invited, remember, so no choice. Making the best of things here though.

She smiled as relief rushed through her. She wasn't safe to be left on her own.

There was a knock at the door. 'Jane!' Her name was whispered.

She grabbed her kaftan and flung it over her head. 'Yes?'

'It's Kate. Fancy a walk? Amy's got to pop down to Sóller.'

'Isn't it a bit hot?' She tried to excuse herself.

'I wasn't planning a trek, just a short explore. Apparently there's a nice circular walk we could do – about forty-five minutes. Linda's staying by the pool.'

After that text mess-up Jane was far too wired to sleep. Goodbye siesta. She swung her legs over the edge of the bed. 'OK. I'll be with you in a minute.'

Walking along a lane edged by olive trees growing on terraces held in place by the neatest of drystone walls, their route ran parallel to the rooftops of Fornalutx below.

'Isn't this wonderful?' Kate flung out her arms to encompass the surrounding landscape. 'I knew it would be gorgeous. She obviously surrounds herself with beautiful things – you can tell that from her website. But this is . . . just heaven. I feel quite different here.'

'I'm hoping for a bit more than trees, pretty villages and sunshine.'

'Like what? Don't be such a misery. If you don't try, you haven't a hope of enjoying yourself. It's very generous of her to have us here.'

Jane laughed. Kate was the only person who ever dared tell her like it was. 'I know. I'm cross because I've just done the stupidest thing. I'm sorry.'

'What?'

'I'm an idiot, I sent David a text meant for someone else.'

Kate raised an eyebrow. 'That isn't so bad, surely? Can't you just explain to him?'

'Not that easy.' She tipped her hat forward to shade her face. 'Not that sort of text.'

'What sort of text was it?' Always curious.

Jane was wishing she hadn't said anything and tried to brush her off. 'Oh, you know.'

'No I don't,' Kate insisted. 'What was it? You can tell me. You know I'm like the grave when it comes to secrets.'

That was one thing Jane had learned long ago. Kate enjoyed gossip but if entrusted with a secret, her discretion was rock solid. 'It's nothing, honestly.'

'Then why are you cross?'

Jane folded in the face of her persistence: another of Kate's sterling qualities. 'It wasn't anything I said. I sent a picture of me in a bikini to a man I've been seeing. At least I thought I did.' Jane picked her way up some stone steps that shortcut the bend in the road as it wound up the hill, fuming at having put herself in this situation. 'In fact I sent it to David by mistake.'

Kate stopped dead, looking torn between shock and laughter. 'Who?'

Jane felt the urge to say something. Unburdening herself would come as a relief after so long but, however tempting it was to offload, she didn't want to hear her friend's disapproval.

'But what about David?' Kate had always had a soft spot for David, found his tiresome old jokes funny. Life would be so much easier if Jane did too, but she had heard them too often and, like most jokes, they had dimmed with repeated telling.

'He has no idea. That's the point. I've been seeing...' She hesitated. 'Well... Rick... if you must know.'

'Rick?' Kate was disbelieving. 'Not Rick, Rick?'

Jane nodded, already regretting she had said anything.

'But you divorced him years ago. It's not true!'

'We met up again at a medical conference years back. It's just sex, nothing else,' she added hurriedly. 'But obviously I don't want David to find out.'

'Just sex!' Kate's disbelief had turned to disapproval.

Jane had expected shock but usually Kate sat on the fence in any debate, seeing the issue from both sides, unable to come down on either.

'How often do you see him?'

'Not often. Two or three times a year. Twice in the last month – but that's an exception.' She wouldn't mention Barcelona.

'But why? I thought you were happy with David.'

'I am, but Rick and I have still got that...' She cast about for the right expression. 'Sexual chemistry. That's all it is. We both know that.'

They were walking side by side, both of them looking at the ground.

Kate kicked a stone so it skittered off the track. 'And now you've given David a clue.'

'But I think I covered up OK.'

'Then why tell me?' Kate tipped her face back to the sun. 'God, I love it here... Of course I won't say anything but I think you're a fool.' She looked towards Sóller, the town further along the valley. 'I wish you hadn't told me.'

Why indeed *had* she said anything to Kate? Because she wanted someone to understand, someone she could talk to in order to understand herself. But she should have known better than to expect sympathy from someone whose views on marriage were traditional. She should have kept her secret to herself.

'How did Amy do so well?' Kate changed the subject.

'Grit and determination. Don't you remember what she was like at school?'

'That cross-country running. How I hated it. But she never gave up, even when it was sleeting and the rest of us had hidden in a barn.'

As they reminisced, a scrappy little dog raced out of a rusty iron gate, straight towards them, barking as ferociously as an animal three times its size. There was a shout and a man ambled out of the gate behind it. 'Jove!' But the animal ignored him and raced towards Kate.

She bent over, her hand out for Jove to sniff, otherwise not moving, waiting till it calmed down.

'Don't touch him!' yelled the man, an American, hopping on one foot as he used a finger to pull the back of his trainer over his other heel. 'Come here, you bloody animal. So sorry.' He ran towards them. 'My wife's dog.'

'Because he couldn't possibly be yours.' A stringy, over-tanned woman in a black crochet bikini, her blonde hair scraped back into a ponytail, appeared at the gate behind him.

At that moment, before they had time to get into a full-blown argument, Jove, who had been sniffing suspiciously at Kate's proffered hand took the opportunity to snap at her finger. Just as quickly, he dashed past her and on up the hill.

'He bit me!' She shook her hand in the air, before squeezing her fingers with her other hand.

'I'm so sorry.' The man drew level with them. He was good-looking in that way some men are when just turning the corner from their best days: greying curly hair, tanned, lean and angular in his shorts and flapping open shirt. His gaze travelled over their shoulder in the direction Jove had taken. 'Are you okay?'

'Of course she's not,' said Jane. 'Let me see.' She took Kate's arm.

'Jove!' The man's wife ran past them, taking no notice of them. 'Where are you? Come here.'

'He'll come home on his own, Sheila. Brendan Barrett,' he said, holding out his hand.

Both women ignored it.

Kate was examining the middle and index fingers of her right hand. 'He hasn't broken the skin.'

'Are you sure?' Jane leaned over to see. 'You shouldn't take any risks with a dog bite. Perhaps you should see a doctor, just in case.'

'I'm sure there's no need for that.' Brendan was frowning. 'Come into the house and wash it. A cup of something.'

'You should keep your dog under control.' Jane shouted at him over Kate's shoulder as she followed him towards the gate.

'It's fine, honestly,' said Kate. 'It was just a shock. He did warn me.'

'Not many people walk along here,' Brendan said as if that was an excuse as he stood back to let them through first. 'Where have you come from?'

'Amy Green's,' said Kate.

'Oh, Amy,' he said, as if that explained everything. 'You've taken a wrong turning if you're on the circular walk. I'll take you back.'

'That's okay. We'll manage.' Jane had taken an instant dislike to these people, but followed him and Kate into the garden. Hidden behind the drystone wall was a low building, the door in its centre wide open. Through the shady hallway was a white-walled living room with a high vaulted beamed ceiling and furniture draped with colourful throws, a dining table covered with books and papers. Pictures hung squint on the walls and over everything hung the faint smell of dog.

'I insist you have a drink – for the shock.' Brendan gestured towards the open folding door that gave on to a wide sheltered terrace and a plunge pool beyond. He spun round. 'But forgive me. The bathroom's this way.' He led Kate back into the hall and out of sight, leaving Jane on her own. She walked through to the terrace, turning as she heard the pad of bare feet on the tiles behind her. Sheila stood behind her with Jove in her arms, the dog's upper lip rolled back in a snarl.

'Your friend shouldn't have held out her hand. He's very nervous.' She stroked the animal's head. 'Shh, baby. He doesn't like strangers.'

Jane pursed her lips. 'We gathered. You're lucky that it wasn't more serious.'

'Shut him in the bedroom, Sheila.' Brendan reappeared. 'Now, what will you have? Sit down.' He gestured towards a table with four white plastic chairs gathered round it.

'Something soft. Lime and soda?'

'Lime and soda it is. Your friend's joining me in a glass of rosé.'

'Isn't it a bit early, Brendan?' The woman returned without the dog, having covered up in a floaty kaftan.

'Guests, Sheila. They're on holiday.'

'But *we're* not.'

He ignored her.

Being with them was uncomfortable despite Brendan's hospitality. He knocked back his wine and poured himself another under his wife's disapproving eye, all the time chatting about the area, the things they should be sure to see, relieved Jove hadn't inflicted any greater damage. In the background they could hear the dog barking from the bedroom. Sheila said little, once or twice looked at her watch. Her relief when Jane suggested they had to get back was embarrassing, although Brendan seemed not to notice. 'I'll drive you.'

Jane glanced at his third glass of wine, glinting in the sunlight. 'No, it's fine. We'll walk.'

'We want to find our way around,' said Kate needlessly as she stood up, leaving her glass three-quarters full.

'Let me at least put you on the right track.'

A bit late for that, thought Jane, taking another meaning from his words. She was the only one who could put herself back on the right path. If only she had the courage and resolve.

9

That first night, we sat outside on the terrace with the paella Carmen had made for us – one of her specialities. The smells of saffron and garlic drifted across the table. Fat pink shrimps jostled with plump mussels in their shells, tender chicken pieces and chunks of spicy chorizo in a mixture of rice, tomatoes and peppers. Above us, the inky black sky was spangled with hundreds and thousands of stars. It couldn't have been more perfect. Superficially, we were getting on better, though I suspect I wasn't the only one feeling the occasional undercurrent of tension. We all recognised there was one subject we'd have to address but at the same time we steered around Mr Wilson and what had really happened. However I was in no hurry and Kate's enthusiasm and energy kept us all on an even keel and the conversation flowing. Even Jane began to loosen up a bit.

As the evening went on, Linda began to emerge from her shell. Keeping her glass topped up seemed to help. The more she told us of her long affair with Mike the more my heart went out to her. What a waste of a life spent waiting on one man's whim. He sounded a total shit but Linda simply didn't see it like that.

'Everyone in the library loved him.' She looked round the table as if challenging us to contradict her. 'He was so good at his job, and getting what he wanted from people. The collection wouldn't have been anything without his contacts. And he loved me,' she said, staring into the middle distance, as she raised her glass again.

'Perhaps he did,' said Jane. 'But people change and start seeing each other in a different way. That's life. It's certainly what I've found.'

I noticed Kate look sharply in her direction before helping herself to some more fruit salad. 'It's not the same for everyone,' she said.

Something had obviously happened between them while they were out. They had returned from their walk full of Brendan, Sheila and Jove but that wasn't it. I had caught Kate looking at Jane a couple of times almost as if she didn't recognise her. I was puzzling over what could have gone on between them, but meeting the neighbours was preparation for the party the following evening. I was used to Brendan and Sheila but they were something of an acquired taste. She was ridiculous about that ratty little dog that she loved so much while poor old Brendan would kill for other female company – and I can't say I entirely blame him. Sheila could be very, shall we say, severe.

'We've been invited to a party tomorrow night,' I said, pleased to see that at least Jane and Kate looked happy at the prospect. 'Our neighbour, William Amos, is throwing one for an artist who's having an exhibition on the island. If you'd rather not go, that's fine of course,' I added. 'But I'll have to put in an appearance.'

'Of course we'll keep you company. All for one and one for all,' Kate said, quoting our childhood mantra. 'I don't think I've ever met a real live artist before.'

'He may not be much of one.' I didn't want too much hanging on William and Fleur's party. 'I don't know his work at all.'

'Does William live here full-time?' Linda had moved on from Mike, thank goodness.

'He's a pianist,' I explained. 'He gives recitals all over the world.'

'I've heard of him,' said Jane. 'Will he play tomorrow?'

'I shouldn't think so. That would rather take away from his protégé, don't you think?'

'I suppose.' Jane looked thoughtful. 'You were good at art, weren't you?' She stopped as if she hadn't meant to say that.

'So were you,' I said, wondering where this would lead.

'I used to love our art classes. Not that I've done any painting since.'

'For one reason only,' said Kate. 'Mr Wilson.'

My heart started thumping faster. Was this the moment?

'Oh yes! I'd forgotten about him.' Jane started playing with the wax that had dripped from the candle onto the table.

'You can't have. You fancied him like mad.' Kate winked at Linda and me.

'I did not.' Jane dropped a little ball of wax on to her plate. She didn't look at me. Only Linda glanced across at me, anxious, but I pretended not to notice. I wasn't ready for a confrontation quite yet – if that was what it was going to be.

'I thought you had a thing for my brother?' I couldn't resist throwing that one in. All of them had found excuses to come with me if I ever mentioned Dan was meeting me after school. He never took any notice of them, though. He barely took much of me.

That made Jane look up, her eyebrows arched in sceptical denial. 'I don't think so.'

'Wasn't that me?' Kate laughed. 'I'd got over it by the time we were in the sixth though.'

'Good to know.' A familiar voice broke in. I leaped to my feet.

'Dan! What are you doing here?'

My brother was standing at the door of the house, looking every inch his unkempt hippy self – yes, still. At least he had pulled his hair back into a tiny ponytail at the nape of his neck. Unlike most men his age – now sixty-three – Dan had never settled down in any conventional way. He had earned enough from working as a carpenter and other odd-jobbing to enable to him to lead the sort of peripatetic life I couldn't imagine.

'I thought you were coming next week.'

'Did you?' He came to the table and kissed me on both cheeks. 'Is that what I said?'

'Yes, in your last email. I've got friends here,' I said as if that wasn't obvious, but I was glad to see him. 'You remember Linda, Jane and Kate from school?

'Of course.' I don't think he did for a second, but his words had the desired effect. As he turned his attention to them, I could sense the girls' interest. His tanned arms were covered with golden hairs, his right wrist banded with two red thread bracelets that were so faded they'd obviously been there for weeks. His flip-flops had seen better days but his shorts and white cotton collarless shirt, sleeves rolled up, were quite presentable. He wore a small Indian fabric purse on a string around his neck.

'What is this? A reunion?' He said each of their names as he shook their hands, one by one, his eyes concentrating on each face: a technique that he'd picked up somewhere that clearly never let him down.

'Yes,' said Jane. I could see that even she was thrown off her stride. 'Just the four of us. We were inseparable then.'

'I remember.' Of course he didn't.

'So why *are* you here?' I insisted.

The girls were transfixed and he knew it. 'We finished the yoga platform sooner than we expected. I'd spent long enough in Goa so I thought I'd come here and see if there was any work to tide me over.'

'Of course you did,' I said as if it was the most natural thing in the world. I loved my gentle, mildly eccentric older brother. I was used to him turning up and leaving whenever the mood and work took him. I didn't care that he hadn't made the sort of success out of his life that others value, and understood that, to him, I was a reliable (and cheap) port in a storm. My success had served us both well and I'd been able to bail him out of financial scrapes countless times, although that role was wearing a little thin. To me, he was the big brother I always wanted. And to be honest, I was enjoying Kate's face in particular, which was all shades of embarrassment. 'Come and sit down.'

'No, you're all right. It's been a long journey so I think I'll hit the sack. Which room am I in, A?'

'You'll have to take the pool house.' Jane was in the bedroom he usually had but I certainly wasn't going to boot her out. Instead he was getting the one that we didn't like using because it was too far from the house and smelled of damp whatever we did to try to get rid of it.

He didn't demur. 'Great. I'm heading there right now.'

'Don't you want something to eat? A drink?'

'I had something in the village on the way up, so I'll leave you to it.' He went back inside, then reappeared with a small backpack and the battered leather carryall that I gave him years ago that went everywhere with him. 'We'll catch up tomorrow.' And with that, he walked towards the pool house, turning with a grin. 'Now no midnight bathing and waking me up.'

'As if,' said Jane, smiling.

'Oh God, I'm mortified.' Kate put her head in her hands.

'Don't be,' I said. 'He was lucky you were being nice about him. There are plenty of other women wouldn't be these days.'

'Do you remember the time we were cornered on a round-about in the local rec by that gang of boys who wouldn't let us off without a kiss or a feel? We must have been about thirteen.'

I laughed. 'We kept on spinning so they couldn't get on but then we were too dizzy to get off?'

'And because you were late home, Dan was sent out looking for you.'

'Ah, my hero brother. The threat of a punch and a few choice words, and they scarpered. If he hadn't turned up, we'd still be there!'

'I hero-worshipped him after that.' Kate was blushing.

'And once word went round I was Dan Green's little sister and you were my friend we were given an invisible cloak of protection.'

'Did he ever get married?' Kate apparently couldn't believe that my dear brother hadn't been snapped up, but she didn't know what he was like. A commitment phobe from birth, but how would any of them know that? They had only seen my parents' marriage from the outside so had no idea of the arguments and fights that had made us the people we were.

'No wife. But kids,' I added. 'Three at the last count, but there may be more he doesn't know about.' I smiled to show that was meant as a family joke. 'Or that I don't.'

'Wow!' said Kate, wide-eyed and possibly disapproving, I couldn't tell.

Linda was pouring herself another glass of wine. A shame she didn't have the same appreciation for the food that she'd picked her way through earlier. Where the other two had lashed into it, voicing their appreciation, Linda had picked out the mussels and put them on the side of her plate, and made a face as if hating shelling the prawns. But she was nervous. I got that. I was pretty nervous myself whenever I thought further ahead than the next minute. How was I going to keep them entertained? How would I broach the subject to find out what I wanted to know without ruining the weekend? For some reason I didn't feel I could just ask, though that would have been by far the most straightforward approach. This was harder than I'd foreseen. But I had time. It could wait.

'What would you like to do tomorrow? We can either laze about here or there's the Saturday morning market in Sóller. We passed the town on our way up here, remember? Or we can explore somewhere else, go to the beach or just go for a walk. Your call.'

'I love a market,' said Jane, sitting up, interested.

'I'd like that too,' said Linda.

'We could walk down before it gets too hot and then my feckless brother can come and get us later.' After all, what else had he to do?

'Would you mind if I stayed here?' Kate looked anxious. 'It's just that I'd love one full day of doing absolutely nothing. We don't have to stay together all the time, do we?'

'Of course not. Whatever you like.' I was pleased she felt able to ask.

'I'll drive you down if it's the walk that's putting you off,' said Jane.

'It's not.' Kate's unexpected earrings swung as she turned her head. 'But as a farmer's wife, I've been to more markets than you've had hot dinners. Trust me.'

'It's not just fruit and veg,' I said, not wanting her to feel done out of anything. 'There's jewellery, clothes, craft stuff – all that sort of thing. And Sóller itself is special.' But I wasn't going to force her. I've always thought the whole point of Ca'n Amy was to be able to do what you wanted there. We came to decompress and I wanted others to, as well – even my colleagues when they came to work here. But we did get better results here. I truly believed that.

We would see.

'That's a shame.' Linda stopped looking out at the mountains where house lights glowed in the distance. Fireflies danced closer by. The distant beat of music reached us from further along the mountainside. 'Shouldn't we do something together?'

'I can always drive down to meet you once you've exhausted the market. But having a couple of hours on my own being at no one's beck and call is my idea of heaven.'

'Then that's what you must do.' Although having Kate there

made being with Jane easier. I guessed Jane wanted shielding from us, too, although I couldn't think why. I was beginning to remember that was the case when we were at school. Even within the short time we'd been back together, snatches of memory were surfacing that I didn't particularly welcome, like the time she asked the others over to her house for a sleepover – but not me. I'd realised something was up by the way she and the others would break apart in the playground, looking secretive, when I approached. But I didn't find out until after the weekend when they all came in with fake tattoos on their arms, talking about the midnight feast I hadn't shared and the ghost stories that hadn't frightened the shit out of me. I was crushed. Or that time when she was picking the players for her football team and I was left till last, and everyone was giggling. And yet, I never gave up wanting to be part of her circle. Why not?

Because being part of it and, when things were going well, having her light shine on me, gave me the best feeling in the world. I could remember that too. She made us feel important, lifting me out of the world I came from and showing me the promise of something else. She was funny, generous, clever and the teachers all adored her. When she hooked her arm in mine as we walked to the sports field or picked me first or laughed at something I said, everyone else looked at me as if I mattered. Until I discovered I didn't matter at all.

What I'd told Kate about what happened after my expulsion can't have been news to her. I was the talk of the school for a while. I look back as if I'm watching another person have that life. Perhaps I should have fought back more but I had tried and failed. My parents had been so proud of my plans to study medicine, and they were desperately upset when it all went wrong. Although I took my A levels at the comp, my grades were hopeless because I hadn't bothered trying. I caved in when I should have fought back.

After that I was a lost cause, and my friends were warned off me. I was angry and alone. And by the time I'd regained my confidence, my life had already gone down a different path. When I thought about it, yes, I was angry that my original ambitions had been sidelined. And here was Jane in the profession I'd dreamed of. I resented that, but there was an edge to her that I didn't remember there being before. I couldn't help feeling something else was going on.

'How's work?' I asked. 'I'm fascinated to know what you do day to day?'

'I see cancer patients, decide on their treatment and keep tabs on their progress,' she said, but didn't elaborate further.

I was puzzled: why so abrupt? Why didn't she want to talk about something so worthwhile that she must feel passionately about? But if she didn't want to, I wouldn't make her. Perhaps we were all keeping some of the truth about ourselves from the others. Perhaps they, like me, wanted to present their best face to the world and escape from whatever they had left behind. I certainly didn't want them thinking my life was less than perfect.

IO

Walking through Fornalutx, the village below Amy's house, Linda felt herself relax for the first time since she'd arrived on the island. Looking around her as they walked down the main road running through the village, she saw narrow cobbled streets and stairways lined by tall, sandy stone buildings with green shutters closed against the heat. Outside front doors, plants spilled from their pots. Although it was early, there were already several tourists wandering about with cameras at the ready. She would come back later to explore.

Amy led them into a little bakery full of groceries, refrigerated drinks and bottles of wine. To the right was a glass counter where all sorts of pastries were on display. On the wall behind, baskets held loaves of fresh bread. The smell of them hung over everything. 'We'll get coffee in Sóller but these *ensaimadas*,' Amy pointed through the glass counter, 'are a speciality of the island. They'll keep us going till we get there. You've got to try one.' An exchange in fluent Spanish resulted in them each walking away with a soft round pastry coiled like a sleeping snake and covered in icing sugar, held in a scrap of paper. 'Don't even think of the calories. We're walking.'

'And sweating,' said Jane, removing her hat and wiping her forehead with the palm of her hand. 'What about stopping for a drink?'

Amy pulled four bottles of water from her backpack and shared them round. 'There. I thought of that.'

Jane looked displeased but didn't say anything. She had never been one for being told what to do, even now when Amy was just trying to give them a good time. Linda wouldn't have minded stopping for a coffee herself and tried to catch Jane's eye. Despite her resolutions, she'd drunk too much the evening before and spent a disturbed night worrying about a lecturer whom she had helped a couple of weeks earlier. She had given him umpteen suggestions of where he might look to find more information about cookery in the nineteenth century, but in the middle of the night, two more had come to her. She had emailed a colleague immediately to pass the info on. That would irritate them because they would never go to so much trouble, but that thoroughness came from her years at the London Library and working under Mike. And now she needed a shot of caffeine to give her a kick start.

Linda was sorry Kate hadn't come because she made everything easier when Jane and Amy were circling each other as if waiting for the real fight to begin. That last year at school held a lot that no one was facing up to. Linda had the opportunity to go over old ground too, but that part of her life and the shame that went with it was so buttoned up inside her that she couldn't imagine ever letting it go. What had happened was part of her now and had done much to shape who she had become.

She sank her teeth into the pastry. *Oh!* Something like a croissant that gave way to a brioche – soft, sweet and delicious inside. She couldn't help smiling.

'Come down here.' Amy took them down some steps, then stopped and pointed. 'Look up.'

Linda craned her neck to see faded red signs painted on the underside of some eaves.

'Those date back as far as the fourteenth century, when

people believed they protected the building against evil. Don't you think that's incredible?'

'I can hardly see them,' said Jane, brushing icing sugar off her T-shirt. Linda had seen her stuff her bun into a bin. You didn't get a figure like that without denial. She took another bite.

The three of them left the village, following the path that wound up the other side of the valley. Amy and Jane were just ahead of her. Obviously they were fitter than she was and nor were their shorts chafing the insides of their thighs.

'How come you went into medicine in the end?' Amy broke the silence as the path evened out at last and they were walking parallel to the valley bottom, the village on the other side. 'I don't remember you wanting to be a doctor. That was *my* dream. Weren't you going to be an actress? I can still remember that *Romeo and Juliet.*'

'When I was Juliet to your Romeo! "Romeo, Romeo wherefore art thou..." God, we were *so* good.' Jane put her hands on her hips and posed with her chin in the air. 'I loved those school plays.'

Amy laughed.

'Because you always scooped the best parts.' Linda remembered how she had longed to be cast as Juliet but ended up as one of the crowd, while Jane walked off with the main part.

Jane looked surprised. 'Did I? I thought it was Amy who was always being picked.' She turned to her. 'Everyone loved you in *The Importance of Being Earnest.*'

'To your Gwendolen.'

Linda remembered that production too. She had been relegated to the wings as the prompter.

'Yes, well. I did want to be an actress then but things changed,' Jane said. 'I joined the Dram Soc at uni but I wasn't good enough.'

'I suppose your dad wanted you to be a doctor.' Amy was

pulling up a piece of long grass from the roadside as she walked. She sounded almost envious.

Jane's father had been an orthopaedic surgeon at the local hospital. 'Consultants were gods back then and he was used to people saying yes to him, but I don't remember him ever pushing me.'

Amy pressed her lips together. 'Hmm.'

'What does that mean?'

'We were all scared of him when we came to your house,' Linda explained.

'He wasn't that bad.'

'Remember when he caught us drinking in the kitchen?' Amy reminded her. 'After that party when your mum had roped us in as waitresses and we went round knocking back the dregs?'

'I don't remember that,' said Jane.

'Probably because you were sick as a dog over the hall floor.' Linda reminded her.

'And his feet. He went ballistic,' Amy went on. 'He dragged you upstairs to the bathroom and we had to follow because we were staying the night and didn't know what else to do. We were terrified. Kate too.'

'If we hadn't been there . . .' Linda let the thought hang in the air. Somewhere nearby sheep bells jangled.

'Are you sure?' Jane looked completely blank. 'Maybe I *should* have been more of a rebel. But when I tried they just yanked me back into line.'

'I wish someone had yanked me,' said Amy.

'What happened?'

Linda hung back, realising this was the moment. Her head was pounding.

Amy stopped walking. 'You can't have forgotten that. I was expelled because no one believed a teacher would do what Mr Wilson did to me. No one would take my word over his. And then I was set up by someone so I was blamed for stealing his watch...' She waited as if she was expecting Jane to say something but she had started to walk ahead. 'I should have done brilliantly but I was so furious about how I'd been treated that I screwed everything up and did too badly to get into university. I didn't care what happened after that. I'd let everyone down. My mum's disappointment was unbearable, so I did everything I could to escape it.'

'And we lost touch.' Jane stepped aside to let a man leading a donkey through. 'I saw you a few times after you'd left but...'

'I cut you dead, I expect. I'm sorry. I didn't want to know. I was so angry with all of you then.'

'That's OK. I understand better now. And if it weren't for Kate making the effort to contact us, we might never have been in touch again.'

'Let's not talk about this any more,' Linda said. 'Not here. We're meant to be enjoying ourselves.' She didn't want them to talk about Mr Wilson any longer than necessary.

'That's true. And anyway, I've moved on.' Amy gazed at Jane's back, then tipped her panama over her eyes.

After that, they didn't talk but concentrated on the walk, on the views back to Fornalutx on the other side of the valley, and towards Sóller. On either side of them the neat terraces were separated by drystone walls; occasional gateways signalled houses hidden in the trees, while well-tended olive groves sheltered sheep who studied them gravely as they passed.

Eventually they descended into another small village. By this time, Linda was gasping for a coffee. Lukewarm water wasn't enough. But the café they came to was closed and they didn't pass another. Amy led them down a pedestrian street that wound between green-shuttered houses towards a tarmacked road signed to Sóller.

'I hope Kate's OK.' Linda swatted an insistent fly. Her legs were aching.

'Left with my reprobate brother? I should say there's little chance.' Amy pushed her hair off her face and replaced her dark glasses. 'I'm sorry he's descended on us. I'd no idea he was going to.'

'Doesn't he ever warn you?' Linda had often wondered what it must be like to have a sibling. Being brought up alone by her aunt had been a lonely business, despite her friends at school.

'No, he's utterly useless. And it probably won't be just a friendly visit. He'll have run out of money or something.' But she spoke with affection.

'Doesn't that drive you mad?' Jane bent over to retie her shoe.

Amy scratched her arm, leaving a white mark on her tan. 'Used to it. He knows better than to ask unless he absolutely has to because he knows I've reached my limit with him. He may get a job round here somewhere and stay at the house rent-free until he's ready to go again.'

'He's family, though,' Linda pointed out.

'Exactly. And I'm all he's got now.'

'When did your parents die?'

'A long time ago. Dad lost his marbles and had to go into a home which was thankfully short-lived. Mum eventually went to live with her sister near Bath. That's why I moved there. That must have been one of the most considerate and brave things she ever did, so we didn't have to worry about her. She was almost blind by then and Auntie Leekie was happy to look after her. She died about seven years later. What about yours?'

'You must remember? My mother abandoned me and Aunt Pat brought me up. We never heard from my mother again.'

'Oh God, I'm so sorry. Of course.' Amy looked stricken.

'Don't worry. I've had a long time to get over it.' As she had everything else that had happened to her when she was a young woman. She wasn't going to tell how she cracked under the pressure of the second-year exams. Or how her boyfriend Smithy had gone off with Briony right under her nose. More abandonment. It never took much to summon up the hopelessness she had felt or the crazy reasoning that, if no one loved her and she was going to crash out of the exams, life was not worth living.

The trajectory of her life had changed after that. Her academic ambitions, which had been sizeable, seemed unachievable after all so she scaled them down. If it hadn't been for Mike picking her out when she was shelving in the university library and then later getting her to help with his early modern cookery collection, she couldn't imagine what might have happened to her. Aware her life must seem a failure to anyone who had once known her, she tried to forget the part of her past which was, as it was proving now, unforgettable.

'Have you ever tried to track down your mum?' Jane hadn't grasped that she wanted to end the conversation. This was how Linda remembered her, always confident she was right, slightly hectoring, making you feel inadequate if you didn't go along with whatever she wanted.

Linda stopped in her tracks. 'Why would I? She didn't want me. I don't want her. And, before you ask – everyone always does – no, I'm not in the slightest bit interested in what she made of her life.' She looked embarrassed. 'I'm sorry, I'm sure you're not that interested either. So no, I don't have any parents, my aunt's in her eighties. I help her as much as I can but it's difficult now.'

They turned on to a main road with a sign to the centre of Sóller.

'Here we are,' said Amy. 'Time for a coffee.' Despite the heat, she upped the pace, regardless of Linda wilting in the heat behind her, wishing she hadn't given so much of herself away.

As they approached the centre, the streets filled with people. They passed stalls selling fresh fruit and vegetables, fish, dried meats and salami, the ubiquitous leather-handled reed baskets, clothes, jewellery, olive oil. Linda's heart beat faster as she looked around. This felt quite different from the markets she knew at home.

They found a table at one of the cafés on the edge of the main square. In front of them, vast cream parasols and stretches of canvas suspended between posts shaded the stalls that hummed with activity. Over the whole scene presided the vast baroque façade of the church standing shoulder to shoulder with the flag-strewn town hall on one side and a bank on the other, while the other three sides of the square were made up of apartment blocks, restaurants, cafés and shops.

'*Dos cortados y un café con leche, por favor.*' Amy ordered for them all.

The waiter took their order, to return with the drinks almost immediately. The three women gazed at the busy scene in front of them. Linda's legs zinged with the pleasure of being still at last. That was more exercise than they'd had for ages.

'Fun, isn't it?' An American voice came from behind them. Its owner had a kind face under his misshapen straw hat and looked like an expat gone native in his unbuttoned white shirt, khaki shorts, and worn navy espadrilles on his feet. For some reason Linda didn't understand, Jane was glaring at him.

'Brendan, hi. Are you going to join us?' Amy gestured towards the fourth and empty chair at the table. 'I heard you met Jane but you haven't met Linda.'

He nodded towards Jane, who avoided his gaze. 'Good morning.'

Linda inclined her head towards him as she lifted her coffee cup. 'Hello.'

As he shook her hand, a woman in a long floaty dress with a yapping dog clutched under her arm joined them. Over her other shoulder was slung a straw basket full of vegetables.

'Wouldn't be easier to leave him at home?' asked Amy.

'Brendan will never stay where I want him.' A hint of a smile cracked the woman's face.

'Oh, ha ha.' He put his arm around her shoulder, disregarding the snarling from under her arm. 'Listen. I'm glad we've bumped into each other because I'd like to make up for yesterday. It wasn't the best start – so, I'd like to invite you all on to our boat.'

Jane didn't look bowled over by the idea but Linda was excited. Why come to a Mediterranean island if you weren't going to see the sea? 'I'd love that.'

'This afternoon?' he added. 'We can take the tram down to the port.'

'We ought to get back,' said Jane, interrupting Amy. 'We've left Kate and Dan up at the house.'

'Dan's here? When did he blow in?'

'Last night. From Goa.' Amy drained her coffee. 'We've just walked down for the market and then he's going to collect us.'

But Brendan was not so easily deflected. 'Tomorrow morning, then, ladies?'

Linda cringed, hating that patronising way of being addressed.

'Or afternoon?' he went on. 'It'll blow the hangovers away.'

Was it that obvious? Linda tried one of the little biscuits that came with the coffee.

'Can we tell you later?' said Amy, quieting any objections from Jane with a raised hand. 'At the party tonight? You'll be there?'

'Of course. It's only a suggestion.' But he sounded disappointed.

After the two of them had got lost in the crowds, Amy turned to the others. 'No one has to go, don't worry. They may not be for everyone,' she gave Jane a pointed look, 'but he's got a good heart. You haven't got long here, but going out on a boat might be fun. We'll see what Kate thinks and what we feel like tomorrow.'

Linda gazed at the crowds, enjoying the sun on her skin and the activity around them.

'Can we explore?' Jane was already on her feet. 'Let's. We could meet back here in an hour?'

Amy showed no sign of getting up. In fact she was getting her phone out of her bag.

'Sure.' Linda galvanised herself. 'I'll come with you.'

Jane barely looked back as she said, 'Let's start with the church.'

Despite realising Jane didn't really want her company, Linda joined her. The elaborate façade, with its large rose window and gothic turrets, soared above the square and suggested something too intriguing to miss.

II

After the others had left for Sóller, Kate cleared up breakfast, despite Amy's assurances that Carmen would be up later. Having staff made her uneasy and helping out was the least she could do in exchange for their stay. Once the crockery was returned to its place on the open wooden shelves, she went to her room to get everything she needed for a morning by the pool. But first she phoned home.

Alan picked up his phone immediately. 'How's it going?'

She could hear the throb of an engine in the background. He must be out on the moors. 'Better. We're going to a party tonight.'

'When are you coming back?' As if he didn't know. 'I had trouble with getting the oven going last night so I ate the stew cold.' Her special lamb stew.

'Honestly, Alan! How hard is it to heat something up?' She tried to control her irritation. 'Perhaps you put the oven on automatic? The instruction manual's in the kitchen drawer. You'll have to look at that.'

He sighed as if this was the most onerous task she could have set him. 'OK, I'll find it. It's not the same without you here though.'

She could imagine only too well. No one to get the oven working. No one to cook breakfast and make the beds. 'I'll be back soon.' She stretched out on hers, looking out at the high grey crags of the mountains on the east side of the valley, the vivid green of the mountain pines, the grey green of the olive trees lower down, merging into the rich deep green of the citrus trees in the valley basin, all of them punctuated by the occasional graveyard green of a yew tree.

This place was a slice of heaven. If only she didn't have to go back so soon.

A speck of an aeroplane left a long white vapour trail cutting across the sky.

Time for the pool and a spot of me time.

'If you can't tone it, tan it.' Her daughter's words flew into her head as she stretched out, feeling the sun on every bare inch of her cellulite. Too late to tone anything now. She was here and the most relaxed she had felt for ages. No husband, no children, no farm, no guilt, and no need of her book. She could just lie, staring at her surroundings and the blue, blue pool.

Behind her was the house, the wide veranda with one end covered by a pergola overtaken by deep red bougainvillea, the other a relaxed seating area with cushioned comfy seats, parasols and low tables. Shutting her eyes, she could hear birdsong and the bees in the lavender. Not a tractor for miles. In the distance, the sound of sheep bells. Someone had lit a fire so the smell of woodsmoke drifted by. She hadn't enjoyed peace such as this for almost as long as she could remember.

A door slammed, startling her out of her reverie. Her eyes opened to see a completely naked Dan advancing towards her. His body was lean, not unattractive, tanned all over. *All* over. She quickly averted her eyes. Almost. Her husband was the only man she had seen naked for years and, fit as he was, he didn't quite come up to scratch beside Dan. As for everything else – there wasn't much competition there either.

'Morning!'

He was still there. She turned back to look at him, surprised that he hadn't run for his swimming shorts or something when he saw her. In fact, he held a towel in his hand and showed no intention of covering himself. She adjusted her sunglasses and held his gaze, careful not to look down.

'Isn't it beautiful?' He flapped the towel in the direction of the mountains. 'I never get tired of it.' He was walking along the edge of the pool quite at ease with himself. He obviously wasn't trying to embarrass her or expecting a reaction of any kind. So, she wouldn't give one. This was just what he did. She tugged at the bottom of her swimsuit to stop it riding up and made herself comfortable. He wouldn't come and sit beside her, would he? That would be impossible to deal with. She observed the muscles in his legs as he walked.

'Have you had a swim?'

She cleared her throat. 'No. Not yet. I'm waiting till I'm much hotter.'

There was a splash. He surfaced into a relaxed crawl. Up and down. Even with his hair plastered to his head, he was still a handsome man. Studying him, now he wasn't looking at her, she could see the boy that they had all known and fancied. The blond mop of hair might have thinned, greyed and got longer but those blue eyes hadn't faded. His face might be weathered and lined but it had at least avoided being buried in a middle-aged layer of fat. That young man was still there.

Eventually he climbed out. 'Fancy a coffee?' He shook his head so spray rained off him, just missing her, then towelled his hair.

'I'd love one.'

'Coming right up.' He left wet foot prints on the tiles all the way into the house.

Well. She had not been expecting this. Her book was less attractive now than ever. Taking advantage of his absence she sat up and rubbed sun cream over her legs, pretending the dimples of cellulite weren't there. She had just started on her arms, when...

'Need any help with that? On your back I mean?' He must have seen her surprise.

'Do you always sneak up like that?'

He put down her coffee. 'Only if I want to surprise someone.' She was glad he had found himself a pair of dry shorts and put them on.

'Why would you want to surprise me?'

'Your face was a picture. Let me help.' He stretched out a hand for the cream.

'I'm fine, thanks.' She popped the top back on the tube and put it back in her bag. Anything else would unacceptably intimate.

He put up a parasol so that it shaded his lounger. 'Are you going in?'

'Not yet.' Sweat pricked her forehead as the heat became unbearable but she was too self-conscious to get in the pool. The last thing she wanted was to swim up and down in front of him. She didn't want him considering her in the way she had him.

'Ah well.' He stretched himself out with his arms behind his head. She could have counted his ribs if she'd wanted to. 'You don't mind if I join you for a bit?'

'Of course not.' There was hardly a choice.

He grunted his thanks. 'So. A school reunion. Whose bright idea was that?' He sounded amused.

'Amy's, actually.' She was unnecessarily defensive.

His eyes gave away his amusement but he wasn't put off. 'I'm surprised you've all kept in touch. She's done so well that people are frightened of her now.'

'Are they?' She didn't believe that.

'Aren't you? Really?'

'No.' Although she had felt better once Amy and the others had left for their walk, but she wasn't frightened. Intimidated maybe. A little bit.

He changed position so he was lying propped on one elbow, his eyes on her.

Feeling uncomfortable and hotter still under his scrutiny, she walked to the pool steps and splashed down them, as inelegant as you like, hardly able to breathe because she was pulling in her stomach so hard. However the water was deliciously cool and once in she felt less self-conscious. As she swam up and down she made up her mind not to be intimidated by either of the Greens. She was here to enjoy herself, and that's what she would do. When she got out, she pulled over a parasol to shade herself and settled back on the lounger.

'I do remember you all, you know.'

'I should hope so.' That sounded sharper than she'd meant to. The coffee he'd brought her, though lukewarm now, was delicious.

'Jane was the leader of the pack then, wasn't she? Amy had such a crush on her.'

'I think we all did back then.'

'But she blew hot and cold, right?'

'Maybe a bit.' But of course that was exactly how it had been. 'It's so long ago, I can barely remember.'

'I can. Amy was once so upset when she was the only one not invited to some birthday do. There was something else she was left out of too.'

'That must have been years ago, long before we got to the sixth form. There was always stuff like that going on back then. The flipside was that there were plenty of others she was invited to. Anyway it wasn't just Amy and it didn't happen all the time. I think we all fell in and out with each other over the years.' Once Jane had told her that no one in their class liked her. That slight had gone unforgotten but no doubt there were others that she was guilty of too. 'That's just girls.'

'Does that make it OK, then?' He pulled an elastic band out of his pocket and pulled his hair back into its ponytail.

'Of course not. But we've survived and got over it.' She wasn't sure why she had to be so defensive but she wasn't going to subject herself to a lecture from him about the rights and wrongs of their friendships. 'Amy's tough.'

'Don't be so sure. She might be successful but not in the way she wanted. You know how her dreams of being a doctor went up in smoke. That still hurts. And someone's to blame.'

'If you say so.' But she was puzzled. 'But if she wanted it so badly why not take the exams later? Being expelled wasn't what stopped her.'

'Wasn't it?' His eyes were darker than she remembered. 'She was thrown badly off course and went off the rails for quite a while. When she was trying to get herself back on the straight and narrow, she didn't have the confidence to do more than help Mum.'

'It happened so long ago.'

'You must know who was behind it?'

He made it hard to tell whether he was teasing or asking her a serious question. She frowned, not trusting herself to speak.

'Amy told the truth about that teacher, you know,' he said. 'She may be many things, but she's not a liar.'

Unlike some, whispered a voice in her head.

'I don't know what happened.' *But you do have an idea*, came the voice again. *You do.* 'It's not important any more though, is it?'

'Something as life-changing as that is always important.' His face suddenly was serious. 'She may look as if she's brushed all that under the carpet but it's still there – just out of sight.' He traced his finger along the line of the paving. 'She could have gone to uni – she'd have been the first person in our family to do that – and she would been a doctor. I'm not sure that having something as big as that snatched away from you is something you'd ever get over.' His voice rose as if he was asking a question, but it wasn't one.

'Perhaps you're right.' She spoke quietly. 'But if she wanted it that badly, she could have done her A levels again later, applied for medical school when she was older.'

'Oh, come on. Have you forgotten? Our parents barely had a pot to piss in. Once Amy started making money it all went to them. By the time she could have afforded to change direction, she was far too entrenched in her business and, dare I say it, too old.' He slapped his hand on the ground. 'Of course she wants to know what really happened. I understand that.'

He was right. Nothing was ever entirely buried in the mists of time. How could Amy possibly have forgotten? Kate had hoped that time might have obliterated that summer from everyone's minds, but that had been naïve.

'Know this.' He sat up, swinging his legs off the lounger so he faced her, leaning forward. 'If anyone hurts her again, they'll have me to answer to.'

'Where were you then?' Kate felt her courage returning. 'Why didn't you help her when she needed you?'

'I'd left home.'

Of course he had. She remembered his farewell party in the basement of a York pub, all dark wood and engraved glass. She and Jane had gone with Amy and stood on the sidelines – his little sister and her friends. No one took much notice of them, least of all him.

'I'd escaped to London, was working in a record shop and living in my first squat.' He grinned. 'I heard it all through Mum and Dad at the time and had no idea how serious it was. I was way too caught up in my own life. It wasn't till I came back and it was all over that I really understood.' He paused. 'If I knew who did for her, I . . . well, I'd . . .' He clenched his fist, then laughed. 'I don't know what I'd do.'

'Well, you don't have to worry about it being one of us.' She picked up her book and opened it to signal the conversation was over.

'That's good.' He lay back on his lounger and hummed an unidentifiable tune that gradually faded away.

Kate was far from asleep. Her mind was buzzing as it tried to grab at the memories that dodged her reach just as she closed on them. She remembered the basics of what happened in that summer of '76 but not the detail any longer.

Dan started humming again, tapping his fingers on the edge of his bed. She cleared her throat.

'I'm sorry. Force of habit.'

'This yoga platform...'

He lifted his head. 'Mmm?'

'Is that all you do now?' Amy had said he drifted from job to job. She could believe that of a twenty-something but Dan was in his sixties, for God's sake.

'I do anything that'll make me a buck or two. That was in Goa. A Canadian guy I know was opening an Ayurvedic retreat there. I offered to help in exchange for a treatment or two, bed and food. Barter works for me.'

'Have you always been...' She stopped, trying to find the word.

'What? Good for nothing?' He grazed his hand over his stubble.

She smiled back. 'Yep.'

'Depends who's asking. I haven't always, although Amy would have everyone think so. I was married – briefly, admittedly,' he acknowledged. 'And I've had relationships since, even got me some children along the way. Arlo's thirty now,' he said in answer to her raised eyebrow. 'He's a lighting engineer. Works for the BBC – steady job. Nothing like me. Takes after his mum. Leaf's twenty-nine. She went to Australia with her mother so I never see her. She's a teacher there. And Jackson's sixteen. He lives with his mum in France.' He looked sad for a moment then recovered himself. 'Yeah, I'm the original Teflon man – no one sticks to me for long.'

'Why's that?'

He laughed. 'God knows. Too many bad habits, too selfish, too prone to temptation – all of the above.'

A burst of music interrupted them. He pulled his phone out of the purse that hung round his neck. 'Yeah, we're fine. Just had a swim and now we're chatting. Sure.' He held the phone out to Kate. 'It's she who must be obeyed.'

She took it. 'Amy?'

'Just checking you're OK.'

'Couldn't be happier. Are you still in Sóller?'

'Yep. Dan's coming to get us, and we'll have lunch at the house again. Brendan's invited us on to his boat tomorrow.' She didn't wait for a reply. 'Anyway, no one has to go, I just thought it might be fun.'

'It would be.' Kate couldn't think of anything she felt less like doing. Being beside the pool was enough for her. She wished Dan hadn't reminded her that Amy might have an ulterior motive for them being there. Now she felt more apprehensive than before.

12

They were in and out of the church in a matter of minutes. Jane's interest in things religious was always short-lived, but she liked to be able to say that she'd been inside various European churches and seen whatever was notable in there. Once through the small door within a huge heavy one, the cool and quiet welcomed them in. A few tourists milled up and down the aisles, intent on the various gilded side chapels that were illuminated by flickering votive candles. Frankincense and polish flavoured the air.

Jane headed straight down the centre aisle to the ornate main altar. She had no time for anything else. She gave it a quick glance, aware that Linda had sunk into a more sober reflection of the gaudy extravagance in front of them. They stared up at the cherubic faces peeking out of gold clouds surrounding the virgin and child. Above them, in an elaborate cupola, flew the dove of peace.

'Done?' Jane spoke briskly. How did all this ostentation tally with anyone's faith? She didn't get it but turned to gaze at the stained-glass rose window above the door they had come in by and took a step towards it. The outside world beckoned.

'Well, I—'

Still smarting from the earlier conversation about her father, she ignored Linda's hesitation. If she wanted to stay to look at the side chapels, Jane could go on ahead and they could meet up later. No one criticised her family. They might not have been perfect but that was for her to say, no one else. Her parents had adored her, their only child, and only wanted the best for her. In return she did all she could to please them, even though she got it wrong time after time.

There was the time when her father found her with the boys who hung out in the playground, smoking dope, drinking cider. He'd come looking for her when her mother got worried when it was getting dark and she still wasn't home. He had leaped out of the car and made her get in, to the jeers of the boys. When they had turned the corner, he stopped the car and slapped her cheek. 'I've been driving around looking for you for half an hour!' She never saw those boys again except to avoid them. When they got home, her mother reacted as always – turned her face away from Jane, making her disappointment clear. They had been hard to please, so she learned early on that bending the truth to get the reaction she wanted was the way to deal with them. Going into medicine had been her last-ditch bid for approval – and it had worked.

'Shopping beckons.' She took a quick snap of the rose window on her phone without looking at it too hard then headed to the door, leaving Linda to follow her.

Outside, enveloped in a wave of heat and noise, Jane felt her pulse quicken in response. She circled the tourists photographing each other on the church steps and went down into the square that buzzed with activity, stopping to take one of her own on the way.

A couple of high-pitched toots announced the approach of a wooden tram on a track that ran through the middle of the square. People scattered as it came through. The four carriages were crowded with tourists waving and looking out of its open sides.

'This way.' Jane threaded her way through the crowds to a long stall covered with bags of every description. 'I love these.'

She picked up one of the straw baskets that Brendan and Sheila had been carrying and slung it over her shoulder. 'I'll take it.' She glanced back towards the café where they had left Amy. She was still sitting at the same table, bent over her phone, engrossed in conversation.

Jane was in her element, mooching around the stalls, exclaiming over handmade jewellery, jams, beefy tomatoes, sponges, locally woven fabrics or turning over objects carved out of olive wood, buying a chopping board for her husband. 'He loves cooking. I'm so lucky,' she explained unnecessarily. Linda bought a rose-coloured scarf.

At a clothes stall, Jane leafed through the racks and produced a blue and white top. 'You'd look great in this.' Anything would be more summery than the dreary tan and taupe Linda had plumped for that morning.

Linda held it up in front of the mirror. Once upon a time, she would have leaped at something like this.

'It's perfect. Really lifts your face. You must get it.' Jane was good at this. Shopping was one of her favourite ways of relaxing.

'Oh, I don't know.' Linda handed it back to the stallholder.

'If you're at all tempted, you should. You only ever regret what you don't buy.' Jane was impatient with any kind of indecision.

'You mean "do",' said Linda, smiling.

'Whatever. Put it on over your T-shirt to get the idea.' She picked it up again.

Linda did as she was told and lifted the garment over her head and slid in her arms.

'See.' Jane clapped her hands. 'It's perfect.' Linda looked brighter, younger, more alive. More like her younger self.

'I'll never wear it to the library.' She turned side to side.

'So what?' Jane looked for the price tag. 'It's only seventy-five euros. A snip. Go on, you're on holiday.'

Linda took one more look at herself and pulled the garment over her head. 'OK! I'll take it,' she said, handing the top to the stallholder and getting out her purse.

'Right top, right decision.' Jane was holding up a fitted yellow shirt against herself. Linda clearly needed her approval so she gave it easily.

They walked away from the stall clutching their purchases with a renewed bond struck up between them. For the next half hour they meandered down the town's noisy side streets where the market continued and shops had their own stalls outside, lingering over the fruit and veg and deciding to buy some strawberries to contribute to lunch.

'It's funny us all being together again...' Jane spoke her thoughts aloud.

'So generous of Amy to have us here. She would have been successful whatever she did – although it didn't look like it for a while.'

'You mean when she was hanging out with the punks? Remember how they used to stand on street corners, intimidating passers-by? They were trash.' Jane dismissed them. 'My parents told me I shouldn't have anything to do with her after that. But all that's so long ago now. Nonetheless, it's odd that she was the one who organised this.'

'Perhaps she wants to set the record straight.' Linda stopped in front of a bakery with a long queue waiting in front of a window full of croissants, ensaimadas, sweet potato cakes, pizza pieces, and much much more. 'Look at these.'

'Set the record straight – what do you mean?' Jane felt a stab of panic.

'Sort out what really happened. She always claimed she was telling the truth about Mr Wilson and his watch. Perhaps she was.'

'He would never make a move on one of his pupils. She must have made that up. He wasn't that stupid.' He had been gorgeous. Jane's first case of unrequited love. In fact, as far as she could remember, her only case. She could picture his chiselled bone structure, piercing blue eyes and thatch of sandy blond hair, a dead ringer for Robert Redford whom they had all fallen for in *The Sting*. Mr Wilson was the next best thing.

But Linda had already walked on. It was funny she didn't want to discuss those days. She had never been so prickly or self-effacing way back when. On the contrary, she had been form captain, sports captain and vied with Jane and Amy to be top of the class. And she had been beautiful. With the perspective of age, Jane now knew that every girl in her late teens was beautiful however they might think of themselves, but then Linda had been the pick of the bunch. Everyone thought so. Straight brown hair, bee-stung lips, and a model figure. They all wanted to look like her. What had happened to all that promise?

They continued past stalls selling everything anyone could want. Shouts from the stallholders punctuated the general hubbub of the crowd, but soon they were back in the square and heading to the café where they found Amy deep conversation with Dan. He was standing opposite her, his hands on the back of a chair, looking as if he were saying something important. They looked up as the two women joined them. Dan shook his head. 'Some women! My sister's a hard nut to crack.'

'Don't say that. I've agreed you can stay for a couple of weeks but then I may be back here with the team to look at our current strategies and new design ideas. You'll have to find somewhere else while they're here.'

'They could stay in a hotel.'

'They could,' she agreed. 'But they're not going to. They always stay at the house. They like it.'

'And where will I go?' Dan sounded like an aggrieved child.

He tipped back the chair and pulled it towards him, its legs scraping along the ground.

'Dan! You're over sixty. You shouldn't be relying on your sister to provide a roof over your head. Don't you agree?' she appealed to Jane and Linda.

'Don't answer that!' Dan's grin was back. 'My little sis is right, of course. I'll move on. Don't you worry.' But despite his agreement, there was an edge to his voice.

Jane thought Amy had a fair point but just pulled out a chair and sat beside her in a gesture of moral support that surprised them both.

'I won't,' said Amy. 'Not even remotely. You've survived the last forty years. God knows how. So I dare say you'll survive the next few. Are you guys ready to go back now? I've got some bits and pieces for lunch.' Amy nodded in the direction of her basket that she had filled with shopping since they last saw her. She stood up and slung it over her shoulder.

'Let me.' Dan held out his hand.

Amy laughed. 'Playing the gent won't make me change my mind.' She handed the basket over all the same.

Lunch was a repeat of the previous day. Spicy *sobrasada* sausage, *jamón ibérico* and other salami, various cheeses and salad. The lightest of rosé wines for anyone who wanted it (Linda), water and soft drinks. Jane had an iced tea. Afterwards, Amy went to do some urgent work in her study while Dan disappeared to his room muttering the words 'yoga' and 'siesta'.

'Thank God, he's gone,' said Jane. 'We can talk now he's not here.'

'He's not that bad,' said Kate.

'Well you've spent the morning with him, so I'd guess you'd know.' Jane tapped the side of her nose with one finger, teasing. 'I just meant that we can't be ourselves and catch up when he's around.'

'We were never friends with him before,' said Linda. 'You all had a crush on him and would have died if he'd said a word to you.'

'Not you?' Jane gazed at her through her dark glasses.

Linda smiled that anxious smile of hers. 'Yeah, well. Maybe a little.'

'There must have been other men in your life apart from Mike.' She wasn't being intrusive, just friendly.

'Of course.' Linda's face closed up immediately.

'No one special, though? You haven't been married? Or got close to it?' Perhaps the change in Linda was only superficial. They hadn't been together long enough to know. Perhaps none of them had changed really. She certainly felt the same.

'Leave the poor woman alone!' Kate interrupted her. 'We haven't come here for the Spanish Inquisition. Why don't you tell us about your marriages instead?'

Infuriated by Kate's intrusion, Jane put down her glass 'Sorry, it's none of my business, of course. I just thought it was all part of being here and catching up. Shall we go down to the pool instead?'

Jane would never confess to the mess of her own personal life. And if Kate were ever to challenge her publicly, she would deny anything to do with Rick. She was still kicking herself for having said anything. What had made her break all her own rules? When she'd finally got to bed the previous night, she had acknowledged to herself that her secret had become too much of a burden, Offloading it on to someone she could trust was just human, wasn't it?

Secrets were hard to keep. And she'd kept Rick a secret for years. She could rely on Kate to do the same whatever she thought. On the other hand, life is short. You've got to take what you want from it while you can, she reasoned. Why submit to a lacklustre marriage if you can find the lustre that's lacking somewhere else and make it work with both men. That was a lesson that many people might do well to learn.

'Why don't we volunteer our life histories when we're ready,' Kate suggested in an obvious attempt to smooth things over. 'Instead of trying to winkle it out of each other when we're not ready.'

Without looking up, Linda nodded. She was clearly holding back something. That made two of them. Perhaps things would emerge later over a glass of wine or two. Jane determined not to let down her own guard again.

They spent the rest of the afternoon by the pool, the time drifting by as the three women lay relaxing with their phone, their book or just lying there in the sun.

Eventually Jane stood up, and pushed her hair off her face. 'When do we have to be ready this evening?'

'The party's at seven-thirtyish. Amy said we'd walk into the village afterwards and have dinner there.'

'I'm going to go inside for a bit, get ready.' Jane wanted some time out, alone.

'Do we need to dress up?' Linda sounded apprehensive.

'No, surely not. This is Mallorca, not the Riviera.' An idea struck Jane. 'Actually I've got something that would really suit you. Come and see.' The top she was thinking of was a mistake, bought in a hurry before a conference in Florida a couple of years back. She didn't know why she'd brought it with her but it might look different on Linda.

'I can't borrow from you,' Linda protested.

'Why not? If you like it, you can have it. It's too big for me really, and it'll suit you, I promise. Come and look.'

The three of them were gathering up their stuff as Dan emerged from his room. 'Nothing like a good siesta,' he said. 'And now a swim. It's not a bad life.'

'We're going to get ready,' said Kate as he began to lower his shorts.

Linda cleared her throat and looked at the ground while Jane stared. He was in good shape.

'You don't want to come in too?' His shorts hit the paving.

'We'll leave you to it.' She kept any note of regret out of her voice.

'As you will.' He dived in and swam a swift length before coming to the side and resting his arms on the side of the pool. 'You sure? It's lovely in.'

Of the four of them gathered in the living room, Jane was pleased to see she had made the most effort. The flouncy dress she'd originally bought for a wedding in the south of France made her feel a million dollars even if it was a little overdressed for the occasion. Amy was wearing a bronze pleated long skirt and cap-sleeved T-shirt with a narrow leather belt. She'd pulled her hair back into a clasp at the back of her head and held a battered panama in her hand. Linda sat awkwardly in the long yellow and white top from Jane's wardrobe. Kate was in blue with those tassel earrings again – they weren't to Jane's taste at all. Tassels! She preferred something more discreet – more gold or precious stone.

'That suits you,' Amy said to Linda. 'You look like the old Linda. You should wear bright colours more often.'

Linda looked surprised and sat a little straighter. 'Thanks.' Her hands knotted and unknotted in her lap.

'Told you.' Jane smiled. 'A bit of colour makes all the difference.'

'If we're all present and correct, shall we go?' Dan appeared, his ponytail neatly curling at his neck, a loose collarless shirt over his shorts and flipflops.

Along the drive and a little way down the road they came to another open gate. Two oriental stone dragons sat on the top of the gateposts, tongues out. A ceramic tile on one of the posts read *Casa Olivo*. Along the driveway, candles in storm lanterns lit the way even though it wasn't yet dark and fairy lights adorned the olive trees. The sound of a guitar came from somewhere ahead of them. Excited, Jane followed Dan and Kate, eager to see where they had come to.

The driveway widened into a generous space where a couple of cars were parked under two palm trees. At first glance, the house was more modern than Amy's, though built in the same stone with the same deep green shutters. Just one storey for the most part gave way to a second at one end. At the open front door of the house, a waiter, in cream shorts and white shirt, stood holding a tray laden with glasses of champagne. Opposite him, a firebrand illuminated the entrance. Just then, a distinguished-looking man came from the house towards them. His face was expressive, extraordinarily lined, and he was smiling in welcome.

'Dan! I didn't know you were here.' He grasped Dan's hand with both of his, before looking at the two women. 'No Amy?'

'I've just arrived.' Dan pulled his hand away, holding it out towards his companions. 'Meet Jane and Kate, two of Amy's old schoolfriends. She's right behind us.' He stood to one side. 'Let me introduce William Amos.'

'Welcome, everyone. Come in.' William gestured at the drinks tray with well-manicured hands. 'Help yourself.'

They took their drinks and followed him into a vast open-plan living room.

'Wow!' Jane said under her breath to Kate. 'I wasn't expecting this.'

The furnishings were elegant, the typical white walls with wooden beams crossing the ceiling. Wall alcoves held exquisite pieces of sculpture, subtly lit. The lighting was intimate, but what made the room special was the wall on the far side where glass doors were folded right back. Beyond, the party was taking place on a wide covered terrace that gave on to a lush-looking lawn. Lanterns hung in the trees and lights were staked in the pots planted with cacti and palms.

'Dan! We haven't seen you for ages' A guy homed in on Dan immediately. 'Julia's here. She'll be so pleased to see you. Julia! Look who's here!' As he was led away, Dan sent an apologetic look over his shoulder as he left Jane and Kate on their own.

'We meet again.' Brendan was undeterred by Jane's frostiest glare. 'Looking forward to the boat tomorrow? It's going to be another lovely day.'

'Have we a definite arrangement?' Jane turned to Kate who had been about to say something, but stopped.

'No pressure. If you don't want to . . .'

'Oh, none felt,' said Kate. 'I think Amy said something about going on the tram from Sóller and meeting you there. I'm looking forward to it.'

'That's great.' He looked at Jane over the edge of his glass. 'No call for you all to come, of course.'

'Here we are.' Amy materialised behind them, denying Jane the pleasure of the last word and allowing Brendan to slide off into the crowd.

'I guess we don't want to stay too long as we're eating in the village, so let me find William so he knows we're here. Will you excuse me?'

'And what are we meant to do?' Jane was exasperated by the way Amy had left them.

'I'm going to look at the pictures.' Linda indicated a series of white screens by the house on which were hung several paintings. She let a waitress top up her glass first.

Jane took a canapé from a passing tray. 'Let's try working the room.' This was one thing she was used to. Years of dealing with complete strangers and putting them at their ease, hosting parties and events, meant she was quite confident about plunging into the fray. With Kate in her wake, she joined a knot of people where a roughly bearded man was attempting to hold a conversation in broken Spanish.

'*Mis pinturas están . . .*' He raked a hand through a wild shock of greying hair, muttering, 'Oh God, what's the bloody word?'

'*Impresionistas?*' someone helpful offered.

'No, no, no. Expressions of a deeper-seated . . .' He gave up and beat the end of his stick on the ground. 'I can't explain. I'm so sorry.'

'Having trouble?' Jane asked.

At the sound of her voice he brightened. 'Do you speak Spanish?' Hopeful.

'Not a word. You must be the painter we've come to celebrate.'

'Yes, William's kindly giving this party for me. I don't know him but my work's being shown in a gallery in Valldemossa that belongs to a mutual friend. Small world.' He scratched at a scrap of dried paint on his waistcoat pocket.

'Are you from here?'

'No, no. I'm English of course but I live in France.' His eyes held Jane's and for a fleeting moment she thought there was something familiar about him.

'But you've always painted?'

'Oh, always. I used to teach, and I still do some private classes. It always surprises me how many people want to learn. Cheers!' He accepted a top-up of champagne and sipped. 'I'd kill for a beer.'

'But it must be so satisfying teaching a subject that everyone likes.' Surely she could do better than this?

'It is, and the more senior students do usually get a lot from it. That does make it very satisfying.'

'I certainly did when I was at school.' Jane realised she wasn't including Kate in the conversation. 'Didn't we?' She watched him consider Kate for a moment, a frown furrowing his brow, before he smiled and held out his hand for her to shake.

'Hello. I'm Jack.'

Jane looked up sharply, but Kate didn't react to his introduction beyond the handshake. 'Kate.'

'Jack Walsh. And you?'

'Jane. We're staying with a friend next door.'

'I hope you'll all come to see the show then. There's a taster over there.' He pointed with his little finger in the direction of the screens where Linda was gazing at one of the paintings. 'I'd love to see you there.'

The gesture disturbed Jane. There was something familiar about it, something she couldn't place.

'If we can,' said Kate. 'We're not here for long.'

'Jack, you must meet Valentin Orlof, I insist.' A tall, reed-like woman wafted up in a cloud of perfume, diamonds sparkling at her throat and on her ring finger. 'He's dying to meet you.'

They watched as he was swallowed up by another group of people.

'Potential customers, I guess,' said Kate. 'And more like the Riviera than you thought! Shouldn't we take a look at his paintings?

But Jane was intent on Jack, disturbed. She didn't know anyone in the art world so it couldn't be that she'd met and forgotten him. Nor did she know many people living in France. 'He reminds me of someone, but I can't think who.'

'Does he? He reminds me of a grizzly bear.'

Jane laughed. 'I've never met one.' But it wasn't that. His beard was self-consciously untidy, growing in all directions, disguising his mouth and the shape of his face, disappearing into the open collar of his shirt. The only part of his face that was visible was his nose, his veined cheeks and his eyes that were disturbingly focussed.

She watched him talking. Obviously they all spoke good enough English for him to be able to manage this time. As he talked he gestured, laughed and had them hanging on every word. He was flirtatious towards the women, collegial towards the men, knew exactly how to get the best out of them.

He moved on to another smaller circle. After a moment, Amy was brought into the circle of admirers by William. She looked across the party to where Jane and Kate were standing but someone in the group said something to her. She threw back her head and laughed. By the house, Linda was in conversation with a couple who looked as if they'd strayed straight off the beach.

'They obviously didn't get the memo about the dress code.' Kate was looking round for the waitress.

But Jane wasn't listening. The longer she stared at Jack Walsh, the more frustrated she was by her inability to place him. He was listening to someone, his head cocked to one side, intent on what he was saying, when once again he used his little finger to point towards the screen. And in that moment, Jane knew.

'Oh my God!' She clutched Kate's arm.

'What's the matter?' Kate tried to shake herself free.

'It's him.' Jane couldn't bring herself to say his name but just watched as Amy said something that made him laugh.

'Who? Who are you talking about?'

All sorts of carefully buried memories were whirling up so fast, they were confusing her. It couldn't be. 'No one. Sorry. I thought I saw someone I knew.' If she were right, telling the others would be opening a can of worms she'd prefer was kept shut. With luck they wouldn't notice. 'I'm just going get myself a glass of water. Want one?'

'No thanks. I'll go and see who Linda's chatting to. We should mingle.' Kate stepped out into the party.

Inside, the house was cool, the atmosphere calm. A waiter directed her to the bathroom. As she shut the door, Jane leaned back against it, bent double, her hands on her knees, closed her eyes and let out a long sigh. Scenes from that long, boiling hot summer of 1976 were jostling for space in her head. She shook her head as if that would rid her of them but they were too insistent. For the last forty-five years of her life, she had erased what happened that summer so successfully that she had as good as forgotten her part in it.

How stupid she had been to come here. If Rick hadn't been so insistent about Barcelona, she would have refused the invitation however hard Kate had pushed.

The way he pointed with his little finger. Back then he had worn a signet ring on it that he tapped against the desk when impatient. Back then, he was a fresh-faced twenty-five-year-old. Back then, he was slim, athletic and so good-looking that nearly all the senior sixth had the hots for him, none more than her. Back then, he was called Jack Wilson. Back then, he had been their art teacher.

She couldn't be more certain.

Unwanted memories came crowding in.

And all she wanted to do was run away and catch the next plane off the island.

13

I got us out of the party as soon as I decently could. I was aware that the others hadn't really thrown themselves into it – why should they when I'd sprung it on them and they didn't know a soul? Although Linda did her best, Jane and Kate stood on the periphery like teenagers at a house party thrown by someone they didn't know. They reminded me of how I felt once at a party at Jane's house. We must have been about twelve or thirteen. Whenever her mother left the room, they bunched together in a tight circle so I couldn't join in. Funny what the mind does. I'd forgotten about that completely until then.

Being together was throwing up memories like that: things I hadn't thought of for years. Of course I wasn't always on the outside. I could equally well remember squishing onto the back seat of the bus home, Jane's gang packed so tight together that Fran and Pam had to sit on the seat in front where we bombarded them with empty monkey-nut shells, and called them names. But if you stuck out the cold shoulder for long enough, Jane would come round and it would be your turn in the sunshine again while someone else got left out. In the meantime Kate or Linda would offer a hand of friendship when Jane wasn't looking. Back then, her attention was something worth waiting for. Now, less so.

There was so much I wanted to ask her but now she was here I found myself holding back, not wanting to hear my suspicions were unfounded, not wanting to ruin things for the others. I was sure now that she was the one responsible for my being branded a thief and a liar, for my expulsion from school. Yes, it happened years ago but I still cared. It had taken me a long time to recover from the labelling and its ramifications. She was the reason my life went off the rails. But I was the one who got me back on them. Now, thanks to Rob, it was veering off them again and I had this irrational desire to sort things out for the record. If I could confront the past, then maybe I had a future. She had got from her life what I once wanted from mine, and I wanted to know whether that had made her happy.

By the time we left the party, Jane wasn't looking well and asked if we'd mind if she skipped dinner and went back to the house. I didn't like leaving her on her own but she insisted and the three of us were hungry. Besides, I wanted to share Fornalutx with them. I'd been going there so long but I never tired of the place. Some people criticise it for being a museum piece restored for the tourists but, to me, it was a beautiful village full of character.

We were shown to a table on the terrace of one of the restaurants on the hill down into the village. Mountains on one side, road on the other but once the tourists have left for the day, very little traffic goes through. Linda and I had to wait for Kate who had stopped by a litter of scrawny kittens that were playing around the entrance.

'That was some house,' said Kate eventually, as she browsed the menu. 'Stunning.'

'I liked the couple I was talking to.' Linda handed me the wine list.

'I don't really know them. They've only been in the village for a couple of years and rent out their house most of the time.' I hoped Linda realised how well Jane's top suited her. She had lost all the self-confidence that I remembered her having. I was puzzled by the transformation from class star to the unconfident, self-effacing person who had come to stay. I had always imagined she would end up running the world, or at least have a hugely successful, high-profile career but something had changed her. I ordered a bottle of *ses Nines*, one of the red wines produced on the island, sensing her need. This man, Mike, had obviously messed her up badly. Or maybe there was more than that.

We ordered quickly. They took their lead from me as I recommended various local specialities. *Pa amb oli; tumbet;* paella; cod and veg. I know. I know. But the last tastes better than it sounds.

'What did you think of the paintings?' Kate asked, finally, once she'd chosen.

'Not much. I was disappointed. William's got such a good eye normally.' I liked to think I had too.

'What about the artist?' said Linda. 'I didn't get to talk to him but he looked pretty wild.' I wasn't sure whether she was disapproving or admiring.

'Jane thought she knew him.' Kate took a mouthful of tumbet. 'This is delicious. What's in it? Onions, tomatoes, potatoes?' She poked at it with her fork. 'Anything else?'

'Aubergine and peppers,' I added. 'How funny, he reminded me of someone too. I wasn't going to say anything because I supposed he must be someone who I'd met through the business. If we hadn't been surrounded by his admirers, I'd have asked him.'

You couldn't see much of his face thanks to that beard but there was something about him. The intensity in his eyes was disconcerting and the way he held his head tilted to one side... no, it wasn't that. The way he gestured. And then, I got it at last. 'Oh my God. You know what it was?'

She shook her head and they both looked at me.

'The way he pointed with his pinkie. There's only one other person I've seen do that. Mr Wilson! You remember?' Of course they did. We'd talked about him only the night before and we all knew we'd be talking about him again before our holiday together was over. 'We used to copy him.' I pointed with mine at the bottle of wine.

Linda was staring at me as if she'd seen a ghost. 'But Mr Wilson wore a signet ring.'

'I know.' I could picture it against my thigh all too clearly, his fingers pressing hard enough to dent the flesh. That feeling of fear that haunted me for so long afterwards returned to me.

But the hand I saw tonight belonged to someone else. Its skin was loose, wrinkled over the knuckles, marked with age spots. Thick blue veins crossed the bones. The nails were bitten right down. But there was no ring.

'He can't possibly be,' said Kate. 'It's just because we're here together that you're imagining it.'

'Maybe.' But those eyes. Sharp and calculating. I was sure they were his.

'We haven't really talked about all that properly,' said Kate. 'Do you want to?'

At last. But why not now? It was time I told my story again. It had been locked away unresolved for too long. A shame Jane wasn't with us.

'Sure,' I said, as if it was the most natural thing in the world, and I was only doing it to oblige them. I waited for a moment while the waiter took our plates and brought the main courses. I sipped my one glass of wine, poured another for everyone else. 'It happened just as I said at the time. You don't remember?'

'Not in detail. To be honest, I haven't thought about it for years. Sorry.' She added the apology when my face must have given away something I hadn't intended. But why should have any of them have held what happened to me in their minds. They had their own lives to lead.

'Mr Wilson was a predator.' I might as well say it the way I saw it.

Linda's fork clattered against her plate. 'No!'

'Maybe that's harsh.' I'd obviously touched a nerve. I was only too aware that most of our contemporaries had a crush on him. 'But he had a position of responsibility and he abused that. He was one of what? Four male teachers in an all girls' school?'

Kate nodded and ticked them off on her fingers. 'Him, Mr Sutton, the Latin teacher, Mr Greaves for physics and . . .' She hesitated.

'Mr Franks for French.' I helped her out. 'How could you forget him? Right name, right job.'

We all smiled at the old joke.

'But none of them took advantage in the way Mr Wilson did. I know he was a young man, but it wasn't right. And still he had plenty of fans.'

Linda reached across me for the bottle.

'But not you,' said Kate. 'I always thought he was OK.'

'Me too,' Linda added.

'He gave me the creeps. I used to watch him flirting as if we were some sort of game he was playing. But I was only interested in my results. I was set on getting into university – the first of my family. Art was an extra because I loved painting.'

My parents had been amazed and quietly pleased by my unexpected ambition that had been born when Mum had gone into hospital with a burst appendix. I had the romantic notion of being one of the people who could make others better, just like the white-coated doctors I saw. 'Maybe he saw my indifference as a challenge. Whatever it was, during that last spring term, he got me alone in the art room at the end of the day. I'd left my cardigan in there and went back to get it. He was at his desk and asked me to come up and sit beside him. I did because I assumed he was going to critique my work. When I sat down, I saw he had a book of photos of naked men and women open on his desk.'

'Really?' Linda didn't believe me.

'Oh, they were very tasteful: arty,' I reassured her. 'But he asked me what I thought of them. I was shocked, and a bit confused. I must have mumbled something but I didn't know what he meant me to say. The next thing, his hand was on my leg, pressing, moving towards my skirt. Remember how short we wore them?' I could almost feel that pressure again as I retold the story.

The others had stopped eating to listen. I hadn't talked about this for so long, but every moment of it was as clear to me as it had ever been. I couldn't stop now.

'Although I'd watched him flirt, I didn't think he'd do any more than that. I couldn't believe what was happening and yet for some reason I didn't move away. I couldn't. But as his hand reached under my skirt and his other touched my right breast . . .' My own hand rose to it as I spoke. 'I jumped up, knocking the chair over. The clatter it made seemed to register with him, then he was on his feet too. "Amy," he said. "Amy. There's nothing wrong with this. We're both adults. You can make the decision I know you want to. Nobody need know." '

'Jesus,' said Kate. 'How could I have forgotten all this? What did you do?'

'Honestly, it was as if I was paralysed. I knew how wrong it was but I couldn't react. It's as hard to explain now as it was then. Then he reached out for my hand and pulled me towards him. "That's how much I want you," he said, and put my hand on his cock through his trousers. "And you want to get good marks, don't you?" '

'Oh my God!' Kate was shocked. Linda was biting her lip, her eyes fixed on me as she listened.

'I was so stunned I didn't react straight away, but then I pushed him as hard as I could and ran out of the room.'

'Is that when you went to the Head?' Linda sounded as if she was blaming me for not doing exactly that.

'God, no. She hated me, remember? Or I thought she did. I'd been reported to her one too many times. I went to the cloakroom, grabbed my bag, and got the hell out of there.'

'And what about the watch?'

On the other side of the valley, a car wound up the road, its lights appearing and disappearing as it travelled the road through the trees.

'So . . . I raced home and decided that I wouldn't say a thing to anyone, convinced that it was somehow my fault. That I'd said something or looked at him in some way that he'd mis-interpreted. Maybe my skirt was too short.' It was, but that was hardly the point. 'If I didn't say anything perhaps it wouldn't have happened.' I looked round them. 'Sounds so daft now.'

'You could at least have told us,' said Kate.

But she wasn't remembering how it had been between us then. We were seventeen and a close-knit group of friends who over the years had survived the bouts of bullying, exclusion, betrayals and secrets but who still scapegoated anyone who fell out of line. And that's what I must have done in Jane's eyes, our leader of the pack. Besides, nothing had happened. He hadn't raped me. His word against mine. No one else had been there, so he could deny it. Just as he did. In 1976, we weren't as clued up about our rights as girls are now. At least not at our school.

'I couldn't.' I didn't want to explain. Their memories would be different and I didn't want to argue over the facts. 'But it didn't take long for Mum to work out there was something wrong. Eventually she wormed out of me what had happened. She was furious—'

'I bet.' Linda spoke at last. But she didn't look up from her plate.

'She phoned Milters to report him. But Milters didn't believe her. I was down as a troublemaker and this was the last straw, and of course she supported her staff.'

'She wouldn't be able to deal with it like that these days.'

'I don't know that she could then, but she did. Anyway . . . He flat out denied everything, so it was his word against mine. And then his watch went missing and all hell broke loose.'

'I remember that. What was it, his grandfather's Rolex or something?'

'A valuable watch that he'd inherited is all I know. He made such an almighty fuss and insisted the police were involved. We all had to have our bags and our desks searched – do you remember how we all stood beside them as Miss Wilford went through them, banging the lids down one by one – and lo and behold, there it was in mine.' I could still feel that stomach-churning moment of discovery. I couldn't believe what I was seeing. 'I still have no idea how it got there, but someone put it there.'

They were both looking at me with varying degrees of interest, Kate most of all. The passing years must have dimmed their memories more than I'd imagined. And why not? This was my drama, not theirs.

'Then what?'

I couldn't help noticing Linda was more challenging than sympathetic. But I didn't have the tiniest scrap of evidence to back any accusation of Jane. I'd have to be more subtle in trying to find out what happened.

'Whatever I said, no one would listen. It was just like when Jane popped that lipstick in my bag so I got the blame for shoplifting.'

'You're not blaming her?' Both of them were shocked.

'Of course not.' I hurriedly smoothed that mistake over. 'Mr Wilson claimed I must have stolen the watch to get back at him when my story about his coming on to me was discredited. I mean . . . it all sounds so ludicrous. Suddenly I had a criminal record, or at least was branded a thief, and was expelled for theft, lying and trying to ruin his career. Goodbye A levels. Goodbye university.'

'But why believe him and not you?' Kate asked. 'There must be procedures that have to be followed when an accusation's made like that.'

I shrugged. 'No idea. But I'd like to know what happened, even now. I've done OK in life...' I looked around me. 'But not in the way I wanted to. That choice was taken away from me.'

'Well!' The word came out of Kate in a long whoosh.

'Of course one of the reasons for wanting to see you again was to be able to talk about it, but there hasn't been the right moment till now. Something's happened at home that's made me revisit things, and I'd like to resolve what happened for my own peace of mind.'

'But you're only talking about it now because of that guy's little finger!' Linda said, thoughtful. 'That couldn't have been Mr Wilson tonight. I'd have recognised him.'

'Jack Walsh?' I shook my head. 'You're probably right. It's just a coincidence that's made me think it was him, that's all. Why would he change his name?' But I knew what I'd seen. Jane must have recognised him too and been shaken by it. She had a massive crush on him back when, always first into the art room and last to leave, desperate for his praise and approval. That I do remember.

'It's an incredible coincidence if you're right.' Katie polished off her cod, straightened her knife and fork on her plate and leaned back in her chair.

'True.' But I couldn't help wondering about Jane's absence. There hadn't been anything wrong with her when we left for the party.

'Why don't you ask William?' Linda suggested. 'He might be able to find out.'

'He'll think I've gone mad.' I could imagine his reaction only too well. 'No, I'll wait in case we feel like going to Valldemossa and the exhibition. I'll ask Jack Walsh himself.'

But I wouldn't. I wouldn't because I was suddenly scared that the answer would be yes, and then what would I do?

We finished our wine, paid the bill and went back to the car. I'd decided I wouldn't put the others through the walk home because it was pretty arduous unless you were used to it. It wouldn't be the first time that the stony steps caused an accident. Rob and Dan had both tripped up more than once when a bit the worse for wear and without the torch. Rob was once limping for weeks.

The house was quiet when we got back. Lights off. Dan had either hooked up with some others for supper or he was in his room. To my slight relief, Jane must have gone to bed. However, when we walked into the living room, before we put the lights on, I noticed candlelight flickering outside on the terrace table. I opened the door and went out to find Jane, wrapped in a pashmina, sitting quietly and staring at the night sky.

'You OK?'

She shook her head. 'Not really.'

I could see she was upset about something. However Kate was right behind me and bulldozed her way in.

'You'll never guess. Amy thought the same thing: that Mr Wilson had risen from the dead.'

Jane's mouth opened and she stared at me, her face pale in the moonlight. It was then I knew I'd been right all along. She had something to do with that watch and my expulsion. Then she remembered herself and adjusted her expression from aghast to interest.

'I did wonder for a moment, but it can't be him,' she said.

'Why not?' Linda had arrived on the terrace armed with four small glasses and the half-finished bottle of wine from the fridge. She put them down and got pouring. 'This OK?' she asked me.

I didn't bother replying, just grabbed a glass and sat down. 'Whether he is or not doesn't really matter.' I took a breath.

It was now or never. 'Did you have anything to do with me being expelled, Jane? It's a long time now but here we are, and I'd still like to know.'

She looked away. 'Of course I didn't. You accused him of offering you high grades for sex. And you stole his watch.'

'You're sure of that?' I could hardly get the words out, I was so angry.

'And then you told me you'd made it all up. Anyway, what does it matter now? It's history, and you've overcome whatever happened. You've got a great life.'

The other two were staring at me, waiting for me to reply. I was so astonished, I wasn't sure how to react. Whenever would I have said that to her? I felt a cold wind on my back.

'Yes, I have got a great life. But, as we're together, I'd like to know the truth now. I'm sure I didn't tell you I'd made it up because it happened. Simple as that.' My word against hers. Just as it had once been my word against his. 'When do you think I told you?'

'I can't remember exactly.' She shifted in her seat, uncertain. 'But I'm sure you did.'

I could see, with the weight of history on her side, the others were wondering which of us could be believed.

'And that's what I told Mum.'

I didn't know what to think, but she had handed me a key.

'You told your mother?' Immediately I could see that she regretted saying anything. She looked suddenly unsure of herself, turning to look at the others for the support they couldn't give.

'Yes.' Defiant now.

'Without talking to me?'

'Of course we must have talked. I wouldn't have said anything otherwise.' But she didn't sound one hundred per cent certain. 'And anyway, he wasn't like that.'

'How do you know that? You weren't in the room with us.'

She sat up straight, clenching her fists, her expression fierce. 'This is just something you've built up over the years and expect us to go along with. Well, I won't. He was, and probably still is a good man.' She appealed to the others. Linda looked as if she was about to say something but didn't. But why did Jane care so much about Mr Wilson? Why did any of it matter to her? Why not the truth?

'What did your mum do, Jane?' I picked up my glass and turned it in my hand, watching the wine slosh to one side then the other.

She sat straight, poured herself a glass, and looked me straight in the eyes. 'Nothing,' she said. 'She did nothing.'

But I didn't believe her.

14

The next day, Linda woke with a light headache, resolving once again to cut down on her drinking. Still lying in bed, she phoned her aunt who was having one of her good days and wished her a happy holiday. The conversation was short but Linda was glad to hear that Aunt Pat was coming round to the carer who had bought her favourite biscuits and done her ironing.

When she eventually got out to the terrace, Amy had already laid breakfast: fresh bread, croissants and almond cake brought up from the bakery by Dan, salami, cheese, butter and jam, and fruit. She brought out fresh coffee and poured them all a cup.

'Brendan called to say he'll have the boat ready at about one-thirty. I thought we could go down to Sóller again and take the tram to the port. It's a bit of a tourist thing but you can't come all the way here and not go on it once. What do you think?'

'I think I'll pass,' said Jane abruptly.

They all looked at her. But her face gave nothing away.

'That is if you don't mind,' she added quickly. 'But I prefer dry land.'

Amy looked put out, then recovered herself. 'Not at all. You must do what you want. Are you two up for it?'

Linda grasped her coffee cup in both hands and nodded. Kate too.

'Great. If we leave at ten-thirty. OK? And of course no one has to come if they don't fancy it.' What did that look she gave Jane mean? Or had Linda imagined it?

'I'll squeeze in an hour by the pool first then.' Kate picked up her breakfast things to take inside. 'I'm getting used to this.'

'Oh, leave them.' Amy jumped up. 'You haven't come here to skivvy. I'll clear up and check my emails before we go.' Her mind had obviously run ahead to something business-connected. She seemed to have more emails to deal with than anyone Linda knew.

'Everything OK at work?' Linda couldn't help thinking of her own predicament.

'Oh yes, nothing that can't be sorted.' But Amy's brush-off lacked conviction. 'I've just got to keep in touch to make sure it's happening.' She started collecting the breakfast things onto the tray.

'I'll come with you, Kate.' Linda picked up her book, trying not to show her reluctance to be left alone with Amy and Jane. She had a feeling last night's conversation wasn't over yet and she didn't much want to be there when it reached a conclusion. They all knew Jane's hold on the truth could be shaky, but would she really have planted that watch as Amy suggested? Or lied to her mother? As for Amy's story about Mr Wilson – she couldn't believe that either. Which of them was telling the truth?

Linda and Kate set up their loungers in full glare of the sun rising above the mountains across the valley. 'Now what?' Linda couldn't resist, lowering her voice so she couldn't possibly be heard from the house.

'What do you mean?' Kate began spraying her legs with suntan oil.

'Isn't a bit awkward after last night? What are you going to do?'

'Nothing.' A long sigh escaped Kate as she lay back. 'I'm

going to enjoy this place while I can, even though I'm not too great on boats.'

'Come with me to Deià then.' Dan sat down beside them. Although he hadn't joined them for breakfast, they had seen him doing yoga at the very end of the garden and left him undisturbed.

'Deià?' echoed Kate.

'Yeah, why not? It's great little place – you should visit. On the coast and very different from here.'

'Sounds great.' Although she would never expect him to, Linda wished he had asked her.

'But I've only got room for one.' He spread his palms in a gesture of apology.

'I don't know,' said Kate, uncertain.

'Oh go,' said Linda. 'You don't like boats and I don't mind them. It'll be hard but somehow we'll manage without you!'

'Really? You don't mind.'

'Not at all.' Being on her own with Amy might be fun, and perhaps by the evening, the general atmosphere would have eased. If only they hadn't brought quite so much unresolved emotional baggage with them.

Looking at the crowd waiting for the tram in the centre of Sóller, Linda hesitated. People were spilling over the pavement, jostling for position, some armed with beach bags, others hanging on to their children. Even in the shade, the heat was oppressive.

'Come on.' Amy led her up the hill to join the crush at its lowest point. 'You'd be surprised how many the tram takes.'

The toot of the tram sounded in the main square below. Immediately the crowd surged forward in anticipation of its arrival, everyone eager to be first on. Up the hill chuntered the four carriages, the few people inside looking braced for the imminent influx of passengers, the driver standing at the front.

As they pulled up, Linda felt herself being pushed forward and up the metal steps into the last carriage. She was about to take one of the wooden slatted seats when a large heavily tattooed man and his family barged in front of her.

'Here!' Amy shouted from behind where she had bagged a seat for the two of them. Gratefully Linda sat down and waited as everyone else settled round them. Soon Amy was proved right and the street was almost empty, with lots of people standing in the aisles and on the footplates at either end of the carriages. Once the tram got moving, jolting and creaking, a light breeze blew through the open windows, and Linda looked out at the residential part of the town as they travelled between blocks of flats, houses and gardens, over the main road, heading towards the coast.

The tram slowed, giving a couple of warning toots so a couple of children and a dog scarpered out of its way. Before long they arrived at the port, taking the last straight section between the long strip of beach and the promenade, and the restaurants jammed with hungry tourists. More holiday apartments were being built beyond the houses on the hillside that surrounded a large natural bay with a marina at its northern end. The sea glittered in the sunlight, children's shouts travelled from the beach; a couple of yachts sailed out to the open sea. The marina was jammed with boats of all shapes and sizes. Somewhere among them Brendan and Sheila were waiting.

Once off the tram, they picked their way through the crowd waiting for the return journey towards the promenade. They walked past a couple of restaurants, the air rich with the smell of frying fish. Even from here Linda could make out the gin palaces moored alongside smaller boats of all shapes and sizes. She could imagine them all on board, convivial, glass of wine in hand, as they bobbed on the open sea. Brendan hadn't struck her as someone with money to splash around, but she didn't know his background or his enthusiasms. This was going to be a more luxurious afternoon that she'd imagined.

As they took a left along one of the pontoons, they spotted Brendan waving. To Linda's relief there was no sign of Sheila or Jove. She and Amy waved back and started to walk a little faster, past the fishermen who had their nets laid out on the ground for repair, and their boats: dirty, smelly, working vessels laden with tackle.

Brendan was standing by one of the biggest boats in the marina. Even with the minimum of seafaring knowledge, she could recognise the Rolls Royce of motorboats: gunmetal grey and gleaming, sleek and powerful. At the stern was a large seating area with a dining table and cushioned sun chairs – ideal for the odd sundowner. Perhaps this afternoon was going to be even more enjoyable than she'd anticipated. Pity the other two for not having come.

'Just the two of you then?' Brendan's disappointment when he realised Jane and Kate weren't with them was evident. Perhaps, to him too, Jane was another nut he had to crack.

But his disappointment was nothing compared to Linda's when he turned and walked away from the boat of her dreams. Still, she reassured herself, there were hundreds of others to choose from: not necessarily as big, but pristine white conquerors of the sea that swarmed with crew, mostly fit young men in shorts, cleaning, painting, sitting having coffee. One of them must be Brendan's. Messing about in a boat had taken on a whole new dimension for her. She clutched the handle of her picnic basket a little tighter.

'Aren't they amazing?' Amy didn't wait for a reply. 'Where are you moored?' she shouted at Brendan's back.

He lifted an arm and pointed, but it could have been at any of a number of boats, all of them considerably smaller than the ones they had passed. He turned a corner and stopped. 'Climb aboard!' he said with a sweeping gesture. 'This is *Reina del Mar*.

Queen of the Sea to you. Isn't she a beauty?' He spoke with real pride.

He must be joking. Surely this boat was far too small for them to spend the whole afternoon on. Less a luxury motor boat and more a tarted-up fishing boat painted a brilliant white with a royal blue canvas strung over the deck for shade. But Sheila and Jove were already on board, stashing a coolbag into the wheel cabin where all four of them couldn't possibly fit should the weather change. If the other two had come it would have been a real squash.

'Don't look so worried,' said Amy behind a hand. 'She's as stable as they come, made for all weathers. Anyway we're not tackling the open ocean, just chugging round the coast to a beach and getting off.'

'Less of the chugging.' Brendan was right behind them. 'Wait till you hear the hum of that engine.'

'Come off it,' said Amy, as she took her first steps on to the gangplank, then held her hand out to help Linda.

As they boarded, Jove, who was tied up on a very short lead, jumped about, barking.

'He'll calm down in a minute. Take a seat.' Sheila backed into the cabin, leaving room for Amy and Linda to settle themselves on wooden benches on opposite sides of the boat. She passed them each a cushion. Linda wedged hers behind her back but all the rocking about was making her queasy. She took a few deep breaths with her hand on her throat and watched as Brendan and Sheila cast off from the moorings so that they could chug (right word!) out of the marina towards the mouth of the harbour. Meanwhile Jove, who had been let off his lead, had settled down in a fleece-lined basked by Brendan's feet.

'Drinks?' Sheila passed out bottles of chilled water.

'Isn't this great?' Amy stretched out her legs and leaned back, her face bluish in the light filtering through the canopy.

Linda used her hand to stop her hat flying off. 'Mm-hmm.'

But it was. As she breathed in the sea air the sickness left her and, after a few minutes, she removed her hat altogether and trailed her hand in the wake of the boat.

'What do you think I should do about Jane?' Amy's question came from nowhere, taking Linda by surprise and making Sheila and Brendan look at her.

'Trouble?' asked Brendan.

'Not really. We were talking about something that happened years ago that we remember quite differently.'

'She has a quite different take on what happened,' Linda said. 'Very odd.'

'I was expelled just before my A levels,' Amy explained.

Leaving Sheila at the wheel, Brendan sat beside her, intrigued.

'Jane says I told her I lied about something, and I'm absolutely sure I didn't.'

'And?'

She left it there with a smile and a shake of her head.

Brendan looked disappointed that she wasn't going to go on. 'But does it really matter any more?'

Linda stared out towards the island's coast, where green-clad mountains dotted with ochre houses and villas rose towards the uninterrupted blue sky. The heat on board was mitigated by the blue canopy and the sea breeze. 'Do you think she'll still be there when we get back?' she asked, although what she really wanted to know was whether Amy was right about the artist. Surely she would have recognised Jack Wilson herself – even from a distance.

Amy was startled by the idea. 'I'm sure she will be. We left it open, and anyway she's not due in Barcelona for another couple of days. She's got a conference there. That was what swung her into coming here.'

'Didn't Kate hint at something else?'

'Did she? I didn't notice.'

'What sort of conference?' asked Brendan.

'Medical. Something to do with oncology, must be,' explained Amy to the other two. 'Believe it or not, I wanted to be a doctor too when we were at school, but things didn't work out that way.'

'Why not?' Brendan returned to the wheel and looked back at them. 'You seem the sort of person who could do anything she wanted. Unlike us.' He took over the steering from Sheila and grinned.

'Because it was a teenage dream and stuff happened. I lost my way for a bit and then, when I perhaps could have taken my A levels and gone to university, it was too late. I was in my thirties and I was getting Amy Green up and running with Rob. I couldn't have let that go.'

'We've lived here successfully enough,' Sheila said to Brendan, looking hurt he'd suggested otherwise. 'We didn't want that sort of success. I've always believed what matters is living your life, being true to yourself. Whether it's having a business empire like yours,' she nodded towards Amy. 'Or opening a shop like ours.'

By those standards, Linda's own life hadn't amounted to much. Had she even been true to herself? Sheila's words found their target. 'You had a shop?' she asked. 'I didn't know that.'

'Not any more. We made and sold silver jewellery, ours and other people's, but the demand fell away and the rents went up.'

'We inherited the house from Sheila's parents who conveniently died and left it to her when we were on our uppers,' Brendan added. 'So we make do by looking after various rental properties on the island for the owners. It's not glamorous but it gives us the life we like.' He gestured towards the island. 'What about you?'

'I'm not sure I do have the life I like. Not really.' Linda thought about the dismissive or despairing looks she received at work when she took too long helping with an enquiry while the queue grew longer and longer. She remembered how much

147

more pleasant her working environment had been when Mike was there. But had she even been happy then? Truly happy? 'I work in the Robin Hood Library in Nottingham, have done for years but I've just been offered voluntary redundancy.' To her surprise, she felt better having it out in the open.

'Oh no! That's awful. You should have said.' Amy grasped her hand.

'I'm trying not to think about it while I'm here.' If only it were that easy. She pulled her hand away. 'But I'm going to have to make a decision pretty much as soon as I'm back.'

'Take it,' said Brendan. 'You're probably thinking it'll be the end of everything. But when I think of those of our friends that it's happened to, not one of them regrets it now. Other things will come to you. Open yourself to the universe, and the universe will give back to you.'

'I wish I could believe that.' As far as Linda was concerned, that was too much like hippie waffle. That wasn't how the world worked in her experience, but Sheila was nodding in agreement. 'He's right, you know.'

'Maybe.' She relapsed into silence with the others in sympathy as the boat nosed its way along the coastline. Eventually they turned into a long rocky cove, with a beach at its head.

'Cala Tuent,' announced Brendan. 'One of our favourites. It's so hard to get to by road that it stays relatively quiet.' He cut the engine and, with Sheila's help, lowered the anchor. 'Swim, anyone?'

Swim! Linda had almost forgotten she had, on Amy's advice, put her swimsuit on underneath her clothes. Somehow she had got used to its restrictions. Without the engine churning it up, the water became a deep greeny blue, lightening to aquamarine at the edges of the cove. Without the breeze from the movement of the boat, she could feel her skin burning in the sun. As Brendan pulled off his T-shirt and dived in, Jove started racing from one end of the boat to the other, standing on his hindlegs in a frenzy of barking as Brendan upended and dived underneath the boat. He emerged on the other side, sending Jove even more frantic, shaking his head and pushing his hair off his face. 'It's bloody marvellous. Come on, ladies.'

The boat rocked as the other two stripped down to their bikinis. Not that Linda would be caught dead in one, but the ruched lycra did make her feel a bit old-maidish. But what could she do but join in regardless? And the sea couldn't be more inviting. As she got to the metal steps, she felt Jove rush at her ankle. Panicked, she kicked out at him. There was a splash and the barking stopped. She was already almost down the ladder, feeling the water like a warm bath, when there was a scream. 'Jove!' Sheila came whirling through the water like a demented bath toy. 'Where is he?'

Linda looked around her. Not far to her right, a bundle of fur was doing a feeble doggy-paddle, its nose just clear of the water.

'Grab him,' shouted Sheila. 'Quick!'

'I thought all dogs could swim,' yelled Amy from the other end of the boat.

'Not this one.' With a couple of clean strokes, Brendan had scooped up the floundering Jove and popped him back over the edge of the boat.

'Not like that!' Sheila reached the ladder and climbed in, bending over, muttering endearments. 'Where's the towel?'

By the time she found it, wrapped up the dog and was sitting cradling him like a baby, Linda had swum up to Amy. They caught one another's eye and smiled broadly. Then Amy winked. Trying not to laugh, Linda rolled on to her back and lay, floating, eyes closed, feeling the water lap against her.

'Race you to the beach,' said Amy.

Race? Linda hadn't raced anywhere for years. But Amy splashed water over her so that she spluttered and overbalanced. Why not? She hadn't forgotten how. Not entirely. As she began to swim, she found the strokes and some of the strength that she'd had when they were young. Together, they pulled away from the boat and swam stroke for stroke, just as they had in the past, towards the shore.

When they arrived at the pebbly, gravelly beach, backed by olive trees, they sat at the edge of the sea, their legs lapped by the translucent water. The pick-pock sound of a game of beach tennis in progress behind them broke the stillness of the afternoon. Linda picked up a stone and skimmed it across the water. One, two . . . five jumps.

'Isn't this perfect?' said Amy.

And it was. All Linda's anxieties had left her and for once, she was entirely in the present. This is what life could still offer her. She didn't have to be the misery she'd become.

'You should listen to Brendan. He's right. Sometimes it's easier to stick in the same job doing what you know because anything else seems daunting. I've seen so many people do that. But it's never too late to change. Other opportunities do present themselves. You'll see.'

Linda's disbelieving sigh made Amy turn to look at her but she kept her face tipped towards the sun. Did opportunities present themselves to women of her age who had only ever had one career, she asked herself. Was there still a chance for her to do something where she would be accepted and that she would enjoy? Perhaps, she thought, perhaps they were right. Perhaps the time had come to start being braver and putting herself first.

15

Kate felt giddy and light-headed as she gripped on to Dan's T-shirt, pressed her knees in against his thighs, feeling the warm wind against her face. He was probably taking the winding coastal road slower than he normally would, given she was riding pillion, but this was thrilling all the same. As they roared up the road out of Sóller, the surrounding landscape grew increasingly impressive as they sped over the mountains until the road ran parallel to the coastline below.

Her heart was in her mouth as they hugged the edge of the road to let something pass from the opposite direction, the land dropping away beside them, across the wooded mountainside to the endless deep blue sea where, in the distance, boats sailed slowly across the horizon.

Ochre-coloured houses clung on to the mountainsides among pines and olive and citrus groves. The road was busy but Dan was focused, slowing down for the twistiest of bends, speeding up again as it straightened. This was the most reckless thing Kate had done for as long as she could remember. How many times had she forbidden her sons from riding motorbikes, terrified by all the horror stories? And yet here she was taking a risk with her own life. The knowledge that she was doing something that Alan and the kids would have insisted she didn't only added to the adrenaline rush.

Dan slowed down, signalled left by an olive grove and turned up a track into a car park. Off the bike, her legs were trembling, her knees stiff and, her helmet off, her hair stuck to her head.

'You can't come to Deià without visiting Robert Graves's house,' said Dan. 'So that's our first stop.'

Kate raked her fingers through her hair despite it being too late to care how she looked. He locked up the bike and they walked along the side of the road as far as a gateway with a ticket office just inside. The next hour was unexpected and fascinating, as they wandered through the house and garden. Kate found out more than she'd ever wanted to know about the author of *I, Claudius*, a novel she dimly remembered reading in her early twenties, and his wives. The whole set-up looked so bohemian and alive.

Dan turned out to be a good companion and guide. He sensed that she didn't need him crowding her and overloading her with information, so kept his comments to the bare minimum, only drawing her attention to things she might otherwise have missed such as some of the ephemera in Graves's office or a letter from T.S. Eliot in the museum. This was the first time she'd been anywhere on her own with a man who wasn't Alan since she got married, and she was surprised by how at ease Dan made her feel. He felt like the best kind of old friend.

Back on the bike, they took a turning down a steep winding road that could only lead to the coast. She hung on for dear life as it twisted and turned, the bike leaning to the left and then the right, stopping for the occasional car coming in the opposite direction where the road was too narrow for both of them. Eventually, they arrived at a crowded woodland car park, where Dan pulled up.

'Just a little further, then we'll have to walk,' he said. 'I think you'll like it when we get there.' Through the car park dappled with sun, down a road exclusively used by those who lived in a hamlet in the woods, until they came to a concrete slipway leading down to the sea, the white hulls of upturned boats lined up down its sides. On the far side of the slipway was a huddle of small stone buildings and, above them, a restaurant, its terrace open to the sea. A faint smell of fried fish hung in the air. Round the corner, a small bouldered beach formed the base of a rocky inlet. At the back of the beach was another restaurant, like the first, packed with diners.

'I thought we could have a swim,' said Dan, checking to see her reaction. 'And then I've booked a table for lunch.' He pointed to the restaurant on the cliff. 'What do you think?'

Before they left that morning, he'd suggested she wear her swimsuit just in case. 'Or you can change in the woods.' So she was all ready. Looking around at the assorted bodies, she realised that there was no need for embarrassment and, after all, he'd seen what she had to offer before.

'Sounds perfect.'

So together they picked their way over the rocks to a spot where they could leave their clothes not too far from the water. She stripped off and laid her shorts and shirt on her towel. Dan gave her a quick, appreciative look. 'You look great,' he said.

'Great's the word,' she replied, immediately annoyed with herself for being so tiresome and self-deprecating.

With the brief 'Don't be silly' and a raised eyebrow that she deserved, he led the way to the sea.

What would Alan say if he could see her now? Before she found the answer, she pushed the thought from her mind. For once, she was enjoying herself without anyone hurrying her up or nagging. Besides, she'd be home in a few days. He'd offered a slightly begrudging 'Enjoy yourself' when she left – so she would. And it wasn't as if she hadn't left the freezer bursting with his favourite meals. Even if he couldn't work the oven. She had done her bit.

After their time by the pool, she didn't feel too self-conscious as she crossed the boulders to the sea. And the sea was perfect, like being submerged in a shimmering opalescent bath where the rocks under their feet were completely visible. Dan was already swimming out towards the boats moored at the mouth of the cove. He turned round once and waved her towards him – 'Come out here! The fish!'

She swam towards him, looking down at the shoals of tiny fish that whisked back and forth around her. From here, the beach looked smaller, dotted with brightly coloured parasols, towels spread out on the baking rocks, people splishing about at the shore, others striking out as they had.

'I haven't been anywhere like this for years. The farm's so demanding that it's hard to take time off.' What she didn't say was that when they did, the holidays she dreamed of were not those her husband looked forward to. Any disloyal thoughts were private. Alan could never slow down, so when not on the farm, he liked to be in a city. He liked galleries, monuments, medieval town centres with maze-like streets in which to wander, places dripping with history and culture. Over the years they had notched up long weekends in Paris, Rome, Vienna, Tallin, Budapest and one or two more.

However she wanted nothing more than this: the nothingness of being in a beautiful place with no calls on her time. She gazed at the beach where people stood or basked like lizards on the hot rocks. Above them the cliffs rose to pine woods that resonated against the blue sky. Paradise. And she was part of it.

They swam back together and sat on the shoreline, saying nothing, the waves lapping over their legs.

'So you like it?' Dan eventually broke the silence between them.

She beamed at him. 'It's perfect. Thank you for bringing me here. Much better than throwing up on a boat.'

'I doubt you would in this weather. It's like a mirror out

there.' He smiled. 'But I'm glad you came. Shall we dry off and have lunch?'

Fifteen minutes later, they'd climbed the steep stone steps to the restaurant and were sitting at a table at the edge of the terrace, overlooking the sea to the other side of the cove with the rhythmic sound of the waves as an accompaniment. A bamboo screen above their heads protected them from the worst of the sun, though Kate's skin was tingling.

'You approve?' Dan poured them some water.

'A hundred per cent.' Kate was feeling quite overwhelmed with the perfection of it all.

Dan raised a hand to the waiter. 'Shall we order? I want to show you more before we head home.'

'Sure.' But the heat had taken away her appetite.

'So?' Dan pulled off a piece of bread and popped it in his mouth, his eyes fixed on her.

'What do you mean?' She looked out to sea, knowing exactly what he meant, but the last thing she wanted to do was talk about what had happened the night before. She didn't want to spoil the day, however selfish that was. On the other side of the cove, a couple were pulling a boat down a short stone slipway from a boathouse in the rock face. In the sea, people were lolling on the rocks, swimming under the sun.

'So what happened last night? Something must have because you're all behaving so weirdly today. Look at you. You're here for a reunion and yet you're all off doing your own thing.'

'Amy and Linda are on the boat together.'

He gave that wicked grin. 'You know perfectly well what I mean. It isn't going as planned, is it? I know my sister well enough to know when she's rattled about something.' He leaned forward, squinting against the sun. 'You can tell me. I do know how to be discreet.'

Kate doubted that.

'And I'm the only one here who knows how to deal with her.'

He leaned back as the waiter put down a whole grilled sea bass and salad for them to share. 'Let me.' He proceeded to fillet the fish and divide it between them before helping them both to salad. 'There. So . . . Amy and I have always been pretty close. You know that, right? Our lives might have taken us in very different directions but I've always looked out for her.'

'You once rescued us in the playground. We've never forgotten.'

'Did I?' He shrugged and speared a chip with his fork. 'But you're not changing the subject that easily. Last night . . .'

'I guess you might as well know,' she said, moving her fish around the plate before taking a mouthful. 'That artist last night?' The fish was delicious, fresh and sweet, and grilled to perfection.

He raised a quizzical eyebrow. 'Jack Walsh. Yeah. I met him. Seemed an interesting guy.'

'Well, you won't believe this but . . . Amy thinks he might be Jack Wilson. I think Jane does too, but she's not admitting it.' She presented him with the fact, like a dog with a bone.

He looked blankly at her. 'And Jack Wilson is . . . ?'

She watched his face change as he cottoned on.

'Not the art teacher at your school?'

She nodded.

He gave a long low whistle. 'Bloody hell!'

'Hard to believe, I know. But Jane and Amy had a bit of a set-to last night. If it's him, he's obviously got a different name but it got us talking about what happened. When Amy asked Jane if she was involved, she claimed that Amy had told her that she'd lied to get Mr Wilson in trouble.'

'But that's not true.' His face set as he banged the end of his knife on the table.

'Well, true or not, it wasn't resolved. Jane was so insistent. I think they were both quite relieved not to have to spend today together. It'll be better after a day apart when everyone's had time to reflect and calm down.' But why would it be? Wouldn't they both want to be proved right for their own reasons?

'You're very sweet.' He scratched his chin, gazing at her for a long moment before looking away.

She felt herself blushing. 'Sweet' was not an adjective applied to her often. 'Not really.'

'We could go down to Valldemossa and find him.' His eyes lit up with the plan. 'Find out for sure.'

'That's not a good idea.' Suddenly the day had lost some of its magic. 'If anyone's going to do that, it should be Amy, not us.'

'Perhaps.' He rapped his fingers on the table. 'I'd have something to say to him if he is this guy. What happened did change her life, and bad karma doesn't just disappear.'

'Please. Can't we just pretend we didn't have this conversation until this evening?' She wanted the day to carry on as it had been without any kind of unpleasantness. All this had happened so long ago that it shouldn't matter any more. Aside from that, she wasn't ready for her adventure to be over. She was enjoying his company, and this new feeling of being alive again.

He picked up his glass, turning it in his hands, as if considering his next move.

She watched him, tense with anticipation.

Then he held it still and looked straight at her. 'All right.'

'All right what?'

'Let's carry on as planned. I said I'd show you Deià, and that's what I'd like to do. And then I'll think again.' He signalled for the bill.

Kate sagged with relief as he dug in his pockets for his wallet. The prospect of travelling to confront her old art teacher over something he may or may not have done decades ago did not excite her. However, she was aware that the matter would have to be addressed at some point but not without

Amy's involvement. What must she be feeling? Although she was often in trouble at school – bunking off, shoplifting (once that she didn't do), wearing too much make-up, skirt too short, smashing the hall window with a tennis ball, painting graffiti on the playground wall – and that time they were both banned from sports for being caught smoking behind the changing shed – she was not a liar.

Amy had been egged on by Jane and competed with her in everything they did, but for some reason she always came off slightly worse. One of them had to be lying now. But Amy's description of the assault was so detailed and she was obviously mystified by the theft of the watch. Why would she have told Jane otherwise? That made no sense. So Jane had to be lying. But that made no more sense. Unless she was just mistaken. Worse, all these years later, Amy still blamed the whole episode for changing the direction of her life, as if her success counted for nothing. Kate had no idea what or who to believe.

'I, er – Christ, this is embarrassing.' Dan held out his hands in supplication. 'I must've left my wallet on the bike.'

He looked so mortified she felt sorry for him. 'Oh, I can pay. Of course. I'd like to. Think of it as a thank you for today.'

'Are you sure?' He passed over the bill.

'Of course,' she said, controlling her expression so it didn't register her surprise when she saw the total. 'It's the least I can do.'

As soon as she'd paid, Dan was on his feet. 'Let's go. Or do you want coffee?' He hesitated.

'No, I'm ready.' She didn't want to leave this idyllic spot but at the same time she wanted to see more of what the island had to offer.

At Deià, they parked on the side of the main road. Dodging the through traffic and the dozens of tourists wandering the pavements, they crossed the road and were soon walking up a hill through a much quieter part of the old town. On the walls of houses were occasional ceramic wall tiles depicting the stations of the cross. As they climbed, sweat trickled down her temple. They stopped for water at a drinking fountain where Dan splashed some over the back of his neck and put his icy hands on hers, so she yelped. Just when she thought she couldn't go any further, they reached a church.

She was standing looking out past two large cannons to the village falling away below them and the view that extended towards the limestone crags beyond, when he took her hand. 'This way.'

She was so startled that she let him tug her in the direction of the church door. Once there, he let her go. She entered the dim interior and planted herself on a pew, pretending nothing unusual had happened. Just the touch of a hand. What was the matter with her? Did he feel the same flash of something between them that she had? She hadn't felt anything for a new man for years. She had written herself off as undesirable, too old, and anyway, she hadn't wanted to open herself to anyone new. The only men she came across were married to her friends – no-go areas even if she had any inclination. But this … this felt dangerous and unexpected and … wrong. She cleared her throat and concentrated on the music being piped quietly through the church – Allegri's *Misereri*. The notes calmed her as she considered the baroque altarpiece, the elaborate tiling and a figure of Christ with what looked like a red tablecloth girding his loins.

Dan was standing in the doorway, waiting for her. Composing herself, she joined him and they stepped outside into the heat of the day again. Around the side of the church, he showed her through two tall grey gates in a wall. Inside, a modest cemetery contained gravestones both vertical and flush with the ground, shaded by yews, olive trees and shrubs. Some of them simply had names and dates scratched in cement, others were more elaborate and finished off with photos of the dead.

Dan sat on a low wall where several English expats were memorialised while Kate explored. They climbed down the vertiginous steps to the terrace below and walked along to the steps back up. When they reached the opposite side of the cemetery, they sat on another wall, looking across the village and surrounding mountains, enjoying the peace.

'Not a bad place to end up,' he said.

'I hope you're not thinking of ending up here soon,' she said.

'I've a few things left to do yet.' His hand rested on the wall just inches from her hip.

When the gate opened to admit a group of chatting tourists, they got up to leave. 'Like minds,' he said. 'And now for something completely different.'

'I'm not sure I can take in any more.' She didn't want too many memories overlaying one another or she wouldn't remember each one clearly.

'I don't think you'll have any trouble with this.' He set off down the hill, taking a different path to the one that had brought them up there And she, like a sheep, followed him, hoping, despite herself, that he might take her hand again. After all, it wouldn't be so very wrong if he was making sure she was steady on the cobbles. But she was disappointed.

Fifteen minutes later, they were walking up a tarmac drive flanked with gnarled olive trees while the greenest manicured lawns she had seen since being in Spain spread out to their left. They arrived at the long wide terrace of a beautiful building. Elegant couples sat at well-spaced tables in the sun or under parasols.

'Welcome to how the other half live,' Dan said in an undertone, then flung out his arms in a dramatic gesture. 'Once manor houses, now a hotel. *The* hotel. The Residencia. Or The Resi to those of us who have drunk here for decades.'

Kate couldn't help comparing her dusty shorts and crumpled shirt with the expensive-looking floaty garment on the woman walking past her on immaculately pedicured feet in expensive strappy sandals. She curled her toes inside her dusty Converses.

'Are we allowed here?'

'Why not? We have as much right as anyone else.'

They were shown to a table at the edge of the terrace, looking towards the hill they had just climbed, the church at its summit. The waitress didn't blink at their appearance although Kate felt an impostor, sitting by the balustrade, pouring tea from a silver-plated pot, offering him a sugared fruit jelly sweet. But nobody questioned their presence, and she began to enjoy herself. 'I could get used to this,' she said.

'I don't meet many women like you.'

The tea splashed into her saucer. 'I'll take that as a compliment. Thank you,' she said, hiding her fluster by mopping up the spill with a napkin.

'You're different.'

'You should come to the Dales. There are plenty more like me there.' Her heart was pounding so hard he must be able to hear it.

He was leaning back against the white cushion, hands clasped behind his head. He smiled that smile again. 'I don't believe that for a moment.'

They were headed somewhere dangerous, tempting but not somewhere she had an inkling she'd be visiting on this short break. She had to change the subject despite admitting to herself she was enjoying flirting with him – perhaps she wasn't quite as past it, as she had imagined. 'Where now?'

'Valldemossa?' he suggested, his smile widening as he winked. Again. He knew exactly the effect he was having on her. And yes, more than anything, she wanted to be back on the bike, speeding through the mountains, clinging on to him, the sun on her arms and legs, his smell in her nostrils.

'I think we should go back,' she said, exerting every ounce of self-control she possessed. 'The others will be wondering where we are.'

16

Jane was sitting on the edge of the pool, legs in the water, the sun bright on her face, the conversation from the night before racing through her brain, when her phone rang. Stretching behind her, she picked it up. She had been miles away, not only preoccupied by the previous night but also that night decades earlier when she came home from school and told her mother Amy had lied about Mr Wilson wanting sex for results. Now she'd been prompted, she could recall quite clearly her mother's outrage. Seeing their art teacher again – if that's really who he was – had triggered more memories than she cared to admit. She hadn't behaved well, that was for certain, and she wasn't sure what she should do about it now.

The ringing of the phone was relentless. She glanced down. *David.* The thought of her husband was a comfort. She too easily dismissed women who talked about their man being their 'rock', but she understood what they meant. David was such a solid presence in her life and provided her with stability and love. Without him, she would be adrift. So why risk it all by continuing her relationship with Rick? This was the question she had asked herself so many times yet failed to find a definitive answer. She was only too aware how wrong and chancy it was. After Barcelona, she would finish with Rick for the last time. After. She lifted her phone. 'Darling.'

'Where are you?' Nothing affectionate, nothing personal. That was unlike him.

'You know where I am. In Mallorca at Amy's, my old school friend's, remember? I told you.'

'I know that's what you said.'

She lifted her legs from the pool, stood up and walked back to her lounger, the phone pressed to her ear. 'What do you mean? What's the matter? You sound odd.'

'Do I? Is that all that surprising?'

'I don't know until you explain.' She picked up her suntan oil and sprayed it on both legs, switched her phone to her other hand so she could rub it in more easily.

'I was at the hospital today.'

'Are you OK?' She stopped rubbing and sat still, waiting for his answer.

'I went with Paul to cheer him on during his chemo.' He paused as if he was about to say something momentous.

'You're such a good friend to him,' she said, breaking the tension. The two men had known each other since university and had always remained close. 'How is he?'

'I bumped into Jonas Fleetwood.'

Jane didn't know the recent addition to the oncology team well but she could envisage him, dark, bearded, committed. 'Nice guy.' They'd all met socially at a party given by one of the other consultants a few weeks earlier.

'Didn't you say you were going on to a conference in Barcelona this week when you left Mallorca?' A chilly finger traced a path down Jane's spine.

'Yes. You know I did.' She shifted position on the lounger.

'He told me the conference was last week and you opted out of it weeks ago so he could go.' His voice was icy calm.

She thought fast. 'This is a different one.' Would he believe her?

'Really?' He didn't sound one hundred per cent convinced.

'I'm not sure Jonas would necessarily know about it. It's a much smaller affair.' She picked at the cuticle of her thumb until a drop of blood appeared. 'Honestly, darling. What on earth did you think I was doing?'

'Who was that text and photo really for?'

Oh God.

'I told you. For you.'

'Honestly.'

She could tell how much he wanted to believe her.

'Honestly. Cross my heart.'

There was a pause. Eventually David broke it. 'Well then, why don't I change things round and fly out to join you? There's a flight I could get on tomorrow morning. I can take the time off and we could spend a few days together.'

Jane's phone slipped from her hand and cracked on the paving. As she scrabbled to pick it up, her mind was racing. They had reached the point that she had always dreaded. This was the writing on the wall for her and Rick. She couldn't risk losing David. She had to stop things now before it was too late. She would get hold of Rick the moment this call was over. Or . . .

'Why don't we wait till after the tribunal? We could go somewhere together then when all this isn't hanging over us?' The words were out of her mouth before she'd even thought them.

'But when do you think we'll hear?' *'We', not 'you'*. The question of a man who supported her in everything she did.

She was ashamed of what she was about to do, despite everything, knowing how devastated he would be if he ever found out. But she had to finish things with Rick face to face. She owed him that. 'Immediately after the tribunal itself. Just let me get through that and then we'll take a long weekend wherever you like.'

'We-ell.' He didn't sound entirely convinced.

'I'll be working anyway. We'll hardly see each other.' The lies fell from her lips as easily as ever. 'You choose where we go. We can book it when I get back.'

By the time she ended the call, her hand was shaking. If she cancelled Rick, she didn't trust him not to say or do something that would reach David's ears. She was also a firm believer that dumping someone by a phone call was a coward's way out. Her duty was to see him one more time and make things quite clear. They were through. After that the tribunal and its result. Then she would be free to start her life with David again. No more deceit. She lay back in the sun, arms by her side. There was nothing she had to do except wait for the others to return at the other end of the day. But despite the beauty of the morning, her head spun with persistent nagging anxieties.

David and Rick.

She would call Rick and prepare him. She would devote herself to David from next week on. She would. Decision made.

The tribunal.

There was nothing she could do but wait it out. But what if they didn't find in her favour? What if her action born from her concern for Paul ruined not only her reputation but her career? Surely the tribunal and her colleagues would be lenient when they understood the circumstances, that she had acted in a moment of madness brought on by concern for her son.

Amy and Mr Wilson.

What did happen? She had buried the events of that summer so long ago that it was hard to remember. Had Amy really told her she had lied to Miss Milton? She thought so. She clearly remembered Amy coming out of school the day after 'it' had happened. She hadn't bothered to take her hair out of its school plait or put on any make-up. Instead she had been white with rage, so furious and upset she could barely speak. As she forced herself back to that afternoon, Jane recalled listening to Amy's almost incoherent account of what had happened, and of her mother's phone call to Milters asking for Mr Wilson to be suspended. Worse had been her own reaction of frustrated anger that she couldn't explain.

Even now, lying by the pool, she could feel that sense of powerless frustration all over again. She clenched her fists against the memory. But her anger hadn't been for Amy, had it? If honest with herself, it had been because Mr Wilson had come on to Amy and not to her. She could barely bring herself to admit the truth. Even now. To this day, none of the others had really cottoned on to the brightness of the torch she'd carried for him.

She had done her best to keep it hidden.

Every art class, she'd wait, eager for his attention, jealous of anyone whom he helped or advised for too long. She would never confess that she was the one who'd buried the sharp modelling tool in a lump of clay so that when Linda, who kept calling him back to explain again the principles of hand-building a clay bowl, banged her hand down on it, the tool went straight through the fleshy bit between her thumb and index finger. Only her scream shocked Jane into realising what a dreadful thing she'd done. And for what? She had thought punishing her friend who was asking for help with her work would be funny. But it wasn't. It was terrible and shamed her.

It hadn't occurred to her that the tool would do anything more than bruise Linda's hand. She hadn't wanted anyone else to have the attention of a teacher whom she fancied and who didn't give her the attention she wanted. How flattered he must have been, being worshipped by a classroom of teenage girls awash with rampaging hormones. All except Amy, and perhaps Linda, both of whom were focused on their academic success to the exclusion of almost everything else. Amy's lack of inerest must have made her a challenge.

How hazy and unreliable memory is.

But what had she, Jane, done? Remembering Amy's outrage

was one thing. But when had Amy confided to her that she had exaggerated what had happened because she thought Mr Wilson's predatory (not a word she'd have used then, but it would have been the right one) attitude to her and the other girls was out of order, and wanted him shocked out of it? That Jane shouldn't tell a soul. She must have done, but try as she might, she couldn't remember the actual moment when that confidence was made.

But that was certainly what she'd told her mother. A couple of days after the event, rumours were travelling all round the school: Mr Wilson was suspended; Mr Wilson was hauled up in front of Miss Milton and they'd had a blazing row as he defended himself; Mr Wilson had left the school; Mr Wilson protested his innocence; Amy lied; Amy only said what other girls could have said; the girls were going to stage a protest on his behalf.

Gradually her memories slipped into place. How desperately she hadn't wanted him to leave. The idea of not seeing him again was unbearable. And the watch. He had taken it off and left it on his desk while he went to wash his hands. It had been the work of a moment to take it and slip it under the books in the nearest desk – Amy's. An act of simple jealousy and fury because Mr Wilson's future at the school was under threat. Nobody had seen her. But the fuss that ensued... When no one owned up, Mr Wilson insisted on making it a police matter.

She used to hang around the classroom at lunchtime or at the end of the day, hoping to catch him. But having seen him last night at William's party, she was hard-pressed to imagine what she once saw in him. Then, he had been handsome, arty in his jeans, a shock of sandy hair, tank top and open-necked shirt with rolled-up sleeves. Compared to the other three male teachers who stuck to traditional suits and rarely joked, he had been a breath of fresh air. He was sex on legs. He smoked cigarettes in a holder, his pinkie crooked. He wore an aftershave that lingered on after he'd moved to the next pupil. When she'd heard the rumour he was leaving, she had been as distraught as everyone else, all caught up in a minor mass hysteria. She remembered going home the day she'd heard. Her mother had been in the kitchen and looked up from the newspaper she was reading. Taking in Jane's distress, she immediately looked alarmed. 'Whatever's the matter? Come and sit down.'

By the time she was at the table with a cup of tea and a custard cream, Jane was shaking with sobs.

'Jane, darling. Pull yourself together. Nothing's that bad. Tell me what's happened.' Her mother was typically to the point.

Interrupting her explanation with loud sniffs, Jane explained. 'Our art teacher... he's going to be sacked... didn't do anything... Amy Green's lying... didn't get good marks...'

When she'd finally grasped the full story and felt the injustice of an innocent man being wronged, her mother was up in arms. She'd been impressed and charmed by Mr Wilson at parents' day, enjoyed how he'd flattered Jane's artistic abilities (which decades later, Jane realised had in fact been limited) and her own, commenting on her sensitive choice of colour in the scarf she wore.

'That's outrageous. Helen' – her mother, a dutiful school governor, was on first name terms with Miss Milton – 'can't be taking Amy seriously. That's a girl who's always been in trouble since day one. You know I've never trusted her.' She folded up her newspaper, omitting to remember the number of times Amy had been to their house when nothing had gone missing or wrong or, when she'd chatted at some length with her, how impressed she had been by her ambition. 'Don't worry, I'll deal with this.' Her hand went to the French roll that she styled every morning and patted the hair in place, a gesture that signified she was about to embark on a mission. She took her role in the local community seriously and was intent on it running the way she believed it should. She made a formidable opponent.

And then the watch was found.

The next thing was that Amy had been expelled from the school. Jane had not seen that coming at all. She had imagined Amy would find the watch and hand it in. But that's not what happened. Her mother had more influence that she'd realised. A subdued Mr Wilson was back in the art room. Like the other girls, she was overjoyed that he had had a reprieve.

However, things were never the same after that. Mr Wilson had maintained a reserve and a strict distance from his pupils from that day onwards. His jokes were fewer, less funny. The more risqué ones were non-existent. If he noticed Jane's deliberate leg crossing – she'd read in a magazine there was nothing more erotic to a man than the swish of a stockinged leg – he made no response. He didn't comment on anyone's appearance. He was very careful. As for Amy... Amy would be all right. And she had been.

Here she was now in Amy's beautiful home, enjoying her hospitality; but thanks to an unfortunate quirk of fate, they were reliving their school days despite her having suppressed the worst of them long ago. Although Amy had been ambitious, Linda and Jane almost always pipped her to the top of the class. Hanging on to this grudge was one thing but, if she was so driven to be a doctor, she could easily have studied and become one. Jane would not take the rap for that.

She went inside to get herself a glass of water, the indoor tiles cool under her feet. She stopped for a while to admire the living room again. Amy had always had an eye. As a kid, she went along with the fads and fashions but had always managed to add her own distinctive take with a bright belt or a clashing brooch. Jane had envied her that. She must have inherited her mother's sense of colour and style: a woman like Mrs Tiggy-winkle, small and round, who wore a pincushion on her chest and was always in their small front room – the one that never got used for best – surrounded by bolts of fabric and dresses hanging from a rail that crossed the back of the room. And in the window where there was the best light, the table with her heavy black and gold Singer sewing machine.

In this room, Moroccan-style fabrics with geometric patterns were striking against the white walls. There were two large landscape paintings of what Jane assumed were local beauty spots. Simple, elegant and timeless: all those clichés. Jane sighed.

On her way back outside, she heard her phone ringing. Not David again! She really didn't want her mind deflected from the immediate problem of what to do about Amy and Mr Wilson or whatever he was calling himself now. And why?

Nonetheless, unable to ignore it she picked up her phone from the lounger. *Rick.* Should she? She settled her hand on her stomach, reassuring herself of its flatness.

'Hello.'

17

What a day. Despite Jove's accidental dip, the four of us had a great time. Sheila was quite laid back for once and Linda was so much more fun than she'd been till then. I began to see traces of the old her coming through, perhaps because we'd escaped the others. And escape was the right word. Jane was a constant background noise to my thoughts now I was sure she was the one who had been behind my expulsion. All I hoped for was an apology – an acknowledgement of the wrong done.

Why not? That's what I hoped for from Rob too. Was that so unreasonable? I wanted my life cleared up before I moved on. I wanted Kate and Linda to know that I wasn't a thief. Dan, too, although he'd always supported me.

If I was worried about anyone, it was Kate on my brother's pillion. Charming as he could be, I wasn't blind to his faults. I knew what he was like around an attractive woman and, although she may not have realised it, Kate was that still. Not the social X-ray that the bloody media still dictates we women should be but gloriously rounded and very much her own person. I was sure Dan wasn't blind to any of that.

By the time Linda and I swam back to the boat, Brendan and Sheila had pulled out our picnic. It was all a bit of a squash on board but perfect. I'd brought some slices of pizza from the bakery in Sóller and some fruit: fat plums and figs. They had chilled water, orange juice and wine, cheese, tomatoes and ham.

That was all we needed. We spread it out on the small picnic table that Sheila provided and got stuck in.

'This is a feast.' Linda looked so chilled. She didn't even have a glass of wine, just ate a little, and sat back, quite content. So if nothing else was to be achieved over these four days, at least that was something. She looked as if she couldn't believe the life she was living. And what's more, I'd thoroughly enjoyed spending the day with her.

The journey home seemed to speed by compared to the journey out. The sea remained like a millpond, and while Brendan and Sheila stood in the cabin, chatting and steering the *Reina del Mar*, Linda and I sat under the blue canopy, trailing our hands in the water, saying little. We didn't need to. Until...

'So what are you going to do?' she asked tentatively.

'About what?' For a moment I thought she meant about Rob and the continuing threat to the business. He'd promised he'd pay the money back, but so far we'd seen nothing. I can't say I was wholly surprised, although if he thought I was going to soften towards him, he should think again. But of course Linda didn't know anything about that.

'About Jack Walsh and Jane?'

'I don't know. I probably should let it go, but I don't want to when I might be so close to the truth. Perhaps I'd feel better if I confronted Jack Walsh and got the apology I'd like from him. After all, if it weren't for him...'

Linda propped herself up with both elbows on the side of the boat, alarm on her face. 'Really?'

'Why not? What harm can he do now?' I was right. There was nothing he could do to me now. The damage had been done long ago. If anyone had anything to fear, it was him.

'I guess so.' She trailed her arm in the water, dabbling her fingers, distracting herself. 'I'll come with you if you like.'

I was surprised. 'Are you sure? It may not be pretty.' I *was* joking but she didn't smile.

'Then you'll need moral support.' Evidently nothing more needed to be said. She'd made up her mind. That was fine by me. I wasn't relishing the idea of a solo confrontation but I needed to do something.

'You're so lucky having all this.' She gestured towards the island, which was looking its best in the evening sun, showering us both with water. 'Ah! Sorry.'

We laughed again.

Despite her initial diffidence, I felt as comfortable with her now as if we were still best mates, plotting how to get tickets to a gig at the local cinema, dancing in our bedrooms to Steeleye Span and Roxy Music, experimenting with make-up, guessing what the questions on the next exam paper would be. There must be something more than Mike behind her loss of confidence but I still didn't like to ask. She would tell me when or if she was ready.

We didn't stay to see the sun go down – a shame, because I've seen some of the most beautiful sunsets in the world from that side of the island and I'd have liked to share that with her – but time was against us and by the time we got home, it was nearly dark. There was no sign of Jane. I discreetly checked her room to find her things were still there, so she hadn't done a runner. When Linda went to change, I made a beeline for my office. Spending a day without access to the internet was wonderfully liberating but now I was itching to be back in touch with the business, checking the daily figures and whether Rob had made a payment. I couldn't let a day go past without that.

My office was on the north side of the house so it was always something of a respite from the heat of the day. Apart from the table that I'd stripped down to the wood, there was my easel and my watercolours, brushes and pencils that I used when I was roughing out a new design. On the table sat my laptop and a heavy green glass paperweight that I'd found in a junk shop. I loved the way the light played on the air bubbles inside it.

Beside it, Rob grinned at me from a holiday we once had in St Lucia. I hadn't quite been able to put in a drawer, as I had with the rest of his photos in the house. I didn't want the others prompted into asking questions about him and it seemed to have worked. Although I was closing my heart to him piece by piece, a little bit of me still wanted to believe that when I got back home, everything would be like it was before. Even though there was no chance. But most of me didn't want that at all, not after what he'd done.

One wall held a large corkboard where I pinned up my designs or pictures and cuttings that I found inspiring. Apart from that, I'd hung one of my favourite paintings of the island and in a corner, an old school photo, and one of the four of us together when we'd been on a school trip to London. I'd found that one after Mum died, stuffed in the back of a drawer.

As soon as I logged into my inbox, I saw an email from Kerry headed *Good news and bad*. Heart sinking, I opened it.

Hope all's well on that beautiful island and that your guests are behaving themselves. Good news is that Rob has made a payment. Bad news is that we're still £100,000 short. I thought you should know rather than wait till you get back. Do you want to take it up with him?

Of course I didn't. Talking to him was the last thing I wanted to do. I didn't want to be reminded of what I once felt for him. Perhaps a little of me still did but I wasn't letting myself go there. What was the point? He had made up his mind to leave me and move in with Morag and her kids. Whether I liked it or not, whether it tore me apart or not, I had to come to terms with it. I hadn't had all that long to digest the news but if I kept busy, it kept the worst of my grief – because that's what it was – at bay.

However, when it came to the business, I had the others working there to think of, so I called him up.

My nerves kicked in as I listened to the dial tone. I had no idea where he was, but I couldn't help wondering. Where could he be that was better than Ca'n Amy? But, at that moment, what I minded about most was the remainder of the money he owed us. Although I didn't want to involve the police, I would if I had to; but surely the threat of prison would be enough to make him pay up. His phone rang and rang, eventually clicking through to his voicemail.

'Rob, it's me. Amy. I've just heard from Kerry that you've paid back one hundred grand. Thank you. I just wanted to remind you that we agreed you'd repay the money in full within a month.' I was about to say something about how much I hoped we'd be able to resolve things but at the last minute I decided to keep it as impersonal as I could and cut off the call. How would this play out? As the weeks passed, I felt increasingly angry with him. Our marriage was one thing but how dare he jeopardise our business and everyone who worked for me as well? I couldn't understand how someone with his financial background could have taken such a stupid risk.

For a while I sat with my head in my hands, filled with an overwhelming sadness. How had we ended up here? But I knew the answer. We had grown apart without noticing what was happening and the spark that once welded us together had fizzled out. Even I knew that once that had gone, it was hard to row back.

I don't know how long I sat there thinking about the good times and bad, about how much I'd miss him. We'd shared our personal and professional lives for almost thirty years. Without his financial skills, Amy Green would never have been the success it had become; but how I thanked God that I'd never given him a share of the business. I thought I was protecting myself in the way I hadn't been able to when I was younger. I was not going to be betrayed by anyone again. Of course I'd paid him well and given him generous bonuses – I just didn't want to share what was mine. He had professed to understand and agree with that. I was wary of people when I first met him. I didn't give my trust to anyone because I didn't want to be let down again. Not even to him. I had to laugh at the irony.

Eventually I decided to rejoin the others. They would take my mind off all this. I blew my nose, fiddled with my hair in the mirror and put on a bit of lipstick. I was reaching for the door handle when there was a knock from the other side. I returned to my desk and shut my laptop as Dan came into the room.

'Got a minute, sis?' He was wearing that eager but apprehensive face that meant he was going to ask a favour.

'Sure. But I haven't got too long as I must make sure the others are okay, because we've been doing our own thing all day.' And I didn't want to hear the usual lengthy preamble that led up to a request. I know that sounds mean, but I'd been there before, remember?

'I noticed.' He winked as if we were colluding in something then came in and sat in my favourite black leather reclining chair. He lay there, head resting on the roll at the higher end. 'Kate and I had a great day though.'

'Dan.' I said his name as if warning him off.

'What? We got along great guns.' All innocent but . . . I knew what he was like.

'She's married and I don't want my brother to be the one who messes that up. We've only just connected again.' I couldn't bear to think what the others would say if I ended up being indirectly responsible for anything like that. Things were difficult enough as it was.

'Don't worry. I like her but nothing like that's going to

177

happen.' He flexed his feet then turned them in circles. 'But I do want to ask you something.' His feet stilled.

'Not money, Dan. Please don't let's have that conversation again. The last time you asked, I made it quite clear.' I was not going to spell out to him how precarious the business was. That was my concern alone.

'Oh come on.' He pushed himself up into a sitting position so he could look out of the window while he spoke. I braced myself. The fact he was avoiding eye contact meant I wouldn't like whatever he was about to say. 'I only need a couple of grand, say five, just to get me back on my feet again. Once I've got work here, I'll be laughing, and I can start paying you back.'

I opened and shut the drawer of my desk, summoning up my most reasonable voice. 'You haven't paid me back the last five. Do you think that might happen first?' I didn't even ask why he needed the money. I might be too easily persuaded.

His head spun to face me, furious but controlled. 'That's a bit low. You know I can't.'

'Then why should I lend you more?'

'For Christ's sake, sis. I need this money. I admit some of it's for debts I shouldn't have run up but Meera's asked for it to help Jackson go on a photography course. Come on. We're family and you're loaded. Look at all this.' He got up and came to stand with both his hands planted on the desk.

I refused to be intimidated by him. 'One, I'm not loaded. Perhaps I am by your standards but we've worked hard to get – and to keep – what we've got. And two, of course I want to do all I can to help you but you've got to help yourself too. I can't always be an easy touch whenever you've run out of funds. Not even for Jackson.' I could almost hear Rob cheering me on. He'd always said I'd been too soft on Dan and that he was a drain on our resources. Again, the irony was not lost on me. However, the five thousand was not the only debt that had gone unpaid. But if I didn't say something now, this would just go on and on. The older he got, the harder he'd find it to find work and he needed to think about that. 'You can't rely on me. I always give you a roof over your head and food when you need it. Why isn't that enough?'

'You can be so hard when you want to be. Mum wouldn't believe it.'

'Then it's a good job she's not around. And don't bring her and Dad into it. This has nothing to do with them. She wouldn't believe that you've done so little with your life.' The words were out before I could take them back.

I watched his eyes narrow and his lips tighten and then he shook himself. 'Below the belt. Being driven isn't the sign of a good person, you know. Not everyone has to prove themselves at all times. If you won't lend me what I need, then I'll manage without. I'll find a way.'

I didn't have time to ask how because he turned on his heel and left the room, closing the door quietly behind him. I sat quite still in my chair. Men and money! How had I got myself into the middle of them? Perhaps I had been too harsh on Dan. He had always muddled through working at this and that, though less frequently the older he got. It was as if he felt he'd paid his dues and now the world owed him a living. I was a convenient pit stop in his world. But my pot wasn't limitless, especially now Rob had stuck his fingers in the till. All this was so hard.

18

The motorbike held no appeal to Linda whatsoever. She stood with her hands on her hips, staring at the dusty black beast, wondering how the hell she was going to get out of this one. Only minutes before, they'd been at breakfast discussing the day ahead.

'I'd like to go over to Valldemossa to see if this Jack Walsh is any good as an artist or not.' Dan had been concentrating on dipping his croissant into his coffee without it falling to pieces, so his face was hidden when he made this announcement.

Had Kate told him about Amy's suspicions, or was he genuinely interested? At that moment, Kate was failing to cut the fresh bread Amy had brought up from the village into even pieces. Instead she resorted to tearing it.

'I'd like to go.' Linda had spoken without thinking. She was curious, the only one of the group not to have talked to him when she, more than any of the others, had her own reasons for wanting to see if he was Mr Wilson or not. Not that the rest of them knew that.

The effect of the previous day had yet to wear off. She had woken determined to put herself first for once, to do what was good for her. She had already phoned her aunt, deflected a barrage of complaints and spoken kindly to the carer. The day was now hers for the taking, and she was wearing her new blue top that Jane had convinced her to buy, just to remind herself of her resolution.

'You must be joking.' Kate had snapped her reply. 'I thought we talked about this yesterday, Dan.'

'Talked about it?' Amy asked, putting her coffee cup down and turning to her brother. 'What's it got to do with you, Dan?'

'Just thinking of you, sis.' For once, his smile didn't register in his eyes. 'Looking after your interests . . . just as you look after mine.'

'Well, that's very kind. But I'm on top of my own interests, thanks.'

'I'm going down there anyway.' Dan poured himself some more coffee. 'And it looks as if Linda's coming with me.'

'Oh, I'm not sure. I hadn't really thought . . .' The last thing Linda wanted to do was cause a row. She didn't understand the antagonism that had surfaced between Dan and Amy.

'Perhaps you should go.' Kate had been silent up to that point, her attention taken by her phone. 'Why not?' she responded to the surprised faces of the other women. 'Someone should go and see if Amy's right and if Linda wants to, well, that's great. We can stay here and make the most of the day. If he is Mr Wilson, then we'll find out from Linda this afternoon, and we can decide what to do about it then. And if he isn't, well, we can forget all about him again.'

'Do you really want to go?' Amy folded up her napkin and laid it beside her plate. 'You don't have to. Stay here with us and we'll have a good day.'

But, sitting on the opposite side of the table, Linda saw Jane's face change as if she'd be disappointed if she didn't go. She was reminded of the days when Jane would fix on someone she didn't want around – it wasn't dislike so much as boredom – and drive them to the periphery of the gang. And then, like the time she was invited to the pantomime party after a week of being left out and ignored, the relief and pleasure of being accepted again made all the heartache and feelings of inadequacy worthwhile. Her knee-jerk reaction was to stay – just because they weren't teenagers any more and she could – but, she reminded herself, she had her own reasons for wanting to find out the truth.

She nodded. 'I know I don't have to. I'd like to though.' There was no need to explain. 'And anyway, I'd love to see a bit more of the island.'

'Fair enough,' Amy said. 'You can go ahead and scout out the truth for us.'

And now Linda was staring down at the offered transport, wondering whether she'd made the right decision. Losing her life or incurring a life-threatening injury was not something she'd factored in. His hand on her shoulder made her start.

'Second thoughts?' Dan rested his other hand on the black leather seat. 'Unimpressed by my trusty steed?'

'Not so much second thoughts as sheer terror.' That was despite Kate coming home the previous night exhilarated by riding pillion, unable to stop talking about it. She had been positively glowing, not just from the sunshine but from inside. Something else had changed her. But, in Linda's eyes, even achieving such a change wasn't a prize worth the agony of its winning.

'Then we'll leave her at home and borrow one of the cars. Hang on while I check with Amy and get the key.' He disappeared back into the house to return with a key dangling from his finger. 'I'm in her bad books so we're not allowed the sporty one. Come this way.'

In the shaded parking space to the side of the house sat a dusty four by four. 'A discreet little number,' he said, raising his eyebrows, as he opened the passenger door and waited for her to get inside.

While he drove, Dan began a running commentary on their surroundings as they travelled down from the mountains, skirting Sóller, through the long dark tunnel, out through a plain of almond and olive groves and then back up into the mountains.

She gazed out at the countryside, so much greener than she had ever expected, and listened to his stories of the island. Chopin had stayed in Valldemossa – 'He came with George Sand and her children and stayed in the Charterhouse. We'll go there.' About the island's only saint – Santa Catalina Thomàs – who was born in Valldemossa: 'You'll see tiles on the houses showing scenes from her life.' He talked about how, if there was more time, they should take the train over the mountains to Palma. 'People imagine it's all lager-swilling tourists, but not at all. There's a beautiful historic heart to the town with so much to see.'

'Have you ever thought of getting a job as a tour guide?' She wasn't entirely joking as she let his words drift through her head.

'Sorry. Was I going on?' He laughed. 'I love this island, that's all. Look, there's where we're going.' As the road wound back up into the mountains, ahead of them was a village of typical stone houses stacked up the side of a valley with an unusual spire at their centre.

'I know you do.' She hadn't meant to upset him. 'I'm interested. Really.'

And off he went again. Did she know that Rafa Nadal came from Manacor?

As she had absolutely no interest in sport whatsoever, no, she didn't.

Eventually she was able to squeeze in a word as he took a breath in the middle of extolling the choir that sang in the sanctuary of Lluc.

'What if he is our teacher?' The question that had been bugging her since they set out.

Dan was jerked out of his description of the former

monastery. 'Who? Walsh? We'll play it by ear. There's every chance he won't be here anyway. Nothing worse than sitting in a gallery overhearing what people think about your work, watching them raise eyebrows at the price and then stroll out empty-handed.'

'I can imagine.'

'I used to turn out some pretty good wood carvings, if I say so myself, and I've exhibited them in a couple of joint exhibitions. That's even worse – when the person you're exhibiting with sells way more than you do. And a good reason for never doing any more.'

She couldn't help laughing. 'How have you managed never to get a proper job?' Visions of the library stacks and her old desk that never met her standards of tidiness floated past her mind's eye.

'Oh, I've had plenty of jobs. I've done practically anything you can imagine from bar staff to carpenter to backstage chippy to joiner to...'

'Yoga platform maker.' She finished the list for him as they entered Valldemossa, passing some large modern housing that contrasted with the picturesque historic face the village had presented from the road up there.

He laughed. 'Yep. I don't know why but I've never had the work ethic and ambition that drives Amy. Different reactions to our upbringing, I guess. She wanted to get out and upwards even after her wilderness years.'

Linda smiled. 'And you?'

'I just wanted an easy life, to work enough to keep body and soul together but no more. Here we are.' He turned right off the busy main street, drove past a crowded car park and found a parking space among the modern residential streets. 'Fancy some sightseeing, or shall we go straight to the gallery?'

Linda suddenly had cold feet. If she was about to meet Mr Wilson again, would he even remember her? Like all of them, her appearance had changed beyond recognition. Whether he did or not, she would have to tell him who she was. Would she regret opening up such a Pandora's box? Would the others forgive her? 'Let's walk around first.'

'I'll take you into the old town, down to the church of Santa Catalina. You'll like it down there.'

'Because I'm so saintly?' She smiled. If only he knew.

He laughed. 'No. Because I think you're a serious soul and will probably appreciate the history. We'll go to the monastery and the Chopin museum after we've done the gallery. Yes?'

Linda agreed. She was looking forward to exploring somewhere new. They walked down a steep hill through the old part of town, through streets whose houses were decorated with the tiles he'd told her about, depicting scenes from Santa Catalina's life, into her gaudy sanctuary and then on to the modest church.

The place was enchanting, sleepy and attractive, where locals chatted in doorways, cooking smells filtered into the streets, stray cats lay prostrate in the shade.

Getting back to the shopping centre where dark red parasols shaded restaurant tables and souvenir shops vied for attention was quite a jolt. But at least the streets were lined with trees that shaded them from the sun and the atmosphere was quite different from that of Sóller. While she looked around her, Dan touched her arm.

'There's the gallery.' He pointed out a modern shop with a plate glass window. 'And it looks like our bird is there for the taking.'

Her stomach turned over. 'Wait.' She pulled him back as he began to cross the road. There was no point delaying things any further. 'Let me go in first.'

He looked disappointed. 'Why? I thought we were in this together.'

'We are. But if it is him, there's something I'd like to say to him on my own before you get involved. You don't mind, do you?' She touched his arm to signal they were still friends. 'I won't be long. Give me a few minutes.' That wouldn't be enough, but it would have to do.

He stepped away from her, into the sunshine. 'Actually there are a couple of things I want to get, so I'll do that and then come back. If you're sure that's what you want to do.'

'It is.' She hoped her smile didn't betray how nervous she felt.

While he walked down the street, she crossed the road towards the point of their visit.

There was no one in the gallery apart from a young woman at the counter. Linda took a price sheet and sat on one of the chairs in the centre of the gallery to read the artist's biography. She looked round at the swirls of paint on canvas that represented nothing she could identify. *Abstract No 5*, she read. *Flight at Sunset*. Only one of them had a red dot beside it. She was in the middle of reading about Jack Walsh, his lack of formal training, his love of the natural world and his desire to communicate that through his paintings, when she became aware of someone standing over her.

'Hello. Can I get you a coffee, a glass of water?' Jack Walsh himself was leaning over her. 'I'm the artist.'

She gazed at him and her pulse quickened. His eyes hadn't changed, nor his mouth, although it was disguised by the shock of hair round it. Amy had been right.

'No, thank you.' She raised her bottle of water from her bag. 'I know you are. I was at the party a couple of nights ago. We didn't meet though.'

'Was a good do, wasn't it? Generous of them.' He sat in the chair beside her.

'In fact, I came to see you, Jack.' The little time she had made her braver. 'Remember the sixth form in York? St Catherine's

School for Girls?' She stared down at her walking sandals and pulled her feet under the chair.

She heard his intake of breath. Yes, he did.

He stood up in front of her. 'Linny?' He sounded shocked, disbelieving.

No one else had ever called her that.

'So it *is* you. The others thought it was.'

'Others?' He took a step back, steadying himself with a hand on the back of the neighbouring chair.

'I'm here with Amy, Jane and Kate. Remember?'

'Dimly.' He rubbed his beard. 'Dimly.'

He must remember them all. His assumed vagueness infuriated her.

'But you do remember me?'

'Yes. I wouldn't forget you. How could I?'

'Although you did forget to ring me after the day I left for Edinburgh. In fact, as I remember it, you didn't phone me again. You didn't return my calls. You only sent me a note, asking me not to bother you.'

'Linny, don't. That was a long time ago. None of that's important now.'

Linda couldn't believe what she was hearing. All the anger she had kept tamped down for years was boiling up. 'I loved you and I thought you loved me but I was so wrong, wasn't I? Those times you just didn't turn up, or you cut something short to go off with "friends", or you didn't phone when you said you would. I chose not to believe what was happening but hoped you'd come round again. When you were back at school and I'd gone to Edinburgh, you sent me that note. How did it go?'

This was something she'd never forget.

This can't go on any more. After what happened with Amy, Miss Milton has her eye on me. I can't be caught seeing you. I'm looking at other jobs, and now you're at university you've got a chance to move on. Don't try to contact me. However you try, I will ignore you. This is for the best, trust me.' She waited for him to say something.

'You still remember it?' He sounded shocked, bemused.

'How could I forget? It was that first term when I realised I was pregnant.' She stopped.

His mouth dropped open. 'Wha . . .'

'I tried every way I knew how to get hold of you. I even came back to York, only to be told by your landlord that you'd moved. I couldn't ask the school where you'd gone and I couldn't confess to my friends. Telling my aunt was out of the question. She wouldn't be able to face the Sunday congregation if she had found out.'

'Linny, I didn't know,' Jack said, moving closer. 'I changed jobs at the end of that term. It wasn't the same after what Amy said. I went to Birmingham.' So he did remember them. Of course he did.

'And I had no idea how to find you.' To her embarrassment, her voice cracked.

Just then a couple of people entered the gallery and hovered in front of the paintings.

'I think we should go somewhere to talk. Come into the office.' He led her through to a small white room with two chairs, a desk and a computer; the only splash of colour was a postbox-red geranium on the windowsill. Metal bars prevented the window opening so the air conditioning was up high, providing a constant background hum.

'Is this the truth?' He took the chair behind the desk.

'Why would I make this up now? I've had years to get used to the idea of your being a liar, of being abandoned by you, of being pregnant on my own. It was pure chance that took us to that party the day before yesterday. Or fate. I certainly wasn't looking for you.'

His eyes were wide. The same eyes that had once looked at

her in a very different way but were now sunken and framed by lines. 'Did you have the baby?' He clasped both her hands.

She pulled them away, folding her arms across her body. 'No.' She glanced at him to see his eyes were shut, his hands clasped tight together on the desktop. 'How could I possibly have had it? I was seventeen. I had no one to support me. I had no money. I arranged an abortion through the health clinic but two days before I was booked to have it, I lost the baby.' The searing pain, the blood, being rushed to hospital – those indelible images flashed in front of her.

He was staring at her now. 'That *was* bad luck, but you recovered. And, after all, it probably was all for the best.'

'For the best!? For the best?' Her voice rose as she echoed him. 'Do you know what they had to do? Of course you don't because you weren't there. Complications meant I had to have a hysterectomy. My chances of ever having children were taken away forever.'

'I don't know what to say.' He pushed his hand through his hair, making it even wilder.

'Don't you?' Was this why she had wanted to confront him when she'd thought there was a chance it was him? Was this the best he could do? No remorse. No apology for not being there when she needed him.

'Do the others know?'

She shook her head. 'I've never told anyone. I was too ashamed. I'd been such an idiot to believe in you.'

'I'm sorry. I'm so sorry.' He put his head in his hands.

She had often wondered what she'd feel if she ever saw him again, never expecting she would. Once she'd realised that he'd gone for good, she understood she had to cope on her own. As for her feelings now, she felt nothing towards him except anger. Any residual feelings she might have harboured over the years had been wiped away on sight. It was hard to reconcile this bear of a man with the art student and teacher that she'd fallen so hard for.

'When they said it was you, I had to see for myself. I never thought I'd see you again.'

'What do you want?' He was sitting back in his chair, gripping the edge of the table.

She grimaced. 'I don't want anything. I just want you to know that what you did as a young man had profound consequences. You ruined our lives, mine and Amy's. Or at least you changed them forever.' As she spoke, a thought crossed her mind. 'Actually, there is something I'd like from you. I'd like you to come up to the house and apologise to Amy.'

He gave a gruff half laugh. 'Now why would I do that?'

'To prove you're a halfway decent human being and because you owe it to her.'

He sat up straight. 'Don't be so melodramatic. I don't owe any of you anything. I was a young man then. You girls were completely up for it. None of it meant anything.'

His refusal to take responsibility and the fact that he saw them as a pack to prey on maddened her. 'How dare you say that? You couldn't be more wrong. Perhaps not to you, but to me and Amy and maybe others I don't know, it meant a great deal.'

He dismissed that with another laugh and a disbelieving shake of the head.

'Why have you changed your name?'

His expression changed, and she thought she saw a glint of fear.

'What are you hiding?'

'Nothing.' His knuckles whitened as his grip on the table tightened. 'I just wanted a new start.'

'Linda! Are you back here?' Dan shouted before knocking on the door and looking round. 'You OK? Oh!' He stopped when he saw Jack.

'This is Jack Wilson, Dan. He once taught us all art. He was just saying that he'd like to come up to the house.'

'So you're the guy who couldn't keep his hands to himself.' Dan's face flushed as he advanced into the room, fists clenched. 'The younger the better, eh?'

'Steady on.' Jack pushed back his chair and stood up, ready to protect himself. 'I was a young man myself. No one was under age. No one said no.'

'Not true. My sister said no, and look what happened to her.' He took a step towards Jack.

'Don't!' Linda stood in his way. 'He's not worth it. Now I've seen him, I can see what a pathetic man he is. Amy should have the chance to see too.'

'And what if I won't come to see her?' He was belligerent now, challenging her.

'What's an apology going to cost you?' Linda couldn't believe she was saying this. Wouldn't it just be easier to leave now she'd seen him, enjoy the unexpected sense of release she was experiencing. Confronting him had been the right thing to do, it turned out, so perhaps Amy should come down to the gallery herself? On the other hand, she was relishing having some kind of small control over him at last. 'I think William would be very interested in the story. He could have this exhibition taken down in hours.'

'He couldn't.' The alarm on his face was gratifying.

'But do you want to risk it?'

19

After she'd been to the bakery for essentials, Amy had left Kate in the village.

'You don't mind, do you? I've got more bloody emails I need to answer, and I want to talk to Jane.'

'Not one bit.' Kate was pleased to be given an excuse not to be there when they locked horns again. 'I need to get some postcards and I'd like to explore.'

The supermarket was easy to find, a little further along the main street on the corner of the village square. Kate chose her postcards carefully from the rack outside. She would be home way before they arrived but at least they would show that she hadn't forgotten everyone while she was here. The supermarket was surprisingly big, much more than the door that opened on to the village square would suggest. Before paying, she wandered up and down the aisles, enjoying the funny ham-and-cheesy smell and checking out the unfamiliar packaging. In the end she treated herself to a packet of biscuits.

She decided to sit down for a coffee and an ensaimada while she wrote her cards so took a table outside the café next to the supermarket. Next to her, a couple were locked in a game of cribbage. Up to her right, above a retaining wall, the church stood solid and square, its small clock tower crowned with a weathervane. Above her fluttered tatty white-and-orange tickertape-type bunting strung from the spreading lime tree by the road to all sides of the square. Down a wide alleyway opposite, two other cafés were beginning to fill with customers. But here outside this one, Kate, definitely had the best seat to watch the goings-on in the square where locals stopped to chat to one another, children ran about and a couple of walkers with sticks and backpack were poring over a map.

She looked down as a one-eared grey cat wound its way around her legs, miaowing for food. She tickled its neck as if it was one of the farm cats. She missed them: Black Bomber; Mandy; Mouser; Tallulah; the Boss. In fact, she was missing home altogether. She envisaged herself and Alan walking across the wild moorland landscape with the sheepdogs at their heel. It was strange to be so disconnected from everything that made her who she was. Of course she missed the kids too, especially Noah and Molly who, though grown-up, still treated their family home as if it were a campsite. As she pictured Noah's room – he was twenty-seven for God's sake – and the constant mess in the kitchen where neither of them ever put anything away, perhaps she didn't miss that side of them so much. At least Kit and Lara were making their own way but Home Farm would always be there for them. Then she remembered Alan's call this morning. He couldn't find a clean shirt. Had he never been into her laundry room? Of course he had. He just hadn't thought to look there where she had left a couple hanging up freshly ironed for him along with everything else he might need. Perhaps she shouldn't complain. In fact, perhaps she should go away on her own more often.

She saw Brendan before he saw her. He was ambling down the steps that led down from the church door on the opposite side of the square. He stopped by one of the souvenir shops, checked his reflection and adjusted the angle of his battered panama, then carried on down. He was wearing his uniform of baggy shorts, an old shirt, espadrilles and the ubiquitous basket. Kate bent over her postcards, trying to look busy. She didn't want her time alone to be interrupted.

'On your own? Mind if I join you?' Before she had time to reply, he had plumped himself down at her table. 'I always have a morning coffee here if I'm around, catch up with friends and acquaintances.' He raised a hand to greet a local woman who was passing – *'Bon día'* – before turning back to her. 'Have you ordered?'

'Not yet.'

'Then let me treat you. Diego!' He called over the waiter and ordered them both coffee. 'Anything else? An ensaimada?'

'If you are, it would be rude not to.' She put her pen on the bag of cards. They would have to wait.

The order was in front of them within minutes.

'Where are the others?' he asked, stirring three packets of sugar into his coffee.

She tore a piece off her pastry and put it in her mouth. 'Jane and Amy are up at the house, and Linda's gone to Valldemossa with Dan. I came down here to have a bit of me time. Something I don't get much of at home.'

'And I've ruined it. I'm sorry.' He picked up his basket as if he was about to leave.

'Not at all. You count as part of this amazing place. I was trying to imagine what it must be like to live here.'

He smiled, his eyes almost disappearing in the creases round them. 'It's like anywhere. It has its marvellous points – sunshine, sea, mountains, beautiful walks – but it has plenty of negatives too. You guys only see what goes on on the surface. You've no idea of the petty feuds, the gossip, the objections to local planning – all that sort of stuff.'

'I live in the country so I know very well. I'd love to think it doesn't happen here.'

'Sorry to disappoint. But I want to know more about you.'

He put his elbows on the table and cupped his chin in his hands. ' How come you've fetched up here?'

'I've kept in touch with the others since school and suggested we met up. I didn't think the others were keen but then Amy invited us here. I loved the idea because . . .' She couldn't tell him about Alan giving her the duvet and her childish resentment that she was being taken for granted. 'I've never been here before,' she finished up. 'I gather the boat trip was a big success.'

'You'll have to come aboard.' He saluted as if to the captain of a ship. 'Will you have time?'

Perhaps she was meant to salute back, but she refrained. 'We're leaving tomorrow, so probably not.'

'But you'll be back?'

'There's so much we haven't had time to see, but who knows.' Kate thought of Dan, sorry she might not see him again. 'Who knows? I hope so.' She pulled herself up short. She wasn't an infatuated teenager or, like Lara, desperate for a boyfriend. Dan was the kind of guy who flirted with everyone, and she had been flattered. Having his attention, even for that short while, had been like discovering an oasis in a desert.

'A walk?'

'I'm sorry?'

'Let's go for a walk. I'm going to visit a friend and I could take you with me and then you could walk back. You won't get lost and it's beautiful up there.'

'Why not? I haven't got anything else to do.' She surprised herself. Her only plan had been to visit the souvenir shop on the way up the hill on her way home, but she could do that later.

He raised his hand for the bill. 'On me. I insist.'

As he stood up, he picked up his basket and planted his hat on his head, revealing a neatly mended tear under the arm of his shirt. 'This way.'

They walked up to the closed front door of the church and turned left through the village along the narrow pedestrian streets. The road widened as they walked out of the old centre, past a wall smothered in blue flowering plumbago. At last they came to a road that led out of town. Voices came from above a high wall to their right along with the clink of cups and saucers. As they left the buildings behind, the land dropped away to their left; drystone terracing, olive groves populated by sheep and their bells, a view across to the other side of the valley where they'd walked down to Sóller. With the warmth of the sun on her skin, the smell of roadside herbs in her nostrils, Kate felt there was almost no better place.

'So how do you find Ca'n Amy?' Brendan's voice startled her.

'Quite beautiful. Amy's got an extraordinary eye. Nothing's—'

'And Amy herself?' He spoke over her, uninterested in a eulogy to Amy's taste.

'She's fine. Why?' Was his interest for small-town gossip or out of genuine concern?

'They've got an odd sort of marriage and I worry about her.'

'Hasn't everyone?' She remembered Sheila and Jove. 'Why do you say that?'

Brendan's face lit up at her interest. 'Well . . . far be it from me, but . . . they're here separately quite often these days.'

'That doesn't mean anything. Plenty of couples have relationships that work better because they do things independently. Allowing each other to be your own person can be a good thing.' Not that she and Alan were like that – until now.

He laughed and kicked a stone to the edge of the road. 'Don't get me wrong but for years, he's brought other women here on and off. I've seen for myself. Not many, and not often. They usually stay up at the house but of course people have noticed. And recently he's brought the same one more than once.'

All this news disturbed Kate. She didn't like the suggestion that Amy's marriage might be in trouble, she didn't want the perfect image to be hiding something so painful. And surely Rob couldn't be so stupid as to think that no one would notice if he *had* brought other women to the island. But that was none of her business. Did Amy even know, she wondered. If she didn't, should she say something? Alert her? But wouldn't that be too intrusive when the way Amy and Rob ran their relationship had nothing to do with her? She didn't like Brendan's attempt to elicit information from her, and she wasn't going to be the one who helped him.

'Perhaps you should talk to her yourself.'

'Wouldn't like to rock the boat – to use a sailing term.' His wink made her recoil. 'We've been friends of theirs for years. He's a laugh, Rob. He doesn't care what anyone thinks. We've had plenty of good times together.'

'Even if I did know anything, I wouldn't tell you.'

He lifted his hat so she could see his eyes avid for gossip. 'I only thought you might be interested in finding out what's going on. For her sake.'

She stopped for a second. 'Afraid not.' But inside, she was dying to know so that she could offer Amy any support that she might need.

He stood still too. 'Ah well.'

Kate was glad to have disappointed him.

'Well, this is where we part ways,' he said as if they hadn't had the conversation at all. 'You can go on,' he indicated a sturdy post with an arrow carved into it for walkers that directed her up a narrow path alongside a low stone wall. 'Or you can turn back.'

'I'll go on for a bit.'

So they went in their separate directions, Brendan turning into a driveway to their left, leaving Kate with her own thoughts. The pleasure of walking alone in the open air, sun on her skin, breeze in her hair, to the sounds of birds and sheep bells, was too great for her to want to turn back.

As she walked, she thought about what Brendan had said. Amy seemed so composed, so on top of her life. Could her carefully curated image of a beautiful woman with a perfect marriage and a successful business be hiding something quite other? How different that was from her own set-up, where what you saw was what you got. Except that wasn't quite true. Alan was a wonderful husband who had given her everything she had ever wanted. As a young woman, she had dreamed of a beautiful country house (tick), a large family kitchen (tick) for her large family (tick). She had wanted nothing more than to bury herself in family life and that was what had sustained her for years until all the children grew up and began their own lives. The thing about living on a farm was that there was never any shortage of things to do. All those sheep needed looking after if they were to make any kind of a living from them. And yet... Like Amy's, from the outside, her marriage was a success but now, if she was honest with herself, the lustre had dulled and cracked. Her mind turned to Dan...

A sudden 'Baaa!' made her jump. At head height, on the top of a drystone wall, a sheep looked down at her, not moving but poised to get on to its spindly legs and run if it had to.

'Don't you judge me,' said Kate. 'A little bit of a flirtation never did anyone any harm. And who knows when I'll get another chance.'

The sheep got to its feet and crapped a neat little pile of droppings before ambling off in the direction of its flock.

'Well, thanks. If that's the best you've got to offer.' If she kept going, perhaps an answer would come to her. With age, one's chances were narrowing all the time. Opportunities came less often so had to be grabbed when they did. That's why she was here, after all.

But, Dan. Was he an opportunity to be grabbed? Or was the

sun going to her head? He obviously liked her. Should she relax and let herself go? She allowed herself a little smile at thought. What harm would it do? The flattery and the fun were a treat, and no one at home need ever know.

When they first got together, Alan did try. He even surprised her with an engagement ring that he had chosen with the help of his mother and sister, although the knowledge that he didn't choose it on his own took some of the magic out of his proposal.

She twisted her rings round her ring finger. The top one was the one she'd had made from a diamond and ruby brooch Alan's mother had given her, the second was the Victorian engagement ring Alan had given her, a sapphire flanked by two diamonds, the third her slim gold wedding band that had never left her finger since the day they married. Her marriage might be frayed at the edges and worn like a favourite piece of clothing, but the warp and weft of the fabric was still intact and strong.

However, if the scissors cutting it were sharp enough...

At nearly midday she turned around and began to make her way back to the village. Her thoughts reverted to Amy and Rob. Amy hadn't talked much about him, but that was some people's way. She had only seen the one photograph of him in the living room that had been removed the day after they arrived. Was that a sign that all of them had missed that something was wrong? Surely not. Kate didn't want any cracks in Amy's façade. She liked the idea that having had nothing, Amy, through her own hard work, now had everything.

20

While the others were in the village, Jane took her iPad to the terrace table and got to work. Obsessing over the identity of Jack Walsh was giving her something think about other than her messy home life, so she started googling with determination. If he really was their Mr Wilson, there must be a reason for him changing his name. Even if done on a whim, that still begged the question – why the whim? Finding the answer took much less effort than she'd anticipated but the reason why was far more shocking.

She took a good long look at the photo of a Jack Wilson taken on a security camera at Gatwick, and another at the mugshot on a newspaper website. There was no doubt that was the man they had all known. His face then, its contours, the way his mouth curved very slightly downwards on one side when he smiled, they were all etched on her memory. He was a little older here, perhaps ten years but not so much he wasn't recognisable. She bookmarked the page and waited for the others' return.

As soon as she heard the sound of the car, she was on her feet. Showing Amy what she had found could be a bridge between them. She didn't like being given the cold shoulder even if they were only giving her a taste of her childhood medicine. Not that Amy had been unpleasant but since the party, she had put a distance between herself and her guests that was uncomfortable. Perhaps something else had happened because, since last night, she'd been more distracted and had dropped her interest in whether Jane had shafted her or not. At least she had in front of the others. Thank God.

Amy came out to the terrace. She looked tired and her smile was strained. 'Kate's stayed to explore but I thought I'd get back. I've got a work thing I need to sort out – one of the shops has a lower turnover than forecast this month, and we're trying to work out why. Also I wanted to talk to you and clear the air. Coffee?'

'Love some. Thanks. But look, I've got something to show you.'

'Let me make the coffee first.'

'I think you'll be interested in what I've found.' Possibly the understatement of their stay. While she waited, made impatient by Amy's lack of immediate interest, Jane watched the bees busy in the lavender growing by the edge of the terrace. A lizard paused, shiny green in the sun, then raced for the shade of a stone. Smoke rose from a bonfire further down the valley, bringing with it the smell of burning wood. Voices rose from one of the orange groves below. Several throaty motorbikes roared along the top road. What was taking Amy so long?

Eventually she reappeared carrying a tray with two mugs of coffee. 'So?' she said, putting them on the table.

'Look at this.' Jane tapped at her iPad, found the relevant page and sat back.

Amy pulled the iPad towards her, angling it so it was out of the sun. She began to read, scrolling down until she'd finished the article. 'Jesus!'

'I know. Right?'

'She was only fifteen! Under age. Are we sure it's the same Jack Wilson?'

'Definitely. Look at the pictures.' Jane was pleased by the effect of her discovery. 'So Jack Wilson must have become Jack

Walsh after he was jailed for running away to Germany with one of his pupils. Not much of a name change.'

'Enough, though. He served nearly three years in prison. No wonder he wanted to disappear. When did it happen?' She looked back at the article. '1986. Ten years after we left school.' Cradling her cup of coffee, she stared at Jane. 'Wow!'

'She did believe she loved him though.' Jane tried to find the girl an excuse. She remembered what that teen infatuation felt like.

'More fool her. I knew there was something.'

Jane looked at the pictures again. 'Now what?'

'I don't know. Do you believe me now?'

Jane couldn't look at her. 'I don't know what to believe. I could have sworn you'd told me you'd made it up.'

'Stop it!' Amy thumped the table. 'We're not seventeen any more. It's over. You don't have to keep on lying.'

'What do you mean?' Jane was genuinely puzzled.

'That's what you used to do.' Amy was quite calm and matter-of-fact. 'You passed on the blame for your shoplifting to me, you copied my homework and passed it off as yours, you often lied about where you were going or who you were with and, of course, we always found out. What Mr Wilson did to me and how he got away with it was terrible, and you lied to your mother about what I said. You must have.' She raised her hand to Jane's objection. 'It's the only explanation.'

But the examples Amy was quoting were all lost in the haze of time. Jane was having trouble recalling any of them. Was that how she was remembered? Her only defence was to hit back. 'Would you have got the grades? Would you have been able to hack the training? Weren't you much more cut out for what you've done? Maybe I did you a favour.' Realising what she'd just said, Jane quickly added, 'If I did anything at all.'

'Jane, please. Look at this.' Amy flicked a finger at the iPad. 'The man obviously had a problem. He was young, girls fancied him and he had his pick until he fell for someone under age and got caught. He did do what I said. So I've got two questions for you. *Why did you tell your mother otherwise?* is one. And *what did she do next?* is the other. This,' she pointed to the iPad. 'This must persuade you.'

'For God's sake. Why can't you leave it alone? Isn't this enough?' Anger and a sense of injustice bubbled up in Jane. 'If you're so desperate to know, I'll tell you. I didn't want it to be true because I fancied him too. All right? I couldn't bear the idea of him leaving so I told Mum you were lying. Is that good enough for you? I know she called Milters but she never told me what she said. OK? Can we let it rest now?'

But Amy still wasn't done. 'Milters was a snob and listened to anything any of the other middle-class parents would tell her. If they said "Jump!" she'd jump. It was parents like mine that she took no notice of. I wouldn't have had a chance and you knew that.'

'Mum knew how much trouble you'd been in at school—'

'Mostly thanks to you.'

'That's not true.' Though she suspected there was more truth in that than she'd like. 'And so Milters believed her, thought it was the sort of thing you'd do, and acted fast before it went further.'

'And his watch? Did you put that in my desk?'

Now they had reached this point, all Jane wanted was for it to be over once and for all. Why pretend any longer? It was in her gift to put Amy straight. 'OK. Full confession. Yes, that was me.'

'I knew it!' Amy looked pleased but her anger soon took over. 'Why? Why didn't you say something at the time?'

'It was just a moment of madness. I shouldn't have done it, but I never dreamed it would go as far as it did. When the police got involved, I was too scared to own up. My dad...'

Even now, she could hear his shouts, imagine him grounding her, withholding her allowance.

'So it was me or you. And bang went my A levels and all those dreams.'

'That's being over the top. They didn't have to. Your parents could have pressed harder.'

'Don't you dare blame them.' Amy banged her fist on the table. 'You know that your mum had Milters's ear every time over the other parents.'

'Then you could have knuckled down for that last term at the comp.'

'No I couldn't. Don't you see? Everything I wanted had been taken away from me. Nobody trusted me. Some girls in the class wouldn't speak to me. My parents' disappointment in me was crushing. That's why I ran away to spend the summer with Dan in London and why, when I came back for my results, I got in with Mick Kirby's bunch. They gave me somewhere to belong while all you lot left for university.'

Jane got up and walked to the edge of the terrace, gazing towards the pool, glittering blue in the sunlight. 'Look, I'm sorry. I am. But we've all done things we shouldn't have and we're not seventeen any more. You must get over this.' She was aware that this was the voice she used with some of her patients: calm, thoughtful, superior. 'Move on. You can't let yourself be defined by something that happened so long ago. Look what you've achieved since then. I shouldn't have done what I did. You're right. But I was a self-centred teenager.'

'Maybe I wouldn't have made it,' said Amy, reflective. 'You did say that last night, and it hurt. But I'd have liked the chance to find out.'

'I shouldn't have said anything.' She flinched under Amy's gaze.

'But you did.' Amy gave a wry grin. 'The only person who's ever dared to say. You never were scared about speaking out.'

'A bad habit.' Though not as bad as rewriting the truth to suit her own story.

'What's haunted me is the knowledge that he got away with it. He was the one who should have been punished. Not me. This' – she swung the iPad round – 'isn't enough.'

'Now's your chance then.' Jane returned to the table. 'When Linda and Dan get back, we'll know for sure whether it's him or not. And if he definitely is Mr Wilson, then you can decide what to do.'

'I think we know he is, don't we? But what? What could I do?'

'It'll come to us.'

Amy was turning her mug in circles, scraping it on the tabletop. 'Were you really so much better cut out than me to be a doctor? I know I didn't have your background but I'd have worked.'

Jane returned to the table and sat down. 'I don't think so. In fact it turns out that, apart from being a bad wife and mother, I'm a bad doctor too.'

Amy's eyebrows raised. 'What do you mean?'

'The wife part, you don't need to know. But next week I'm up in front of a tribunal . . .' She put her head in her hands as she spoke so she couldn't see Amy's reaction. 'I might as well tell you because anyone will soon be able to read about it online if they want to.'

'Whatever happened?'

Jane took a breath. 'It was all about my son, Paul, and Elaine his fiancé. She and I don't get on: controlling, and extremely ambitious.'

'Nothing like her mother-in-law then.' Amy pursed her lips. 'Joking!'

'OK. I asked for that.' She looked up and smiled. 'Anyway . . . She's on the way to being a pretty hotshot financial lawyer as far as I can make out but he needs someone more gentle.' Jane couldn't bear to think of her son being under the thumb of anyone, especially a woman with whom she didn't see eye to eye; although she had to admit, it would be a rare woman who would be good enough for Paul. 'Anyway, she got pregnant. For a moment, I thought everything was going to work out after all. David and I were thrilled at the thought of being grandparents, but then she miscarried at fifteen weeks. Paul was devastated, and so were we for them, but she brushed it off as if it didn't matter. "Stuff happens," she said. Stuff happens!' Jane was as outraged now as she had been then.

'But having a baby when you're starting out on a career that matters to you isn't necessarily the best plan, and she was probably putting on a brave face.'

'I wish that was true.' Jane sighed. 'But I know it's not.'

'How?'

'I looked up Elaine's hospital record. God!' She looked to the sky as if he would appear and help her.

'Is that so bad?'

'Bad?! Looking up a patient who isn't in your care breaches every patient confidentiality rule in the book. It was a moment of pure madness. I was upset, I wanted to see why she'd miscarried, if there'd be any longer-term effects. I told myself I'd be able to comfort Paul better if I knew. Perhaps a bit of me didn't believe her. I don't know. It took a matter of minutes to find out she'd been admitted for a termination.' She brushed away her tears.

'Oh, Jane.'

'She'd lied to all of us, including Paul.' It momentarily registered that it was odd to be complaining about something she had just been accused of doing herself. But this was different. 'Once I knew, I didn't know what to do with the knowledge.'

'What did your husband say? Did you tell him?'

'David was appalled that I'd used my position to get

confidential information. He said I should forget what I'd found and pray no one noticed what I'd done.'

'But they did?'

Jane shook her head. 'Worse than that. David was right, of course, but when I had dinner with Paul one night, he was so distraught about the "miscarriage" and how well Elaine had dealt with it – what a saint she was – that I told him the truth.'

'You didn't!' Amy's shock made her feel even more ashamed.

'I'm afraid so. One glass of wine too many and I let the cat hissing and spitting out of the bag. He was even more appalled than David.' She could still see his face, white with fury, as he pushed his chair back, desperate to leave the table. 'I thought he was angry with Elaine, but he wasn't. He was angry with me. He confronted her of course. She couldn't deny it so naturally he felt betrayed, hurt that she hadn't confided in him. They nearly broke up over it, not that that would have been such a bad thing in my view, but they didn't. If anything it's brought them closer together. Paul didn't speak to me for months. Even now, I have to be incredibly careful what I say in case it's construed as criticism. David's no help. Just says it's my fault and I'll have to wait it out.'

'And Elaine?'

'Oh God. You can imagine. She was justifiably furious with me and told her parents. They encouraged her to make an official complaint to the GMC. So that's what she did. Next stop tribunal.'

'Isn't there a way round it?' Amy sounded more sympathetic.

'Nope. There's a record of who's logged in to every file and when. There's no way I could deny it, and once the GMC are involved, that's it. My reputation and my career are on the line.'

'God, Jane. That's terrible.'

'What's terrible is that I jeopardised everything I had with one stupid mistake, driven by my love for Paul. But it's their life, not mine. I should have left well alone. I see that now.'

'But your career's not really in danger?'

Jane wondered how much schadenfreude lay behind Amy's question, but perhaps she was asking from genuine concern. She gave her the benefit of the doubt. 'Who knows?' she replied. 'They could strike me off or suspend me or they might give me a warning. I'm hoping for the warning, of course, but this wait is no fun.'

'This is so weird, the four of us have somehow managed to get together just as our carefully constructed lives are falling apart.' Amy threw back the last of her coffee.

'Yours too?'

'Mine too.' The mug landed on the table with a bang. 'Rob's left me. Not only that, he's been stealing from the company.'

'You're kidding?'

'I wish I was. I wasn't going to say anything to any of you but . . . well, what does it matter? He's been having an affair with someone who works with us and he's going to live with her and her two children. A ready-made family – exactly what he always said he didn't want.'

Jane registered the bitterness and hurt in her voice. 'What are you going to do?'

Amy gave a wan smile. 'Please don't tell the others. I shouldn't have said anything.'

Jane nodded. The one thing she was supposed to be good at was keeping confidences.

'Do what I've always done. Carry on. I had this silly idea that if I found out what happened when I was expelled, I'd feel stronger about coping with what he's done.'

'And do you?' Jane sat quite still, waiting for her reply, understanding for the first time the long-lasting repercussions of her actions.

'I think so.'

'I hope I've changed.' Jane folded her hands on her lap. 'I never thought for a second of the impact on you, just about me.'

'I hope you have, too. Otherwise I feel extremely sorry for your patients.'

They were laughing as her phone signalled a text. 'Hang on. It's Kate.' Amy picked it up and read the message. 'She's in the village and wondering if anyone wants to go out for lunch.' She looked at the time. 'I wonder if I've got time to—'

'Why don't we get out of your hair for a while?' Jane was glad to have a reason to leave. 'I'll meet her down there.'

'But you don't know where she is.'

Jane gave her a look. 'Er, sat nav, phone. I think we'll manage.'

Amy hit her temple with the heel of her hand. 'Doh! But only if you're sure.'

'It'll be an adventure. You do what you need to do and we'll catch up when we get back.'

Jane enjoyed driving the silver Golf they'd hired and was soon on the road that took her down to the village. Unburdening herself to Amy had helped, letting her see for the first time how her behaviour had repeated itself over the years. What a ghastly child she must have been. She had loved being ringleader and had done what she needed to do to keep the position, albeit at the expense of others. But now she saw how that behaviour had continued. Yes, she did like getting her own way, and she would lie if it helped her achieve that. She had been selfish and thoughtless, acting only out of self-interest but perhaps it would work out for the best. It wasn't too late to learn. In the end she and Paul would be reconciled. He would see her punished. He would understand that she had only been acting in his best interests. She wouldn't be able to bear it if that didn't happen.

21

I'd never expected Jane, whom I remembered as being so contained and controlling, to open up like that. To me of all people. Respect. That impetuous moment and what followed might well have ruined her life. But I couldn't help thinking that it was so like the time she stole the watch and planted it in my desk, and lied about me. She only thought of the consequences for herself, no one else. She seemed to understand that now, but I doubted she would ever change. It was too late for that.

Once she had left, I went straight to my office. I skyped Kerry straight away but there was no reply.

Why had I told Jane about what Rob had done? I had meant not to say anything but the pressure was intolerable. I'd been doing my very best to put on a good show but inside I was cracking up.

Suddenly I didn't feel so confident about how everything would turn out. How would I manage without him? Really. We had been together for nearly thirty years. It wasn't long after we met that I'd formulated exactly what I wanted my shops to be. Amy Green would sell my own textile designs but also pieces of furniture and accessories that would go towards creating a certain look. We had been introduced by a friend who thought we'd get on – those matchmaking skills surprised all of us. We hit it off from the moment we met for a drink in a pub near his flat. Rob was tall, sporty and though not conventionally handsome, he had a great sense of humour and a way of looking at me that made me laugh and go weak every time. He was working in the finance department of Jolly's in Bath and was pretty full of himself.

What else did I love about him? So much. But most of all, his wild enthusiasms. On a Saturday morning, he might announce that we were going to London or Bristol or one of the Cotswold villages for the weekend. He'd buy extravagant treats to liven up our suppers of scrambled eggs or baked beans until he took up cooking as a hobby. But that didn't come until we were living together. I let him choose our first house, the pretty little Georgian cottage in Wingfield, just outside Bath, and in exchange he let me furnish it from top to bottom using all the junk shops and sales that I knew. We'd spent weekends restoring pieces of furniture, trailing round car boot sales together, or going for long country walks when we talked about our hopes and dreams.

So many people asked where I got the bits and pieces I collected that I began to dream of having a shop, turning my hobby into a job. When I told Rob, he thought it was a brilliant idea. Without his belief and backing I probably wouldn't have dared to embark on it. We found the first shop together – small but in a position where there would be passing trade. At the beginning, he helped me with the financial side of things and then as the business expanded, he took it over altogether, and eventually he took it on as a full-time job.

And now he had thrown it all back in my face. Our marriage too.

We had weathered that time when I had an affair with Lenny, a short-lived and terrible mistake with one of our suppliers who reminded me of Steve McQueen. Rob and I hadn't been getting along and when the opportunity presented itself... He had strayed too when he met Fran, a woman we met at a dinner party. She was recently divorced and was an example to us all: exuberant, flirty and fun. 'I'm not letting any man get me down,' she said to me. 'At least he's not going to see it if he does.' I should take a lesson. There may have been others since then, I've no idea.

We worked all night and all day when we were setting up the business. In a way Amy Green and the staff who worked for us took the place of any family we might have had. We certainly gave them all the hours we could. When we weren't with them, we were thinking up new ideas, new lines, new ways of expanding our market. God, it was exciting and exhausting and everything in between. And now he was throwing all of it away and threatening what we'd built as a result.

I picked up my tiny pink flamingo watering can and watered the pot plants on my windowsill.

Outside the sun was high in the sky. As I was wondering where the others could have got to, I received a text from Jane.

We're going to drive down to Deià. Back later this pm. OK?

Good. That gave me a little bit more time to steady myself. This wasn't something I wanted to share with them.

I quickly tapped back, **Of course.**

I left my office and wandered round the house, my hand drifting to things that reminded me of Rob. So much of what was there we had collected together. The fabrics were all my designs from the Moroccan inspired geometrics in the living room, to the parrots in the downstairs loo and the flower silhouettes in the pool room. All of them told me a story about where we were in our relationship when they were made. Of course, there have many others before or since, some we reissue and some let fade into oblivion. The Moroccan patterns I made when Ca'n Amy was almost done up, and we went to Marrakesh for a long weekend. The parrots were part of the first tropical collection I designed after we expanded from our first two shops in Bath and Bristol and branched out in Cheltenham and it looked as if business was going to boom. We celebrated by going to the Caribbean for a week. The flowers I designed the year Rob had his fling with Fran. They're pretty, monochromatic against a pale grey background, but they remind me of how bleak I felt at the time. And that in turn reminded me that I'd felt the world was ending before and I'd got through it. I had to hang on to that memory if I could.

Thinking back to those few days with Linda, Kate and Jane, I suppose I was still in some kind of shock, even though Rob had dropped his bombshell weeks before. I kept telling myself that I had to hold it together so I didn't spoil the weekend for the others. But there were many more factors than just me at work of course. They each had their own reasons for wanting to get away, but coming here hadn't been a way to escape them. They had brought their problems with them. I don't know why any of us ever thought such a reunion would be anything other than a terrible idea that would unsettle us all.

I went out to pick some tomatoes in the wired-off enclosure round the side of the house. The vegetable garden might be small but the plants were laden with fruit and gave off that wonderful sharp grassy smell. As I put the tomatoes in the basket I'd brought out with me, I was aware of someone standing outside the enclosure. I turned to find Linda standing watching me, her face expressionless.

'It is him,' she said. Just that.

To my astonishment, a couple of tears ran down her face. 'Sorry.' She wiped them away.

I left the enclosure, tying the gate on place with the frayed string. 'What's happened?'

She pulled herself together. 'Long story. I thought I'd got over it. Turns out not as much as I'd imagined.'

'Over what? You didn't fancy him as well? But it was years ago.' That couldn't be the reason she was so upset.

'I know. Silly of me.' She dug the toe of her sandal into the earth and twisted it back and forth.

'Jane found out why the name change.' This was something we all should know.

She looked up. 'Which was?'

As we walked back to the terrace together, I told her the story, all the while wondering what had happened. I couldn't remember her ever having hinted that she had a thing for him. I almost wanted to laugh. Kate was the only one of us who had emerged unscathed. And here we all were over forty years later discovering the truth about our art teacher for the first time and how all three of us had been affected by it.

Linda's reaction to the story of his arrest and imprisonment was hard to read. She stared at the mountains, lost in thought. Then... 'I've thought he was many things but I never thought he'd go for someone under age; though why not, I don't know.'

'What things are you talking about?' I had no idea what she was getting at. From where we were, we could hear Dan splashing up and down the pool. He must have gone straight there when they got back, leaving us to talk. Occasionally his sensitivity took me by surprise. 'You did believe what he did to me, didn't you?

'Actually, I didn't, not at the time.' She turned to look at me, her brown eyes sad.

'But why not?' I'd always assumed she had been quietly on my side. 'I thought we were best friends.'

'We were, but I was far too wrapped up in him to believe he would ever be capable of behaving like that. Sex for grades.' She shook her head. 'I had no idea.'

'What do you mean "wrapped up in him"?' Not her too.

She hesitated, rubbing the palm of her hand as if it was

going to provide the answers. 'I suppose you might as well know. None of it really matters now.'

'None of what? And it obviously does matter. You're upset.' We walked to the terrace and sat at the table. I put the tomatoes in the shade of a sago palm.

She managed a short laugh. 'I was having an affair with him, and none of you knew.'

I was stunned. 'You were having an affair? With him?' It was inconceivable. How could she have been? We were all four friends and knew everything that went on each other's lives. We played together, talked about the boys we fancied together, revised together, argued together, made up together. She couldn't have had an affair without one of us registering it.

'I really was. It began at the beginning of our final year and went on into that first fabulous summer holiday when we were free after the exams.'

I didn't bother to remind her that summer hadn't been like that for me at all. I had disappeared to London to stay with Dan, angry, rebellious but with my tail between my legs. 'But you never said a thing.' How wrapped up in ourselves we must have been not to have noticed.

'I was head over heels in love with him – or I thought I was – and didn't want anything to spoil it. I knew it was wrong and we'd both get into terrible trouble if we were found out, and it was easy to keep a secret once A levels were over because you weren't around and Jane's parents took her and Kate off to Greece to celebrate the end of school.'

I remembered how my invitation on that holiday hadn't been so much withdrawn as dropped like a hot stone. Not that Jane's parents would ever have much wanted me to go away with them. I would only have been invited on Jane's insistence, and the moment things blew up with Mr Wilson, that was when everything went wrong.

'Until then, I just kept quiet. It was quite fun watching

everyone getting their knickers in a twist over him, all the time knowing I was the one he had chosen.'

I winced as I remembered his hand on my thigh again. 'So what happened?' I was mesmerised, unable to believe what I was hearing.

'We had a couple of almost blissful months – no more snatched moments out of the classroom, but time I could spend with him in his flat, quite the little homemaker. I chose not see him pushing me away.' She sounded bitter now. 'We didn't go out much in case we were seen but I didn't care. I was convinced it was only a matter of time, that he would get one of the jobs he was going to apply for and we'd go wherever he was employed together.'

'You were going to live with him? But what about your degree?' I was having difficulty getting my head round all this.

'He said I should go to Edinburgh, as planned, that we'd be together in the holidays. In my heart I knew that wasn't really what he wanted.' The smile she gave me was so sad. 'But if you don't want to see the cracks, you don't. God! I was so young.'

'Tell me about it.' I understood exactly what she was talking about. I had ignored the widening cracks in my marriage in the same way. 'So what happened?'

'I'd been in Edinburgh for a few weeks when I discovered I was pregnant.'

I couldn't speak. So I was far from alone in having my life changed by that man. But Linda had never come to find me to share our misfortunes, so I had never known. When I came back to York from London, no one wanted to know. I assumed she'd be the same so I never looked her up. That came later, thanks to Kate. We sat in silence for a moment, the sheep bells tolling in the distance somewhere, the breeze rustling the leaves of the big old carob tree by the wall.

'And then?' I asked as gently as I could but I needed to know the answer.

'It turned out to be an ectopic pregnancy that ruptured.'

Even I, without any experience of pregnancy and the risks, knew how serious that could be.

'So I had to have a hysterectomy. Days after my eighteenth birday.' She let that sit there for us both to consider.

To think of the fuss I'd made over my expulsion. What had happened to me was nothing compared to this. My life had been easy compared to Linda's whose was irreparably damaged. Not only had he broken her heart, left her to deal with the pregnancy on her own, she had been left unable to have children. This was so very much more serious.

'I had no idea.'

'Of course you didn't. I kept that secret too. One or two people in Edinburgh knew but I hadn't been there long enough to make many friends. That came later. I didn't want anyone at home to know in case it got back to my aunt. And anyway, although I was bereft when he abandoned me, and could have done with an old friend, I felt a fool. How could I have been so stupid? I thought you'd all laugh at me. But I was young, naïve and I believed everything he said. When I heard what had happened to you, I refused to admit to myself it could be true. But I should have known. I should have seen what happened to me coming.'

'How could you?'

'And now I've seen him again for the first time since then.'

I listened, intent on her story of visiting the gallery with Dan.

'So now he knows. And, weirdly, I feel so much better having it out in the open.' Her face lightened. 'I didn't even feel it was a weight until I confronted him and then realised something had lifted from me. Just as I feel telling you after keeping it buttoned up for years.'

'How have you coped?' I tried to put myself into her shoes, but it was impossible to imagine.

'The hardest thing of all was coming to terms with the fact that I'd never be a mum. Having that choice taken away became more significant the older I got.'

She sounded so sad that I wanted to hug her but felt she might not welcome that, so sat quite still, letting her talk.

'It was fine until I got to that age when my friends were having families and I could never ever be one of them. I never met a man who didn't want a family at some point, so I never married. As a result, I tended to keep myself to myself more and more. I was friends with Mike for years before we slept together. At one point after that I even believed we might live together but by then we were too old to have children and anyway he had his own. Then, in the end, he plumped for his wife, his children and his grandchildren. And that, of course, is the other thing: I'll never be a grandparent either.' Her grief was painful to see.

I couldn't help thinking how Rob and I had made that decision not to have children together. We had been in a café overlooking a Devon beach, watching the sea roll in.

'I can't imagine how we'll have time for children and all this,' he had said.

'I don't want them at all,' I finally admitted. This was something I had thought long and hard about. I didn't feel that rush of affection or love or envy when with other people's kids. 'I must've missed out on that maternal gene.' I looked at him nervously, waiting for him react. I was so scared he would think I was unnatural, that he would run a mile.

Instead his face relaxed and he smiled. 'That's a relief. We're on the same page then. Unfortunately we'll have to have a life that involves long sybaritic holidays; going out whenever we want to until as late as we like; doing exactly what we want. We'll have more money so we can live in beautiful places, own beautiful things.'

The relief I felt was unimaginable. It turned out we wanted

to throw all our energies into the business and, when we weren't working, to enjoy the fruits of our labour. We watched our friends with their children, and heard how much they envied us, our lifestyle. The decision was right for us. But if we hadn't had the luxury of choice ... perhaps it would have been different. Perhaps in the end Rob was feeling something of what Linda was saying, and I wasn't enough for him any more.

I gave her feeble smile and got one in return. 'I think we need a drink. It's a bit early, but ...'

'A drink would be just right. It's been a helluva a day.'

As I got to my feet, there was a knock on the terrace door. Between us, we must have left the front door open, and someone had let themselves in and walked through the house.

'Can I come in?' A man's voice.

We turned together.

And there, leaning against the doorpost, cigarette between his fingers, cane tapping against his deck shoes, straw hat cocked on his head as if he didn't have a care in the world, was none other than Jack Walsh himself.

22

Linda froze. She hadn't expected to see Jack again. But Amy showed greater presence of mind by getting up as if she was going to welcome their visitor. Whatever she was feeling, she kept to herself.

'I think we definitely need that drink now,' Amy said, instead of a welcome. 'Linda, can you give me a hand?'

'Can I sit down?' he asked. He pointed towards the chairs with his cane.

'No,' she replied. 'Wait right there until we're ready to talk to you.'

Linda followed her into the kitchen, admiring Amy's self-control and chutzpah. 'I suggested he saw you to apologise but I didn't think he would.'

'If that's why he's here.' Amy got a bottle of gin from the cupboard. 'I think we need something strong. There's tonic in the fridge. How dare he just walk in here with no warning?'

For the first time, Linda noticed how tired Amy looked. Despite the effort she made with her appearance, she couldn't hide those shadows under her eyes. As she got out a couple of limes and sliced them on the cracked chopping board she asked: 'What do you want to do? Shall we send him away or listen to what he has to say?'

Linda thought as she got two bottles of tonic and put them on the tray. This man had blighted both their lives in different ways. This might be their last chance to say what they had always wanted. 'We should listen. We've both waited years for this.'

Amy considered, nodding, her lips pressed hard together. 'Okay. We'll do it together. All for one and one for all. Right?'

Their old schoolgirl mantra had never meant more than it did at that moment. Although this trip had thrown up far more than any of them could have anticipated, Linda felt sure this renewed friendship would last.

They emerged together, Amy carrying the tray; Linda, bowls of pistachios and olives. The heat of the early evening wrapped itself round them. From the terrace, Linda could see Dan, covered in a hippy throw studded with tiny mirrors that glittered in the sun, asleep in the shade beyond the pool, quite unaware of what was going on at the house.

'Come and sit down.' Amy showed Jack to the table where he took a seat with his back to the view, letting the two of them sit opposite him, as if they were on an interviewing panel.

'You've done well for yourself,' he said as Amy poured the drinks.

'I don't imagine that's why you've come.' She slid his gin across the table with such force that it slopped over the edge of the glass. 'Perhaps you'd better tell us why you have.'

Her self-control was impressive.

'I've come to apologise.' He held his hands in supplication before removing his hat and putting it on the table.

Amy looked at it with such distaste that he moved it to his knee. 'To which of us?' she said.

Jack looked taken aback, as if he hadn't considered the two of them would have confided in each other so soon. 'Both.'

'Forty-three years too late, I'd say.' Amy was not going to give an inch.

Linda realised she had nothing more to say to him so sat silent watching the two of them square up to each other, waiting for this to be over. If the Sóller valley split open and swallowed her, she'd be happy.

'I know. I should have been braver.' He moved his head from side to side, considering. 'I should have done all sorts of things.'

'Or not.' Linda spoke at last. The release of having her own secret in the open made her braver.

'Give me a chance.' He held his glass in both hands, looking at them over its rim. 'It wasn't easy making the decision to come up here. But, Linny, you persuaded me.' He cast an uncertain smile in her direction.

She didn't respond. The gin slipped down her throat as her confidence returned.

'Sorry, but I think I must be missing something. Are you asking us for our sympathy?' Amy gave a disbelieving laugh.

Jack looked uncomfortable. What sort of reception could he have imagined? 'No. I, er... well, I want to apologise.'

'Sit tight, Linda. He's had a long time to practise this, so it should be good. Fire away. We're listening.'

At the other end of the garden, she saw Dan sit up and look in their direction. After a minute or two he lay back down but remained facing their way so that he could see if he was needed.

'I'm sorry.' Jack kept looking from Amy to Linda and back, shifting in his seat under their gaze. 'I am.' He leaned his elbows on the table and clasped his hands, nudging his chin with them, waiting for their forgiveness.

'That's it?' said Amy. 'After all this time, you think that's enough? What you did to me was unforgivable, although I built the fallout into something that was more significant than perhaps it deserved. But what you did to Linda was worse. For that, all she gets is sorry? Do you really think that's good enough?'

'I'm all right. Really. We've spoken.' Linda hurried the conversation on.

His hands fell to the table so the glasses jumped. Linda

steadied hers then stared at him, trying to see the young man she had known but there was nothing of him there. His eyes were expressionless. There was nothing of the sorrow he was professing there. She looked away, disappointed.

'Can I try to explain?'

'This should be interesting. Please.'

Amy's animosity was wearing thin. Linda wanted to get this over with as quickly as possible, realising that Jack must have come with an ulterior motive. She didn't believe he was here just to humiliate himself. Couldn't Amy see that?

'Look . . .' he began, reasonable in his appeal. 'I was a young man, and I was extremely pleased with myself, I'll admit that. I'd landed a breeze of a teaching job that allowed me to carry on with my own painting. I was a novelty in St Catherine's, and I enjoyed the status and the sort of celebrity that came with it. I was flattered, didn't think, and took advantage of my position.' He took a sip of his drink.

'I'd say,' said Amy under her breath. 'Go on.'

Twisting his fingers together, he went on. 'OK. I abused the responsibility that, at the time, I didn't take seriously. But I was only twenty-five. Gimme a break. I was only human and did what any other twenty-five-year-old would have done. You were the only one who wouldn't play. Of course, if I could go back and behave differently, I would.'

'How many were there?' Linda asked, dismayed by his admission.

'Don't misunderstand me.' He held up his hand. 'Only one or two. I forget now. And nothing terrible happened, just a bit of harmless flirting.'

'It was anything but that.'

Linda could tell Amy's control was close to breaking, so she stepped in. 'We know what happened to you, about your prison sentence.'

That surprised and alarmed him. 'How? You never said.'

'Google made that easy,' Amy snapped.

'I loved her. Or thought I did.' His face reddened.

'That's what you said to me.' Linda couldn't help returning to that long hot happy summer when she had felt the same way, when he had told her he loved her, teaching her all sorts of things she had never been taught in in any classroom.

His eyes fixed on his hat, working his hand round its brim. 'During my time in jail, I was made to think about what I'd done – not just what put me there but of the others, including you, who came before. I was banned from the classroom for life.'

'I should hope so.'

'It couldn't happen again.' At last he hung his head. 'But I wanted you to know that I didn't just make life difficult for you, I ruined my own. A jail sentence has plenty of side effects. My parents disowned me. My friends moved on. Luckily for me I met Anika.' At that point he looked up again, his eyes brighter. 'She's Dutch and was running a chocolate shop in Béziers where I—'

He was interrupted by a snort from Amy who looked as if she was about to explode. 'We don't need your life history, fascinating as your relationship with Anika may be. Honestly? I've heard enough. I think you should go.'

'She was the one who put me back on track. I'd paid the price for what I'd done. I moved to France and started painting again, thanks to her. We got married. I even teach privately now. Adults,' he added swiftly.

'She sounds a saint but that's not why you're here,' said Amy. 'Linda and I need to talk. We know where to find you. Thanks for coming up to see us.' She took his glass and returned it to the tray, making it quite clear the time had come for him to leave.

He didn't get up immediately but sat twisting his hat around on his lap.

'Anika mustn't know any of this,' he said as he got up. 'I don't know what she'd think if she knew and I don't want to risk her finding out. Can we keep it between ourselves?'

'So that's why you're here.' Amy looked incredulous. 'Doesn't that rather devalue your apology?'

'Not at all.' His hands fumbled on the back of his chair. 'I meant everything I said.'

'I think you should go before one of us says something we might regret.' The sun glanced off her glass as she turned it on the table.

After he'd left, Amy sat back in her chair. 'Wow! I can't believe that just happened. You okay?'

'I think so. You?' In fact Linda was feeling quite braced by the whole experience. Whatever she had thought her life had been until now had been tossed in the air and landed having taken on a quite different shape. 'But didn't you want an apology? I thought you would.' She slapped a mosquito that had landed on her arm. A tiny bead of perspiration ran down her face.

'That was never going to be a proper apology. That wasn't about you and me. That was about him. Self-justification and his need to be exonerated by us. He'd like us to say it didn't matter, that we're okay now. He'll go to sleep tonight, his conscience clear. He's apologised so that's enough. And Mrs Chocolate will hug him and tell him he's done the right thing – if he tells her any of it.'

Linda couldn't help laughing. 'I don't remember you being so harsh.'

Amy tipped her head so her face was in the sun. 'Do you believe him?'

'I'm not sure.'

'I mean about the wife. Do you think she even exists? I don't trust him at all.'

'Surely he wouldn't lie about that.'

'Who knows?' She stretched her arms behind her head. 'What a day.'

'Has something else happened? You don't have to tell me, of course.' But she would be disappointed if she didn't.

'No, I'd like to talk about it. I've already told Jane and I felt better for it. Turns out getting things into the open can be a good thing. In a nutshell, Rob's been stealing from the company and he's leaving me. There.' She leaned over the table, cradling her head in her arms.

Linda didn't know what to do. Kate would have immediately hugged Amy, but she wasn't comfortable presuming an intimacy she wasn't sure they had. She looked to Dan for help, but he must have gone into his room when he saw he wasn't needed. As she dithered, Amy recovered herself.

'I'm sorry. This isn't going to help anything.'

'But what happened?' Linda passed her one of the paper napkins on the tray.

'Long story.' Amy blew her nose but then began to talk.

As Linda listened, she felt as if she had returned to the role of close friend at last. Amy wanted the ear of someone who would listen for as long as it took, who would say nothing and not judge. After today, they would both be bound by one another's secrets. If Amy didn't tell, neither would she, so she listened gripped, horrified, sympathetic, appalled.

'So,' Amy drew to a close. 'You see nothing's perfect in paradise after all.'

'What next? You're not going to let him get away with it, are you?'

'The money or running off with my so-called friend?' Looking thoughtful, Amy picked an olive from the dish, tossed it in the air and waited, mouth tipped up and open, till it dropped straight in. 'I'm not sure there's much I can do about him going off with Morag. The more I get used to the idea, the less I'm surprised by it. We haven't loved each other enough over the

226

years. Funny – without children, I thought we would. Don't they get in the way of love, sometimes? As for the money: he's said he'll pay it back but he hasn't yet. I don't want to involve the police but we'll have to soon.' Her eyes filled with tears but she kept them under control.

'I don't know what to say.'

'There isn't anything *to* say. But you've got to admit, as far as I'm concerned, this rather puts our "Mr Wilson" ' – she loaded the name with disdain – 'into the shade. At least as far as I'm concerned it does. Although you must feel very different.'

Linda thought about it for a minute. She stretched out her arms, twisting her wrists as if handcuffs had just been removed. 'I'm not sure I do. When I realised it was him, that was a shock. But I'm over that now. We're the same in that what happened then is something that's coloured my life and that I've built up into something that it doesn't deserve to be any more.'

'But losing a child . . .'

'It wasn't like that. Not really. I had to face facts and was making my own life possible. The truth is that I never met anyone I wanted to have children with. By the time I hit the menopause, everyone I knew had kids and the fact that I came so close to having one once really hit home. I could have been a mum. That's when I started thinking about Jack again.' There was a deep buzz and she dodged sideways as a hornet flew past her en route to the eaves of the house. 'But actually seeing him has made me realise that I've let it rule me more than I should. Not that the whole thing hasn't been enormously significant in shaping me but . . . well, all sorts of things do that. Life throws you those curve balls and you've got to find a way to get on nonetheless.'

Amy laughed. 'You wise old woman. Well, this weekend has been full of curve balls. What will you do when you get back?'

'Go back to the library and make a decision. Being dead wood doesn't make me feel great so perhaps I should take the money.' Although she didn't feel particularly confident about that choice. Then what?

'I'm sure you'd find something new'

'At my age? People aren't crying out for librarians in their sixties.'

'Do something different?'

'Like what?'

'Come and work for me. You must be pretty organised.'

They both looked at one another, equally astonished by the suggestion.

'As what? You're hardly going to be hiring people just at the moment.' The thought of working in a completely new area was as dizzying as it was unlikely.

'Except that we've just lost two directors at a stroke. There may be something. I don't know what just yet.'

'But I couldn't do fill either of those roles.' Linda grinned. The idea of herself going out and promoting Amy's brand was funny. Working alone at a desk was what she did best. 'But I appreciate the thought.'

'I'll think on it and let you know.'

'Halloooo!' Kate's voice carried through from the living room. 'Anyone here?'

'It's the cavalry – too late. We're out here,' Amy called before smiling at Linda. 'I don't think they need to know everything, do you?'

'It's all safe with me. They're your secrets to tell, not mine.' Although a little of Linda longed to let the others know how close the two of them had grown in such a short time and what it was that had brought them together.

Jane and Kate burst through the door carrying shopping.

'We ended up in Sóller again. Delicious tapas lunch. And we saw the Picasso and Miró ceramics in the station. Loved them.' Kate was beaming.

'And let's not forget I almost totalled the car.' Jane pulled out a chair and sat down.

'You didn't?!'

'On the way back. Those mountain roads are a nightmare.' She caught Kate's eye. 'Oh, OK. I forgot just for a second and drove on the wrong side of the road. Just for the shortest of distances but this maniac...'

'Came round the corner exactly where he should have been,' added Kate. 'And by some God-given miracle, we survived because there was no one else on the road. So we went back into Sóller for a bit of retail therapy.' She brandished a bag. 'Souvenirs for the family.'

'And something for me.' Jane unravelled a deep blue scarf patterned with silver stars.

'Anything happened while we've been away?' Kate nodded towards the empty glasses. 'Bit early for the hard stuff, isn't it?'

Linda and Amy exchanged glances.

'Nothing much. We had a visit from Jack Walsh. You've just missed him.'

'You're kidding!' Jane sat down.

'What did he want?' Kate followed suit.

'To apologise,' said Amy. 'To say that prison changed him. To be forgiven.'

'And did you?'

'Forgive him? No. If I need to forgive anyone, it's you.'

Jane looked alarmed. 'I thought we'd talked about this, resolved it.'

'We had. But seeing him has brought it all back in even clearer detail. All those times when you chopped and changed between us so none of us ever knew when we were or weren't in favour.'

'It wasn't like that. We were all friends.' Jane was almost pleading.

'Were we?' Amy looked at the others for their agreement.

'Steady on,' Kate interrupted. 'I think this has gone too far now. Perhaps this isn't the best moment to have this conversation.'

'Perhaps it is the best moment. I hoped to find out what happened, and now I know. I'm not talking about the watch, that's one thing. But if you hadn't prevented the truth about him getting out, other lives might not have been harmed.'

Linda froze. Surely Amy wouldn't break her promise to her so soon.

'You're not suggesting I'm to blame for his abducting that girl? That had nothing to do with me. That was ten years later.'

'Not just that.'

Linda found Amy's foot with hers and pressed hard.

'This is ridiculous.' Jane's entire demeanour had changed. 'When I left we'd discussed what happened and I'd apologised. What's happened?'

'I've just realised how responsible you were. Don't you see? If anyone had listened to me, everything else might have been avoided.'

'I've had enough of this.' Jane slammed her fist on the table. 'I didn't want to come here in the first place. I was only doing Kate a favour.'

'What?' Kate was astonished. 'That's not true. You came because it gave you an excuse to go to Barcelona and . . .' She stopped as Jane turned on her.

'I'm not going to listen to any more. I'm going to pack and find somewhere else to stay.'

'You do that.' Amy was incandescent.

Linda couldn't move, transfixed and terrified by the argument.

'Amy, don't do this.' Kate put a hand on Amy's arm in an attempt to calm her down only to have it thrown off.

'I'm not doing anything except pointing out what should have been pointed out a long time ago. Lives were changed because of what you did, and it's important you should be taken to task for that.'

'Which lives are you talking about? Yours? I'll say it again, you'd never have made it through medical school.'

Suddenly Linda came to life, unable to tolerate such an unjustified attack on Amy. She may not have backed her when they were seventeen but she could at least do that now. 'She's talking about me.'

'Don't, Linda. You don't have to say anything.' Amy held up her hand.

'What are the two of you talking about?'

'I fell pregnant, and he was the father . . .'

Jane paled. 'That's not true.'

'There you go again,' said Amy. 'Sometimes you should believe what you hear. Not all of us are like Elaine.'

Or you, Jane. But Linda kept her thought to herself.

At the mention of her son's girlfriend, Jane got up from the table. 'That's enough. I didn't tell you about that so you could tell everyone.'

'But we're old, old friends,' said Kate. 'We should be able to talk to each other without worrying that one of us will break confidences. What happened, Linda?'

Linda could tell her concern was genuine. 'A miscarriage.' Easier not to tell the full story. That was enough.

'You poor thing, I'd no idea.' Kate leaned across and hugged her.

'I didn't want anyone from home to know. That's why I stayed out of touch for a long while. It took me all that time before I could face anyone. And then you wrote to me. By then I didn't need to say anything.'

Jane got up from the table. 'You were lucky.'

The other three gaped at her.

'You can't mean that.' Amy looked horrified.

'I meant she was lucky not to have had the child. Imagine.

231

At seventeen or eighteen with university ahead of you. But I'm sorry that it happened. What was it? A one-night stand or something?'

'Jane! You're impossible.'

But Linda felt quite calm, glad they were all seeing the real Jane. Growing older had not done her any favours, it turned out. 'Actually we were together for months. I used to watch you mooning over him, and I'd hug my secret to myself, pleased that I was the one he'd chosen.'

Jane raised her eyebrows as if she didn't believe her.

'More fool me. I know.' Linda gave a sheepish smile.

Both Amy and Kate smiled back.

'Fascinating, but I think I've heard enough. I'm going to my room to work out what to do next.' Picking up her bag and new scarf, Jane went inside, leaving the others open-mouthed.

Linda breathed a silent sigh of relief, glad that she hadn't had to go into any more detail about the pregnancy and its results in front of her.

'God! She's even more impossible than I remembered,' said Kate. 'Do you think I could have a gin?'

23

About half an hour later Jane came downstairs, pale and red-eyed, suitcase in hand. But far from being contrite, she was combative, determined.

'Don't go,' said Kate, who happened to be in the living room, looking through one of Amy's interiors magazines while Linda and Amy were getting ready for the evening.

'Why not? None of you want me here now and, to be honest, I don't want to be here either. For a moment I thought it might work and that we'd all be friends again but too much has happened. And far too much significance has been loaded on to two tiny things I said and did – when we were at school, for God's sake. More on that than on the watch, which I admit was bad. But even so, get over it. The way your life turns out is down to you, not anyone else. You've got to make good the cards you're dealt without blaming things that happened in your past.'

Kate was astonished. 'That's harsh. You can't expect everyone else to live by your impeccable standards.' Jane's endless refusal to take responsibility for her actions by blaming everyone else was maddening.

'I can.' She stood even straighter. 'I've found a room in one of the village hotels. I'll be much better off there.'

'But what about supper?' There'd been talk of going down

to Sóller. 'Why don't you at least join us? Don't let's end it like this.'

Jane gave a short laugh. 'I don't think I'd be welcome, do you?'

Of course, she was right. Having all four of them together now would be awkward at best. Things should never have been allowed to go this far. Somehow, with an opportunity to clear the air, they had only got much more convoluted and recriminatory. Kate should have done something to smooth things over, but what? As the only one who hadn't had any interest in Mr Wilson – why not? Everyone else had. Perhaps there was something wrong with her. However, for some reason, she felt it lay with her to find a way through this. But perhaps it wasn't too late. 'Of course you would. I think the others were in shock after Jack Walsh turned up. We should have been here.'

'As for the miscarriage story . . .'

'I'm sure that wasn't made up.' Linda had given her the sketchiest outline of what happened. Why wasn't Jane more sensitive? For someone whose job was dealing with the public in a compassionate and knowledgeable way, she showed surprisingly little empathy for her friends.

Jane jangled the car keys from her fingers. 'I'm going to take the car. I'm sure Amy will take you and Linda to the airport.'

'This is silly. Don't do this. Take everything back to your room and stay to sort this out.' Kate put herself between Jane and the door.

'I've tried. I thought Amy and I had resolved things this morning but, whatever Jack Walsh or Wilson or whatever he calls himself has said, has stirred it all up again. I'm not going to take all the blame for Amy and Linda's lives not turning out the way they wanted. It's ridiculous.'

'Aren't you missing the point? All she wants is for you to acknowledge what you did, that's all.'

'I did that, and look where it's got us. And now I've got

other things that I need to deal with, if ever I'm going to sort out my own life. No, this really is the right thing to do – for all of us. Please.' She waited for Kate to move out of the way. 'I'll see you back home, if I don't bump into you at the airport.'

Kate was dumbfounded. She thought she knew Jane better than that. Did she mean her affair with Rick was causing problems? That wasn't so surprising. How do you run two men at the same time with so many other commitments? Never mind whether you should or not. If she were to have an affair, the secrecy would last for about two minutes before she blurted out something that would give her away. Believing in truth and transparency had its disadvantages.

'Penny for them?' Dan walked in from outside. 'What's been going on?'

Kate was pleased to see him: the one apparently sane person there. 'You've no idea.'

'Then come outside and tell me. I saw Jack Walsh was here, but I decided I should keep my distance. Drink?'

'I'd love a water. Although after today . . .'

'Don't worry, I'm not going to force you.' His wink made her nothing but nervous.

When he reappeared, carrying a bottle of water and one of beer, she had moved to beside the pool where she sat on a lounger. Somehow being away from the house out of the range of Amy and Linda felt more comfortable. Their experiences with Jack Walsh had bonded them and, now Jane had gone, being alone with them made her feel the odd one out. Instead she found herself wanting to confide in Dan and ask his advice. She felt a natural kinship with him. Whether that was because they'd known each other since childhood or because they simply clicked, she didn't know. Whatever it was, she was enjoying it.

'So, what's going on?' He stretched out on the lounger next to her, hands clasped behind his head.

Under his T-shirt she could see his ribcage rising and falling

235

with each breath. How badly she wanted to touch him, but of course never would.

'What have I missed?'

'Seems that Jack Walsh—'

He stiffened at the name, sat up and picked up his beer. 'We saw him this morning in the gallery and he was up here this afternoon. Amy seemed to have everything under control so I kept my distance.'

'I don't know what went on at the gallery but apparently he came up here to apologise, and it's upset everyone. Jane's left in a huff.'

'What?' The hint of a smile crept across his face. 'So everyone's true colours are coming out after all? That didn't take long.'

'It's not like that.' She wished she hadn't said anything. 'Jane's got a lot on her plate at the moment and needs to be somewhere she can sort herself out. It's got nothing to do with the rest of us.'

'Do I really believe that?' He tipped his head back and took a long swig of his beer. 'I met Jack Walsh this morning. Nasty piece of work, although Linda seemed to have got his measure. I was impressed.'

'She was always quite secretive.' That must be the understatement of the century. An affair with Mr Wilson. Pregnant. How come none of them noticed? It seemed impossible.

'I didn't think he'd drive up here for a moment.' His brow furrowed. 'How was Amy?'

'Angry.' She watched him tap his fingers against the bottle again and again. 'Unforgiving.'

'Of course she was.'

'There wasn't anything you could have done. And perhaps it's a good thing that she had the chance to confront him.'

He grinned at her. 'You're such a thoughtful person. I love that about you.'

Was she? Kate puzzled over his comment, wondering what he really meant.

'Do you fancy having supper tonight? Just the two of us?' His beer bottle scraped on the paving as he put it down.

'Oh I don't know...' But that would be exactly how she'd like to spend the evening, getting to know this intriguingly enigmatic man better. But, given it was their last night, she would run the risk of alienating Linda and Amy. But, but, but...

He tipped his head to one side, his eyes fixed on her in a way that made her fizz with anticipation. 'Up to you.'

She closed her eyes, shutting out her surroundings. She pictured Alan, stocky, often muddy and tired from going out to find a lost ewe with the dogs, no fashion plate but reliable, solid – her man.

'I should wait for the others,' she said. 'It's our last night after all and Amy's booked the table in Sóller. We're having *pintxos*.' She said it as though Amy hadn't had to explain to her that pintxos were a version of tapas.

'Then come for a drink first.' He leaned forward so that when she opened her eyes they met his, washed-out blue like chips of sea glass. 'Please.'

'I should change,' she said, swinging her legs round so her feet were on the ground and she was sitting up. But what harm could a drink do?

'We could pop down to the village early and they can pick you up on the way. Go on. There's something I want to ask you.'

She imagined herself back on the motorbike, hanging on, wind against her face, pressed up to his back. But – she stopped herself – what did he want to ask her? As there couldn't be a future in any kind of close relationship, he must just enjoy being with her. And, after the previous day, she could be confident it would be fun. But what would Amy and Linda think? She was old enough not to care. 'OK. Give me ten minutes.'

'Sure.' He smiled and she could feel his eyes on her back as she walked up to the house.

In her room, she showered quickly, finger-dried her hair, and paired the prettiest kaftan top she had brought with a pair of white linen trousers. The tight and tingly skin that went with being out in the sun too long put her in a holiday mood. She kept her make-up minimal and, as an afterthought, spritzed herself with cologne. Lime, Basil and Mandarin seemed in keeping with where they were.

In the corridor, she hesitated then went to Amy's room and knocked on the door.

Amy was sitting on her bed, towel wrapped around her, phone in her hand. The room was beautiful: minimalist like the rest of the house, but the little touches that Amy was so famous for made all the difference. The only splash of colour in the room came from a pomegranate-patterned cushion cover in the off-white armchair, a couple of landscape paintings and the brass Moroccan pendant shade in the centre of the room. On the floor a faded antique rug covered varnished floorboards. A wooden heart hung from the bedside light. Otherwise everything was white, even the curtains that framed the window and the doors to a Juliet balcony.

Amy looked up at her with such an expression of sadness that Kate crossed the room and hugged her, then pulled away.

'Hi,' Amy said quietly. 'This has been quite a day.'

'Are you OK?' She looked anything but.

'Not really. It's Rob. I wasn't going to say anything but I've told the others so I might as well tell you, too.' Quickly she regaled Kate with story of her disintegrating marriage and Rob's theft from the company. Kate listened, appalled. 'He's only paid back some of what he owes us. I gave him a month – perhaps that was unreasonable – but if he doesn't repay us, we're going to have to involve the police. That's the last thing I want to do but it's me or him.' She smoothed the duvet cover with her right hand.

Kate gasped. 'You're exaggerating.' She sat on the bed beside her.

'I wish I was.' She stilled her hand. 'So I'm just taking a few moments out to straighten out my head. But it sure puts everything else into perspective.'

'Of course. Is there anything I can do?'

'Short of killing Rob? I don't think so, but thanks. This is something I need to sort out on my own.' Amy stared at her hands, turning the thick gold band on her ring finger. 'But you didn't come in to hear that. I'm sorry.'

'Don't be silly. I just wish there was something I could do to help. But Dan's asked me to go for a drink with him before dinner. I thought I would. Is that OK, though? I'll happily stay if it would help.'

'You're getting on well.' Amy looked enquiring.

Kate forced an embarrassed laugh. 'There's nothing like that going on.'

'I wasn't suggesting there was or I'd be warning you off. Reliable he ain't. But go, of course. We'll pick you up on the way down.'

'Are you sure?' Kate didn't want to leave her.

Amy nodded. 'Are *you*? He can be a bit of a Lothario, so watch yourself.' Her eyebrows rose in warning.

Heat rose to Kate's cheeks. 'I will. I'm just enjoying catching up with you both.'

'Only teasing. No, go. You're looking great. That green suits you.'

Once on the bike, Kate realised her mistake in wearing the white trousers. By the time they dismounted at the village square, there was a long smear of oil on her inside calf. Dan took her to the bar on the opposite side from where she had sat

239

that morning. Now it was doing a booming trade, filled with people who looked overdressed for dinner in such a modest place. They found a table and ordered two Aperol Spritz. The square was busy, illuminated by the orange street lamp on the church wall. Underneath it, a sign announced some kind of fiesta and a stage had been put up during the day. The bunting fluttered in the breeze.

After their drinks arrived, Dan leaned towards her as if he was about to say something significant. Something gave way in the pit of her stomach.

'You know how much I like you,' he began.

Oh God! She should have listened to Amy's warning and stayed at the house. She didn't and yet she so did want to be propositioned by him if only to remember what that felt like. What was wrong with a little harmless flirting? 'No' was a word that was available to her, she reminded herself. 'Do you?' she said, her voice a quaver.

He looked shocked. 'Of course I do. I remember you from when you had pigtails – how you've changed since then.' He pulled in his chair as a family squeezed past him.

'I should hope so. It would be sad if I hadn't.' With pigtails was not the way Kate had hoped to be remembered. Especially not by him. She would rather be thought of as the sultry one. Fat chance of that. She was more the everyday, jolly, sporty one to the others. However, at least she was remembered. That was better than not at all.

'I feel our friendship's developed over the last couple of days.' He ran a finger back and forth over his lips as if considering what to say next.

This was going much faster that she had expected. 'Yes,' she said, wishing something more articulate, more inviting had come to mind. But her focus was on his side of the conversation, not hers. There was burst of laughter from the stage where a band of children were attempting some acrobatics under the watchful eyes of their parents.

For a moment, they stole his attention too, before he turned back to her. 'So.'

'So?' she echoed. 'What do you mean?'

'So you agree?' He reached his hand across the table.

She stared as if it was some sort of gigantic foreign insect. Should she take it? When she didn't, he withdrew it again in favour of his glass.

'I'm married,' she said, her voice a nervous treble.

'What?' He jerked to attention and put his glass down, turning it in the wet on the table. 'I know that. What's that got to do with anything?'

'I just thought...' But what had she thought? Her heart was beating at a hundred miles a minute and that had obliterated any coherent thought process. She should never have put herself in this position. She had encouraged him and now, however she responded, they would both be embarrassed.

'I brought you here because there's something I want to ask you.'

Could a pulse pump itself into a standstill? If so, hers must be almost there. She composed herself, trying to look considered, interested. She lay her hands on the table so they looked steady.

'You can say no, of course.' His hand ran back over his head, stopping at the ponytail.

Oh God, he actually was going to ask her if she... if she what? What should she say to him? What did she want to say? She felt as giddy as one of her daughters before a new date. As she turned her head to look at what was going on in the square again, she could feel the weight of Lara's earrings as they swung with the movement. She was the one who had got herself into this situation, she would have to be the one who got herself out.

'I'm wondering if you'd like...' He paused as the same

family as before squeezed past in the opposite direction having failed to find a table.

'Yes?' She felt breathless, almost faint, took a sip of her drink.

'I'm wondering if you would...' He looked down at his knees, as if he was bracing himself to say the next bit.

She waited, apprehensive, expectant.

'...lend me some money.' He finished off. 'I'd pay you back as soon as I could, of course.'

She stared at him and began to laugh. Had he any idea what she had been expecting? They'd only known each other for two or three days, and how close she had come to making an absolute twit of herself. Of course he hadn't been about to ask her, a married, sixty-year-old (just!) mother of four to embark on an affair. She looked down at herself: the top that strained across her bust, her stomach almost resting on her thighs, the slick of oil on her white trousers, two bunions and orange-sherbert nail varnish. She was no catch – even to the most fertile imagination.

'What's so funny?' He sounded hurt, confused.

'Nothing. It's just that I thought...' But she couldn't control her laughter as she watched light dawn in his face.

'Oh no, you didn't think I...' His appalled and amused expression said everything, but he wasn't laughing.

Time to retrieve her dignity. 'What do you mean?' She pretended to cotton on, raising her hands in denial. 'Heavens no.'

That smile was beginning to creep across his face, making his request less surprising. 'You don't mind me asking, do you?'

'Not at all.' Her relief was tinged with bitter disappointment but at least he had asked for a decision that was easier to make. Of course she would help him. 'How much are you talking about?'

His grin went from piratical to sheepish at once. 'Five grand.'

A scream went up from the square as a little boy fell from the platform, fortunately to be caught by an adult standing nearby. A woman started shouting and gesticulating, furious that nobody had been supervising the child. Kate was thankful for the distraction. It gave her a second to compose her features so her shock at being asked for so much didn't show. By the time the drama was over, she had recovered herself.

'I'm afraid I don't have that kind of money. If only.'

'Can't you lay your hands on it for me somehow? Please.' His hands were clasped in front of him. The romantic bohemian hero had disappeared to be replaced with a sad, elderly man reduced to begging from his sister's friend. She actually felt sorry for him.

She shook her head. 'I'm sorry. I'm a farmer's wife, not a banker's. We don't have that kind of money sloshing about. Have you asked Amy?' Immediately she asked the question, she could see she'd made a mistake.

His expression darkened. 'What do you think? I'm her brother, and I'm desperate but she wouldn't lend me a dime.'

'But that's a lot of money.'

'Do you think I don't know that?' To her astonishment he pushed back his chair and stood up.

'Can't you manage with less?' She could probably find a couple of hundred for him.

'No. I owe a guy I met in Goa. I needed some of it for my youngest son's mother for a photography course he's going on. The course and the equipment he needs mounts up. And some of it for myself. I thought I'd be paid something for the platform.' He looked defeated for a moment.

'I'm sorry.'

'If you won't help me, I'll have to find someone else who will.' He looked around as if expecting that someone to materialise. 'I'd better get on. The others will be here soon.' He took off across the square as if escaping an argument.

If he was hoping she'd have second thoughts, stamping off like a teenager and leaving her with the bill to pay was hardly the way to encourage them. Kate couldn't help being reminded of her children and how often she'd had to deal with them flouncing out of a room when they didn't get their way. The greatest flouncer of all was Kit, with Molly coming in a close second. 'Mu-um.' She could hear the word divided into two syllables to signify how unreasonable she was being. Ignoring them worked best and that's what she'd do now, so instead of chasing after him she remained at the table, nursing her drink, musing on the day's events and waiting for the other two.

At last Linda came walking up from the main road. She looked terrific in Jane's cast-off top, quite different to the woman who arrived on the island only days before. When she spotted Kate, she came over to her, smiling. 'Amy's waiting in the car park. We've decided that whatever's happened, we've got to grab what's left of our time here and make the most of it. Are you game?'

That was so good to hear. She would not let Dan's change of attitude spoil things and perhaps the three of them at least would leave the island friends. She raised an arm for the waiter. 'Of course, I'm totally game. Just let me pay for these drinks.'

24

By the time she reached the hotel, Jane was already regretting her decision to leave Ca'n Amy. Walking out on the others would only confirm to them her guilt over her role in what had happened to Amy and Linda. And she did feel guilty. They had made sure of that, even though they should take more responsibility for what happened in their lives. But did she honestly believe that? Or was that merely her absolving herself? She had a horrible feeling she knew the answer. Although, as a doctor, she had talked to so many patients that she understood better than most what made people behave they way they did. Or so she thought.

She found the hotel down a narrow street running below the main road. When she phoned, they had told her a last-minute cancellation meant they had one room available that night and she had jumped at it. She rolled her case, bumping it over the cobbles, from the car park below the village and into reception from where she was shown to her room. To reach it, she was taken back into the street and into the adjoining building. The hallway was imposing: high ceilings, an antique sideboard, some ancient agricultural tools (Kate might have known what they were), funky light fittings. Her room was just off it.

When the door shut behind the porter, she suddenly felt very alone. The room was not one of the light and airy ones she'd seen advertised on the hotel website, but was small and dark with narrow French windows that gave a sliver of a view of the mountains. The bed took up most of one end of the room, but there were a couple of chairs and a table at the other. She sat down and got her phone from her bag. Footsteps thumped across the floor of the room above her.

She desperately wanted to talk to someone about what had happened but, not knowing any of the women she'd spent the weekend with, no one at home would understand. She couldn't call David after their last conversation. He was the one person who would listen and sympathise but it seemed wrong to use him as a shoulder when she was lying to him about so much else. And that was the reason for coming here alone. She had twenty-four hours to get her head round her own situation and decide finally whether to end her affair – was that what it was? – with Rick or not. Or could she get away with it for a while longer? After all, they didn't usually see each other that often. Going to Barcelona was a reckless one-off that wouldn't be repeated. After their phone call the previous evening, he had emailed detailing the ways they were going to enjoy themselves. She felt hot with anticipation just thinking about them.

She stared at the face of her phone, then called up Rick's number. The dial tone was a series of long beeps. So he must already be there. Waiting for her. For the first time in their long relationship, she didn't feel that familiar thrill of expectation, of desire.

He picked up quickly. 'Darling! I wasn't expecting to hear from you. Is everything OK?'

'No.' She rarely cried but, to her surprise, tears were rolling down her cheeks.

'What's wrong? I can hear something's up.'

He might not be David but his voice was still a comfort.

'Everything.' She reached for a tissue from the box on the table, telling herself to pull herself together. Now was not the moment to fall apart. 'And nothing,' she added.

Above her, the footsteps were louder than before.

'We'll put it right when you're here. You're going to love this hotel. The room has everything and it's round the corner from a couple of top-class restaurants.' He was such a sybarite. All he cared for were the luxurious trappings of life. And sex. But, pleasurable as those things were, there was more to life than that. That was the difference between them.

'We can't go on like this,' she said. 'David suspects something. I'm risking everything coming to Barcelona'

There was a silence from the other end of the phone. From upstairs as well.

'Why didn't you say something before? We could have cancelled.' He wasn't shocked, just matter of fact. She suspected he could and would move on from their relationship in a heartbeat. She wasn't the only woman who could satisfy him and he had never had any trouble in finding others. She heard herself take a deep breath.

'I think we'll have to stop seeing each other.' There, she'd said it. The footsteps stopped and started again above her. She pushed open the window to let more air into the room, into her head.

'But not today? Not now I'm here?' He knew her too well. 'Sounds like you could do with some fun before you go home.'

Within minutes he had persuaded her that it was too late to back out. Just a few days of sex, sunshine and the high-life and then it would all be over. If only the prospect filled her with more joy. Instead she felt an overwhelming sense of guilt towards David although something still stopped her acting on it.

There was no point unpacking, and staying in this depressing room for the rest of the night was out of the question. She had noticed a bar that served tapas in the main square so she would go there and people-watch. She grabbed her bag and keys, and left. As she was locking the door, another one slammed above her head. Whoever was up there was making their way down the winding stone stairs.

She was straightening up as someone reached her floor. She was aware of a man walking past her but as she turned to follow him out of the building, she stopped dead. Even from behind, his build, the shape of the head, the checked cotton shirt and cream chinos were all achingly familiar. It couldn't possibly be.

'David?' The word emerged as a shocked whisper.

He had just put his hand on the door to the street but let it drop to his side as he spun round. 'Jane! What the hell are you doing here? You said you were staying with Amy.'

'I am. I mean I was.' She had never heard him sound so suspicious. 'But what are you doing here?'

'I could ask you the same thing.'

'The four of us fell out over something that happened at school – we all remembered it differently – and so I left a couple of hours ago. I was lucky there was a room here.'

He scratched his head. 'You mean you walked out without sorting things out.'

'Kind of. It's complicated. But why are *you* here?' Though the answer was obvious.

'I've come to find you.'

'But why? I'll be home in three days. What's happened? Is Paul all right?'

He put his hand back on the door handle. 'I was about to go to that bar in the square and phone you. But we can talk there instead. Fancy it?'

'I was going there too. Or we can talk in my room.' She indicated the door. 'Except there's someone upstairs doing a clog dance.'

'I'll take my shoes off next time.' He allowed himself a brief smile. 'Let's go out. It'll be easier to say what I've got to say on neutral ground.'

'Christ, David. What is it?'

But he was already out of the door and walking up the cobbled street. He paused to wait for her. 'Are you here on your own?'

She slipped her hand through his arm, but could feel him resisting the contact. 'Of course I am. We've just had a row and I had to get out. Coming here turns out to have been a big mistake. You'll never guess who's on the island.' Not that she had ever told David about Mr Wilson. What had there been to tell, since she hadn't given the man a thought for years? But she would tell him now.

However he showed no interest, just carried on round the corner and up the main street to the square, saying nothing. She felt more nervous with each step.

At the square, they went to the bar to the right of the plane trees where there was a free table tucked up beside the church wall. As they sat down, Jane saw Linda on the other side of the square, walking over to where Kate was sitting on her own in one of the opposite bars. They exchanged a few words and Kate paid before they walked off down the hill, smiling and chatting. If only they had never met Jack Walsh, she could be with them, heading into Sóller for a jolly last supper. Except David would have caught up with her anyway. As it was, she seemed to be on the brink of something dramatic. She ordered a white wine to his Estrella.

David looked around the square. 'Pretty place.' He squeezed the end of his nose, a telltale sign of his anxiety.

'David!' Jane couldn't wait any longer. 'Please tell me why you've come. I'll be home straight after the conference and I thought we were going to plan a holiday then.' The lies came without her trying. 'What's happened? You're frightening me.'

'I know there isn't a conference. That's what's happened.' He stared at her, challenging her to deny it. Wanting her to deny it.

'But...' Despite all the activity in the square, and children racing about the makeshift stage, they were in a bubble of their own. Nothing else mattered as she struggled to find a reply, wondering how to give him what he wanted. 'How...'

'My computer crashed last night when I was in the middle of checking a pitch. I had to move on to yours otherwise I wouldn't have got it to Pete in time. While I was working on it, you got an email alert from Rick headed Barcelona.' He paused, as if hoping she might jump in with a reasonable explanation.

Jane couldn't speak. She certainly couldn't explain as she wilted inside, remembering what Rick had said.

'I opened it. You'd have done the same, wouldn't you?' He looked at her long and hard. 'I know you would.'

Did he mean in the same way she'd looked at Elaine's notes? She took a sip of her wine, but it tasted like vinegar now.

'So you're meeting him there, in the Hotel Neri, I gather. I don't think we need to go through what else he said. You must have read that for yourself.'

Right then, sudden death would be preferable to the memory of Rick's description of what he wanted to do to her, things she and David had never come close to doing. The thought occurred to her for the first time that perhaps she was getting on a bit for such shenanigans. But was there such a thing as being too old for experimental sex?

'I couldn't wait for you to come home to discuss it, and I couldn't do this over the phone. I had to come out here and find you. How long's this been going on?' His question broke into her train of thought and, as it did, the world slid away from her as her head emptied of everything except for an overwhelming rush of panic. Would they ever be able to find their way back to each other after this?

'The funny thing is I'm not even angry. I'm sad,' he said, laying both his hands on the table.

And hurt. He must be hurt that she had lied to him and betrayed him time and again. And angry. She would rather he were angry. She wanted him to shout at her, hurt her back. Anything would be better than this awful controlled calm. The little emotion betrayed in his face was underwritten with grief and exhaustion. She wanted to reach out and touch him, but feared his rejection.

'You see, I thought we had a good marriage.' He ran his finger down the stem of his glass.

'We do.' She almost choked on the words. Not because she didn't mean them but because she did. 'We still do.'

'No, Jane. We don't. Who can have a good marriage when one of a so-called partnership is still fucking their ex?'

She flinched at the fury in his words. At last. She couldn't help looking around to see if anyone had overheard him. But despite the harshness of the question, his voice was low, restrained. Around them, people were talking, laughing, eating and drinking, enjoying their holidays.

'I never thought I'd say this but I can't trust anything you say. You've breached patient confidentiality and you must have lied on plenty of other occasions about Rick. Have you?'

How could she explain what she and Rick had together and that it didn't impact on her marriage to David? Except for the fact it had. How could she make him believe that it wasn't an affair, that it was just sex? That it was nothing more than a spark of electricity and a jolt of self-belief that she no longer got from him? That all they enjoyed was physical gratification, nothing more. There was no deep or fulfilling emotion involved in their exchange, nothing like what bonded her and David. And that was what mattered. Now she was in danger of losing everything, she saw that she should never have challenged her love for him. Once again, she had been too selfish to see straight.

He was biting his bottom lip, waiting for her reply.

'Yes, I have.' All her energy drained out of her.

He visibly tensed before putting his head in his hands.

She hurried on. 'But not often. I promise.'

251

'Do you love him?'

She could hardly hear him but shook her head. 'No. There's nothing like that between us at all. I love *you*.' She stopped. Speaking about their emotions was not something either of them did easily. If one of them ever tried, the other would laugh it off. But not this time.

'You understand why I had to come?' He looked up at her, his eyes earnest as he pleaded for the right answer.

She nodded. 'I think so.'

'If you go to Barcelona, our marriage is over.' He clenched and unclenched his right fist. 'When we get home, I'll file for divorce. If you come home with me now, I'd like us to start over.'

She went from despair to elation in a heartbeat. He was putting the decision about their future into her hands. But he hadn't finished.

'Coming here was a knee-jerk reaction. I didn't think about what I was doing until I was on the plane and by then it was too late to go home.'

'But you don't do knee-jerk.' She couldn't help an affectionate smile. In all the years she'd known him, he'd thought every decision through. Even when it came to proposing to her, a travel company had arranged their trip to Iceland and the special journey to Gljúfrabúi where he had got on to one knee in front of the waterfall. Planned spontaneity – that was what he was good at.

'Perhaps it was about time. But I've thought about nothing else on my way here except what I was going to do and say when I found you. I don't want us to separate. As far as I'm concerned, we share too much that I don't want to give up and, although some people might think I'm bonkers, I do still love you. If you want out, now's the time to say. If I'm not doing something right then tell me, and I'll try to change. That's how much it matters to me.'

She studied his face with its familiar contours, less defined than they once were but distinctive all the same: his hooded eyes embedded in laugh lines; his nose straight and pointed, widening a little near the top; his dark thick eyebrows; his wide narrow-lipped mouth with even teeth. She knew every mark from the tiny thread veins on his cheek to the chickenpox scar by his ear. How he bit his bottom lip if he was angry. How his left eye narrowed a little more than his right when he laughed.

'I'm so sorry,' she said. 'I don't know how it happened.' She didn't want to hurt David any more by telling him the truth. 'I've already told Rick it can't go on.'

His eyes lit up for a moment then the light faded. 'But you were still going to Barcelona? To see him? You were still going to pretend you were working?'

'Yes.'

'But why?'

'Because I'm an idiot.' She didn't have the words to explain. 'Because I've taken you for granted. I know I've lied and done things I shouldn't, and I'm sorry. I really am. I want us to try and forget what's happened, and start again too.' She sounded like someone who'd walked straight from the pages of a romantic novel but for once at least she was speaking the truth. By coming here, he had showed her how much he cared. How could she not be moved by that? As a result she was almost stripped of pretence. Almost.

The relief on his face was a pleasure to see. 'You'll tell him you won't go?'

'I'll tell him.'

'Now?'

'What? In front of you?' But she could tell how much it mattered to him. She got out her phone.

'Why not?'

Typing quickly, she wrote:

> Won't be coming to Barcelona after all. David and I are
> spending a couple of days in Mallorca. We can't meet
> again

'Will this do?' She held out her phone so he could read the message, worded so Rick would understand what had happened without David realising.

'Fine,' he said, immediately looking out at the square, but he looked as if he was a million miles away. After a moment he came to. 'Have you sent it?'

She held out her phone, pressed send and they heard the whoosh of a message being sent through cyberspace. 'Yes.'

'You said we were spending a couple of days here?' He looked puzzled.

'Why not? I've got the days off and now we're here . . . so, if you can, we might as well start the way we mean to go on. Together.'

'No.'

She was startled by his forcefulness.

'I want to go home,' he went on. 'We can't just pretend nothing's happened by having a nice holiday and brushing it all under a rug. We need to get back into the real world and sort out where we've gone wrong.'

'But we could do that after a break.' The thought of a few more days in the sun, putting things right, appealed to her.

'Absolutely not. For one thing, I've got a presentation on Friday and need to prepare with the guys for that. I mean everything I've said but we're going home.'

'But my flights . . .'

'We'll change them online, and then we can have dinner.'

There was no point in arguing. Once his mind was made up, changing it was a work of weeks. She raised her glass, the wine less vinegary now. 'I give in. Shall we go back to the hotel now and sort it?'

'Perfect.' He held out his hand for her to take.

She did, feeling its familiar warmth and solidity. They were going to be all right. They had so far managed to avoid the in-depth analysis of their relationship that she so dreaded. The last thing she wanted was to be driven into a corner where she would be pushed to tell him the home truths that should be left unspoken. The dread word 'counselling' had not been mentioned. Whatever anyone said, she didn't believe that baring one's soul and telling all was necessarily a recipe for success. Some things were better kept to oneself. If she were careful, she would get away with this.

'Let's go to one of the restaurants up the hill. The guy in reception told me the first one on the left does great fish.'

She hesitated. Situated on the side of the main road, anyone sitting there could easily be seen, but Amy, Kate and Linda were going into Sóller so there was no danger they would bump into them. And Dan would probably be visiting friends. 'Let's try it.'

After he'd paid, they set off to the hotel. She felt the weight of her phone in her bag. She couldn't help wondering how Rick would reply.

25

By the time we got to Sóller, I was exhausted. The past few days had taken their toll. This had been so far from the reunion I'd thought it would be. Yes, I wanted the answers to my own questions but I'd got a lot more than I'd bargained for, as had everyone else. At least we'd got rid of Jane. I'd run out of patience with her and the other two were leaving the following day. I would miss Kate and Linda but I only had to hold it together for twenty-four more hours. I could do that.

I prefer Sóller by night when the town empties of people and the main square is at its best. I'd chosen the pintxo restaurant not far away where the alleyway outside it was packed with crowded tables. We were given a table at the back and I ordered wine and water immediately. Still reeling after so many revelations that had put my own teenage problems into the shade, and worrying away about the Rob situation, I was pretty much functioning on autopilot.

'And then there were three,' said Linda, raising her glass of Rioja in a toast. As we all clinked glasses, I couldn't help reflecting how far she and I had come since she arrived. I'd been too ready to dismiss her then, far too quick to judge, but over these few days I'd discovered a new respect for her. More than that, I liked her. What had happened to me when I was seventeen was bad, but when all was said and done, I had moved on from it and made a good life for myself. What happened to her was so much worse. She had endured so much: promises made and promises broken, but she had survived. And even in the short time she'd had on the island, I could see she was feeling better about herself. I had an idea about a job for her but, whatever happened, I was resolved to keep in closer touch with her from now on.

'I've loved it here,' said Kate. 'Thank you.' She blew a kiss across the table at me. 'I'm sorry I couldn't lend Dan the money he needs but—'

'He asked *you*?' My brother had got through his life, largely living off his wits and me, but as far as I knew he'd never tapped any of my friends for cash. He must be more desperate than I realised. I should have listened to him, asked questions, because this was embarrassing. 'I'm so sorry. How did he take it?'

'Not well.' She shrugged. 'He stormed off and left me in the bar.'

'He's probably trying his luck with William.' Dan was shameless. 'But he won't have any joy because I've already briefed him. I don't want to give Dan any more money unless he's earning something for himself. I'm doing him a favour. No, really.'

The other two had begun to laugh.

'You sound like the frustrated mum of a teenage son,' said Linda.

'That's what it feels like sometimes.' And it did. Dan relied on me, always had, but I couldn't rely on him for much in return.

'The funny thing is that I thought he fancied me,' said Kate, beginning to smile. 'He was so lovely. And . . . I even thought I fancied him. It was kind of like being back at school but this time everything was going the way I used to want it to. Except it didn't.'

'I'm sure he does,' I said. Kate might have put on a bit of weight but she hadn't lost her looks or her personality. Part of

257

her charm lay in the fact that she didn't know how attractive she was.

'He just wanted your money more.' Linda shook her head. 'Bloody men.'

'Mine's not so bad, you know,' said Kate. 'I was so fed up with him when I came out here, but this break's been enough to make me see that he just needs a few minor adjustments and I'm going home to make them.'

'Poor man! I feel sorry for him. But can people ever really change?' Judging by Dan, I doubted it. I wondered about Rob and whether he'd had affairs that I'd been too blind or too stupid to cotton on to.

'He'd better,' she said and raised her glass in a toast. 'Here's to our new lives.'

'Good luck with that.' Linda's scepticism about men was hardly surprising, I guess.

'Wish I'd had the chance.' I hadn't meant to sound so self-pitying, but the knowledge that Rob had gone for good washed over me like the sea at high tide. Having the others round me had helped steady me and made me see that I had let what happened to me at school get way out of proportion. If Linda could survive what happened to her, I had done more than that. And now Rob had gone. I would survive that too. However desperate I might feel, I had to pick myself up – as impossible a task as it seemed – and remake my life. I would get that money back and make sure everyone who worked for us was still employed by the end of the year. I would. As for Jack Walsh: Why had I spent so much time brooding over the bloody man when I would have been better concentrating on what was happening in the present?

'The past is a different place,' said Linda, sounding almost wistful. 'I've made so many terrible errors of judgement – and look where they got me. All I've got left is a job where my days are numbered and my aunt to look after. Apart from the fact that being with you has made me realise that I should moderate my drinking,' she raised her glass with a grin, 'my future isn't exactly sparkling.'

I wasn't sure what to say.

'Let's drink to that. To your dreary future' said Kate, making us all laugh as we clinked glasses. 'Can't you persuade her to go into a home?' Forever practical. 'It's just finding the right one that's hard. One friend's mum was adamant about staying in her own home but then she fell and broke her wrist, and was persuaded. Now, instead of sitting home alone, she's always at an art class, playing cards, going on an outing or having her hair done. Loves it.'

'Sounds like my idea of hell,' I said, before I realised how unhelpful that was. 'But perhaps I'll feel differently at that age.'

'I've tried, and she won't consider it. At least the new carer seems to have got her measure. Thank God.'

We all stared as food was brought to the table next door to us. It smelled good.

'Shall we go inside and see what they've got left,' I suggested.

'Yes.' Linda put down her wine and led the way into the wood-panelled bar. For a moment we forgot our conversation as we chose from the cold pintxos that were left along the counter by the window. Outside, we put the coloured cocktail sticks that came with them into a container so we could be billed later. We took ages to order the hot ones, unable to decide between the battered octopus, the salmon tataki or the prawns in dough with wasabi foam. In the end we had the lot. When they came, each plate looked so beautiful, it seemed a shame to dismantle them. But we did.

Over supper, we rallied as our conversation revolved around how our perspectives on our own lives had started to change over these past days. Extraordinary in such a short time, but true. By chance we'd come together at various turning points in our lives and each of us had been kickstarted into seeing ourselves a little differently and how life might be changed. Our mood was positive, forward-looking and warm.

'You know what you should do, Amy?' Linda was markedly more positive. 'Do something new. Set up something in Spain? I mean, why not? You love it here – what could go wrong?' She stopped. 'What is it?'

Kate was gazing at something happening at one of the tables nearer the road as if she'd seen a snake. 'It's Jack Wilson.'

I glanced quickly over my shoulder to see him and a younger woman taking a table near the main road. I suppose I shouldn't have been so surprised. The restaurant was a highlight in the town. Linda was less discreet and was staring hard. 'I don't want to sit in the same restaurant as him.'

'He hasn't seen us. Take no notice.' Kate put her hand on Linda's shoulder.

I sympathised. Even though he was at the other end of the alley, I felt uncomfortable too. Given his impact on our lives, it didn't seem fair that he should be living his as if nothing had happened. I didn't want to think about how he'd messed up his own as well. 'Let's get the bill,' I suggested. 'We can go for a coffee in the square instead.'

'Good idea.' Linda signalled for the waitress. 'Though I don't see why we should be the ones who have to move.'

As we left, squeezing our way through the tables, there was no way of avoiding his. I hoped that we'd pass him without drawing attention to ourselves. Linda, however, had other plans.

'Hello, Mr Wilson. Fancy seeing you again,' she said loudly enough for him to hear. 'Holidaying with a friend?'

I was embarrassed, but delighted to see him knock his water glass flying. He recovered himself enough for a gruff, 'This is my wife, Anika.'

'She looks so much younger than you but I suppose that isn't so surprising, given your history.'

Anika was blotting her skirt with a napkin but stopped immediately. 'What does that mean?' She looked at Jack, puzzled. 'Why do they call you Mr Wilson?'

'I thought he might not have told you. Perhaps you should ask him to be more open with you. I'm sorry we can't stop for longer.' She swept out, with Kate and me rushing out as best we could behind her. I was aware of Anika sitting, mouth slightly open, bemused.

'Who is that?' she said, staring up at me as I went by.

'Just someone I knew a long time ago. No one who matters.'

If I hadn't been so averse to public scene-making, I would have picked up his knife and stabbed him in the chest. Instead, perhaps wisely, I raced round the corner with the other two where we high-fived each other.

'I shouldn't have done that.' Linda looked worried. 'That was a terrible thing to say.'

'Of course you bloody should.' Kate clapped her on the back. 'That's the very least he deserves.'

When I woke up the following morning, I decided I would go to the gallery on my way back from the airport. We had gone on talking about Mr Wilson over coffee, and agreed that he shouldn't get away scot-free. He may have paid for what he did to the fifteen-year-old, but he hadn't paid back Linda for what he did to her. An insincere apology was not enough. I was glad Linda hadn't overheard the way he dismissed her the previous evening, but I was furious too, and wanted to do something, though I was unsure what.

Before we left, Dan emerged from the pool house and joined us for breakfast. He was beaming like someone who'd just won the lottery as he sat in Jane's place. After a couple of minutes, Kate left the table and walked to the other end of the terrace.

'You'll be pleased to know that a friend of William's from

the party has asked me to build him a wood cabin, so I'll be gainfully employed for a couple of months at least.' Thank God for William. He knew what was needed and was generous enough to find a way of providing it.

'That's great. Where?'

'Pollença. So I was just thinking if I could base myself here and use your car, I could begin to pay off my debts.' As if we'd never had that conversation, but this was the way he got through life.

I was irritated by his assumption that I'd let him stay. But of course I would. I'd had to postpone the work meeting we had planned at Ca'n Amy – too much that still had to be sorted out at home – so there was no good reason why he shouldn't. That aside, I wanted him to pay off his debts. 'Of course you can.'

'That's great. Thanks, sis. I knew I could rely on you in the end. And there's one more thing I need to do. I owe Kate an apology.'

I was so glad he'd come to that decision on his own.

He went over to Kate who was photographing the view. They talked together briefly and at the end they were both smiling. A kiss on each cheek seemed to cement whatever had been said.

'It would never have worked,' she said with a little regret as I drove us down the mountain. 'I'm too much of a homebody now.'

'Don't do yourself down. That's not such a bad thing to be.' In the rear-view mirror I watched her stare out of the window.

'But I've never done anything much with my life. I look at the three of you and wish I had.'

'And I've never made a comfortable family life,' said Linda. 'I've never worked on a farm. So which of us is the worst off?'

Kate leaned forward to talk to us. 'Neither, I guess. What are you going to do when you get home?'

'You mean about the library or Aunt Pat?'

'Both.'

Linda turned round in her seat so she could talk to us both more easily. 'I haven't decided about work. I'm so tempted to cut and run. What Brendan said on the boat about no one regretting taking redundancy really struck a chord. I've been thinking about my one or two friends who have, and they've got new things on the go. It's a big risk but—'

'—but it's a risk to stay. We've only got one life, so we'd better make the most of what's left.'

We both groaned.

'Don't say that!' said Linda.

Kate pulled a face. 'But it's true.'

I glanced at Linda. 'But I'm going to try to find something for you.'

'I didn't think you were serious.'

My eyes were back on the road as we entered the tunnel. 'I can't promise anything, but I do have an idea. I'll ask around, too.' I was determined to help her if I could but didn't want to raise her hopes too high.

'Really?' She sounded disbelieving but pleased.

'I've got to talk to Kerry first. What about you, Kate?'

'What? When I get home?' She smiled to herself. 'I'm going to talk to Alan about going away together. It'll be a miracle if I can get him off the farm but I will try.'

'Good for you. And you, Amy?'

I sensed Linda glance at my profile as she waited for my answer.

That wasn't difficult to give. 'I'm going to sort out Rob and the money because I'm determined the business shouldn't suffer, and then I'm going to make a new life.'

'I'm going to send you some dates so we can meet up again. Maybe you could both come to Yorkshire?' Kate sat back, smiling.

Discussing what we might do there meant the drive to the

airport whizzed by. I walked with them into the terminal, kissed them goodbye and watched as they went into Departures together. They both stopped for a second to wave for a last time and then they had gone. But I was happy to think that we'd see each other again.

And then I drove to Valldemossa.

When I walked into the gallery, I found Anika studying the paintings. She moved like a dancer, gliding from one to the next, stopping and looking intently at each one. Her hair was tightly knotted at the nape of her neck, showing off her long neck and straight back. The room wasn't large but it was well lit and the few paintings were spaced out round the walls. They were riots of swirling colour that looked as if they had been spun in a washing machine. They were far too abstract for my taste although his use of colour was exciting.

I cleared my throat. 'Hello.'

The alarm on her face showed that she recognised me. 'You're one of those women from last night. What do you want?'

'I'm curious about the paintings, and I thought I'd come and see Jack. But I'm more than glad to see you.'

'I don't want to talk to you. He'll be here in a minute.' She headed towards a door at the back of the gallery, then stopped as if she had remembered something.

'Why were you all so rude? How do you know Jack?'

This was my opportunity to put the record straight. Should I take it? For her sake as much as for our own. 'He was our art teacher at school. We haven't seen him since then but we never forgot him because of what he did.'

'What did he do?' She looked terrified. 'It must have been very bad if it still matters so much.'

'It was. For one of us it was literally life-changing. For me? Well, I was just put on a different path to the one I thought I'd follow.'

'Life-changing, how?' Her fingers fluttered to her throat.

'I think you should ask Jack. But don't let him dismiss Linda as someone from the past who doesn't matter. She does matter. Just like the girl he went to prison for.' Perhaps I shouldn't have said that but it slipped out.

She took a couple of steps towards me, her face aghast. 'What?'

'How old were you when you met?'

'Nineteen. Why?'

'And he was what?'

'Forty.'

I shook my head. So until he met her, he hadn't really changed. 'Just talk to him. Find out the truth about the man you're living with. That's all.'

Anika turned away just as the door opened.

'Amy!' Jack stood framed in the doorway, not at all pleased to see me. His right fist clenched and unclenched. Behind him the dappled street was busy with tourists, none of them giving a second glance to the gallery and what was going on inside. I was glad I had the advantage of surprise.

'What are you doing here?' He must have hoped he'd seen the last of us.

'I'm interested in seeing your work after all this time.'

Anika went over and took his arm. She was tiny, birdlike compared to the man he'd become. He didn't say a thing, just scratched at his beard and stared at me. I can't remember anyone ever looking at me with such loathing and with such underlying apprehension at the same time. That gave me a great sense of achievement.

I walked up to a painting, a splurge of bright colours but from a reddish palette. Sunset.

'Perhaps we should talk in the office.' He spoke as the door opened and a couple wandered in off the street.

'No, it's OK. I've said all I've come to say.' I acknowledged Anika with a nod.

Now he looked alarmed, as well he might. 'What do you want from me?' He leaned against the wall for support. 'I've apologised. Isn't that enough?'

'For you, perhaps. But that was just words. Nothing can make up for happened to Linda and the way you abandoned her.'

Anika gave a little gasp and looked up at him for an explanation.

'But that's what young men do,' he protested, spittle landing on his beard.

'*Some* young men,' I said. 'Others wouldn't have broken—'

'You don't need to say any more.' He went over and held open the door. 'I'd like you to leave now.'

'With pleasure,' I said, hoping that what I'd said to Anika was enough at least to make his life difficult for a while.

'Now what?' He took a step towards me but I wasn't frightened. He was less menacing and more fearful. 'Are you satisfied now?' He looked down at his wife whose expression was changing. She unhooked her arm from his and stood aside.

'I don't know,' I said. 'This has been way more interesting that I thought it was going to be. You'll have to wait and see.'

As I stepped outside into the sunshine, I was pleased that I had been able to do for Linda what she would never have done. I felt bad for Anika. I didn't want to upset her life, after all she was the innocent in all this, but wasn't it better that she knew who she was married to? I was justifying my secret-spilling in the name of the sisterhood. But she had done nothing to me and I did realise that I was not the one to make that call.

As I walked down the main street of Valldemossa, alive with people sitting outside at the cafés, going in and out of the souvenir shops, I felt a spring in my step that I hadn't felt for a while. I thought ahead to home. I would be able to cope with what lay ahead. I knew that now. Rob deserved what was coming to him. I'd made the company's position completely clear. But before I had to deal with it, he had two days in which to organise his finances while I would enjoy my last couple of days at Ca'n Amy.

26

The last leg of the journey home was a lonely business. Having said goodbye to Kate at Victoria Station, Linda didn't feel the relief she had been anticipating at being on her own again. She had imagined being on the train with a paper and a plain KitKat, enjoying the journey and being able to reflect on the past few days. Instead she was surrounded by a rowdy gang of football fans on their way home who made her feel even more alone. She missed the company of the others much more than she'd anticipated: the joking, the support, the easy familiarity that had developed.

She had only been home half an hour before she went to collect Sacha. As soon as she'd returned and shut the front door, she opened the door of the cat basket. If she was hoping for the welcome of a returning hero, she was disappointed. Sacha showed her displeasure at being locked away by ignoring Linda as if she had been banned to the Antarctic instead of to a cage with a heated floor, and a menu of Linda's choice.

'Okay. You be like that. I can wait.' Linda went to the treat drawer and, within minutes, Sacha was eating out of her hand. 'Silly.' She took the small pile of mail and sat on the sofa with a cup of tea, while Sacha settled beside her. Already they had fallen back into their routine. After a while, they went into the garden and Linda was soon cutting back, weeding and thinking about the bulbs she would plant in the autumn. But over everything hung the thought of her first day back at work. She had one day's grace before she had to face her colleagues: one day in which to stop swithering and make her final decision.

'There was so much fighting talk in Mallorca,' she told Sacha, whose ear flicked as a fly landed on her. 'I'm not sure I'm brave enough to go through with it. What do you think?'

Staying at the library, continuing to work on the enquiries desk was not an attractive prospect but at least she'd have a job.

But for how long? Amy's voice rang in her ear.

And if you're not enjoying it, is it worth it? Kate supported her.

Take the money. Life's short. Even Jane threw in her tuppence worth.

'Stop it, all of you. Let me make my own mind up.' She helped herself to another chocolate biscuit, the thing that accompanied the best decision-making, and switched on the TV.

'And what about Aunt Pat,' she asked Sacha. 'If I don't have a job, perhaps I should look after her. After all I owe her pretty much everything.'

Sacha jumped off the chair and headed for her food bowl. But, but, but... becoming a full-time carer had never been part of any plan.

The following day, the hour-long drive to her Aunt Pat's gave her plenty of time for thought. She didn't want to become her full-time carer, but that might be financially expedient if there was no money coming in. When her aunt was younger and old age seemed an impossibility, even she had said Linda must never give up her independence for her or anyone else. To say that after she had given up her own to bring up Linda made her self-sacrifice all the more remarkable. However, without a job, without Mike, Linda would have no real reason not to. The thought of selling up to go and live with her aunt broke her heart. However she remembered Kate's words – 'We've only got one life' – and crossed her fingers on the steering wheel.

When she arrived at the terraced Victorian cottage, she let herself in. 'Hi there! Aunt Pat!' she called. 'Where are you?'

'In here.' Her aunt was in her favourite chair, a rug tucked round her legs, a morning games show blaring from the TV. Beside her were the remains of her breakfast, blackcurrant jam smeared among toast crumbs, an empty cup of tea. She was dressed, a cardigan done up unevenly over a shirt that looked as though it might have been slept in. Her hair, once such a pride and joy, was now so thin and grey her scalp was visible. Always a woman who took pride in her appearance, she had even made a stab at her make-up. Linda couldn't help loving the belligerent but kind old woman who had given her so much and who was so reduced by age.

'Are you ready?' She pointed the remote at the TV and turned it down a fraction, though they both still had to shout to make themselves heard. 'We're going to see Judy, remember?

'I don't want to go.' She was pouting like a small child.

'We don't have to stay for long.'

With a lot of tutting and muttering, her aunt kicked off her slippers. 'Pass me my shoes, but I must be back in time for *Father Brown*.'

With her aunt's arm linked through hers, Linda took her out to the car. Perhaps once she saw Fairstead House, she might reconsider. Talking about what they did in Mallorca, omitting all mention of Jack, took up most of the journey until they eventually pulled into the gravel driveway of a large Victorian building. Fairstead House could never be called cheery but exuded the grim fortitude of an institution. Black drainpipes angled down its red-brick façade, and the windows stared expressionless at the outside world.

A woman who Linda took to be Judy appeared at the front door. Tying her hair back in a ponytail emphasised her wide smile. 'Pat! I'm so glad you're here. I thought we could go and

sit in the sunroom. I've ordered tea and the fruitcake you like.'
She offered her arm.

In the corridors they passed young visitors, a tea room, a
room where a small art class was going on; in another a few
elderly people were watching TV; in another, tables were laid
for dinner.

Her aunt refused to look anywhere but straight ahead. However she mustered a smile when they arrived in the sunroom.
Large, airy and well-furnished, it opened on to a large garden
with a lawn like a bowling green that was surrounded by glorious overflowing herbaceous borders.

While they had tea, Judy was effusive in her praise of the
place. Linda just sat back and listened, wishing her aunt was a
more malleable soul. As Judy talked, drawing her aunt out of
herself in a way that she never could, Linda drifted into thinking about her own predicament. Wasn't the most important
thing to have control of one's own life? Before Linda realised
what was happening, Judy had persuaded Pat to see one of the
vacant bedrooms, and they were leaving her in the last of the
late summer sun.

When they rejoined her, Linda tried to quiz her about where
she'd been.

'Very nice. But not for me.' For the first time, they heard
uncertainty in her voice.

On the way home, Pat said little before dozing off, her head
hanging forward, looking as if its weight would snap her neck.
Linda didn't dare hope that visiting Fairstead House would
have changed her aunt's mind. Once made up, there was little
anyone could do until she was ready.

The following morning, she was up at six-thirty, as usual,
wondering what her first day back at work would bring. She
dressed in her smartest blouse and black skirt, then changed
her mind. Pulling them off and chucking them on her bed, she

271

took the blue top she bought in Sóller instead, pairing it with some pale grey skinny trousers. Just the change of clothes made her feel as if Amy, Jane and Linda were coming into work with her. They made her feel braver. The three women had made her question what her life should be about. And the answer? Instead of trying to please others, she must try to live life for herself. Easier said than done though.

As soon as she walked through the door of the library, she was aware that she was getting more than the usual sideways glances. Within minutes, Frankie, her only real friend there, had taken her to one side.

'Watch out, Simon's on the warpath, and you're in his sights. Stella's complained about you taking too long to answer queries. She says she doesn't have time to deal with the resulting queues.' That was probably a fair criticism because Linda did get caught up in each enquiry, pursuing the leads as far as she could. That was the aspect of the job she enjoyed most. The people she helped thought she was fantastic. Others did not.

Simon, Mike's replacement, had wasted no time in reorganising the systems and introducing new programmes to attract new users. The whole place was being rearranged and reclassified – against Linda's advice. She had been made too aware what a lowly position she held in his esteem. She was part of the old guard and just about tolerated on board the gleaming new ship, no more than that.

'I'm only just through the door. What else am I supposed to have done?'

She didn't have long to wait for an answer. Simon barrelled round to the reception desk where she was working that day, his approach heralded by the click of his heels and his brisk cough. He stood in front of her, all angular legs and arms like a giant stick insect, looking down his patrician nose at her.

'Have you got a moment, Linda?'

The expected answer was not, 'No.'

Having exited from the document on which she was working, she followed him through the stacks to the small windowless room they used for meetings. The overhead neon light was unforgiving and the books and papers piled on the shelves needed a thorough go-through, but that wasn't her job. The coffee machine responsible for the gallons of indifferent coffee that she'd drunk over the years sat on the side, not working.

'So.' He waited for her to sit opposite him. 'Good holiday?'

Why was he asking a question, when they both knew he had zero interest in the answer. But she would play along. 'Fine. Thank you.'

'While you were away, it came to my notice that the way you manage your time on the desk...'

As she listened to him drone on, she was struck by a flash of understanding. At once it became abundantly clear what she had to do. 'Can I stop you there?' she asked.

'Well!' His long fingers reminded her of spiders' legs as they skittered on the table. 'Do you have something you want to say?'

'I do,' she said, feeling the words bubbling up. 'I never wanted to work on the desk, as you know, but... I've enjoyed giving people as much help as they need. But whether or not I take too long needn't worry you any longer, nor any other aspects of my work here, because I've decided to apply for voluntary redundancy.'

He sat bolt upright as if he'd received an electric shock in his bony nether regions. 'You have? Are you sure?' A smile began to twitch at the corners of his mouth.

Seeing it, Linda knew she had made the right decision, whatever happened to her. 'Quite sure,' she said. 'There are various things I want to do with my life, and staying on here isn't one of them. When funding was withdrawn from the Tom Florence project, that should perhaps have been my moment, but I'm taking it now.'

'Then you must—'

'I know. I must go to HR and sort it out. Thank you, Simon. It's been a pleasure.' As she left the room, she felt as if she was ten feet tall with adrenaline fizzing through her.

The HR manager was able to see her immediately. Their chat was brief. A payment calculated against her long service and three months' notice – and that was generous, she was told. She could take the rest of the afternoon off, but he'd see her to discuss the finer detail in the morning.

She left the building without saying anything, even to Frankie. The only people she really wanted to see and discuss this with were Amy and Kate, although phone or email weren't the same as face-to-face. By the time she was unlocking her front door, her euphoria had begun to wear off and a fear of the future was creeping in.

'I'll find something,' she said to Sacha when she got home, trying to sound calm when inside she was quailing.

But the truth was, she didn't want to find another library job. As time passed, the more certain she became of that. What she had been reduced to was not the job she had once enjoyed. Instead, she had been given a chance. This was the break she needed so she must use it wisely. Three months and a tax-free pay-off would keep her going for the immediate future until she found something. She could always work in a shop if she ran out of money first. But would she?

By the weekend, her time in Mallorca had already assumed a dreamlike quality. Linda could barely believe she'd been there at all. But the proof was in her continuing changed attitude. Getting up on Sunday morning, she shut the door and padded to the kitchen to go through her usual routine: feed Sasha; put kettle on; make cup of tea; make toast and marmite; return to bed with both, and the post. The weekend lie-ins were the best part of the week. Sometimes she went mad and added a boiled egg into the mix, but not that day.

Back in bed, feet warming up, Sasha purring beside her, Radio 4 on almost too quiet to hear, Linda began to open her mail: bills, an invitation to a library event – another reading and Q&A with an author in whom she had no interest whatsoever – and a couple of catalogues that she threw across the room, missing the bin. 'You wouldn't believe it but I used to be so good at games,' she said.

Sasha purred.

Next was the laptop. Answering emails in bed was a luxury she was going to be enjoying more often until she was lucky on the job front. But first she went to the *Guardian*, to see if any librarian jobs she might be suitable for had been posted since she last looked. However half-hearted she might feel, she was at least qualified for some of them. As a beggar, she couldn't afford to be a chooser. Nothing suitable stood out so she opened her inbox. Immediately, her eye went to an email from Amy replying to the one she had sent the day she took redundancy.

> Linda!! What news. Congratulations. You won't regret it, I'm sure. I'm going to keep my eye out for you. I'm sorry I didn't reply immediately; I went straight back to work yesterday, trying to hold things together till we get the money from Rob. Not looking good on that front but, with Kerry, I'm feeling positive.
>
> But I need to tell you what happened about Jack Wilson. I did go back to the gallery after I dropped you off.

Linda snapped shut the laptop. She didn't want to read what Amy had done, she'd rather hear in person, so reached over her breakfast to her phone and called her. Could she have changed her mind about saying something despite what they'd agreed? But why? Linda hadn't wanted any more confrontation.

Naming and shaming was not how she wanted to deal with Jack. He'd been to prison, he seemed contrite. She'd seen him, she'd told him what happened. He knew. That was enough. It was over. She wanted to leave it in the past where it belonged.

Amy picked up immediately. 'You've got my email, then? There must be a huge question mark hanging over his career now, I imagine.'

'I haven't read it all. I'd rather hear it from you.'

'Well, OK, but don't go mad.'

Linda braced herself, slipping down the pillow until she was almost lying flat. She listened to Amy's account of what happened in the gallery, shocked and thrilled at the same time.

'That was a terrible thing to do.' Although she had sympathy for Anika, she could not help sharing Amy's delight in her account of what she had done.

'I know.' Amy didn't sound the slightest bit contrite. 'But she should know who she's married to.'

'But it's not up to you to tell her.'

'I knew you wouldn't like it. I didn't go in there meaning to say anything. It just slipped out.'

'Did you see him again, after that?'

'God, no. I stayed up at the house for two heavenly days and came home yesterday. If I'm honest, I do feel a bit guilty but I'm back here now so I can't do any more damage.'

Linda couldn't help smiling. She was right. Jack deserved what he got. Maybe he would be lucky and his relationship with Anika would be strong enough to withstand having the knowledge of who he really was in the open. 'But you didn't say anything to anyone else?'

'No!' As if she would. 'Well, I might have said something more to Dan just before I left.'

'Amy! You said you wouldn't.' She was hopeless.

'But I thought you'd like to know.'

'Of course I would.' But in fact she didn't really want to

know anything more about Jack or to talk about him. 'And you? How are things?'

'Difficult.' There was a sigh at the end of the line. 'But not insurmountable. I'm having a make or break meeting with Rob. He's called wanting to talk, but I've put him off till next week. I've decided I want to divorce him as soon as I can. I'm going to see a lawyer.'

'You're not going to wait till the dust settles?'

'What's the point? I want a clean slate.'

Linda knew her breeziness was only masking Amy's hurt. She had seen that at the villa. Even if she hadn't, she knew for herself that you could fight the pain of rejection and lost love as hard as you liked but it took a long time to disappear. And then she realised that she hadn't thought too long about Mike for days and her life had been all the better for that. He had done her a favour by being so decisive about their break-up. He hadn't wavered once. From now on, she would follow suit. She would not waste any more time mulling over what might have been. By taking her redundancy, she had taken the first step into a new future of her own. Like Amy, she was going to move on.

27

Alan had sent one of the lads to collect Kate from the station because he was too busy preparing the ewes for sale. As they drove along the lane to the farm, the familiarity of the undulating moorland was balm to her spirits. She might miss the mountainous beauty of Mallorca's Serra de Tramuntana and the company of her old friends, but this was home. There was the oak tree that the boys once always badgered her to let them climb, the gateway where Red, their terrier had escaped from the car, the drystone walls that Alan and the boys had spent hours of their lives maintaining, the field where she and Lara had once spotted a sheep in labour and had gone to help. The ewe had died, and they'd reared the lamb – Lara called it Florrie – at home. Everywhere she looked, there were landmarks from her life.

As they rounded the corner into the farmyard, Kate looked at the place she belonged through new eyes. The old grey stone farmhouse had been in Alan's family for three generations now, the outhouses and the old barn where they kept the sheep during the hard winters. In the yard, there were bits of old farm equipment that Noah should have repaired during the summer, alongside the hay baler and one of the tractors. She got out of the Land Rover and took a deep breath of moorland air, guessing what might await her indoors.

Sure enough, the kitchen was a shambles. Some washing-up

had been done, but not the burned saucepan on the counter, nor the one with something unidentifiable stuck round its sides, or the plates and mugs in the sink. The remains of lunch had been left on the table so one of the dogs had finished off the ham leaving the evidence on the mat by the Aga. Clothes were strewn over the back of chairs. The stone floor was covered in muddy footprints. However hard she tried to instil a sense of house pride, it was ignored.

From now on, things were going to be different. Instead of falling back into her old role of cook and bottlewasher, she sat at the kitchen table, unearthed a pencil and paper, cleared a space, and began to write a list of chores for Noah and Molly that would help her. As for Alan, she would do her best to make him understand.

That night, while he was showering, Kate slipped on the new pyjamas she'd splashed out on in the airport. She'd browsed the lingerie in the branch of Victoria's Secret, dazzled by what was there. Alan would think she'd taken leave of her senses if she surprised him with something as flimsy and lacy as some of the things on display. No, this was enough. She'd bought them while Linda was in the Ladies.

She looked down at herself. Perhaps if she stretched out a bit more. The coming-home steak supper they'd had sat heavy in her stomach. If only she hadn't had the pudding, too, but it would have been antisocial not to keep him and Noah company.

The handle of the bathroom door turned. Alan emerged in his stripy pyjamas, took one look at her, and actually blushed. 'Wow! What's happened to your usual kit?'

At least he'd noticed something was different. That had to be a start. 'I thought we could inject a bit of spice into our life.'

He sat on the edge of the bed. Not the desperate lunge that she'd imagined in her wildest fantasy. Worse, he looked puzzled.

'You don't need to do this, you know. You look lovely whatever you're wearing.'

'Do I?'

'You know you do.'

'How am I meant to know if you never tell me?' A buzz of irritation went through her. But no. She must not spoil the evening. This was important.

'Of course I have.' He slapped her thigh and left his hand there as if she was a prize heifer. 'Lots of times.'

'Maybe thirty years ago.' She couldn't remember when he had last said anything of the kind.

'But you know that's what I think,' he protested. 'I don't need to keep telling you. You don't keep telling me how infinitely desirable I am either.' He grinned and flapped up his pyjama top.

Just for a second, Dan's bright eyes and piratical grin flashed into her mind before she hurriedly blocked him out. 'Oh, come here,' she said. 'This is silly. I only wanted to give you a present to remember. Your birthday's coming up.'

He went to his side of the bed, singing 'When I'm Sixty-Four'. He broke off as he got under the duvet. '*Do* you still need me?' he asked, thoughtful. 'You've been a bit odd since your birthday.'

'You're imagining things,' she said, climbing in to join him.

'I know I'm a bit of an old fool, but I do love you, you know,' he said, taking her by surprise. He lay on his back, hands behind his head. 'I may not show it or say it enough but as far as I'm concerned nothing's changed since we got married.'

That made her feel terrible. Terrible and stupid for dolling herself up in a way she didn't need to. At her age and stage, that was never going to change things. And this wasn't the moment to give him a lecture about taking her for granted. He loved her in his way. Was it selfish to want more?

'Shall we?' She turned to look at him, lying prone, eyes closed, mouth slightly open.

'Mmm . . . I think we should.'

She knew the familiar moves that they had done nothing much to vary over the years. If it ain't broke . . . Sex with him was like a boarding a train that always took the same route to arrive at the best destination. That night was no exception.

Afterwards, they were lying side by side and Kate was wondering how to suggest adding something new to their usual repertoire without hurting his feelings. In her head, she had gone through this countless times, but in reality it was not as easy as it should be.

She snuggled up to him and kissed his ear 'Next time, do you think we . . .'

Before she got any further, a great rumbling snore shook the room. He was sound asleep. She pulled away, amused despite herself. Well, there was always the morning.

But when she woke up, Alan was getting dressed. Outside, dawn was just breaking. She groaned.

'A few days off and you've been softened,' he said. 'Shall I bring you a cup of tea?'

What he was hoping was that she would then get up and make him and Noah breakfast before they set off for the sales. The ropes were all too familiar to her. 'I'd love one.' She rolled on to her side as if she was going back to sleep.

He came round to her side of the bed and kissed her cheek. 'It's good to have you back.'

'It's good to be back. Perhaps I will get up after all.' She threw off the duvet and so another day began.

After a day of the normal farm chores and a run to Helmsley for some shopping, Kate was delighted when Lara turned up with Molly, having picked her up from work and given her a lift home.

'How was it, Mum? I want to hear everything.'

'It was great and I brought you these.' Kate held out two charm bracelets that she'd bought with Jane in Sóller. The girls dangled them from their hands, pleasure on their faces.

'Cool,' said Molly, laying hers on her arm. 'Thanks, Ma.'

'I want to hear how it went.' Lara was fastening hers round her wrist, then holding her arm in the air and turning it back and forth. 'I love this. Thanks so much. But tell us . . . What were they like? Did you wear the earrings? Did you have a villa with a pool? Take any photos?' All the questions that Alan and Noah had been too tired to think of the previous evening. That had been more of a supper, collapse in front of TV and doze, go to bed sort of affair.

At the kitchen table with cups of tea, the dogs at the hearth and two of the cats asleep on the pile of ironing, Kate told them about her rare holiday.

'A motorbike, Mum?! Did you fancy him?'

'Don't be silly, of course not!'

But Lara's raised eyebrows showed she'd answered that a little too quickly.

'He was nice, but not for me. Your dad's the one I've signed up with and nothing's going to change that. And anyway all Dan wanted, apart from showing off the island, was to borrow money.'

'What a tosser,' said Molly.

Kate smiled. 'Perhaps he is, in a way. He's never married and probably never will. I wouldn't like to live like that.'

'I would. Imagine travelling round the world. If it's Tuesday, it must be Bangkok.' Molly leaned back with her eyes shut. 'I'd love to ride an elephant.'

The other two burst out laughing. Molly's changing ambitions always made them laugh, especially the more outlandish ones.

'What? What have I said?'

'Nothing,' said Kate, putting her arm round her youngest daughter and kissing her cheek. Being here, in their untidy, dubiously clean kitchen surrounded by her family was where she belonged.

'Being away confirmed to me how much I love it here. But...' She tapped both hands on the table for their attention. 'I've decided it's time for one or two changes round here.'

Both girls looked at her, dismayed.

'It's time you contributed a bit more, Moll. I don't mean rent, but I thought you might cook one meal a week, and keep your room tidy.'

'What about Noah? His room's a pigsty.'

'Pot. Kettle,' Lara said, dodging out of Molly's reach. 'Good for you, Mum.'

'Don't worry. I'm going to have a word with him too.'

Being taken for granted belonged in the past. If she could make one or two small changes to the domestic routine, it would be better for all of them.

'God, Mum,' Molly was looking disgruntled. 'Perhaps better if you don't go away too often if this is what you're like when you get back.'

'She's right, though,' Lara said. 'Perhaps we do take you a bit for granted. But you're our mum, what do you expect?'

Kate smiled. She was already thinking about her next plan. The next day she would start looking for a weekend break for her and Alan. He would object but she would insist. That way Noah would learn he was trusted with the care of the farm, and Alan might begin to let go a little.

And if he couldn't always get away, then she had proved to herself that she could do her own thing if she wanted. And she would again one day. She had a feeling that she hadn't seen the last of Amy and Linda. Of Jane, she was less sure.

28

David and Jane had been walking on eggshells around each other ever since they'd arrived back in Oxford.

The morning after they got home, Jane had gone straight to the hospital as early as she could to catch up with anything she had missed, while David went into the agency to get on with his own work. Within a couple of days it was as if nothing had happened, except of course everything had happened and neither of them knew how to deal with it. David's impetuous dash to save their marriage, all the thoughts and promises they'd made in Fornalutx belonged to another reality, one that had nothing to do with the life they lived at home.

The first night David went to sleep in front of the News, and she left him there so she could go to bed on her own. After that, back at work, they'd return in the evening in time for a scratch supper then fall into bed and straight to sleep with only the most cursory of exchanges. In bed together, despite their mutual assurances about new starts, they didn't make love but lay side by side like two silent marble effigies.

Meanwhile Rick had been insistent: texts, missed calls and emails all saying the same thing: *What happened?* Naturally, he was angry that he'd flown to Barcelona and been let down. Eventually Jane caved in. She couldn't write to him because there was too much to say. She owed it to him to give him the explanation he deserved face to face. He deserved that at least.

If he understood what had happened, he would leave her alone. David need never know.

They met at his flat after work, despite her knowing this could be a mistake.

When he opened the door, he looked serious. 'What the hell happened? I took that time off and paid a fortune for that suite . . .'

'I know, I know. I'm sorry.' She followed him into the living room, sat in one of the Swedish designer chairs and explained, all the time having to remind herself why she was there. Whatever he said, she was not to succumb to anything. He poured her a glass of champagne.

When she'd finished, he poured them another and chinked his glass against hers. 'Come with me.'

When he went into the bedroom, she followed, despite herself. Just one last delicious time.

Two hours later she left, ashamed and angry with herself. How could she be so certain she wanted to be with David and then deceive him so thoroughly? She had no answer. She should have arranged to meet Rick on neutral territory but had been frightened of them being seen together. At least David would never know. And she was not going to see Rick again. That they had agreed.

'Where have you been?'

She had never seen David look so fierce. He was in the kitchen, hunched over, slicing a piece of bread.

'I had to stay late. I wanted to see a patient who was operated on this afternoon, and I had some notes to finish up. How was dinner?' The lies came easily.

'Cancelled at the last minute. Their MD's flight back from Frankfurt was delayed. When I heard, I'd thought we might go out instead and talk. We've barely spoken properly since we got home.' He put the knife down. 'So I'm doing beans on toast instead.'

'I'm so sorry.' She pulled out a chair and sat at the table, leafing through the day's post. 'That would have been great.' Although conversation between them seemed to be harder with every day that passed.

'But we couldn't because you were ... Where were you again?' He was frowning, thunderous, staring down at her.

'At work.'

'Why do you do this?' He shook his head, as he turned to put the bread in the toaster.

'What?' That visit to Rick would cost her everything. She should have known better.

'Lie.' He rubbed his head and sighed. 'I phoned the ward at six-thirty.'

Her pulse was racing. That was half an hour after her day ended.

'They paged you until someone told me you had gone home. But you weren't here. I know that because ... I was. Which begs the question, Where were you?' He held up his hand. 'Don't answer that. I've got a pretty good idea.'

'It was late night shopping so I—'

He hit the table with his hand. 'I don't want to hear any more. You were with Rick again, weren't you?' He closed his eyes as if he couldn't bear the sight of her. 'Just tell me.'

She nodded.

'Say it! Tell me the truth. After I came to Mallorca and after everything we said then, did you go to see him again? I can't believe you'd do that.'

She had to defend herself in the face of his incredulity. She had to make him understand. 'Yes! Yes I went to see him. But only because I had to tell him face to face that it was over. I thought it was cowardly and unfair not to'

'That text wasn't enough for you? You just couldn't resist.'

She couldn't bear his disdain and disappointment.

'Did you have sex?'

She couldn't look at him. 'Yes.'

'I'm sorry? I didn't hear you.'

'YES!' she shouted. 'Is that better? Yes, we had sex. Where are you going?'

'Out!' He was already at the kitchen door. 'I can't go on like this. I need to think.'

'But your supper...'

'What? My beans on toast?! You have them. I expect you've worked up quite an appetite.'

After the front door slammed, Jane sat for a while, head in her hands. What could she do? She had just thrown away everything that mattered to her. And for what? She thought back to Rick, and the way he had stood in the hall when she was leaving.

'You were right,' he said. 'That was the last time.'

She looked at him puzzled as he helped her into her coat. 'Meaning?'

'When I got your text, I began to think about us, about where we were going. You were right. It's been fun but it's time for something new.'

Light dawned straight away. 'Whose tights were those in the bedroom?' She had picked them up, mistaking them for her own.

He shrugged. 'Just someone I met recently. You're not an exclusive arrangement. You know that and I don't want any difficulties.'

She hadn't anticipated this turn of the tables at all. Because of her desire to treat him fairly, she had jeopardised everything. Not quite everything, she reminded herself. Not yet. The tribunal was being held that week.

How would Paul react if she and David split up? He loved his dad and was fiercely protective of him. She couldn't bear the thought that the negative feelings he already held for her would be compounded. David had given her a chance and, despite her best intentions, she had blown it.

She had to talk to someone otherwise she would never be able to unscramble the thoughts racing round her head. She ran through a mental rolodex of her friends. She had always compartmentalised them, never wanting anyone to know everything about her life. Kate was the only person she had told about Rick, the only person who might listen. As her old school friend, Kate had remained at a remove from her work colleagues, so anything she told her was safe, but she hadn't returned the couple of calls Jane had made to her since they had arrived back home. For the first time, Jane wondered if that might be deliberate. They hadn't parted on the best of terms but Kate knew what she was like and would understand her reasons.

Kate's phone went straight to voicemail again. Jane ended the call without leaving a message.

She tried David next, but got his voicemail too. Where would he have gone? The pub? Was he wandering the streets? Visiting a friend? But who? What he said made sense. They needed to do some straight-talking, something that she found so difficult. In medicine, there was nowhere to hide. She had learned that the hard way when she'd had to give patients bad news. She had hoped experiencing that had brought her a degree of self-knowledge, but when it came to her personal life she still took refuge in pretence. Going to Mallorca had pointed that up. How ashamed she had been made to feel over her past behaviour, although she had done her best to hide it.

She had to explain to David that she recognised her own failings and that her affair with Rick really was over. She began talking to his voicemail. 'I'm so, so sorry,' she said. 'Please come home. You know I find it hard to talk, but I know you want to and we must. Perhaps we should see a counsellor...' She could hardly believe she was suggesting it. 'So we'll have a neutral space and someone who'll mediate. Going to see Rick was a stupid mistake. I thought I was doing the right thing by telling him in person, but you're the one I should be talking to. I understand that now. I do want to try to put things right – if you'll let me. One last chance.'

When she ended the call, she was despairing. It was too late. Following her to Spain had been his last-ditch bid to keep her, and only days later she had thrown it back in his face. They would never come back from this.

She made a cup of tea, her hands trembling, and took it up to bed with her. Not that she would sleep. But there seemed little point in doing anything else. In bed, she tried Kate again. No reply. She switched the light off and lay in the dark, listening out for the sound of David's key in the front door, his tread on the stairs.

When she woke, dawn was breaking. She rolled over to see if he was awake so she could begin her apology. But his side of the bed was empty, unslept in. Immediately, she got up, wrapped her dressing gown round her and went to the spare room. She turned the handle carefully so as not to wake him. Inside, the curtains were wide open, as she had left them, and the early light shone on another empty bed. She checked Paul's old room: empty too. David hadn't come home.

She checked her phone for messages. Nothing.

A while later, she called Paul. The phone rang on and on. She was about to hang up when he answered. 'Yeah?'

Seven-thirty and still not up.

'Paul, it's me.'

'Mum! It's early. What do you want?' She could tell he had rolled over and the phone was suffocated between his ear and the pillow.

'Have you heard from Dad?'

'What?! It's first thing in the morning. Isn't he with you?'

Perhaps phoning him had been unwise. She didn't want to

alert him to anything wrong between her and David. 'No. He's away for the night and not answering his phone. If he calls, would you ask him to call me?'

'Mmm, sure. How was Spain?' In the background, Elaine was saying something. 'Look, I've got to go. I'll talk to you soon.' He ended the call.

But he wouldn't speak to her soon unless she called him. That was the way these days. Elaine didn't like him speaking to her and if she could engineer a way for it not to happen, she would. And Jane couldn't blame her. What she had done was unforgivable, but she had apologised profusely. Surely her soon-to-be daughter-in-law would forgive her with time, especially after Jane had paid the inevitable heavy price. Just one more day to the tribunal and after that the case would be on the MPTS website for all to see.

With a heavy heart, she showered and got ready for work. There would be a small backlog of emails to attend to before her morning clinic, one of the most challenging but rewarding parts of her job. However grim she felt, she could not let those people down and she could be nothing but professional, keeping her own problems to herself. As she drank her black coffee, she thought about the day ahead, the patients depending on her to be there to discuss the treatment of their cancer and help them navigate their future.

The morning passed quickly, one patient after another, some of whom she had been seeing for some time, each of them equally absorbing. She did her best to reassure, explain and comfort where she could. Watching people fight cancer was both hard and humbling. Their bravery and stoicism in the face of the illness could be extraordinary. After a snack lunch, she went on to the wards to see her patients who ranged from an elderly woman in the very last stages of life, surrounded by her large Turkish family, to a young woman in her thirties whose cubicle was covered in cards from her friends and photos of her Westie which was inexplicably called Marrow.

'I can't wait to get home,' she said. 'I want to see Marrow.'

'I'll see you after your next scan,' said Jane, knowing that there was little chance of her surviving much longer than that. But if a patient didn't want to know their own life expectancy, she didn't tell them.

There was the usual mountain of admin and Jane made her way through it with the ruthless efficiency for which she was known, updating patient notes, reviewing lab work and contacting colleagues to discuss individual cases. As they were short-staffed that day, she had called a couple of patients to ask them to come in to discuss their results. By seven o'clock, she was exhausted. Only then, did David's whereabouts and the looming tribunal re-enter her thoughts.

She drove home, let herself in and checked the landline. No messages. Where had he got to? She tried him and Kate again but neither picked up. Her behaviour in Spain may not have consolidated those old friendships but surely Kate wasn't the sort of person who would drop her because of that. They'd been friends for too long. But as the evening wore on and she thought about what had happened and been said in the last week, she felt a terrible, creeping sense of loneliness. With little effort on her part, she had succeeded in alienating everyone; her friends and, most importantly, her husband and their son and his fiancée. It was all very well having the admiration and gratitude of her patients, but that counted as nothing beside the love of her family.

She took her baked potato and tuna through to the living room where she curled up on the sofa and switched on the TV. Her plate sat on the coffee table, the potato untouched, as she surfed the channels unable to get absorbed in anything. What had she done with her life?

A hot bath and early bed didn't do much to improve things.

Through the night she tossed and turned, unable to get David, Paul, Amy, Linda and Kate, and the impending tribunal out of her head. It was as if everything had coalesced into one huge testing ground that, for once, she didn't think she would survive.

In the morning, things looked as bleak. David still wasn't answering his phone. He had never ignored her before and, as far as she could see, it could only mean one thing. But he would have to come back at some time and she had to be here when he did, even if it was to hear the worst. The tribunal was at noon – the other thing that demanded her attendance.

She was sitting hunched over a bowl of uneaten cold porridge and a cup of tea, when she heard a key in the lock. Her stomach flip-flopped. This was it. This was the end of her marriage, timed perfectly to coincide with the end of her career.

'Jane!'

'In the kitchen.'

The tenor of David's voice gave little away. But when he came in, she could see how tired he looked. His face was grey with exhaustion, his features gaunt.

'Where have you been?'

His eyebrows rose. 'That's not a question you have any right to ask. But since you do, I went to the Premier Inn. I wanted to be alone to think.'

She poured him a cup of tea and slid it across the table. 'Did you get my message?'

'Yes.' He nodded his head slowly. 'I didn't want to talk to you until I was clear about what I wanted to say to you.'

'I'm so sorry. I made such a stupid mistake.'

'Yes, you did.' He drank his tea and screwed up his face. 'It's cold.'

'I'll make another.' She stood up.

'No, don't. I'll get one on the way to work.'

'You're going to work?' Was that how important their marriage was to him now?

'It's the last thing I want to do, believe me, but there's a diversity meeting I have to be at, at nine-thirty. I wanted to come home first.'

Her stomach flip-flopped again. *This was it.*

'I've lain awake all night, thinking about you, about us. I thought when I came to Mallorca that I made my feelings clear.'

'You did,'

'Not clear enough, it seems.' He rubbed his cheeks with both hands as if that would energise him.

'I'm not going to see Rick again. He knows that now.' She spoke quickly to would silence him.

'No, you're not.' His eyes fixed on hers. 'I must be mad, but I want to give us one last chance. I don't pretend to understand why you've needed him in your life, so perhaps your suggestion of counselling is a good one.'

'When Rick and I had counselling, all we were told was that there was no hope for us.' Those ghastly hour-long sessions where their mediator ultimately had to announce defeat.

'There's nothing more I can suggest, except I can help you find the least painful way to separate,' she'd said, brushing her hands together.

'Then perhaps we need to inject a little more pain into the proceedings.' His face was stony. 'Counselling and compromise. We're doing this on my terms or not at all. We need to talk honestly about all this and we need help to do that since we don't seem to be able to on our own.'

She hung her head in agreement. 'All right.' Relief swelled up in her. He hadn't forgiven her but they would be all right, and this time she wouldn't mess things up. Coming so close to losing him had made her realise even more how much he meant to her.

'Last chance. I mean it.' He left the room and went upstairs where she could hear him showering and getting dressed.

When he reappeared, he looked more like himself, spruced up for the office. Standing in the doorway as he put on his jacket, he said, 'I'll meet you at eleven-thirty.'

'Why?'

'I'm coming with you. You don't seriously think I'd let you face the tribunal on your own?'

She stood up and flung her arms round him, feeling his resistance give way. 'I really don't deserve you.' How, after Rick, she had found such a generous, kind man was a mystery to her.

'No, you don't!' He put his arms round her. She relaxed into their warmth and familiarity. 'Don't look so glum. It won't be as bad as you think. You're a bloody good oncologist. You know that, and so does everyone else. This was one awful moment of madness that deserves a warning but not a suspension. They'll surely understand that. And if they don't, we'll appeal.'

She heard that 'we' and smiled up at him. Despite everything, she still had him, and that was all that mattered.

29

In the two days I spent at Ca'n Amy alone with Dan, our relationship slipped back into calmer waters. Having found employment and a source of income, he relaxed again, so much so that he barely reacted when I warned him: 'Don't ever tap my friends for money again.'

He just gave a lazy smile. 'But they're not really your friends, are they? Not any more.'

'They are now.'

In such a short space of time, that was quite an achievement, but I did believe that's what had happened. Three of us had bonded all over again and, if nothing else, we'd got a better grasp of Jane and who she was. We might be far from the same people who had hung out together as children and teenagers – life had seen to that – but underneath there was an unbreakable bond and understanding between us.

'Even Jane?'

'Let's just say I'll definitely be seeing Kate and Linda again.'

He laughed. 'So are you going to tell me what happened with the famous artist?'

And I did. I didn't need to tell him about Linda's part in the story (that was hers to tell) but there was plenty more to discuss. I had a funny feeling that I could leave the island and Dan would take pleasure in doing something to scupper Jack Walsh.

Sure enough a couple of days after I got home, I received his email.

Been seeing plenty of our old friends before starting work

That was so typical. Having a good life always came first.

Unfortunately I found myself telling them about Walsh
and his past. I don't think you said it was secret and of
course there's plenty online about him, if you look. I have!
Brendan and Sheila were all for live and let live. 'The man's
paid his dues,' was Brendan's take – idiot. But they never
saw the effect all that had on you. I won't forget the
angry, defeated Amy who crashed in our squat that boiling
hot summer, and how long it took you to get over what
happened.
William didn't like the story at all. He had a quiet word
with Johnny and let's just say that the exhibition has closed
and Walsh has left the island. I suspect, actually know,
Johnny is spreading the word through his contacts in the
art world so exhibitions might be harder for him to come
by in the future. I hope so. His wife's still here. Someone
told me she's staying on the island for the summer and
keeping her yoga classes going. Sheila had a flyer for them.

I felt uneasy about Anika. I worried that I'd been too hasty. I
didn't want to destroy her marriage but to let her know who she
was married to; but perhaps that wasn't my job, as Linda had
said. I consoled myself with the thought that if the marriage
was solid, surely this was a hiccup they would be able to get
over. If not, we'd done her a favour, though she might not see
it like that quite yet. And I have to admit I was delighted about
the exhibition.

My first day back at work, I had a call from Rob: the first

time we'd spoken in weeks. Just the sound of his voice made me anxious, but I reminded myself I had to be strong.

'Can I come and see you?' He sounded odd, morose. 'I need to talk.'

'What about? All I want to hear from you is that you've repaid what you owe in full.'

Suffice to say that the following week, Rob came to the office. I wasn't keen on meeting him at home but neither did I want a public confrontation.

When I picked him up from our tiny reception area, I was shocked. This was not the man who had left me. Here was someone with all the stuffing beaten out of him. He looked awful: unshaven with a grey pallor, and he'd lost weight. We went into my room where we sat at the round table where we'd held so many meetings together in the past. But I had to harden my heart against nostalgia.

'Are you all right?'

'No.' He sat opposite me, hunched in the chair, unable to look me in the face. 'I've made a terrible mistake.'

He looked broken, and my heart went out to him. But...

'I want us to get back together.' His head lifted, his eyes full of hope.

This was not what I'd expected at all. Nor was my reaction. If he had asked sooner, perhaps I would have given way. But not now. I'd spent so much time thinking about us, about our relationship and where I had gone wrong. There wasn't a way back for us.

'I'm sorry, Rob. I don't think that's a good idea.' Nonetheless that was such a hard thing to say.

His expression changed. 'Why not? We can go back to the way things were. Just a bit of an effort and we'll be fine.' He looked around him at the office that had been so familiar and dear to both of us. That might sound odd, but so many decisions had been made there. His eyes stopped on the shelf where our wedding photo and a photos of us on holiday in Hong Kong used to be. I had removed them. Otherwise the room was as he knew it, a comfortable working space with the same furniture, same pictures, same books, although I had moved a vase his mother had given us into a cupboard. However he didn't comment.

'No.' I remembered my conclusion to all my deliberations about the future. 'It's gone too far. You stole from us so you could set up in competition with Morag. How can I forgive that?'

He hung his head again, shamed. 'I know. I've been so un-believably stupid. But couldn't we at least try? Please.' Through the glass tabletop, I could see his fingers clasp and unclasp together. 'I miss you.'

Seeing him like this was awful but, despite my sympathy, my heart hardened in the face of his desperation. I knew him well enough to know there was something else that he wasn't saying. 'What's happened? Has Morag changed her mind?'

'No.' He pulled himself upright, businesslike suddenly. 'OK. I'll be honest with you.'

I knew he was about to say something I wasn't going to like. And sure enough . . .

'I can't raise the balance of the money. I thought I'd raised sufficient investment but it's fallen through. Morag's spent a lot on the shop and stock so we need to start trading before we recoup. We're going to have to ask for more time. Please.'

If that's what they were relying on, it could take years. Had he forgotten that I'd built a business from scratch too? I knew what it was like, and how much graft and self-belief it took, how much investment with so little immediate return. I had to be firm. If I bent now, I would lose the respect of my colleagues, and of myself. How dare he? Cushioning their inability to repay in full in a blether of self-recrimination and love for me. Although the word 'love' hadn't come into it, I reminded myself. He didn't want me back at all. He wanted to save himself. The realisation strengthened my resolve.

'Rob, I'm sorry. I gave you a month, almost six weeks ago. Tomorrow morning I'm going into the office and I'm going to have to ask Kerry to initiate criminal proceedings. I have to, you must see that. We need that money.'

'So do we.' He was angry now. Frightened too, I expect. I'd seen Morag lose her temper once when something went adrift at work. It wasn't pretty.

'But it's not yours to take. Don't you see that? It's not mine either. Believe me it breaks my heart to do this, but I have no choice. I've tried to be as fair as possible.'

'You knew a month was an impossible ask!'

'I didn't know that. I hoped that between you, you'd find it somehow. Or even that you still had it.'

He didn't stay for long after that. We didn't have much else to say. I was saddened watching his forlorn figure walking away but I was furious too. Had he honestly been going to leave Morag for me? Of course not! His attempt to win me back had been just a ploy to buy them time.

I went into work the next day and told Kerry to report the fraud formally.

'Thank God!' was her response. 'I didn't think you'd be able to do it.'

'Nor did I,' I admitted. 'But I can't let him get away with it.' I felt sick at the thought of his possible jail sentence, however short, but I had to keep reminding myself that by defrauding Amy Green, he had been acting against me and everything we had held dear.

'I'll make the relevant calls this morning.' She made a note on a pad in front of her, then looked up as if she was expecting me to let her get on with it.

'Actually there's something I want to run by you.' I had to

299

do this while Mallorca and everything that went with our island reunion was still fresh in my mind. As I explained my idea, Kerry's expression changed from dubious to enthusiastic. By the time I'd finished, she was nodding her head.

'It's a great idea but can we afford it? Shall I run it by Ed?' Ed was our new financial guy who had stepped into Rob's role and was putting us back to rights.

So it was that four or five days later, I called Linda.

'I wasn't expecting to hear from you so soon.' But she sounded pleased.

'How's it going?'

'I'm almost a free woman. Just over a couple of months to go but I think they'll let me go earlier. Imagine.' She paused. 'I've no idea what I'm going to do but I'm excited, although nervous too.'

'Then I've called at exactly the right moment.' I was bursting to tell her my idea. 'Even though we've had to put our expansion plans on hold while we sort out the financial side of things, we do need an archivist. We're always getting requests for designs, often from way back and it's all a bit hit and miss. So if we had someone who could make a database and archive all our stuff with digital images and swatches and so on . . . Well, that would help us no end.'

'And you want *me*?' Her disbelief was almost comical.

'Well, *I* do. You've got all those cataloguing and digitising skills, haven't you? But you'll have to come and meet Kerry and Ed and the team. I've a hunch you'd be perfect. What do you say?' I was on tenterhooks for her reply.

'Are you sure?'

'Of course I'm sure, otherwise why would I have called you?' I mustn't let my impatience show.

'Then, yes.' She began to laugh. 'I'd love to come and meet them.'

'What about your aunt?' In my excitement, I'd forgotten her.

'Is she a consideration? I don't know how much of this could be done from home.' I was annoyed with myself that I hadn't thought that aspect through.

'She's a consideration all right, but I think it may be okay. She's warming to the idea of a home I took her to the other day. Anyway, I haven't got the job yet so don't let's jump ahead too soon. But she's keener than she was and I think we might be able to arrange things.'

She must have known she had the job really, but I didn't think I should admit that any interviews were merely a formality.

That evening, I let myself into the house and for the first time I didn't feel racked with loneliness. For some reason, I felt it welcome me in as if we weren't waiting for Rob to come back too. I had briefly considered selling it and moving somewhere smaller that wouldn't have its history, but I loved the place. Slowly, I was getting used to being there on my own. If I'm honest, I had been on my own for much longer than from the day Rob made his announcement. We had been leading separate lives for longer than I had cared to admit.

On the doormat was a scatter of envelopes. Only one with a first-class stamp looked of any interest. I took them into the kitchen where I took one of the bar stools and sat at the island. I'd removed the skeleton clock that reminded me too much of Rob and that night, and hung an outsize black-and-white photograph of the lighthouse at Cap de Formentor in its place. I shunted the mail to one side of the work surface, apart from the one handwritten. Inside was a card with the picture of a long drystone wall cutting through a rolling landscape dotted with sheep. It was from Kate. What she couldn't write in the card ran on to an enclosed sheet of paper.

So this is what you're missing! Beautiful Yorkshire! Just to say a huge thank you for having us all. Got home safely and have settled back into farm life as if I'd never been

away. But haven't forgotten resolutions!! Changes are
being made. Small at first!

Haven't heard from Linda but Jane has called me a
couple of times. I haven't called back. We did see her at
her worst, and I'm sure I'll feel better about her in time
but, just the moment, I'm not sure what to say to her. I
think I'll leave it a while longer. Is that bad? She did leave
a message today though. Seems the tribunal gave her a
warning. So she hasn't lost her job. That doesn't sound so
bad to me but apparently it goes on her record and can be
seen by anyone who bothers to look her up. Reputation,
reputation, reputation! Anyway . . .

And what happened to Jack? Did you see him again?
And Dan? I'm afraid I made a bit of a fool of myself but
I enjoyed being with him even if he did have an ulterior
motive all along.

I took a tangerine and began tearing off the skin. I couldn't
hold Dan's behaviour against him for long. If he didn't behave
in that way, he wouldn't be the brother I loved. Of course I'd
helped him out with yet another loan in the end, but only
after making him sit down and go through exactly what he
needed and why. Five thousand pounds had been a hopeless
exaggeration so I lent him the right amount. He's the only
family I've got left now and he's never going to change. I'd just
have to get used to it.

I've been wondering how we can get together again. Not
immediately of course. Do you remember I suggested
that you came here? A far cry from Mallorca, but we do
have a small cottage that we rent with Airbnb. It's quite
comfortable and if you came next spring . . . I know it's a
long way off . . . but the land is coming back to life, and the
lambs . . .

I felt myself smiling. I might have plenty of local and professional friends, but I was so glad to have these two women back in my life. I had a feeling they were going to be there for good.

I got out my own cards from my desk drawer, each showing one of my designs. I leafed through them until I found the one I wanted for Kate: the blues and greens of my seascape collection. Thinking about the following spring, which would be here before we knew it, and the possibility of another weekend with them, I took my pen, and began my reply.

Acknowledgements

So many more people are involved in the making of a novel than the writer so my thanks go to:

My extraordinary and tireless agent Clare Alexander who always offers the soundest of advice and has had my back at all times. Clare Hey, my patient and inspiring editor, and of course all her team at Orion, with a special mention of Alainna Hadjigeorgou, Olivia Barber and Amy Davies. Once again, Sally Partington was the most eagle-eyed of copyeditors.

Julie Sharman for plotting and planning as we walked, and whose medical experience I plundered yet again. Lizy Buchan and Janet Ellis for being the staunchest of friends and readers. Anne Welsh and Rebecca Jones who helped me understand more about librarianship. Neville Pereira, Richard Sloan and Andrew Blake for answering my questions about fraud. Lisa Comfort for advice on setting up a business. Lucy Atkins for her knowledge of Oxford. Bill Wright for introducing me to Fornalutx and Miranda McMinn for telling me about Deià and more. Any mistakes are mine alone.

And thanks of course to my family and friends, especially my husband, who put up with me and my ups and downs while getting this story down.

'I adored *An Italian Summer*... A most beguiling read'
Jilly Cooper

Second chances begin with a first step . . .

Sandy is in her fifties, and at a crossroads in her life: she's a teacher and respected by her pupils, but she feels she is being sidelined in favour of younger colleagues. So when her mother dies, leaving her a sealed envelope addressed to an unknown woman living in Naples, Sandy decides to head to Italy to resolve the mystery by delivering the letter herself.

She books herself on to a small sightseeing trip from Rome to Naples and the Amalfi Coast, hoping to meet some like-minded people along the way. Who is the mysterious woman she is searching for? And will Sandy find friendship, or even love, along the way...?

Help us make the next generation of readers

We – both author and publisher – hope you enjoyed this book. We believe that you can become a reader at any time in your life, but we'd love your help to give the next generation a head start.

Did you know that 9% of children don't have a book of their own in their home, rising to 13% in disadvantaged families*? We'd like to try to change that by asking you to consider the role you could play in helping to build readers of the future.

We'd love you to think of sharing, borrowing, reading, buying or talking about a book with a child in your life and spreading the love of reading. We want to make sure the next generation continue to have access to books, wherever they come from.

And if you would like to consider donating to charities that help fund literacy projects, find out more at www.literacytrust.org.uk and www.booktrust.org.uk.

Thank you.

hachette
CHILDREN'S GROUP

*As reported by the National Literacy Trust